# FAMISHED

## an Ash Park novel

## MEGHAN O'FLYNN

PYGMALION PUBLISHING

Distributed by Pygmalion Publishing, LLC

IBSN: 978-0-9974651-1-2

*For my father, who raised me lovingly—and quite
normally—and who should not be blamed
for the twisted nature of my work.
I love you, Daddy.
Always.*

*Focus, or she's dead.*

Petrosky ground his teeth together, but it didn't stop the panic from swelling hot and frantic within him. After the arrest last week, this crime should have been fucking impossible.

He wished it were a copycat. He knew it wasn't.

Anger knotted his chest as he examined the corpse that lay in the middle of the cavernous living room. Dominic Harwick's intestines spilled onto the white marble floor as though someone had tried to run off with them. His eyes were wide, milky at the edges already, so it had been awhile since someone gutted his sorry ass and turned him into a rag doll in a three-thousand-dollar suit.

*That rich prick should have been able to protect her.*

Petrosky looked at the couch: luxurious, empty, cold. Last week Hannah had sat on that couch, staring at him with wide green eyes that made her seem older than her twenty-three years. She had been happy, like Julie had been before she was stolen from him. He pictured Hannah as she might have been at eight years old, skirt twirling, dark hair flying, face flushed with sun, like one of the photos of Julie he kept tucked in his wallet.

They all started so innocent, so pure, so… *vulnerable.*

The idea that Hannah was the catalyst in the deaths of eight others, the cornerstone of some serial killer's plan, had not occurred to him when they first met. But it had later. It did now.

Petrosky resisted the urge to kick the body and refocused on the couch. Crimson congealed along the white leather as if marking Hannah's departure.

He wondered if the blood was hers.

The click of a doorknob caught Petrosky's attention. He turned to see Bryant Graves, the lead FBI agent, entering the room from the garage door, followed by four other agents. Petrosky tried not to think about what might be in the garage. Instead, he watched the four men survey the living room from different angles, their movements practically choreographed.

"Damn, does everyone that girl knows get whacked?" one of the agents asked.

"Pretty much," said another.

A plain-clothed agent stooped to inspect a chunk of scalp on the floor. Whitish-blond hair waved, tentacle-like, from the dead skin, beckoning Petrosky to touch it.

"You know this guy?" one of Graves's cronies asked from the doorway.

"Dominic Harwick." Petrosky nearly spat out the bastard's name.

"No signs of forced entry, so one of them knew the killer," Graves said.

"*She* knew the killer," Petrosky said. "Obsession builds over time. This level of obsession indicates it was probably someone she knew well."

*But who?*

Petrosky turned back to the floor in front of him, where words scrawled in blood had dried sickly brown in the morning light.

> *Ever drifting down the stream—*
> *Lingering in the golden gleam—*
> *Life, what is it but a dream?*

Petrosky's gut clenched. He forced himself to look at Graves. "And, Han—" *Hannah*. Her name caught in his throat, sharp like a razor blade. "The girl?"

"There are bloody drag marks heading out to the back shower and a pile of bloody clothes," Graves said. "He must have cleaned her up before taking her. We've got the techs on it now, but they're working the perimeter first." Graves bent and used a pencil to lift the edge of the scalp, but it was suctioned to the floor with dried blood.

"Hair? That's new," said another voice. Petrosky didn't bother to find out who had spoken. He stared at the coppery stains on the floor, his muscles twitching with anticipation. Someone could be tearing her apart as the agents roped off the room. How long did she have? He wanted to run, to find her, but he had no idea where to look.

"Bag it," Graves said to the agent examining the scalp, then turned to Petrosky. "It's all been connected from the beginning. Either Hannah Montgomery was his target all along or she's just another random victim. I think the fact that she isn't filleted on the floor like the others points to her being the goal, not an extra."

"He's got something special planned for her," Petrosky whispered. He hung his head, hoping it wasn't already too late.

If it was, it was all his fault.

# TWO MONTHS EARLIER

## THURSDAY, OCTOBER 1ST

The killer looked at the ceiling, listening for the call of a night bird, a cricket, a barking dog. But the cemetery was silent, save for the moaning of the wind and the whispering rustle of leaves outside. These were the noises of the dead.

The one-family mausoleum was made of thick white bricks turned gray with age and reinforced with mortar and stone. The walls were a barrier against the outside sounds of gunshots and throbbing bass lines emanating from cars with rims larger than their wheels.

The walls also muffled any sounds that might have tried to escape the small room.

The silence shimmered through his lungs, focusing him. Soon the burgeoning sunlight, birthed from a vast bloody womb, would announce that today was the present and it was time to move beyond a past that seemed so close in these early morning hours.

He closed his eyes and let her image come rushing back at him. Would she still look the way she did inside his head? On the surface, it was a simple question, but it toyed with him, stirred his curiosity and roused an unbridled rage that seared his very soul. He could see her face as clearly as if she were standing before him now—her alabaster skin, the vibrant green of her eyes, iridescent like the Mediterranean Sea.

*Bitch.*

He looked down. This girl was a poor substitute. The slab of concrete bearing her weight was barely wider than her hips, so it had been no burden to cuff her wrists and ankles to the sturdy wooden pillars beneath. Families had once placed the ashes of their loved ones here for a final goodbye before stuffing them into the wall for all eternity. Now it was a real altar, heavy with sacrifice.

Her eyes were unseeing and blank in the dim light. The creamy white of her skin would eventually become translucent as death took over, blending her flesh into the gray stone upon which she lay.

*But not yet.*

He ran his fingers over her breasts, flattened from years of malnutrition. A roadmap of abused veins ran the length of her arms. Her drooping mouth gaped, a string of drool dripping down her wasted face. Dried tears streaked her cheeks.

He had never understood tears. In her case they seemed all the more repugnant as he'd merely finished what she had already been doing to herself. They all tried to deny it at the end, but every one of them wanted this. Even the one he hadn't killed. His neck muscles went rigid, as stony as the altar. He had done everything she had ever asked of him. Would have continued to if she hadn't gone.

*This is for you, cunt.*

He trailed his eyes down the girl's chest to the yawning gorge that had once been her belly. The skin lay peeled back, revealing his prize within the emaciated cavity.

He touched the stomach and it slid like a nest of maggots, writhing away from the light. The still-warm jelly that surrounded her innards sucked at his hand. He slid his fingers over the shiny glass exterior of the organ, gripped it gingerly, and pulled. Resistance, then release, as the surrounding tissue gave way. He bent closer and palpated the surface, pinching, prodding until he felt the familiar firmness, the proof that she was just as disgusting as he'd suspected.

Then the scalpel was in his hand, and there was only the dissection, reverent and precise, the taste of iron on his tongue growing stronger with each inhale. His brows knit together in concentration. The blade sliced cleanly, smooth as a finger down a lover's cheek, as he opened the tissue, inch by inch, toward his prize. Then it was free, writhing in a gooey mass of greenish-yellow mucus and reddish-brown tissue, toxic with her essence. He removed the wriggling creature slowly. His mouth watered.

*There you are, you little bastard.*

---

Radio silence. Then static, like a thousand locusts humming in my ears. The pillow was ripped from my hands and someone screamed, the sound strangled and choked. It was me. It was always me.

I opened my eyes in the dark, panting, clutching at my chest, shirt balled in my fists, the panic hot and white and unrelenting. Next to me, Jake snored softly, oblivious. I watched the covers rise rhythmically with his breath. A demonstration of his ability to not give a crap about anything.

I rolled away from him onto my side, knees hugged tight against my wildly hammering heart. The skin of my arms and legs was dewy with sweat. A scar on my ankle throbbed and stilled just as abruptly.

*You're not back there, Hannah. You're here. You're here.*

But I wasn't here, not all the way, not ever. Even on my best days, I could still hear him, my first love, my only hate, whispering in my ear *I'll find you, you little whore*. I could still smell him—the stink of sweat and some musky, dirty, vulgar thing lingering long after the nightmare, trying to choke me as I lay in the filmy pre-dawn gloom.

I raised my eyes and blinked back tears as the alarm clock swam into focus. Five-fifteen. Two and a half hours until I had to leave for work. Two and a half hours to get myself together and not be so fucked up, or at least find a way to act less obviously crazy. But acting was hard. Most days, I'd rather just disappear into the background. I fantasized about slipping from view, a lithe mass of dark hair, wide mouth and green eyes fading to a transparent whisper, then only the scenery behind, as if I had never existed. If I could force this disappearing, I would. Then maybe I could stop running.

I sucked in a deep breath, my heart expanding and jerking sharply like an agitated blowfish in my chest. Slowly, carefully, I dragged myself away from Jake to the edge of the bed, keeping my eyes on the door in case someone burst through it and grabbed me by the throat. At least Jake would wake up and help me, or I hoped he would; I was counting on him for that part. Probably the one thing I could count on him for. I hoped I was worthy of at least that much.

I swung my feet off the bed, toed around for the slippers below, and crept to the bedroom door, cringing against the chill on my clammy skin, alert for the slightest sound. *Nothing*.

Panic's chokehold lessened to a subtle pressure. *Jesus*. If neurotic freaks ever ended up being cool, I'd be ready for the red carpet. I crept down the hallway toward the living room, pretending I was Scooby Doo on the trail of a creepy amusement park owner. Silliness wasn't the only way to chill out, but it was one way. And it worked… sometimes.

Other times the panic ended up strangling me.

I paused in the hallway, listening, and flicked on the light. Shadowy, amorphous shapes solidified into a familiar scene: the couch, the table, a pack of Jake's cigarettes. I scanned the apartment for the slightest movement. Nothing, not even behind the window curtain. No noise outside. A hint of Jake's lingering cigarette smoke harassed my nostrils and the dusky memories shivered away.

I checked the window lock anyway, snaking my hand behind the curtain and pulling it aside so I could poke at the tab with a trembling finger. Below me, the street was empty, the patch of frosty grass along the sidewalk glowing amber under the streetlight. I dropped the curtain, picked my way back through the living room and groped the deadbolt on the front door. Locked.

My purse sat on the table. I pulled my phone out of it and my heart seized and restarted as I tapped in my code. No creepy text messages. No threatening voicemails. Nothing.

I pushed my purse aside and jumped at the sound the strap made when it slid and hit the table. In the kitchen, the overhead light bounced off the refrigerator and cast a weird, flattened circle of light on the floor. I concentrated on it as I waited for my heart to shrink and drop out of my throat.

*Cake. I should bake a cake.* Because isn't that where everyone's mind goes after a horrible recurring nightmare and panicked lock-checking? But I was being practical. Now I wouldn't have to stop at a bakery on my way from work to the women's shelter, and Ms. LaPorte would get a nice birthday surprise. I still owed her. Probably would for the rest of my life.

I shuffled to the cabinets and carefully pulled out cake-making supplies. Once the mix was emptied into the bowl, I cracked the eggs and zoned out, there but not, baking on autopilot. People got over stuff, right? They left it behind them. Eventually I would forget how the clasp on my duffel bag jangled as I ran for the bus station, chest heaving with sorrow and loneliness and abject terror. Eventually I would forget the way his calloused hands felt against my windpipe. I grabbed the whisk and attacked the mixture in the bowl. Each ingredient added brought the batter one step closer to something better, just like each day took me one step farther from where I had started. I wasn't as delicious as cake, but I was surely an improvement on who I had been five years ago.

Ten minutes later the cake was baking and I was on my way to the shower. I got ready in the dark, easing drawers open and closed to avoid waking Jake. Unless I startled him, he wouldn't be up until well after I was gone and his first cigarette would kill any lingering vanilla in the air. Which was good, especially today. He had no idea where I went after work and the cake would raise more questions than I ever wanted to answer.

## THURSDAY, OCTOBER 8TH

On the morning of his forty-ninth birthday, Edward Petrosky awoke with the remnants of liquor thick and woolly on his tongue. The dawn had brought a gray film that settled on him like fingerprint dust. He stretched, hauled on his clothes, and tripped over frayed carpet to the bathroom.

The mirror over the sink revealed a weathered forehead topped by thinning hair the color of salt and shit. In blue jeans, sneakers, and a gray button-down shirt, he probably looked more like a retired gym teacher than a detective. But that was appropriate; he hadn't felt like a detective in a long time.

Petrosky brushed the fuzz off his tongue, willing his bleary mind to connect with his legs, and headed for the kitchen. In the living room, the suede sofa sat, scuffed and battered, against one wall. Next to it stood a wooden end table, its cigarette-burned top hidden under a tattered copy of some fitness magazine he'd stolen from the dentist's office, and a half-empty (aw, hell, three-fourths-empty) bottle of Jack Daniels.

He ignored the itch to grab the bottle and hauled himself through the doorway into the kitchen, where his daughter's old princess nightlight lit up the stovetop in rose. He swallowed away the ache in his chest and flicked the light switch. Cabinets that had glowed dusty pink now showed their true state, covered with nicks and dings over top of the three refinishing jobs completed at the behest of his ex-wife. She had left the month after Julie's death—before the last coat of paint had dried—still screaming: "Why can't you find who did this to her?"

Julie's thirteen-year-old body had been found broken and mangled after being ravaged for two days by feral dogs. She'd been strangled to death and discarded like a piece of trash.

13

Petrosky had left the room before the coroner could finish with the details—probably the only reason he was still functioning at all. His ex-wife certainly hadn't helped him stay sane. Or sober.

"If we didn't live down here, this never would have happened!" had been her favorite assault because she knew it cut him deepest. And she was right. That shit happened far less to rich folks. He should have worked harder. Now he had less reason to. He fucking hated irony.

He grimaced at the cabinets and shut off the overheads. On the wall, the nightlight flickered, the only candle on his pathetic cake. Petrosky grabbed his keys.

*Happy birthday to me.*

His unmarked Caprice smelled like stale fries, old coffee and resentment, like any respectable cop's car should. Through the windshield, the clouds were pregnant with rain—or maybe snow. You never could tell. October around Metro Detroit was a crapshoot: sometimes warm, sometimes frigid, usually miserable. In the distance, the sun peeked through heavy layers of cloud cover and bathed the street in light. But Petrosky saw the sickness the sun illuminated. The sun's rays couldn't wash away the grime that covered humanity, couldn't conceal the barbs in people's brains that led them to strangle their children, beat their wives, or leave their best friends lying in the gutter, life shimmering from their limp bodies through the manhole covers. By now, the blood underneath the city probably flowed like a hematic river.

Out the passenger window, the Ash Park precinct grew larger, two stories of the dullest dirt-colored brick, home to donuts, pigs and paperwork. On the other side of the street, a matching building proclaimed *Ash Park Detention Facility*, only partially visible behind the lake fog that crept over their tiny part of the city every morning.

He swung into the lot in front of the precinct—an acre of cement, and not one close spot. *Typical.* Stray pebbles crunched and spun from under his tires as he drove to the back of the lot and parked under a streetlamp. It blinked out for the day as he killed the engine and opened the door.

Petrosky glowered at the light and shoved his keys into his pocket. The air brushed at his cheeks with damp fingers, the wet seeping into his sneakers as he clomped toward the building.

On the sidewalk, two familiar silhouettes stood close—not close enough to arouse the suspicion of the masses, but Petrosky knew better. Shannon Taylor was a firecracker of a prosecutor with a perpetual knot of blond at the base of her neck and an ice-blue stare that could cut you in half. Severe black and white pinstripes covered a bony frame that could probably use more home-cooked meals, or at least a few donuts. She wouldn't get either of those with Curtis Morrison.

Morrison was a rookie in the detective unit and still wore pressed blue slacks, though he'd at least traded in the traditional blue uniform shirt for a black crew-necked sweater. He'd relocated from California after getting some fancy English degree. Since they'd met last year, the guy had spent their down time trying to feed Petrosky granola and hounding him to join his gym. Petrosky was perfectly content with carrying twenty years of stake-out donuts around his waist. He assumed he would continue to decline until he finally retired, and then it would be too late to give a shit anyway.

Not that he gave a shit now.

Petrosky stepped onto the curb.

"Leave my rookie alone, Taylor," he barked.

Morrison jumped like he'd heard a gunshot. He was more physically imposing than Petrosky at a chiseled six foot one, but he had a surfer boy smile in a perpetually tanned face, and blond locks too long for any self-respecting cop. Perfect for beach going, though. All that was missing was the bong.

Taylor smirked. "That still works on him, eh?"

"Still."

Morrison grinned. "I always get jumpy when I see that

ugly mug of yours."

Taylor leveled her gaze at Petrosky. "I was just filling in your better half on Gregory Thurman."

"That asshole needs to go away forever," Petrosky said.

"He won't. Few months maybe, based on the physical evidence we had. Child abuse, but not rape."

"I gave you the girl! What the hell happened?"

"She told *you* he raped her every day for five years. But she won't tell me, and she sure as hell won't tell a jury."

"Fuck." Petrosky glanced at a stray piece of concrete near his shoe. He fought the urge to kick it.

"You have a way of getting female vics to talk, Petrosky. If you figure out a way to keep them talking, let me know."

Petrosky glared at her. In his peripheral, Morrison opened his mouth, closed it again, and looked at his shoes.

Taylor adjusted her bun and brushed imaginary lint off her suit jacket. "Speaking of talking, I've got a date with a working girl later. She'll serve some time. Keeps asking for you, Petrosky. Says you bailed her out before, thinks you'll do it again."

"I didn't do shit."

"You don't even know her name."

"I plead the fifth."

"I have the paperwork."

"I'm sure she was innocent that time. And anyways, sex isn't a crime."

"It is if you get paid for it." Taylor glared at him. "And it's dangerous. If we get them off the streets, we can help them."

"How very utopian. But it isn't her fault when someone else is abusing—"

"I prosecute the abusers too."

"Right. Sometimes." Petrosky's phone buzzed in his back pocket. He ignored it in favor of watching Taylor's left eye twitch.

"If you want out of sex crimes, bailing out working girls is the way to do it," she said.

"Who says I want out of sex crimes?"

16

Taylor crossed her arms as Petrosky's back pocket buzzed again. He snatched out the phone, glanced at the text message and jerked his head from Morrison to the direction of the parking lot. "We've got a call. Get moving, California."

Morrison nodded goodbye to Taylor and stepped off the curb. Petrosky followed.

"I'll be down in a little while to get your working girl, Taylor," he called over his shoulder. "Do me a favor and have her ready, would ya? And remind her to put the wrong address on her paperwork so she's harder to find when she skips bail."

"Fuck you, Petrosky." Her heels clacked away until the only sounds against the pavement were Petrosky's sneakers and Morrison's rubber-soled somethings, probably made out of hemp or whatever the hell they made shoes out of in California.

"Consorting with the enemy, surfer boy?"

"She's on our side, boss."

"That she is. But she's still a fucking lawyer."

"I guess." Morrison didn't look convinced. "So what kind of call did we get?"

"Some kids found something over on Old Mill. If we hurry we'll beat the medical examiner."


The cemetery was in an older part of town where residents had started demolishing abandoned homes and raking up the dirt to plant gardens. Across the street, a defunct workout facility sat next to a Chinese food restaurant, each furthering the need for the other, yet both one step away from being turned into a cabbage patch.

Petrosky parked in the road. The entrance gate to the cemetery hung from one hinge and shrieked as Morrison pulled it open. Petrosky winced. *Whispering Willows, my ass.* The gravestones were cracked and crumbling, etched with faded epitaphs about the beloved deceased: *William Bishop, forever in our hearts*, though the barren grounds around the plots suggested that poor Mr. Bishop had been very much forgotten. Through the fog, toward the center of the grounds, stood a small stone building—a poor man's Taj Mahal.

Crime techs milled about in the brown grass outside the building, tweezing bits of dirt and leaves into baggies. One— a kid with insect eyes and boy band hair—saw Petrosky and Morrison and waved them over. "You won't be able to get in with anyone else. It's pretty small."

Hooker heels and a tiny swath of cloth, maybe a tube top, lay discarded outside the door. Probably the reason they'd called him. Sex crime or not, no one else cared about prostitutes.

Petrosky ducked into the building. The air was thick, heavy with the tang of metal and rotting meat and other noxious fumes he didn't want to consider. A row of tiny doors the size of apartment mailboxes, presumably niches for ashes, lined the back wall, keeping silent vigil over the cement room. Below the niches sat a waist-high stone table on concrete pillars, probably used for flowers. But there were no flowers today. Only the girl.

She was on her back on the slab, arms and legs bent awkwardly and tied together between the table legs. Her swollen tongue protruded over blackening lips that pulsed as if she were trying to talk, but that was only the maggots, writhing in her mouth. It had been a few days. How long exactly would be determined by the medical examiner, but he was guessing at least four or five days based on the lack of rigor mortis and the blisters on her marbled skin. Deep gouges that looked more like knife wounds than split flesh scored her arms and legs. Someone had beaten her badly before killing her. If she had been untied then, they'd at least get some skin samples if she had slashed him with her nails.

*Someone's baby girl.* Petrosky's stomach roiled and he patted his front pocket for a spare antacid but came up empty. He inhaled through his nose and clenched his jaw.

The knife wounds continued onto her torso. Her abdomen had been torn apart. On top of her thighs lay coils of intestine, some of them shredded like strips of bacon. Another organ, black and jelly-like, sat on her chest, the side wall torn, fluids oozing from beneath it.

Petrosky bent to examine the restraints binding her wrists and ankles. Metal cuffs, easy to come by, though forensics would have more on the specifics later. Dark stains dripped over the slab and onto the floor, which appeared clean, or at least bore no discernible prints. She had bled a great deal in that little room. Hopefully she had been unconscious.

From the doorway behind Petrosky, Morrison's camera phone clicked. "Holy shit."

Petrosky straightened. "Suck it up, California, this is the job." Not that surfer boy would be getting the full brunt of the smell halfway outside the room.

"Got it, boss." Morrison aimed the phone again and snapped a photo of the letters on the right wall, inky and dripping.

> *A boat beneath a sunny sky*
> *Lingering onward dreamily*
> *In an evening in July-*

"Is that paint?" Morrison asked.

"I doubt it." Petrosky backed out into the cool, muggy air.

"Detective!" The bug-eyed tech stood near the corner of the building, holding out two plastic bags. "Got a purse with I.D. We're dusting the area now."

Petrosky noted the purse, laying on the ground next to a tube of lip balm and a pen. "Needles?"

"No, sir."

"Pills?"

"No, sir. Just some condoms, a little makeup. And this." He held up one of the bags.

Petrosky peered through the clear plastic. "Meredith Lawrence. Morrison, you got your notebook?"

"You know it, boss."

"Seventy-three eleven Hoffsteader, apartment one-G." Petrosky nodded to the tech and headed up the path toward the car.

Morrison fell into step beside Petrosky, hippie shoes

squishing through the grass. "You think it's like… a psychopath?"

"Maybe. He's calculating. Aggressive. Not what you'd normally see in a crime of passion. I think we can be certain that he took her here to kill her since he had the cuffs. And there aren't any clear signs of struggle around the building. Even the clothes by the door are in one piece. Either she knew him and trusted him enough to follow him in, or she was already unconscious when they got here."

"What would motivate someone to—to cut her open like that?"

Petrosky shrugged. "Whatever she did, she didn't deserve this."

"I can't imagine anyone does."

Petrosky ground his teeth and studied the mournful clouds.

*It's okay, Hannah. Just breathe.*

I breathed. It didn't help. Probably because there was a big difference between entering employee files into a computer database and telling someone to get the hell out.

The paperwork rustled with a thick swoosh that sounded like the whisper of a thousand jerks before me getting rid of inconvenient people. It was the swoosh of the executioner's axe over Marie Antoinette, the swoosh of Hitler throwing a swastika like a ninja dagger at a disobedient solder. Though I was probably nicer than Hitler. I hoped.

I pulled the phone to my ear and punched in the numbers. "Mr. Turner?" My voice quavered. *Darn it.* "We need to see you down in HR… yes, I will meet you here… Thank you." Clunk went the phone receiver, like Marie Antoinette's head.

Turner was one of seventy or so engineers the Harwick Technical contract house employed, and one of thousands we contracted out worldwide. He would be at my desk in five minutes, or as long as it took to get from his floor of big projects and design deadlines to my tiny piece of Hell.

*Human resources: where happiness goes to die.*

I rustled through the papers one last time, stood, and took a step toward the entrance of my office.

Well, not really an office. Unlike in the rest of the building, where you could touch your neighbor from your desk, the cubicles here were spaced for privacy—little islands in each corner further segregated by chest-high opaque acrylic. The partitions were low enough that you could still see who picked their nose while they typed. You could also tell who liked their dogs, who had children, and who was in that awkward in-between phase where a new child made a previously devout pet owner decide that it was just a stupid

21

dog after all, leaving them to tuck Chihuahua pictures behind fresh shots of chubby babies. Maybe it made them feel less guilty about their shifting priorities.

The wall to the side of my desk was covered by an old cork board. I had put it there just in case I ever got a dog, though worrying about Jake was enough for now. On my side of the room, my best and only friend Noelle stared at the computer in her corner. Across the room from Noelle, Ralph's bookish glasses wobbled as he attacked an acne eruption on his cheek. In the corner behind Ralph, Tony was nearly invisible, his chalky skin and pale blond hair disappearing into the white of the room. I had never spoken to him, not once in four years. When I'd first started at Harwick, I tried smiling at him, but he swiveled his chair away. Noelle had said he was autistic—but maybe I just had spinach in my teeth. Neither would have surprised me.

The only other person in the room was Jerome, the security guard, who was summoned on an as-needed basis to our part of the building. His ebony skin and shaved head glistened under the fluorescent lights. I often wondered how much trouble I would get into if I were to rub his head like a shiny Buddha, but I didn't have the guts to find out.

Jerome watched the door, Noelle watched the computer, Ralph glanced at the fingers he'd pulled from his pimply face, and none of them noticed me and my shaking hands. Maybe I had already started to fade.

Through the glass wall between my office and the hallway, David Turner approached the door. Turner was tall, with protruding eyes, a beak-like nose, and thin lips pulled into an uneven line. In contrast to his unimpressive face, his gray suit and tie were neatly pressed and impeccably matched. He strode with the confident gait of a man who knew his own worth.

He would not maintain that confidence for long; they never did. It was like watching a balloon deflate every time. I usually deflated with them, leaving me feeling spent and hollow.

Turner pulled the door open and looked at the other workers, who steadfastly pretended not to hear him or know why he was there. Clearly unaware of the nature of my job, he smiled at me and marched to my cubicle.

I drew myself up to my full five-foot-four inches. I wished I were taller. Magic beans. I needed magic beans. Or an earthquake. I paused, hoping for some catastrophe to strike, so someone else could pick this up later. Nothing.

*Figures. Way to go, Michigan.*

He sat, and I did too, lest I end up looking like even more of an overbearing asshole. My heart scampered around like a pissed-off weasel. I cleared my throat, readying my speech from the training manual script. "Mr. Turner, unfortunately your services are no longer needed. As of today, you will no longer be an employee of Harwick Technical Solutions. We will mail your final paycheck to the address on file. You will have fifteen minutes to gather your belongings and make your way to the parking lot. Security will assist you."

The color drained from Turner's face. "But... I... I haven't had any complaints since I've been here. I have a wife, two kids. There must be a mistake."

I averted my eyes, hoping he'd think I was giving him time to process, but my motivations were selfish: I needed to focus on something else before my heart blew up. In the middle of the desk was a corner of paper I must have torn from the folder earlier in a subconscious attempt to curb my anxiety. Across the top of the desk, the three ceramic owls that usually stared at me quizzically were glaring like I had shit on their waffles. My favorite was a horned owl missing an ear. I had stowed the ear in a desk drawer, intending to glue it back on, but had since decided I rather preferred his one-eared imperfection. Plus, it made him look less smug.

"Is there anything I can do?" Turner's voice cut into my owl assessment. "If I understood the problem..."

I blinked. His frustration was palpable, his fists clenched, and I resisted the urge to duck. A bruise on my arm throbbed.

*You've got this, Hannah. You're okay.*

Turner's eyes flicked to the security guard.

I followed his stare, relieved to see we had Jerome's full attention. Jerome always made me feel safer, like he could somehow shield me from anything that might come through the doors. If only he could protect me from the psychos in my past. My heart lurched drunkenly against my breastbone.

Jerome approached the cubicle. "Mr. Turner, you will have to come with me." His voice was the texture of wet silk.

Turner stood slowly.

I pushed the papers toward him. "I need your signature at the bottom of this form."

Turner signed it, barely glancing at the few lines of text, and walked from the cubicle toward the main doors. In seconds, he was eclipsed by Jerome, the guard's gleaming bald head the sun to Turner's gray misshapen moon.

I took a few deep breaths. Human resources wasn't the perfect job for me, but the guards and the locked entrance made it safe enough. And it was far, far away from… *him*.

*Lovers ain't nothin' once they go south.* I couldn't remember where I had heard that, but it was more poignant than most of the nonsensical songs about true love and happiness and beauty and bullshit.

I looked at the clock in the lower corner of my computer screen. Half an hour. Would my chest palpitations ever relent? Maybe I should pound on my breastbone, gorilla style, to subdue my heart. But I'd just end up looking like an idiot.

"Hannah?" Noelle leaned over the partition. Her blond hair floated in silk strands over blue eyes and full lips made even more supple by pinkish gloss. Men followed her with their eyes, if not their actual penises.

Even I couldn't help staring at her sometimes.

I forced a smile and moved my hand from my chest to the desktop before Noelle thought I was playing with my boobs.

"I'm going to grab a coffee, then take some dismissal forms back to the filing room," she said. "Do you have any more?"

"Sure do. I'm the most popular person here today. As

long as popular means everyone wants to punch you in the throat."

Turner's dismissal papers required my signature as the bearer of bad news. It was like signing a death certificate, as if before that moment, nothing had happened that couldn't be taken back. Adding the final signature always made me feel like the biggest douchebag. Maybe coroners felt like that too, with their endless parade of dead-on-arrival cadavers.

I scrawled my name on the form.

*Rest in peace, Turner.*

*Stop thinking crazy shit and say something.*

I looked at Noelle. "I like the pink gloss, by the way. It looks like you blew a dude made out of cotton candy." *Crisis averted.*

"Cotton candy doesn't talk back. Hey, you going to the company picnic tomorrow?"

"Oh… yeah, I think so."

Noelle squinted at me. "What's up with you? You look like someone just killed your dog."

"I don't have a dog."

"Something happen with Jake?"

I pulled my sleeve over my wrist, folded the cuff into my palm and tucked my fists into my lap. My sweaty handprint remained on the desk top.

"Did he find a job yet?"

*Is littering the house with fast food wrappers a job?*

Noelle stared at me.

"No. It's not Jake. It's just… this." I nudged Turner's termination papers on the desk.

Noelle nodded, her silver earrings swinging. "You want to go out somewhere tonight? It'll take your mind off of it."

"Nah, I told Jake I'd be home early."

Noelle's eyes darkened, and my breakfast skittered around in my stomach.

"Soon, okay?" I said.

"Sure. Here, I'll take those papers." She smiled and I watched her go, swaying her hips to unseen music.

I turned back to my computer and glanced again at the clock. Twenty more minutes and I'd be on my way home to the man I loved, or at least, was pretty sure I loved. And he loved me back, as long as I didn't make him mad, which happened more than I wanted to admit. But he was the lesser of two evils. No matter how much of an asshole Jake was, he wouldn't kill me. That had to be enough since I couldn't take Jerome home. Maybe I did need a dog. Not a Chihuahua though. Those things are yappy jerks.

I set my jaw, pulled the keyboard closer and went back to work.

———————

Dominic Harwick sat at his desk, his manicured fingers tapping on the keyboard as he finished reviewing the newest batch of engineering resumes. It was a menial task, beneath him, but it was necessary; each individual represented a dollar amount he would not forget.

He had begun a startup engineering staffing firm fresh out of Harvard. When the recession hit, he put his inheritance to work for him, buying up property in California, Texas and New York. But he'd finally settled on Michigan as his home, unable to convince himself to abandon the glorious buyer's market that had developed in the blighted Detroit Metro area. A few years later, Harwick Technical Solutions had acquired international acclaim by securing a staffing contract from a large aeronautical corporation, prompting local papers to ask, *What Recession?* when covering the construction of his ultra-modern, four story contract house.

His father would have been proud, though he'd have gotten nothing more than a curt nod from Rupert Harwick. Dominic could still picture his stocky legs, his barrel chest and the salt and pepper hair he had kept buzzed close to his scalp. Even if he had let it grow, no one would have dared call him anything other than 'Colonel,' 'Mr. Harwick,' or 'Sir'.

Dominic reviewed the last resume, made a note, and shut down the computer. The screen lowered into a special compartment inside the desk, leaving the opaque glass desktop perfectly pristine. Across the room, leather-bound books sat next to gleaming modern sculptures on custom glass shelves, all now cast in the orange glow of twilight from the floor-to-ceiling windows behind the desk. An oil painting of Duke, his Great Dane, hung beside a door of the thickest oak money could buy.

While the rest of the building was full of glass walls and low partitions to encourage openness and cooperation, his office was shut away from everything and protected by a bulldog-like secretary who let no one enter without his approval. An army of assistants kept his life just as he wanted it: uncomplicated, predictable, and efficient.

Dominic glanced at his Rolex, stood, and walked to the window. On the glass near his right hand, a smudge left behind by the cleaning crew sullied his view. He frowned.

*Distasteful.*

Dominic peered past the offensive blemish. Below him, a large employee parking lot ended in an expanse of rolling hills that sloped down to meet the water. By day, he could see the lake peeking from behind the tall oaks, maples, and firs that surrounded the five-acre complex. At dusk, the west-facing windows provided an overture to day's end. But these were not the reasons he had chosen this space for his office.

For several minutes, all was quiet. Then he saw him.

David Turner emerged from the building carrying the contents of his desk, his jacket, and, from the look of his hunched shoulders, his pride. He fumbled with his keys, popped the trunk of his car and hoisted the box into the back. As he closed the trunk, he wiped his eyes with the back of his hand.

Yesterday, Dominic had overheard Turner bragging to a fellow worker about his track record at the company.

"Six years of service," Turner had said, "and not one complaint."

People who got too comfortable became unimaginative workhorses and rarely came up with anything new. They were bad for business. Sometimes when Dominic fired people like that they seemed relieved, leading him to suspect an inherent boredom with their daily tasks. Turner did not strike him as that type of person, but Dominic suspected the man had some type of emotional connection to the company beyond a simple paycheck, something that would keep him there regardless of his motivational level. And he knew it wasn't Turner's wife, whose makeup-covered split lip at a fundraiser last week spoke volumes about her ability to influence her husband.

Turner would have no trouble landing another job, and quickly at that. Yet, the man was crying. If allowed to, he would have stayed well past his usefulness.

The idea made Dominic's back tense. He turned from the window, plucked his briefcase off the floor, and left the office, each step on the open stainless steel staircase echoing his departure like a drum roll.

Near the bottom floor, another set of footsteps sounded. He paused in the stairwell and watched as Hannah Montgomery appeared around the bend and hurried toward the glass doors to the parking lot, hair flying behind her, feet tapping at a nervous pace against the tile. Despite her constant deer-in-headlights demeanor, he had never once regretted hiring her. She was quick. Predictable. Reliable. Efficient.

Unlike Turner. Dominic smiled and continued down the stairs.

She startled at the sound of his footsteps and dropped her purse. By the time Dominic reached her, she was on her knees scooping items back into her bag. Practical things: a wallet, car keys, sunglasses. She avoided his gaze as he bent and handed her a standard issue blue checkbook. Their fingers touched. She snapped her hand away as if he had shocked her.

They stood and she shouldered the bag.

"How are you this evening, Ms. Montgomery?"

She met his eyes, then looked at her shoes. "I'm fine."

She was an intriguing girl.

"I got your email the other day in response to my request for new ideas in staffing recruitment. You had some great suggestions."

She looked at him again, and this time her eyes lingered on his face. "Really? I mean, thank you, Mr. Harwick."

"I am already implementing some of them. As you know, I believe that the people who work for me are the lifeblood of this company. There's nothing more crucial to its continued success than quality hires. I'm glad to have people like you on the team."

Her face and neck reddened, as did the small swath of chest near her clavicle. "Thank you, sir."

"Have a great night, Ms. Montgomery." He watched her disappear through the glass doors to the parking lot and headed for his private garage below the building.

*Hannah.* It was a lovely name. He wondered if her skin felt as satiny as it looked.


Dominic was still considering her when his Aston Martin crunched up the limestone drive to his expansive home of white concrete and glass. In front of the house, life-sized marble nudes looked forlornly over the grounds amidst a sea of lilies and vibrant red bee balm on its last blush of the year. Not a single weed, as it should be.

He entered through the mudroom and removed his shoes to avoid marring the white marble floors that ran the length of the first level. The lights flickered on as he strode past a roomy half bath, through the kitchen, and into the living room, where a four foot high blown glass sculpture in blue sat on an iron table between convex white leather sofas. No coffee table. A television was hidden in the ceiling, though he usually had better things to do with his time. The Colonel had admonished those who spent their days on frivolous pursuits. Not that Dominic had ever argued with him about it.

He took the open steel staircase at the back to the second

floor master suite which was as open as the first floor, save for a bathroom and a gym at the back. He changed his clothes, returned to the mudroom to tie on running shoes, and took the door to the back porch.

Like everything else, the black paint on the porch was a conscious decision–even the door to the outdoor bathroom where he cleaned off after running was the same deep, sooty color of his Great Dane.

Duke had been a pup when Dominic had taken him from his dying father. Nothing makes a man more trustworthy than a dog, the Colonel had said. As always, his father had been spot on.

Instead of running circles around his four acres of meandering waterfront property, Dominic jogged through the gate, down his drive and into the road. Duke followed at his heel, keeping pace through the quiet streets as the sun painted the sky with stripes of violet and fuchsia.

A young mother pushing a baby carriage piled high with blankets smiled at him as he passed. He nodded in her direction. A few blocks later, an elderly man tending to some end-of-season gardening gave him a friendly wave. Dominic waved back and the chill air kissed his exposed hands.

A few blocks from his home, open wrought iron gates welcomed him into the neighborhood park. The breeze off the manmade duck pond brought with it the scent of dead and dying cattails, and with them, the memories of summers on Lake Michigan, his father at the helm of their sailboat.

He headed toward the pond, watching the withered grass along the side of the walk. Winter was coming early, but Dominic felt no anticipation for the upcoming holidays. There would be no tree, no gifts, no family gatherings. Those days were gone.

As he passed a wide curve in the path, a woman came into view. She leaned over to stretch her legs, her spandex pants leaving nothing to the imagination. Diamond and amethyst rings sparkled on her fingers and a small dog yipped around her heels on a ridiculously tiny leash.

Dominic did not recognize her face or the perfectly symmetrical breasts that swelled under her zippered top. She must live elsewhere, and from the way her gaze lingered on his expensive running gear, he guessed she probably lived in a less affluent subdivision.

He ran past her, three steps, four steps, five, giving her time to start running, then glanced back and feigned surprise, both that she was still watching him and that he had been so unfortunately caught in his stolen look. He turned his face forward again and slowed his pace to match the *thwap thwap* of her approaching sneakers behind him. She bumped his elbow. Cheap perfume and another, undeniably female scent cut the earthy aroma of decaying foliage. Her lipsticked mouth turned up at the corners, playing coy.

He didn't buy it. "Hello," he said.

"Hi."

Their sneakers beat blithely against the pavement.

"Do you run here often?" she asked.

She was into clichés. He could do that.

"Yes, Duke here seems to love it. Well, that and the lovely animals he finds to play with."

*Nothing made a man more trustworthy than a dog.*

"Yeah, Tootsie enjoys that as well." She gestured to the tiny dog at her heel, scrambling to keep up.

*Tootsie.* He kept his grimace to himself.

"How about you? Do you like the view out here?" She winked.

Dominic tried not to sigh at the stale innuendo. "Yes. I have a thing for Pisces women."

Her eyes widened. "How did you—"

"Something in the elegant way you carry yourself." *And the birthstones on your fingers.* "Sorry if I was staring, but you are exceptional."

She smiled. She liked that.

They always did.

31

Two miles and a shower later, Dominic took her out to a small Italian bistro. Women were all the same in the way they expected him to impress them. He did not disappoint. He bought her wine while he drank sparkling water and regaled her with witty anecdotes and tales spun to show how interesting he was, with an emphasis on his financial success. When dinner was over he stifled a yawn and took her back to her house, ten miles from the park.

"I don't usually do this," she whispered as she pulled him through the front door.

They always said that. Why, he wasn't sure. It wasn't as if it would alter the outcome—or what he thought of her.

He watched her carefully, determining her likes and dislikes before she verbalized them. It was basic science, the flush of blood in certain areas of the body, subtle arching, accelerated respiration. When she began to scream his name, he pushed her further, heightening the experience to an art form as he drove himself into her. He raised his face to the window as she panted her way through her orgasm.

Later, as she slept, he went into her bathroom. Soap scum ringed the tub. Spots blemished the mirror. He stepped into the shower, turned the water to scalding, and scrubbed his body until his skin was raw. Then he pulled on his clothes without drying himself and walked out of the house. By the time he climbed into his car, her name was barely a memory.

# FRIDAY, OCTOBER 9TH

Petrosky grimaced at the man in front of him.

Preliminary research indicated that Meredith Lawrence didn't have much in the way of friends, jobs or family. All she had was recently eviscerated organs, her blood on a mausoleum wall and this asshole in the doorway.

"What do you mean she's dead?" Ronnie Keil stood blocking the front door of his apartment, staring blankly through Petrosky with the beady eyes of a reptile. The sweet haze of recently smoked marijuana wafted around Keil's pasty face from the room behind him.

"Mr. Keil, I know this must be difficult for you, but we need to ask you a few questions about your girlfriend."

"Questions about what? I didn't do it."

Petrosky exchanged a glance with Morrison. "No one said you did. But, we do need to know where you were yesterday. You sure weren't here."

Keil's snaggletooth scraped against his fat bottom lip. "I worked all day at the shipyard. After that I went to the bar on Rosenthall for my cousin's birthday."

Petrosky had verified Keil's work information the day before. "What's your cousin's name?"

"Gerald."

"Last name?"

"Keil, same as mine."

"Phone number?"

He told them.

Morrison flipped a page in his notebook.

"Tell me about Meredith. Anything you think might help," Petrosky said.

Keil's eyes were blank, more than marijuana stoned. Pills,

downers, maybe. Down the hall, a door slammed and someone cursed. Morrison glanced toward the sound. Keil stared, slack-jawed.

"Mr. Keil? What can you tell me about Meredith?"

"Oh uh... she was real pretty. Nice to most people unless they looked at her the wrong way."

"Had she mentioned meeting anyone new recently?"

"I don't think so." He paused. "She was kinda bitchy sometimes. You think someone killed her for that?"

"I doubt it," Petrosky said. "Did she ever go out to clubs?"

"Nah, nothing like that. She mostly just hung around here. Do you think it was someone she... like... knew already?"

"We're just covering all the bases, sir."

"Oh, well, she didn't know that many people anyway."

"Did she have any family? Any friends?"

"Her mama died when she was little. Never had a daddy."

No daddy. Not that a daddy would have been able to save her. Petrosky popped his knuckles against his hip and grimaced at the empty pocket where he used to carry his cigarettes. "No parents? Was she in foster care in Michigan?"

"Yeah. I dunno for how long or where, she didn't talk about it."

"How long were you together?"

Keil looked at the ceiling, thinking. "Maybe four years. Not quite."

"And in all that time she never mentioned where she grew up?"

He scuffed his foot on threadbare carpet. "Once she said she had a foster father who beat her up, and she ran away. That was before she met me."

"Brothers, sisters?"

"Just the kid but she hasn't seen him since we gave him up."

"A kid?" Petrosky's eyes snapped to Morrison. Morrison shrugged and shook his head. "What kid?"

"She was pregnant when we met. Had the kid, kept it here for a little, but she wasn't cut out for that. She took him to the church downtown, I think. The one where they have the orphanage."

"What was the child's name?"

"She called him Jessie, but I don't know if it stuck. He was only a few weeks old."

Morrison's pen scratched frantically against the notepad.

"The date?"

"No idea. Late August, maybe? September? She talked about needing to get the kid warmer clothes because it was getting cold. But we didn't, just put him in a blanket with all these little ducks on it and then she took him." His bottom lip quivered. Either the drugs were wearing off, or the police presence was shocking Keil into sobriety. Or he felt guilty about the kid.

"Who was the father?"

Keil swiped at his eyes. "No idea. She didn't either."

"So, a boy. And she took him to the church?"

"Yeah the big one right down the way. With all those troll things. I think it was the only one she could take him to. Not all of 'em take kids." He sagged against the door frame. "She's really dead?"

"Yes, sir."

"Like, dead, dead? I just thought she found an overnight. She was happy when she got one of those."

"I'm sorry for your loss."

"Aw, shit." Keil put a hand to his chest.

"Do you need to sit down?"

Keil lowered his hand to the doorframe and gripped it until the knuckles turned white, but he shook his head. "No. I'm okay."

"We'll make this as quick as possible, Mr. Keil. We need to know where she was the night before last. Who she was with."

"Working." Keil glanced at the wall and dragged his eyes to the floor, looking everywhere but at them.

"Mr. Keil, we have no doubt she was working the street. What I need to know from you is where she was standing when someone picked her up and killed her."

Keil's jaw worked, but sluggishly. "I'm not sure. Maybe Ventura? She was usually up there. If she went anywhere else, I dunno."

"Tell me about the overnights."

"Every now and then someone would pay her for the night, to stay there. Rich assholes with hotel rooms, I think. She always came home not worried about money for a day or so."

"Any idea who they were?"

He shrugged. "No, it was never the same person."

"When was the last time that happened?"

"It's been months."

"She have friends that she hung out with? Anyone you knew?"

Keil shook his head.

"How did she not have any friends?" Morrison asked.

Petrosky cleared his throat and kept his eyes on Keil. "Often in domestic violence situations, women are isolated from their friends and family in order to keep them from revealing the situation."

Keil stared at Petrosky, but said nothing. Morrison turned back to his notepad.

"Anyone she might have seen that night?"

"I don't know, man."

"Where were you the night before last between the hours of twelve and three a.m.?"

"Um... I think I was here."

"Anyone with you?"

Keil looked over Petrosky's shoulder, into the hallway. "Yeah... uh... Darcy."

"Last name?"

"Evans."

"Who is she?"

"A... friend."

"Meredith know you had a special friend, Mr. Keil?"

He stared.

"Did your girlfriend like poetry?" The bloody poem on the

36

mausoleum wall was a wild card Petrosky didn't want leaked, but Keil would be too nervous to tell the press… if he even remembered the question later.

Keil's eyebrows lifted. "Poetry?" He shoved his hands in his pockets. Keil probably had cigarettes. He'd probably let Petrosky bum one.

Petrosky narrowed his eyes. "Where does Darcy live?"

Keil raised an arm, feebly pointing to a door three apartments down from his. "Wait… uh, just wait a little, man. Her husband's home. Saw his car out the window."

"That doesn't bother me any," Petrosky said.

Keil's jaw dropped. He took the card Petrosky offered, but his eyes darted nervously toward the door across the hall.

"Sorry for your loss."

Keil looked once more down the hall and closed the door. The lock clicked into place.

"What do you think, boss?" Morrison asked as they walked toward the other end of the hallway.

"He's a dick, but he's telling the truth. Popping pills and coming off downers will make a person honest, if not a little confused. Good for us. He mentioned her overnights, then freaked out when we asked what she did. And the kid thing… he'll probably regret sharing that when he sobers up. We'll find out in a minute if his alibi checks out."

"I liked the way you snuck the poem in." Morrison lifted the knocker and dropped it. In a neighboring unit, a dog barked and someone yelled at it to shut the fuck up.

The man who answered the door dwarfed them both, his dark shoulders as wide as the doorframe, button-down shirt stretched over biceps that would make Hulk Hogan jealous.

"Afternoon, sir." Petrosky flashed his badge. "I'm Detective Petrosky with the Ash Park PD. I'm looking for a Darcy Evans."

The man's brows furrowed but he backed up and waved them in. "Of course, officers. Come in."

A black leather sofa sat against one wall beside a gleaming glass table with a Tiffany lamp that looked nice enough to be

37

real.

"Darcy! Some visitors for you!"

Petrosky studied a series of black-and-white photographs on the wall that appeared to be the insides of abandoned buildings. *Interesting*. Perhaps they had some photos of abandoned mausoleums.

Petrosky turned from the wall as a woman emerged from the back room, her black hair braided in neat rows. Her smile faded when she saw the badge. "Isaiah, what's going on?"

Isaiah shrugged his beefy shoulders.

"We're looking for information on Meredith Lawrence, your neighbor across the hall," Petrosky said.

Evans's shoulders relaxed. "Oh thank God. I thought someone had died."

"She did, ma'am."

Evans covered her mouth with her palm.

Morrison stepped forward, touching Petrosky's elbow. "Do you think we should do this in private?"

Her hand dropped to her chest. "Why?"

"Because it concerns Mr. Keil," Petrosky said.

Evans shrugged. "I don't know what you're getting at, but there are no secrets between me and my husband."

"Then let's jump right in," Petrosky said. "Ms. Evans, were you with Mr. Keil the night before last, between the hours of twelve and three?"

"In a manner of speaking—if you count him lying passed out in the hallway and me trying to wake him every twenty minutes as being together. I finally got Isaiah around three and he helped me get him into the house and onto his own couch. Though I think he slept through that part."

"Mr. Keil seemed more than a little concerned about me coming over here today."

"I can take this one," Isaiah said. "The one time we spoke, I told him that he needed to get his shit together and stop worrying my wife before I came after him. I wasn't... serious. I just hate to see her upset. She'll sit up all night, thinking he's going to die of an overdose outside our door."

"Did you know Meredith Lawrence?"

Isaiah shook his head. "Not at all."

Darcy sighed. "Not really, just in passing. We talked occasionally in the laundry room, but it was mostly complaining about the laundry machines not working and stuff. She was usually coming in when I was going out to work."

"And you work where?"

"I'm a photographer. I keep weird hours sometimes. Just ask my poor husband. He usually comes home for lunch so we can spend some time together."

Isaiah put his hand on the small of her back.

"What do you do, sir?"

"Molecular biologist."

Petrosky glanced around the apartment.

"You want to know why we live here? With guys like Keil? Student loans. We're saving for a house. And Darcy wants to write a book."

"Anything else you can tell us about Meredith, Mr. Evans? Mrs. Evans?" Petrosky watched them as the silence stretched, but there were no sudden shifts in movement, no alterations in breathing, no wandering eyes. Only slouched shoulders and furrowed brows—worry, but not defensiveness.

"The only thing I can think of that was different is that she seemed... sad," Darcy said finally. "Not a normal life stressor kind of thing, but real, deep sad. Something in her eyes. I take lots of pictures, so I notice that stuff. I just wish I knew why."

Isaiah wrapped his arm around her shoulders and pulled her to him.

Petrosky held out a card. "If you think of anything else-"

"Thank you. I hope you find who did it," she said.

Isaiah opened the door for them.

"We'll do our best, ma'am," Petrosky said.


Two more hours of door knocking gave them nothing new. Apparently, Meredith Lawrence had been invisible.

Hopefully her baby wouldn't be so elusive. If they could find the baby's father, all the better, particularly if he felt that Lawrence took his child from him. If Petrosky ever found the person who took his little girl, he'd do worse than slice them open and paint the walls with their blood.

Morrison clicked his seat belt. "So anyone can just drop off a baby and leave?"

"Safe Haven laws. You leave a baby in a safe place, like a fire station or a church instead of a dumpster, and you're not under obligation to answer questions. After a few months your parental rights are terminated and they set the kid up for adoption. Don't they have those laws in California? You'd think surfers would be first in line to drop off kids so they could get back to playing ukulele or whatever the fuck you people do."

"Yeah, they have the laws. But I never played ukulele, so I never paid much attention."

Petrosky ignored the smile in Morrison's voice and watched the sky roll around them, the clouds heavy and dark. He glanced at the temperature gauge on the dash. Forty-two. No snow today. Rain. Tomorrow was supposed to be warm, and when the sun came out, everyone would grin and talk about how glorious the weather was for October, as if this didn't happen every goddamn year.

Beside him, Morrison tapped on his phone as the church came into view. Through the windshield, gargoyles reached for the sky on stone spires above church doors that looked too massive for human use. Petrosky wondered if maybe you had to build 'em big to invite God in, but he wouldn't know anything about that; God had abandoned him a long time ago.

Petrosky pulled into the parking lot and took a space in front of the main door. Their footfalls crunched against the grand stone stairs. Above them, stripes of stained glass arched toward the thunderclouds, reflecting muted blues and greens and pinks. Morrison pulled the front door open with a *whoosh* and Petrosky followed him in.

The air inside burned with the sickly sweet aroma of

incense. Walls and windows repeated their footsteps back to them as they walked between the rows of pews toward the altar.

A door opened and shut behind the pulpit. A bald, rotund man with white eyebrows approached them, shoving his glasses up his bulbous nose, a white robe and long purple scarf swishing in his wake. "Can I help you gentlemen?" His voice was whisper quiet, perhaps a testament to years of sitting in a confessional.

Petrosky flipped his badge and stuck it back in his pocket. "I'm Detective Petrosky, and this is Detective Morrison. We're looking for information on a child that may have been dropped off here three years ago."

"Dropped off?"

"Part of the Safe Haven law."

The man pushed his glasses up his nose. "I see. Why don't you gentlemen follow me to my office and we'll see if there is any way I can help you." He turned, and they followed him through a back hallway, past ornate bronze and gold fixtures and oak walls glistening with furniture polish. At the last door, he stopped, unlocked it and waved them in.

An intricately carved oak desk dominated the red-carpeted room. On the top corner of the desk sat gold-plated wax stamps, blotters and sheets of rolled parchment. Stained glass windows bounced chartreuse light off a gilded Jesus crucified on the back wall, wrists bleeding gold, mouth agape in an eternal scream.

"Quite the place you have here," Petrosky said.

The priest lifted one corner of his mouth and settled behind his desk, pressing his fingertips together. Petrosky and Morrison sat in red wingbacks across from him. The chairs felt like satin. From the roof above, the muted rattle of rain began and intensified until it rang through the room like buckshot on tin.

"As you surely know, gentlemen, those who leave their children with us are not required to give information, and often don't."

41

"Understood. We're just hoping."

"For what exactly? Most of these children have gone on to successful placements with adoptive parents, some within this very congregation."

"We're not looking to take the child back," Petrosky said dryly. "His mother was slit open from end to end and we have reason to suspect that the father may be responsible."

The priest's jaw fell open and his hands dropped into his lap.

"Your name, sir? For our records," Petrosky said.

"Ernest Bannerman the third. Father Bannerman to our parishioners."

"Mr. Bannerman, can we get a look at those records?"

The priest pushed himself to standing and walked to a squat file cabinet in the back corner of the room. He slid out the bottom drawer, retrieved several thick folders, and returned to the desk where he flipped the top one open.

"We haven't had many, that's for sure. We've been lucky, I suppose. Only about twenty since the law came into existence." He scanned the top sheet, turning it over on the desk. "Do you know if you're looking for a boy or a girl?"

"A boy. Jessie. About three years ago, late summer or early fall."

"Ah." Bannerman replaced the page, closed the top folder and slid it and the second folder onto the desk. The bottom folder rasped as he pulled the top cover off. One page turned. Then another.

"Hmm."

"Got something, Mr. Bannerman?"

"No, no, not yet. We had two girls come in three years ago October. Another in December." He flipped a page. "I don't see anything else from that time. No boys, no Jessie. Are you certain of the year?"

Petrosky looked at Morrison, who nodded.

"Let's do a quick check of the other years," Petrosky said. "Four years up to two years ago."

Bannerman paged through another file, opened a third and

paged some more. He shook his head. "Most of these are older boys, winter or spring, a couple more girls."

Petrosky scowled. "We'll need a copy of that information for our records."

Bannerman's eyes went steely.

"I can get a warrant, but taking all that extra time won't help me find a killer who is still on the loose."

"I'll jot the information down for you." Bannerman pulled a sheet of stationery from his desktop and a pen that appeared to be made from an animal tusk. All God's fucking creatures. Apparently that one wasn't worth saving.

"Any other places around here that she could have taken him to?" Petrosky asked as Bannerman wrote.

"Downtown there's a fire station on Anderson that's listed as a Safe Haven." Bannerman made a final note and handed the paper to Petrosky, who folded the page into his pocket and stood.

"Thank you for your time, sir."

"Father." Bannerman straightened his shoulders.

"Whatever," Petrosky said.

Outside the church, rain sheeted, rattling the glass and making the stark tinny sound Petrosky had heard in Bannerman's office. He pulled the collar of his jacket tight against the wind and hustled to the car, littering the dash with tiny spots of water from his coat as he climbed in and jabbed at the heat controls.

Morrison was silent, tapping on his phone.

"You doing that texting thing with Taylor? None of that hanky panky shit during work."

"No, boss." Morrison didn't raise his eyes from the screen.

Petrosky turned onto the main road and watched the gothic church give way to a similar building that now belonged in equal parts to a legal practice and a bank. They passed a lot full of weed-ridden gravel. Then a gas station. Then a fast food joint. Only eight more restaurants to go and they'd be at the precinct. He stopped at a red light.

"Baby boy found dead on October twenty-third four

blocks from Lawrence's apartment," Morrison said.

"Lots of babies are found dead, Morrison. But we'll follow up."

"He was wrapped in a duck blanket, according to the news reports. They ran a picture of the blanket instead of a dead kid."

Petrosky squinted at the grainy image Morrison held out to him. He could barely make out a tattered blanket covered with yellow and orange ducks, graying with filth.

Petrosky turned back to the road. "Looks like we need to haul Keil back in for questioning."

"He gave us an awful lot of information for someone trying to hide the fact that he left his girlfriend's kid to die three years ago," Morrison said.

"True. But not all killers are smart." Petrosky tried to picture Keil in the mausoleum, dopey eyes staring at the wall as he painted words in blood: *A boat beneath a sunny sky*, *Lingering onward dreamily…*

Petrosky shook his head. "If she was the one who left the kid, daddy might be pissed at her. So far, Keil's the last one to see her alive and he might know more than he thinks he does."

Above them, the light turned green and Petrosky hit the gas. "There's a burger joint up here on the left. We can get it to go, hit the precinct to look up that poem, and head back to Keil's place."

"You want soup and salad?" Morrison looked up. "I know a place with awesome vegetarian chili."

"Unless it has dead cow in it, I don't want it."

Nothing but the pitter patter of sludge on the windshield. Petrosky glanced over.

Morrison stared at his phone, brows knit together in a mask of concentration. Probably a California thing, worrying about poor, abused cows. Maybe. Petrosky craned his neck to see the screen.

Morrison lowered the phone and Petrosky straightened and stared out the windshield.

"We don't need to stop at the precinct. I've got it."

"Got what? You sending PETA after me?"

"The poem. It's from *Through the Looking Glass*. Circa eighteen-seventy-one."

Petrosky raised an eyebrow. "Rare?"

"An original copy? Maybe. And our guy might have one if he's that into it. But the poems are available anywhere as evidenced by me pulling it up in two minutes on the web. I read it at some point in school, probably undergrad. One of those what's-the-meaning-of-all-this-shit kinda thing. I think I read it younger, too."

"Younger?"

"It's the prequel to Alice in Wonderland."

In Petrosky's mind, the gory letters on the wall morphed into a children's book, pages fleshy and oozing. "We'll hit the libraries tomorrow, make some calls, and see what we can come up with."

"Crazed professor?"

"Doubt it, but they might know something about the literature angle that we're not thinking about, even with your fancy-ass English degree."

Morrison didn't take the bait. "The words at the Lawrence scene are only the first few lines. The poem has seven verses, boss. That worries me."

"It should, Morrison." The rain relentlessly hammered the car, as if the clouds were attacking. Petrosky pressed harder on the gas.

Six more. That worried him too.

∗

The clock glowed five minutes until quitting time. Robert Fredricks popped his knuckles and studied the three-dimensional quarter panel blueprints on his computer screen. The design wouldn't win him any awards, but it was what his lead had asked for. And the job was a prime gig even if his asshole boss found something wrong with this design the way he had last time.

The call had come unexpectedly: "Can you come to Michigan?" Robert didn't remember signing in with the head hunters at Harwick Technical, but he assumed he must have. Even if it had been a paperwork mistake, he'd figured it was about time for his luck to change. He had packed up his basement apartment of meager belongings and taken a bus that same week. He wasn't in the main building on the lake, but it had only been a couple years. You never knew what might happen tomorrow.

At precisely five-thirty, he stood and threaded his way through the array of cubicles, down the elevator, and to the parking lot. His Nissan stuck out in the sea of Chryslers. The taupe and black granite building behind him cast a long shadow over the lot.

"Hey!" Thomas Norton waved his hands, a cheerleader above the rows of cars. Thomas had a cubicle in the same department, across the aisle from Robert. When Robert had started at Harwick Tech, Thomas had been the first person in the room to say hello, loping over on stocky legs with his mop of sandy hair shellacked to his head like a helmet. Thomas hadn't stopped talking since, though that wasn't what bothered Robert. It was Thomas's eyes, big and brown and all-knowing, the kind that seemed to peer into your soul. Robert hated that feeling, even the merest hint that someone could guess his most private thoughts. But, if Thomas had even the faintest idea what went on in Robert's head he wouldn't be smiling as he approached. And the women—shit, if *they* knew what Robert was thinking they'd run screaming into the night.

"Yo, Jimmy! We still on for drinks later?"

*Idiot.* Robert smiled. "You bet."

Thomas grinned like a fifteen-year-old girl with a cock in her ass. "I'll have a seat waiting."

Robert climbed into his car. *Jimmy. Ugh.* He hated the name, but it was necessary now that he could no longer use his own. The world was not a friendly place for ex-cons. Not that it had been particularly friendly before his arrest. He gritted his teeth and pulled from the lot.

He had always been bad. There had always been a filthy wrongness lurking within him, despicable and abhorrent, waiting to be exposed. He could remember the exact moment he discovered the truth of it.

He had been adopted into a pious family in southern Mississippi where the air was so thick in the summer it was like breathing underwater. Their old plantation house was surrounded by gnarled oaks— "hanging trees," his father called them, because of the slaves who had once strangled to death in the boughs. As a child, he often watched the wind rusting the branches with rapt attention, squinting until he swore he could see the bodies swinging. Even walking to the bus stop, something ominous always tainted the air, a wisp of energy not yet departed from the place, a tingling on his back whose origins he couldn't quite pinpoint.

Especially under those trees.

Sometimes he could feel the weight of the whole place bearing down on him, concentrated in the glare from his father's eyes. They were the eyes of a prophet, an angel even, at least if you asked the women of their congregation.

His father was not those things.

Despite his unknown heritage, Robert possessed those same eyes. He also had thick black hair and a finely boned face with a jaw wide enough to be attractive, or so he had assumed from the way the girls at school watched him. He wondered if they knew fornication was a surefire path to Hell. Desire was a manifestation of the Devil, his father would say, a ploy for the souls of the weak-minded.

Then it had happened to him, an unfamiliar tingling in his thighs as he watched his sixth grade teacher write Shakespearean verses on the blackboard.

> *But there's no bottom, none,*
> *In my voluptuousness: your wives, your daughters,*

47

*Your matrons and your maids, could not fill up*
*The cistern of my lust.*

Since then, his lust had never been sated, each libidinous thought weaving into a frenzied net set to wrench him kicking and screaming into the ring of fire. As a child his fingernails had gouged into his hardened flesh at these thoughts, bringing him pleasure and pain and pleasure again. Even then, he'd dared hope he might be normal someday. But then he'd been caught, hand on his body, palm still working, and his father had entered the room solemn-faced and carrying a willow switch.

"Train up a child in the way he should go: and when he is old, he will not depart from it," his father had said over and over again, a mantra to excuse the suffering he would inflict.

When his father yanked him from the bed and slung him to the hardwood floor, Robert knew there would be no absolution, particularly when the first blow from his father's fist landed hard against his spine. When his father ripped his shirt from his body and he heard the singing rod as it whipped through the air, he knew he was a dirty, rotten sinner. And when the willow slashed deep into the delicate skin of his back, over and over again, he cried out, because in his core, he knew God would have no mercy on someone like him.

He was bad. Disgusting. Unlovable. Unforgivable. There was no hope.

And without hope, there was no longer any point in fighting his carnality. Then oh, how it had grown. Like a beast in his belly, filling him, consuming him, eating him alive.

A car horn blared, startling him back to the present. Robert's erection was turning his pants into a prison.

Someday he'd find The One. She'd forgive him his thoughts, his actions, his deviousness. She'd understand his lust and appease his demons. She would save him from himself.

The light was green. The horn honked again. Robert waited for yellow and gunned it just as the light turned red, clearing the intersection amidst the bleats of horns belonging to other angry motorists.

He glanced in his rearview mirror and adjusted his zipper. Heat spread through his lower body.

He had to find the girl.

## Saturday, October 10th

The sun warmed my face and turned lake water ripples into a carpet of glitter thrown by an unruly child. The outdoor end-of-summer picnic at Harwick Technical was a vast improvement on the conference rooms we'd turned to last year when the picnic had been rained out.

Noelle sat alone with a plate of food at a table overlooking the lake. Closer to the building, children giggled on inflatable bounce houses. Their parents talked amongst themselves, feigning calm, but poised like meerkats ready to leap at the slightest indication of danger, or, more likely, hair pulling and unauthorized spitting.

I took my plate to where Noelle was sitting and claimed a spot across from her. Ribs, potatoes and corn, the best picnic food money could buy. At least I assumed that was true; I was certainly not a picnic connoisseur. If such a thing existed, that would be my new occupational goal. It would have been better than typing up employee files between bouts of crushing people's dreams.

"You don't have to look so pissed to be here," Noelle said. "I mean, you need to get out of the house sometimes, right? Explore the world. Get away from Ja—"

"I'm not pissed. Just hanging out." I took a bite of corn on the cob, feeling a little pissed. "Besides, Jake was busy today. He went over to his mom's house." A corn kernel escaped my lips and landed on the table. I wiped it away, pretending it was Jake's mother, the real reason I had told Jake this party was mandatory. At least he hadn't wanted to come; having Jake around would have made me feel extra horrible when my boss's presence turned me into a blubbering imbecile. I scanned the field for Mr. Harwick, but that sinewy mass of

50

handsome was nowhere to be seen. Bummer.

"Gotcha. Well, see? You wouldn't have been doing anything anyway." Noelle speared a piece of chicken. "Can I ask you a question?"

I shrugged. "Shoot."

"Why do you put up with that guy? He sits around all day, visiting with his mom and who knows who else, while you work to—"

"I love Jake for things besides money."

Noelle cocked her head. "What, like his cooking? Didn't he once cut the tops off the broccoli and serve only the bottoms?"

I winced. "He tried."

"I guess you must love him for his brains."

The corn rolled around in my stomach. "Everyone deserves a chance, right? And he's there for me when I need him."

Noelle snorted. "Like a faithful lap dog, only way more expensive."

"Faithfulness is important." My ears warmed. "Besides, it's his other attributes that keep me coming back." I winked and hoped it didn't look forced.

Noelle glanced across the field and back at me. "He must have a golden dick, then, for all the shit you put up with."

"Nothing golden now, but believe me, we tried. That sparkly paint was way too itchy."

"Jesus, Hannah."

"Jesus would never do the things I make Jake do to me." My ears cooled. The corn settled. I set the half-eaten cob on the plate and grabbed my fork.

"You're probably right about that. Plus he always had all those apostles following him around."

"He has a long staff though," I said. I smiled, and this time I meant it.

"So I hear." Noelle stared past me and straightened her shoulders, her boobs torpedoing toward someone at my back.

"Good afternoon, ladies."

I startled and dropped a forkful of potatoes at Mr. Harwick's voice. *Nice going, Hannah.*

He stepped around to the head of the table, his eyes deep blue oceans flecked with a lighter shade of gray. His aquiline nose cut through the middle of his face above lips that were just shy of pouty, now twitching up in amusement. The blue suit he wore was immaculate, right down to the silver cufflinks and navy-striped tie. Did he ever wrinkle? Each element of him registered, but separately like the flickered images from an old silent movie.

"Afternoon," I said. Noelle said it at exactly the same time, ensuring that we sounded like wannabe twins, or maybe synchronized talkers. Synchronized talking, an Olympic sport like synchronized swimming, only way lamer. If that was a thing, I had another job aspiration. But I couldn't think about potential jobs or anything else when Mr. Harwick's eyes were staring into mine and making my world disappear, which was probably totally unhealthy but I didn't care. Such was the nature of fantasy men, right? I waited for him to walk away like he always did. He had probably heard that little crack in my voice. Shit, maybe he knew about my weirdness.

But he was still there, staring at me with that amused expression. God, were his eyes always like that? They were *sin*-sational. Was that a word? I wondered if I could dive into them and swim around for a while. And if he'd notice me taking a dip in his eyeballs. And how Jake would feel about that.

*Maybe Jake can come too!*

*That's what she said.*

*Christ. Stop it, Hannah.*

"Enjoying the party?" he asked. His eyes twinkled and I wanted to touch them. But eye poking would surely hurt him and make me look flat-out crazy.

"Very much. It's pretty nice of you to feed the whole place," Noelle said.

He turned to her, and the hold he had on me disappeared. I fought the urge to slump under the table and hide.

"I appreciate the things all of you do," he said. "Might as well show my appreciation with coleslaw and chicken." He looked back at me and rubber bands wrapped around my chest, like that rubber-bands-around-a-watermelon trick where you add more and more until it blows up. If I exploded, it wouldn't be as hilarious as the watermelon thing. But it might make it to America's Best Home Movies or whatever that show was called.

Noelle nodded. "Yeah, the chicken is pretty good."

And there were those eyes again.

"How are you enjoying it?" he asked me.

"Nothing *fowl* about it," I said, and fire spread from my cheeks to my neck. *Nice. Super classy.*

Mr. Harwick laughed. My heart somehow managed to speed up and slow down at the same time.

Noelle cocked an eyebrow at me and shook her head. She cut into a potato with a plastic knife.

"I even got real butter, because with butter there is little *margarine* for error." Mr. Harwick winked at me.

I was a fish gasping for air; I couldn't close my mouth.

"Have fun ladies." Mr. Harwick turned in the direction of the building.

*And there he goes.*

"He's fucking delicious," Noelle whispered. "Weird sense of humor, but delicious." She was watching me closely, eyes darting from me to his receding back.

*I'd like for you to stay, but I love to watch you leave.* Damn, someone else had said that right? It wasn't me. I would never think such a thing. I had a boyfriend, and I loved him.

I swallowed hard and nodded at Noelle.

When the event wound to a close, I skittered to the back of the parking lot, rubbernecking for signs of danger like an inquisitive—or extremely paranoid—giraffe. To my right, a woman with a baby on her hip unlocked her car. Beyond her the lot was gloriously empty.

*Clear.*

My Buick's windshield was the only shiny element of the vehicle, the luster from its burgundy paint long ago stripped away by years of winter salt. I slipped the key into the ignition, pulled out of the lot, and headed for the freeway.

A few times a week I was a goddamn liar. Jake would throw a fit if he knew I still volunteered at the domestic violence shelter instead of working late like I kept insisting I was. I had been staying there when I met him, ruined and lost, stocking shelves at the drugstore where he worked. Maybe he wanted me to leave that part of my life behind as much as he wanted to leave behind the fact that he actually worked when we got together. And though I might have chosen a more creative name, I couldn't let The Shelter go. They needed my help. Plus, it was hard to feel sorry for myself in the midst of so much suffering.

I clicked on the radio.

"—in other news, a local woman was found murdered in an Ash Park cemetery. Police have identified the woman as twenty-one-year-old Meredith Lawrence. If you have any information—"

I wonder what she did to make him mad.

I clicked off the radio with shaking fingers. *Well, fuck.*

I could almost hear his voice oozing like pus from some hidden corner of my brain: *I'll find you, Hannah. Don't ever doubt it.* And the weasel was back, sprinting around in my chest like he was on meth. I squinted through the windshield, waiting for his snarling face to appear against the glass, his nose irrevocably twisted from the lumber yard accident, his eyes that looked just like… mine.

*Get it together, Hannah. He would have found you by now if he was looking.*

I glanced down at my purse, searching for protection. I needed to pick up more pepper spray, though someone in my apartment building would surely complain; the last one dropped and broke in the stairwell, leaving everyone with runny eyes for days. Could lip balm be a weapon? Maybe if he startled me in a parking lot somewhere I could whack him over the head with my journal. My therapist thought writing was a good way to get in touch with my feelings—had the woman known more about my history, she might have prescribed more than a pencil and paper.

I pulled a deep breath into my lungs and held it. *I will always be broken.*

Broken but funny. Well, maybe.

*Dominic laughed at my joke.*

On my dashboard, a one-armed panda bobble head gave me a jiggly nod as I veered off the freeway. Litter-strewn residential streets crackled and crunched with empty Faygo pop two liters and broken beer bottles. Beside the shelter loomed an abandoned school, plywood windows surrounded by crumbling red brick.

The shelter itself was a lump of gray, but the back facade was covered with bright, lewd graffiti—as if a deranged city planner with a can of spray paint had walked up and said, "You know what this place needs? A giant orange dick."

I parked in front of the tangerine penis and got out, surveilling my surroundings for crooked noses hidden in the shadows.

*Crack!* Something snapped at the back of the lot, where trees were steeped in evening dim.

My elbow smashed against the car door and I pressed my back against it, trying to do that hold-your-keys-between-your-fingers-like-a-weapon thing. It didn't help. An icicle shuddered up my back. I squinted into the trees.

Not a movement, except for a few rustling leaves.

I locked my car with my key-claw, dashed into the building and punched in the code to quell the alarm.

"Hannah!" Ms. LaPorte's swishing eighties pantsuit almost glowed, the electric blue and white as unabashed as their wearer. A whitish-blue perm rose from the top of her head like a snow-capped mountain peak.

The ice in my back thawed. "Hi, Ms. LaPorte. How are things tonight?"

"Good. We have a few new girls, but it's been pretty quiet. I was just getting supper on."

"I'll help you. Brandy still sleeping?"

"Yes, dear."

Brandy Lovelle was Ms. LaPorte's one full-time employee; green hair atop a thin, bird-like frame, wiry arms sleeved in tattooed ink, lip ring glinting when she pulled her mouth into one of her ready smiles. She worked the overnights, starting around ten o'clock when Ms. LaPorte left to go home. Brandy was usually asleep in the evenings when I came by, which was a bummer because I suspected she was all kinds of awesome.

I followed Ms. LaPorte down the narrow hallway and into a tiny but functional kitchen outfitted with scuffed appliances. One wall had a hole cut in it for serving food, the chest-high opening finished with a large piece of plywood and covered with a floral tablecloth.

"How's Mario?" I asked.

"He's fine, dear. Just watered him."

I stepped to the makeshift counter and ran a finger over one waxy leaf of the philodendron. Mario was poisonous inside, but if you just admired him from the outside, he was beautiful. Kinda like some people.

*I'll find you, Hannah.*

I shifted my weight, let go of the leaf, and peered down the hallway toward the back door.

Ms. LaPorte hustled to the stove and cranked off the heat. The huge pot spluttered protests and speckled her shirt with reddish-orange. "Chili night. I should have known."

I grabbed the faded apron from the hook on the wall and held it out. "You take it, Ms. LaPorte."

"No, dear, I don't want you ruining your pretty sweater."

"I have a backup." I tugged off my sweater like a bored stripper just trying to get to the point, revealing a long-sleeved T-shirt underneath. *Bow chicka bow wow*. "Problem solved."

Ms. LaPorte's smile was cut short by wailing coming from the front room. I handed her the apron and walked through the open doorway into a space that resembled an elementary school cafeteria, right down to the row of metal cafeteria tables that cut through the center.

Dragging those tables from the school next door in a moment of anarchistic fervor had been my proudest episode of vandalism. Then, in a decidedly un-thief-like way, we had painted the walls a sunny yellow, knowing full well the nature of our work meant that the place had never felt truly friendly. Still, we tried, and that's what mattered.

Around the perimeter of the room, women talked in groups of two of three. A few had small children clinging to their legs. Two little boys sat on the floor running matchbox cars over the linoleum, their mothers looking on silently.

A tight mewl sounded near the front door—another little boy, about six. He gave me a sidelong glance and buried his face in his mother's leg. She watched me with a mix of desperation and practiced suspicion.

"I'm Hannah," I said softly as I approached. "Do you need a doctor?"

The woman poked gingerly at her head. Her black hair would have been lovely had it not been caked with dried blood. "No."

"Do you need the police?"

Her features twisted in anger. "They's the reason I got this." She gestured to her head. "Trey didn' like that I called 'em on his ass yesterday. Shoulda never done it. Wasn't even that bad."

The child sniffled again, and the woman bent and whispered in his ear. He wrapped his bony arms around her and she picked him up and cradled him against her chest, his head resting on her unbloodied shoulder.

I waited, feeling like an intruder, heart aching. There was so much hurt in that embrace, but there was love too. I envied them that even as I reminded myself that I was there trying to help people not get their asses kicked. We didn't receive state funds and weren't under obligation to report, but seeing guys get away with hurting these women made me stabby. She looked back at me and I realized the other women in the room were watching me too.

I swallowed hard. "It's up to you," I said. "We won't force you to file a report. We're here to provide temporary sleeping quarters and a nighttime meal." I lowered my tone. "But if you need to get away from someone, a police record may be helpful."

The woman shook her head. "It ain't gon' do no good."

"Down here they never show up until it's too late anyway," called a gruff voice. Behind me, the short, squat woman who had spoken sat with her hands folded over her protruding abdomen. "Then he's back at you before the next day is done."

The other women nodded their agreement and I resisted the urge to nod along.

Ms. LaPorte emerged from the kitchen, wiping her hands on the apron tied to her waist. "Thirty-three minutes is no kind of response time at all," she said. "Let's have a look at you, dear."

The words echoed in my ears. It was the same thing Ms. LaPorte had said to me nearly five years before when I had arrived at the shelter with two T-shirts, a pair of jeans and a fluttering in my abdomen that wasn't nerves. *Do you have a game plan?* She had asked. I'd nodded. *Yes. And it needs to happen soon.*

*Let's have a look at you, dear.*

My knees wobbled. *Relax, Hannah. No one knows who he was. Not even Ms. LaPorte.*

*If he knew where you were, you'd be dead already.* My hand shifted to my stomach as if the kid was still in there, waiting to eat me from the inside out like a fleshy Pacman.

The woman and her son disappeared with Ms. LaPorte into the communal bathroom. I trembled all the way to the kitchen. *Deep breaths, Hannah. Deep breaths.*

I ladled chili into bowls and placed them on the counter, trying to still my shaking hands by repeating to myself, "I'm not cold, I'm just a little chili," but the mantra helped very little. When all had been served, the women sat and talked amongst themselves in solemn camaraderie connected by an unspoken need for peace. They were almost friends, the pain they shared a tenuous alliance that still left them disconnected enough to feel lonely.

I understood. In high school I'd hung out with an eclectic mix of misfits: Marianne with her sausage arms and cherry red eyeglasses, Jillian with her flaming orange hair, and Monique who wore long sleeves in the summer and a smile even when her eyes were bloodshot. All of us had been hurting, but hiding it, while we tried to belong somewhere. The best thing we had going was when I'd tell them the jokes my dad taught me.

"Why don't cannibals eat clowns?" I would ask excitedly. "Because they taste funny!"

Thanks to my father, I also knew all the dirty jokes. Without other prospects for friendship, my mismatched group wouldn't tell on me. But I still kept the nastiest ones to myself. The cleaner jokes I told with an air of conspiratorial secrecy.

"An airplane is about to crash, and a lady jumps up and says, 'If I'm going to die, I want to die feeling like a woman,' and takes off all her clothes."

I would pause, gauging how effective the joke was by the vibrancy of Jillian's cheeks.

"When she's naked she says, 'Is there someone on this plane who is man enough to make me feel like a woman?' A man stands up, removes his shirt and says, 'Here, iron this!'"

Their giggles always made me smile. But our relationships were as fragile as those in the dining room now, especially since we never saw each other outside of school. These women would never see one another again. Did they have someone at home like I did back then? When my mother put in extra hours at the dentist's office where she worked, I at least had my father to play Monopoly with, though he never gave me any indication I was good at the game.

"Don't worry about it, darling. You're just not quite smart

enough," he would say, and I would nod, sure he was right. And when I would admit my hurt over never seeing my friends outside of school, he would smile knowingly and put his arm around me. "I understand, honey, but no one can ever really love you the way I do. You don't need anyone else but your old man."

And I would giggle and tell him that he wasn't old. It was also true that his protection and love would never have an equal. My friends did not appreciate me the way he did, and the rest of the school didn't even know I was there at all. So I would throw my arms around him and kiss him, vowing never to disappoint him.

It was a vow I had broken. Terribly. Irreparably. But I had real friends now, or at least one.

I should get Noelle a present. Maybe new earrings. She had been there for me from the day she started at Harwick Technical Solutions. She'd probably even listen if I ever got the guts to talk to her about anything important. Friends mattered, even when they had awesome torpedo tits and hated puns.

I watched as the women pushed aside their trays, cold, faraway expressions barely disguising the hopelessness they probably felt at the thought of leaving the shelter, or maybe at the thought of leaving their mates.

They weren't good enough. They had disappointed someone. Probably themselves.

I grabbed a rag and attacked the counter. *I will not turn into this.*


Driving from the shelter to my apartment was usually the most relaxing twenty minutes of my day. In fifteen miles, downtown caved to suburbia, with libraries and apartments across the street from professional buildings, all decorated with only moderate amounts of penis graffiti. Signs for gas stations and fast food restaurants twinkled on either side of the road, the colors on the signs crisper than they'd been in the heat of summer when they had to compete with the fog of muggy air. I passed the comic book store. Lucky's pizza. A cell phone repair shop. And there it was: the little apartment building that could.

Somewhere along the way I'd gotten stuck in five stories of red brick, six units to a floor, a place that just about screamed "I'm here for now but not forever"— at least that was what I'd told myself when I moved in. The building sat on a residential street across from some kind of second hand kiddie clothing store that I had never ventured into and probably never would. In the back, the parking lot bordered another road and yet another gas station. Because what city is complete without four gas stations per block?

I parked in the back and ran up the cement steps, the October air chilling my bones even after the heavy door had swung shut. The smell of onions and old socks permeated the stairwell and hallway on the third floor, much better than my pepper spray, but still gross. I hoped the smell wasn't coming from my apartment.

The door latch clanked. On the television, tires shrieked and a woman yelled something unintelligible. Steam rose from a pot on the stove.

"Hey, babe!" Jake said from the couch. "I was just going to make some of those noodles you bought the other day. I brought pasta sauce from my mom's."

I scanned the apartment, mildly concerned his mother might jump from behind a chair, howling like a banshee, dripping cigarette ash all over the carpet. I glanced at a burned spot on the rug. Like mother like son. "Thanks for starting the water. It's been a long day."

Jake nodded, his eyes on a reality show about wrestling crocodiles. A plume of smoke billowed from his nostrils. "Yeah, sure. Hey, I was talking to my mom and she says we should move down by her after we get married."

"We can't afford to move right now, Jake."

"Well, yeah but one day we might be able to." He didn't raise his eyes from the screen.

61

"It takes time to move up at work," I said to the back of his head. *Plus you could get a job, too. You know, like you've been promising to do for months.*

"Yeah, I guess. Can you get the plates? I'm beat."

I slid dry noodles into the water, poured the sauce into a pan and set the table. Jake kept his gaze on the TV. I resisted the urge to hurl a plate at his skull. Sometimes I hated the way he acted, but having someone next to you made you harder to strangle; at least I assumed that was true. I stalked back to the kitchen to test the sauce. Hot, but store-bought.

Jake was at the table when I returned with the meal.

"Thanks, hon. I love you, ya know."

"I love you, too." I clutched my fork tighter than necessary.

*He's always been there for me, even when I was difficult and crazier than I am now. Maybe I should just agree to marry him and get it over with.*

What was I waiting for, anyway?

Mr. Harwick's smiling face popped into my head, telling me I was a great worker, helping me pick up the stuff from my purse. I tried to distract myself from the warmth in my lower body by shoveling pasta into my mouth.

I did the dishes alone, half listening to the murmur of Jake's television program.

*I love him. I need him.*

The pasta did a nervous dance in my abdomen. Jake's mother was probably trying to poison me. Very Snow White-ish except I didn't have any knee-high friends to mine coal or help me with the goddamn dishes.

I dried the last dish and walked into the living room. My mouth was dry.

Jake stared at the screen.

*I love him. I love him. I love him.*

*Prove it.*

I sat and put my arms around him. He turned, gripped my

shoulders and pushed his mouth onto mine, prodding my tongue like an imbecilic iguana. His tongue tasted like stale cigarettes and Pabst Blue Ribbon. I fought a gag and waited for a tingle, heat, something. I felt nothing. Not that I ever did. Not that I had any reason to expect better.

I wondered how much that case of beer had put me back.

When Jake came up for air, I pulled off his T-shirt and felt a twinge of guilt when Dominic's face flashed in my mind again, helping me, complimenting me, smiling at my lame jokes… No, not Dominic. Mr. Harwick. I grabbed Jake harder.

*I love him.*

Jake pulled away and yanked at our clothes, tossing them into a pile on the floor. His member jutted from his body like a thick diving board. Well, not that thick. Let's not get silly.

*You're going to poke someone's eye out with that thing.*

I wanted to giggle, but couldn't because he was pulling my head toward his crotch. I tried to plaster on a seductive smile but only managed a muted sigh. Not that he would have noticed either way.

*I bet Dominic would be better at this stuff.*

*Mickey Mouse would be better at this stuff.*

*Nothing sexier than bestiality.*

*Shut up, Hannah, and get it over with.*

I closed my eyes and opened my mouth.

---

Even after all these years, Robert could hear the priest's voice in his head, louder than the girl's anxious breathing: *—and the sinners shall pay for their transgressions, the adulterers, the fornicators, the scourge of the earth in their filthy enterprise burning for all eternity…* But the priest was not there now, and, if he were, he would be on his knees screaming unanswered prayers to the heavens.

The girl sat on the bed, her legs wrapped around Robert's hips. Her ash-blond hair was demurely braided over one slender shoulder, resting at the top of two perfect breasts the color of cream. He imagined her skin would taste like cream as well, rich and velvety on his mouth, her sweetness intensifying as he trailed his tongue lower, seeking the heat of her being, each flick making her moan in ecstasy—

The priest's voice got louder, accelerating in pace, like a crescendo toward damnation: —*the heathens who do not know God are doomed to succumb to earthly sin, to embrace lust not honor, passion not holiness, Hell not Heaven*—

Robert took a breath, trying to ignore the words and pretend, just for a moment, that he was a good person, a person worthy of compassion. Perhaps this new girl would find him worthy in a way others never had. He began a poem for her inside his head.

> *My heart expands at your nearness,*
> *Like a balloon begging to be broken,*
> *Yearning to spill our love over the world in rivers of happiness.*

Hope lit in his chest, hope that this creature would forgive him, that she might be an angel who would help him purge his sins before they swallowed him forever. He thrust into her, deeply, slowly, savoring every inch of her.

She moved against him. *I forgive you.* She didn't say it, but Robert felt it, saw it in her glistening eyes. He caressed her face and rotated his hips, each thrust bringing him closer to salvation.

*I forgive you.*

He stroked her breast gently, thanking her for her mercy.

She winced. *Winced.*

She was one of them. She'd be pleased at the thought of sinners thrust down into the pits of Hell. Sinners like him.

Rotten. Unlovable. Unforgivable. He might as well embrace his true nature, enjoy his lechery, for there would be no enjoyment in eternity.

Not for one like him.

Robert pulled himself from her depths and plastered his palm over her mouth before she could vocalize her judgment.

Pimples ripe with pus reddened across the bridge of her nose.

*Fucking cunt. She will pay. And dammit, she will like it.*

Robert grabbed her hair and yanked her forward, off the bed. He kicked at her shins until she knelt before him, worshipping him in the way others worshipped their God, a God that would condemn him and torture him until he could take no more, an agony to be repeated for eternity.

He forced that agony on her, slapping her, splitting her lip. Her sobs echoed through his brain like music, hypnotic and rich. As the blood ran into her mouth he shoved himself into the opening, moaning as she cried, accelerating his pace until he choked her with his seed.

*—and the righteous shall rise again, pious on the Earth until they are embraced into the kingdom of Heaven.*

He pulled the whore's head back, and she stared up at him, lashes wet, freckled skin stippled with hatred, each pock mark like a mouth brimming with accusation. Her glassy eyes told him all he needed to know.

He raised his hand. She would not forgive him. She would not absolve him. His fists clenched, his muscles aching for release of a different kind.

She cringed and turned her head.

*No. Not now.* Robert brought his fist down on the bed behind her and smiled when she yelped. *Stupid fucking whore. This was all her fault.* He tossed money at her and went to take a shower.

She would not be there when he returned. They never were.

Rotting garbage and animal urine curdled the air. The silence resonated with the eerie heaviness of a ghost town, if you were prone to fanciful bullshit. Petrosky wasn't. He squinted at the house.

The building was beyond repair, part of a housing project long abandoned by any developer or landlord. Even panhandlers would not come out this far to squat for a night when they had to trek five miles back in the morning to beg for their breakfast.

*So why here?*

Behind him, rubber soles on gravel crunched closer.

"Morning, boss."

"California."

"I brought you some coffee and a protein bar. I'll get them after we finish up here."

Petrosky grimaced.

"Come on, boss. You'll like it."

"That's what you said about tofu. I will take the coffee though. Later." Petrosky walked up the front steps, Morrison at his heel.

"He killed another one pretty fast, didn't he?" Morrison said.

"Too fast." Only ten days between murders, highly unusual even for a serial killer. They ducked through the front door, kicking up dust and mold that sat, itchy, in Petrosky's throat.

"I don't like this."

"I bet she liked it less." Petrosky glanced around the living room where pieces of roofing tile had tumbled haphazardly to the splintered floor. He followed the low hum of voices and the phosphorescent ricochet of flood lights down the groaning basement stairs, and inhaled deeply when he reached the lower floor. The scent of mushrooms and dank earth clung to the back of his tongue. A dull sheen lit the basement windows from the outside, the sunlight struggling to illuminate through years of filth.

The woman lay prone on an old dining table, wrists and ankles each bound to a different table leg with leather restraints. Blond hair fanned around her head, mussed as if she were merely asleep, but there was no mistaking the vacant death stare in her hazel eyes.

A few techs bustled around the dim space, tweezing and bagging and scraping. Petrosky ignored them and scanned the victim's extremities. Graying skin covered her arms, and the fingers of her left hand were contorted like a claw on the table. Stiff. No maggots yet. She hadn't been dead for long. "Do you have a positive ID?" Petrosky asked no one in particular.

"Jane Trazowski," someone behind him said. "She's in the system, got a couple charges for solicitation of prostitution. We need the family for a positive ID but Connors here recognized her from a domestic violence arrest where her kids were—"

"Fine." Petrosky said. He cleared his throat and dragged his eyes over her belly. Her abdomen had been hacked apart revealing gelatinous blobs of organs and the slick sheen of intestine. Like the first body, the long whitish tube was splayed open, a sheet of bloodied tissue, more torn and gnarled in some areas than others. Either their guy had been pissed, or the rats had gotten to her already. Petrosky squinted at the ruin. Probably both.

"Damn. I feel bad for them." Morrison's voice was irritatingly nasal.

Fucking surfers. They always sounded high. Though maybe he was just trying not to breathe through his nose.

"You feel bad for who? The woman or her kids?"

Morrison's face went red. "Both."

Morrison would have to cut out that blushing shit before

67

he was allowed to handle any perps. Too much visible emotion and suspects would eat him alive.

The stairs wept behind them with a shuddery *scree*, and Petrosky and Morrison turned to see Brian Thompson, the medical examiner, coming down the last few steps. He was tall and lanky with perpetual five o'clock shadow and teeth like a mule. He nodded at Petrosky and approached the table reeking of cigarette smoke—good tobacco, none of that pepperminty menthol bullshit. Petrosky's mouth watered.

"Suspect used standard metal clasps to keep the skin peeled back while he worked." Thompson circled the table, gray eyes wandering like he was bored as fuck to be there. "You can get them from any hardware store. Usually these guys are perfectionists. While the dissection is pretty meticulous, there is a brutality to it that goes beyond the simple cuts themselves. See this here?" Thompson gestured to a series of scrapes visible along the underside of the body. "Splinters in the skin. Looks like she was rubbing against the table, trying to escape."

Petrosky peered at the cuts. "You think she was captive for a while before—?"

"Yeah, like the first. He didn't just murder her and then play around with her insides. She was probably alive when he removed her organs, though I will need to complete the autopsy to confirm abdominal surgery as the cause of death."

Upstairs, the telltale clank and rattle of a wheeled gurney approached the basement steps. *Can't put it off any longer.* Petrosky swallowed over the knot in his throat, bent and craned his neck to see the underside of the table. Copper stung his nose as he read the poem, each line written on a different board in block script. Here and there, the splitting lumber had skewered a chunk of something dark and gory and almost alive. Rotten wood. Perhaps a piece of paintbrush. Maybe skin.

> *Children three that nestle near,*
> *Eager eye and willing ear*
> *Pleased a simple tale to hear-*

68

Petrosky straightened. Evisceration, shock, death. This fucker had tortured her. She'd been in agony. She had begged for her life. Julie probably had, too. An invisible rope tightened around his throat.

*Children three that nestle near...*

"How many kids did she have?" Petrosky asked.

"Three," said the tech from the floor.

"He knew this one," Morrison said.

"Or of her. Maybe Lawrence too." Petrosky let that sink in. "Let's find out where these ladies spent their time."

The shelter was in a shitty part of downtown, but it looked surprisingly well-kept if you ignored the spray paint. In the back parking lot, a spry sixty-ish woman broomed debris from the walkway. She looked up as Petrosky and Morrison approached.

Petrosky flashed his badge. "Ms. LaPorte? We have a few questions—"

"Our girls lives belong to them alone, sir." Her lips were a thin line.

Petrosky stiffened.

"Ma'am, we're following up on the murder of a woman who spent some time here. We were hoping you could help us," Morrison said.

LaPorte's free hand clamped over her mouth.

*Way to go, surfer boy.*

Morrison shrank under Petrosky's glare.

"Who? When was she here?"

"Jane Trazowski." Petrosky tried to keep his voice non-threatening. "She was here last week, Thursday. We think she may have left Friday morning."

LaPorte shook her head. "I wasn't here, had a touch of the flu. You'll have to ask Hannah or Brandy. Brandy's out at an appointment but she'll be back later."

They followed LaPorte down a back hallway to a small kitchen. A thin woman stood at the counter, shoulder blades visible through her shirt on either side of a long dark ponytail as she scooped macaroni and cheese from a metal dish. She turned toward them.

Cotton plugged his throat. *Julie. Jesus fucking Christ. No, not her, but—*

Everyone was looking at him. He nodded at Morrison. *Take it, California.* There was no point trying to speak; his tongue had become a useless dehydrated mass on the floor of his mouth.

"Good evening, ma'am. I'm Detective Morrison and this is Detective Petrosky. We're trying to get information on a Jane Trazowski who may have been here a few weeks back."

*She's not Julie.*

The girl, not Julie, the girl, bit her lip. "Um... I'm not sure. I don't always get names."

Petrosky pulled a picture from his folder and showed her. Her mouth fell open. "Yeah, I... what happened?"

"She was killed."

Petrosky winced at Morrison's bluntness.

Hannah froze. It was the type of shock Petrosky often saw when he told someone their loved one had died, but it seemed an overreaction in this circumstance. Unless this girl was closer to Trazowski than she was letting on. *Interesting.* Petrosky tried to wet his lips with his tongue but his mouth was dry.

LaPorte put an arm around Hannah, who seemed to be having trouble taking in air.

"I... she had some really nasty marks on her. Bruises and... stuff. She said it was from a bad—" Hannah's eyes flicked to the officers.

It was a guilty look. *Very interesting.* "She's beyond trouble at this point," Petrosky said, low but even. "Help us catch the person who hurt her."

Hannah took another breath and blew it out. "She said it was from a guy she slept with. He paid her enough for her rent, but she was afraid to go home because he knew where she lived."

70

"Do you remember anything else about him? A name?"

She looked at the ceiling, the way lying perps sometimes did. It was how they accessed the creative center of the brain. But what would this girl have to hide?

*You're just fucked up and imagining shit, Petrosky.* This girl wasn't a suspect. Whatever she was hiding had nothing to do with this case.

She met his eyes. His stomach jerked against something sharp, like he had ingested barbed wire. *Those eyes. She's not Julie. Julie's dead.*

She shook her head. "No, no names. It never got that deep. Sometimes they don't... want to talk."

"Do you remember exactly what she said?"

"Um... some rent check mother... um... got caught up in something... I'm not sure. It wasn't that, but... something like that. I can't really remember." Beneath her nose, her lips quivered and stilled.

His arms ached to hug her and tell her it would all be okay. Petrosky ground his teeth, returned the photo to his folder and pulled out another. "How about her?"

LaPorte and Hannah stared at the image, frozen.

"Ladies?"

"Is this another one? Another... victim?" LaPorte asked.

Questions, no answers. That didn't sit well with him. "It is, ma'am. Do you know her?"

LaPorte shook her head.

Petrosky turned to Hannah.

Hannah bit her lip, eyes radiating uncertainty as she glanced at LaPorte. "No."

"Are you sure?"

"I... think so. I mean, we see so many and we don't always get IDs or whatever. Some of them are really scared."

But were they afraid of their exes or of someone else stalking them, hunting them down? "Scared?" Petrosky asked. Clean and non-specific. Sometimes it was what you didn't say that tripped people up.

"You'd be frightened too if someone you loved was

beating on you." LaPorte stepped in front of Hannah, her finger jabbing at the air between them. "You'd be afraid if the police didn't help you when you called them. These ladies are allowed to be afraid."

Faces appeared at the hole in the wall behind Hannah—some clean, some battered, all inquisitive.

"We'd like to ask around here, if you don't mind."

LaPorte bristled. "As a matter of fact, I do mind. You have no right to go poking around into these women's lives, and I'll be damned if—"

"Let me rephrase: This is a police matter. We will be interviewing everyone here in an attempt to trace our victim's movements."

LaPorte's spindly fists formed balls. Beside Petrosky, Morrison stopped writing.

"Do you have a room we can use?" Petrosky asked.

LaPorte walked to the door. "Do your dirty work out back."

If a voice could cut flesh, Petrosky would have been on the floor with a severed jugular.


They drove to the precinct in silence. Eight women in the shelter. Three identified Trazowski from her visit earlier that week. One recognized Lawrence, but wasn't able to identify where she'd seen her.

And then there was Hannah. He could still almost see her face—strained and pale. Shocked, but more than shock. She was afraid. Someone had died, yet he hadn't given her a reason to think she'd be in danger any more than losing a loved one signals that you might be next. So what was she so afraid of? He yearned to know, to fix it, to take away the fear.

Cement barriers whizzed by the window. She looked so much like Julie—how Julie would have looked if she had been allowed to grow up.

*Too bad you couldn't save her.*

*Get it together, asshole. Bury that shit.*

He could almost taste the whiskey, feel the fiery comfort of it in the back of his throat. But a drink was the last thing he needed. He had a job to do.

Morrison swung into the lot and tossed Petrosky the keys, heading through the glass door to the precinct. Petrosky huffed up the interior flight of stairs after him, vowing to smack the shit out of anyone who dared suggest he go to the gym.

On the top floor, a hallway to the left led to the chief's office and a series of conference rooms. The rest of the place crackled with the controlled chaos of too many crimes and not enough cops. Detectives and plain-clothed officers sat at the dozens of desks in the bullpen, filling out paper reports and typing frantically on old PCs, trying to get the fuck out of there because they'd promised their wives they'd be home in time to see the kids off to bed. Petrosky had done that too, before Julie was taken from him. He'd give anything to do it again.

"What's up, Morrison?" A short, stocky man in police blues smiled and clapped Morrison on the back before shooting a nervous glance at Petrosky. His teeth were too small, like someone had buzzed them off halfway down.

Morrison shook the guy's hand. "What's up, Pete? See Annie this morning? I think she was looking for you on the Jackson case."

"Oh, really? I'm on it." A final goofy grin lit his mahogany face, and Pete something-or-other was gone.

Petrosky started for the center of the room, for his desk. "How do you know all these people?"

"I meet them in the gym."

"That where you get your girl talk in, California?"

"Pretty much."

The chair squealed under Petrosky's ass as he sat. Morrison grabbed a chair from his desk across the aisle and plopped into it looking like a lap dog: eager, inquisitive, expectant. Might as well throw him a bone. "Morrison?"

"What's up, boss?"

"LaPorte come off confrontational to you?"

"Sure did, boss. I think maybe she's had some bad experiences with cops. Type of place, maybe. Protecting the girls."

"Maybe." Petrosky's fingernails beat a rhythm on the desk. "Maybe something else is going on."

"Boss?"

"Two girls, similar backgrounds. One definitely stayed there, one possibly around before her death, and you don't cooperate?"

Morrison cleared his throat.

"What is it, California?"

"I thought it was weird that LaPorte didn't ask about safety. If I found out that someone who stayed at my place had been murdered, let alone two people, I'd worry about the guy showing up again. Even store owners sometimes ask about extra police protection after a robbery, or at least request a few drive-bys. Why wouldn't she?"

Petrosky stopped tapping. "Nicely done."

"Thanks, boss."

"What's your take on the girl?" Petrosky's stomach twisted. He needed a bottle of Jack Daniels. He jerked open a drawer and pulled out a roll of antacids instead.

"Jumpy, probably in shock. Wanted to help, but I don't think she knew much. I'm sure she's seen a lot over there."

"Agreed." Petrosky unwrapped an antacid and popped it into his mouth. It coated his tongue with chalk.

"So you think there's something fishy about LaPorte?" Morrison said.

LaPorte was fiercely protective of those girls—she hadn't killed one. But to refuse to cooperate in a police investigation, knowing the victim had been there? Something was happening at that place, something everyone there nervous about. Including Hannah.

Petrosky frowned and swallowed the mess on his tongue. "Let's find out."

## TUESDAY, OCTOBER 13TH

Noelle sipped her coffee, willing the caffeine to enter her bloodstream ASAP. The morning had been shitty enough already. The second she'd walked in the door, her manager had come over to interrogate her, giant teeth flapping in the breeze.

"I noticed you had a few files left the night before last."

She'd sat straighter. "I thought I could finish them the following morning. I didn't have too much lined up, and the work day was over."

"The overseas offices are on a completely different time zone. Some needed those reports to begin the next day and you put them another day behind." His beady eyes had radiated disapproval.

"I'm sorry, sir." She'd hung her head.

"Don't let it happen again. There are plenty of people who can do this job." He had marched away, clenching his ass as if he were trying not to shit his pants.

Noelle's cheeks were still burning from the episode. She took another sip of coffee.

Hannah poked her head over the cubicle wall. "Everything okay?"

*No, I'm just blowing everything. As usual.* She was ashamed to admit it, but Hannah's willingness to pick up the slack was probably the only reason Noelle was still employed. And Hannah's support in her personal life was probably the only reason she was still sort of normal. Sort of.

Noelle loved her. Maybe more than she should.

"Everything's fine," Noelle said, drawing her lips into her best smile to prove that it was true. She held the manufactured grin until Hannah nodded and went back to her desk.

75

But everything wasn't fine. She didn't want to lose this job. She couldn't go home to a customer service job in a small town where nosiness was written into the charter. She could hear the meddlesome locals now: "I'm so sorry about your mother. How are you holding up?"

She would have to bite her tongue to keep from responding. Those assholes just wanted the story. Noelle's father being unfaithful was juicy enough, but her mother swallowing a bottle of pills over it was delectable.

Here in Ash Park, no one knew, not even Hannah. Noelle's life before Harwick Technical belonged to someone else, shoved into a closet in the corner of her brain. That was also where she hid Mr. Cantonelli, big shot attorney with sausage fingers and breath that reeked of sauerkraut and coffee. New York: where the buildings were as high as the crack addicts and stiff as the boss's cock, especially if you were desperate enough to do *anything* not to have to return to your nosy hometown and your father's disapproving stare.

Things had fallen apart as quickly as they had come together. She'd worked hard both on and off her feet, and Cantonelli had still given the promotion to some redheaded bitch.

He had paid for that one.

Noelle had brought him coffee that night for the last time. "Just so you know, Harry, I'm pregnant. I'm pretty sure there's a case there for sexual harassment, right?"

His face had gone from disbelief to outright terror.

The next morning she had clicked on the television. "And in breaking news, a local attorney was found dead late last night in his office by the cleaning crew. Foul play is not suspected."

She had faked a resume and gotten in at Harwick Technical before Mr. Cantonelli's body was in the ground. Faker or no, there was no one to dispute her credentials.

*Not anymore.*

Noelle's heel was doing a wild dance under the desk. She closed her eyes and saw Cantonelli behind her eyelids, his

76

bulldog face contorting in ecstasy above her.

*I'll make sure you get that job, honey.*

Then Harry's face turned into her mother's, eyes open and vacant, vomit on her pillow like the day Noelle had found her.

*Fucking slut*, her mother said.

*You weren't any better, Mom.*

*I got a house and a family out of it,* her mother sneered. *What the fuck do you have?*

Noelle opened her eyes. Her boss walked by the glass doors.

She picked up her coffee cup and wondered if it would smash through the window and actually hit him if she threw it hard enough. Her fingers tightened on the mug, as if all her fury was pooling in her hands. She was going fucking insane. Noelle slammed her cup against the desk and coffee splashed over the brim.

"Noelle?" Ralph, her coworker across the way, was wringing his hands next to her cubicle.

"I was wondering if"—his eyes dropped to the floor—"if you might want to go out sometime? I mean, I know I've asked you to do stuff before, but I just keep… hoping?"

Noelle took in Ralph's nerdy glasses and weak, vulnerable gopher face. Her first day there, he had watched her breasts as she panicked at the stack of paperwork. Her jaw clenched in anger.

"Sure," she said, trying to look excited.

Ralph's face lit up. "Really? I mean, great! Let me know where I can pick you up." He almost skipped back to his cubicle.

*Asshole.*


The next night, they ate at a small Italian restaurant off Orchard Lake Road.

"So what do your parents do?" he asked.

"They're in real estate."

"Cool. It's a good area for that. They live nearby?"

"No. They live in Texas," she said, hoping she would remember the information later.

"Oh."

After dinner she let him walk her to the elevators in her building. "Good night, Ralph," she said, pushing the button as she turned her back on him.

"Good night."

The following week he took her to a Tigers baseball game. His excitement was palpable as she sat with him behind third base. She stifled a yawn.

"Do you like baseball?" he asked.

"Sure," she said.

"My ex hated it. But then again, she hated me, too. Thought I was unstable, when really, she just couldn't keep up with me." He had a laugh like a donkey's bray.

Couldn't keep up? *Right*. Noelle kept her eyes on the first baseman as he reeled back to catch a ball and missed it.

Ralph cleared his throat. "My brother always liked to play baseball. Do you have any siblings?"

"No." She wondered what her brother Steve was up to these days. She hadn't spoken to his self-righteous ass since he'd called to tell her their father had died. She had hung up on him before he could tell her about the arrangements.

Ralph cocked his head. "You okay?"

Noelle plastered a smile on her face. "Of course. Why wouldn't I be?"

Ralph followed her to the lobby again that night. She let him kiss her softly on the cheek. "Good night, Ralph."

"Good night."

Later that week he took her out to dinner at an Indian restaurant downtown. The coconut curry was delicious.

"Where did your parents meet?" Ralph asked.

"A real estate conference."

"Was it love at first sight?"

She tried not to look bored. "Yes," she said.

When dinner was over, he took her back to her apartment and walked her through the lobby to the elevator again. She saw the affection in his eyes, the ache, the longing, the adoration. He was in deep enough to suffer.

"Well, I guess this is good ni—"

She put a finger on his lips. "Would you like to come up?"

Desire brightened his eyes. "Yes," he said, breath already ragged with anticipation.

She awoke at three the next morning with the weight of his arm pinning her to the bed. Her skin crawled where his arm made contact with her flesh. She shimmied from underneath him, padded into the kitchen and sucked down a glass of water at the sink, considering whether she should wake him and throw him out, or just wait until morning when he would leave on his own.

Her mind wandered to the night before, and how he'd been so willing and eager to put his tongue between her legs. She smiled.

*I'll wait until morning.*

Monday morning, Ralph approached her as she entered the office.

"Hey, Noelle!" He moved closer to put his arm around her.

"Hello." She sidestepped his hand and walked past him to her desk. The blank computer screen reflected her perfectly curled hair and smooth features. Not a hint of exhaustion as in previous weeks.

He followed her. "Is everything okay?"

She turned on the computer. "Yep." She watched her reflection morph into the Harwick Technical logo and stared at the sign-in window until Ralph finally walked away.

Hannah poked her head over the partition. "So… how'd it go this weekend?"

Noelle shrugged. "You know, same old same old."


The next day, there were flowers on her desk when she arrived at the office. Ralph stood by the water cooler, waiting for her reaction. She dumped the flowers into the trash and watched his face fall.


Thursday morning, Ralph was waiting for her at her cubicle. His face was drawn and there were bags under his eyes, but his mouth was set in a furious line.

"Hey," he spat.

"Hey." She turned on the computer and stared at the screen as it booted up.

"Did I do something wrong?"

Two priors:She could see his fists in her peripheral vision, clenched at his sides near her desktop.

She shook her head. "Nope."

His breath whistled through his nostrils on a long, deep inhale. He sighed it out. "I just… I really like you. I thought we had something good going. I mean, I know it was only a few dates, but—"

"Yeah, sometimes things just don't work out."

"This is tearing me the fuck up," he said.

She shrugged, refusing to look at him.

"Can't we just try again?" His voice rose. "Maybe dinner? A movie? I feel like I'm going insane. I can't think about anything else. I'm on Xanax for Christ's sake." He was practically yelling, loud enough for everyone in the office to hear him. Not that Hannah would be all judge-y about it. And Toni never said shit.

80

"No thanks, Ralph. I don't think you can make me happy."

But as she heard him stomp away, she did feel a glimmer of satisfaction. Not happiness exactly, but close enough. Good old Ralph... that boring fucker.

Maybe the next one would be more interesting. Find the right guy and you could get him to do anything.

*Anything at all.*

Hannah peeked into her cubicle. "Xanax, huh? Are you okay?"

"Yeah, I'm fine. Sometimes, they just like you a little more than you like them, right? Maybe one of these days we can go out, take my mind off all this."

Hannah nodded uncertainly and disappeared behind the partition.

Noelle turned back to her computer and tried to hide her smile.

## FRIDAY, OCTOBER 30TH

Petrosky stared across the cherry desk at Dr. Stephen McCallum. The department psychiatrist was Santa Claus in the off season, at least two-hundred-and-fifty pounds, with ruddy cheeks and a head full of curly white hair that matched his beard. No red coat, though; McCallum's green button-down shirt and brown tweed jacket strained against his bulk.

"Do your victims have any common acquaintances?" McCallum asked.

"Nope."

"Any promising physical evidence?"

Fuck no, there wasn't. No fingerprints on any of the restraints, but tons of random prints all over the crime scenes, probably from kids smoking dope or squatters. "At the Trazowski scene, we found fingerprints all over that basement from some guy who had a previous arrest. Crack addict, says he slept in the basement once, shit in a corner. The restraints are expensive and the dissection meticulous enough that I don't think corner shitter is our guy."

McCallum nodded. "Agreed. What else?"

"No sexual assault, no murder weapons found, and no witnesses. Trazowski and her kids were pretty much ghosts; I've got nothing on her movements until she arrived at the shelter, and less than a day after she left, she was filleted in the basement of a house she has no connection to. The father of Trazowski's kids is currently doing four years in New York on a series of B and Es and he didn't know Lawrence." So not a pissed-off father situation. That would have made his life too fucking easy. "As for Lawrence, she had an abusive boyfriend with eight previous arrests for domestic violence, but he's got an alibi the night of the murder. She had two

82

priors: one for domestic violence and another for prostitution. Then there's her abandoned kid."

Petrosky blinked hard against the headache that was taking root in his temples. "The kid died of hypothermia, no signs of violence, but I turned it over to the prosecutor's office in case they feel like going after Keil. I don't think much will come of it."

McCallum leaned forward in his chair and folded his hands on the desktop. "That bothers you."

"Of course it fucking bothers me."

"Because you'd give anything to have your kid back, and here people are throwing them away?"

"Because it's fucked up, that's why." Petrosky had seen McCallum himself after Julie died. Mandatory leave, they'd said. Fucking bureaucratic bullshit.

"Has the anger abated any?"

"Goddammit, McCa—"

"I'll take that as a no. Remember, anger can be a symptom of both depression and complicated grief, but it's not something to ignore. Drinking still under control?"

"Everything's under control," Petrosky said tightly. He rubbed a hand over the stubble on his cheek. "Let's get back on track here."

"Fine, have it your way. Lawrence, then."

"Lawrence. No family and no friends that the boyfriend mentioned." A lack of acquaintances wasn't uncommon in these situations, but it made Petrosky's job far more difficult. Fewer friends around, fewer ways to trace a person's movements. Fewer leads. He sighed.

"Okay, so not much to go on there. Anyone else who might provide you with some leads?"

"Maybe," Petrosky said. "What's your take on LaPorte?"

"Her file is very interesting. The early arrests for protesting and civil disobedience aren't especially concerning given the time period. However, when paired with other symptoms, trouble with the law can be a sign of antisocial personality disorder, the clinical diagnosis related to

83

psychopathic tendencies. The later arrest for the murder of her husband certainly fits that bill."

"It was dismissed as self-defense. When a man stabs you with a kitchen knife, you're allowed to bludgeon him to death with a tire iron."

"I happen to agree," McCallum said wryly. "And running a non-profit shelter for abuse victims speaks to empathy and a history of victimhood as opposed to someone with antisocial personality disorder. Whatever attitude made you suspicious of her is more likely related to her protecting those under her care than an admission of guilt."

That much was true. LaPorte wasn't a suspect. But between LaPorte's defiance and Hannah's anxiety something still felt wrong.

"What about the poems left at the crime scenes?" McCallum asked. "From what I understand, that poem is open to interpretation, and hotly debated. The whole book is a psychedelic Freudian's dream."

Petrosky had gleaned as much from Morrison's assessment last week: "The poem he's using is from the end of the book. The whole thing's pretty weird, so it's hard to tell what he's saying. If I were him, I would have used the Walrus and the Carpenter. All those poor oysters."

"So you're saying you're the Walrus?" Petrosky had asked.

"Koo koo ka choo, boss."

So much for a fancy-ass English degree.

McCallum laced his fingers on the desk. "The poetry is a conundrum, but the typical profile for this type of crime still fits. White male between the ages of twenty-five and thirty-five. A planner, intelligent, probably well educated in this case. Someone shrewd, calculating."

Petrosky nodded. "Could the dissection be related to the fact that both were mothers?"

"If he were dissecting only the uterus, the reproductive organs, I'd say yes. But according to the medical examiner's reports, he dissected the stomach, the intestines, and in one case, part of the esophagus. Almost as if he's looking for something there."

Petrosky pictured the gaping hole in Trazowski's abdomen, envisioned someone rummaging around, hands submerged to the wrists, forearms coated in gore. His gut clenched. "What would you look for inside someone's stomach?"

"Something he fed them, perhaps, or maybe he wondered what their last meal had been. Or maybe he's just interested in the mechanics. While the dissections were deliberate and rather precise, there were some small tears around the incisions, so I'd guess that he simply lacked the medical knowledge to complete the job perfectly. And the fact that they were alive when he cut into them speaks to an underlying rage or past slight. You might be looking for someone who was hurt by a maternal figure. Lack of attachment in these cases is prominent."

"So our guy had a shitty upbringing?"

"Possibly. But some psychopaths are born without the ability to emote, while others only show sociopathic behaviors after severe abuse or neglect. Either type can end up killing people in fairly horrific ways. It's hard to tell which category this individual would fall into since the presentation is generally the same."

So their killer was likely a younger male, not a physician, who possibly, but not certainly, suffered childhood abuse or neglect. The abused became the abusers, if they lived long enough. Everyone had a motivation. Not that this excused leaving a murdered child to be torn apart in a field. Petrosky's chest tightened and he settled into the anger, letting it focus him. He needed a lead. He needed to think.

How did the killer choose his victims? Both women had a history of arrests for prostitution as well as drug charges. They were similar physically, with thin bodies and blond hair, though that wasn't hard to find.

Petrosky cracked his knuckles and the noise startled McCallum's hands off the desk. *Jumpy mother fucker.*

Petrosky eyed him, be he recovered quickly, leaning back and steepling his fingers beneath his chin in official shrink style.

"You know, this guy is a goddamn stereotype. Kill the hookers. Like that hasn't been done."

"Whether it's the prostitution thing or not, there's something about these women," McCallum said. "They remind him of someone. And whoever it is, he's killing her over and over again."

"You think he killed the original?"

"Perhaps. But maybe he couldn't. She could have died of some other cause. Or maybe she got away and he doesn't know where she is."

"Let's hope someone got away." Petrosky stood. "The next one won't unless we find him."

McCallum shrugged his fleshy shoulders. "That's your department, Ed. Not mine."

McCallum walked him out, huffing as he tried to keep up.

Petrosky kept his eyes on the hallway in front of him. He needed to find a more solid link between the victims, or at least someone else who knew something. It was either that, or wait until the guy chopped up someone else and left a clue. If he left a clue. Hannah Montgomery, the young woman who had been a spitting image of Julie, flashed through Petrosky's mind. He pushed the image away and opened the door.

Icy air brushed his face, but the wind was laced with the smell of grass and earth, a stubborn summer still rasping its final breaths.

"Later, Ed. And I'm here to help you work things through, on this, or—"

"I know, Steve. I know."

Petrosky flipped his collar against the breeze and headed for the precinct.

"Petrosky!" Shannon Taylor's long jacket flew behind her like a cape as she hurried toward him across the lot.

"You looking for my rookie again, Taylor?"

She stepped onto the curb. "Yeah. Where is he?"

"Out. Tracking our vics."

"He's good, Petrosky. Got an eye for details."

"I know. But he'll be better."

"You're taking a lot of time with him. You feel bad because his dad died, or—"

"Did you need something, Shannon?"

"No 'Taylor' anymore, huh?" She smiled. He didn't.

"All right, so I have a defendant in holding across the street. Former or current prostitute, arrested on domestic violence, claiming self-defense."

"And? She need someone to bail her out and you thought you'd ask me?"

"She says she's been over to the shelter. Knew one of your victims—Trazowski. Kinda shaken up about it."

Petrosky squinted toward the street. The detention center hulked in the background. "You been pulling information from my rookie?"

"Just talking."

"How long's she got?"

"Transfer later today to the William Dickerson facility. I told her we'd probably cut her some slack if she cooperated with your homicide case."

"I'll check it out."

Taylor started toward the precinct.

"And, Taylor?"

She turned.

"Don't mess with Morrison."

"I'm not messing with him. He's nice. And unlike you, he doesn't try to hide it from everyone."

"Thanks for the helpful tip, Taylor. I'll let Baker know you said she needs to plead the fifth and focus on changing her name before you lock her ass up."

"You're such an asshole." She turned on her heel and walked away, cape-coat flapping behind her.

It was the same goodbye every time. He smiled at her back and crossed the street toward the Ash Park Detention Center. Halfway across the road, an oncoming Chevy honked at him. Petrosky stopped in the street, forcing the driver to halt with a squeal of brakes. He flipped open his badge. Deciding that asshole looked appropriately chagrined, Petrosky left the street for the detention center where a lady cop with a bored expression checked him through the metal detector inside the front door.

Inside, the waiting room looked like the DMV but felt more miserable, if such a thing were possible. Behind a counter surrounded by Plexiglas, a man with ghost-white skin and a face flat enough to have been run over with a steam roller raised caterpillar eyebrows, too indifferent to bother asking what Petrosky wanted. *A. Cook* glinted off the badge on his chest.

"Cook."

"Petrosky."

"Need a form. Got a few questions for one of your detainees."

Cook pulled a yellow carbon sheet from a drawer and slid it through the Plexiglas slot. "You make them sound like they're on their way to Guantanamo."

"Some of them might as well be for all the good this place'll do them." He scrawled on the form and Cook pulled it back through the slot, a yellow tongue retracting into a Plexiglass lizard.

"Give me ten."

Petrosky moved to the blue-upholstered chairs, set in rows across the middle of the room. Three seats away, a mother with stringy orange hair fed gummy bears to an overwrought toddler, probably waiting for daddy to be brought to the visiting area so they could pretend they were a family for thirty minutes. Behind her, a woman in a business suit picked at a hangnail with a faraway look on her face. Waiting on a brother or a father, Petrosky thought—someone far removed from her own station in life, but whom she just couldn't let go.

The door next to the Plexiglass-enclosed counter clacked open and the previous round of visitors emerged, all from different walks of life, but all wearing the same expression:

forlorn, defeated, depressed. Behind Petrosky, the exit whooshed open and closed, open and closed, bringing with it fresh bursts of misty winter that he could barely smell over the stench of hand sanitizer, dry toast and cheap perfume.

He took his place in line with the others, behind the woman in the business suit. She'd abandoned her hangnail and was now twirling her short, dark curls with such ferocity that Petrosky expected one to snap off in her hand. The toddler was wailing somewhere in the back, a warning siren for his mother to run for the exit before whomever they were seeing sucked her down too. She hushed the child as they walked single file through another metal detector and into a holding pen between two bulletproof doors, then into the sterile-looking interior hallway that led to the visitor stalls.

A young black officer with a drawn face and a full beard stood in the aisle holding a list. "Chapman, second stall," he said, gesturing with the paper toward the first hallway. The woman in the business suit raised a hand, stumbled forward and disappeared down the aisle.

"Baker, end of the line."

Petrosky followed the officer's finger to the last stall, where Sarah Baker stood waiting for him on the other side of a chest-high cinderblock wall. He peered at her through the thick black mesh that ran from the top of the wall to the ceiling. She was thick and stocky, the kind of girl you'd want on your side in a street brawl.

She edged her face forward and squinted, as if trying to get a better look at him through the mesh screen. "Who are you?" Her voice had the low husky quality of a lounge singer.

"Detective Petrosky. I heard you might have some information on Jane Trazowski."

"Oh, that." A wet slap, the pop of bubble gum. "I met her at the shelter over there on Hamerstein."

"LaPorte's place."

"Yeah, her and me were talking at dinner one night. She was real beat up. Bruises everywhere. Couldn't hardly eat on account of her lip, all busted up. Even had those marks on her wrists, the kind from rope or whatever."

"She'd been tied up?"

"Yep. Said the guy paid for the night but he was into some kinky stuff. Gave her twice her normal."

"Did she describe him?"

*Pop.* "She said tall, I think. Not muscle-y like, but tall."

"Hair?"

"I don't remember. I don't think she said."

"Eyes?"

*Pop.* "She just said tall and that he was an asshole. Told him to stop and he said he already paid her so she couldn't say no."

*Entitled fuck.* "Sounds like an asshole, all right."

"So was it him? The one that killed her?"

"We don't know. Where'd he pick her up?"

She shrugged. "Didn't say."

"Tattoos? Anything?"

"Nuh uh. Nothing like that. Just that he was mean and she was afraid to go home because he might know where she lived."

"So he picked her up close to her house, then."

Pause. "Well… I dunno. Maybe. Or maybe he dropped her off. I'm not sure."

"How long were you there with her?"

"She left the day after I got there. You can only stay ten days at a time, but I think she was only there one or two."

"Where were her kids?"

"I dunno."

"Why didn't she bring them with her?"

*Pop. Pop. Pop.* Petrosky waited.

"I only really talked to her that once at dinner. Didn't even know she had kids."

"What'd you have?"

"What?"

"For dinner."

"Burgers." *Pop.* "They were good. The assistant toasted the buns and stuff."

90

"Assistant?" LaPorte had called her "Hannah" at the shelter. Now his file referred to her by her last name. "Ms. Montgomery?"

"Uh... yeah, whatever. She was real nice."

Ms. Montgomery, the assistant, not Julie, his daughter. His stomach tightened anyway as he remembered the shock of the resemblance. "I'm sure she was nice. I'm sure they all are."

"Sometimes they aren't on account of them being hurt. It makes people mean. Some of us anyway."

"Hurt?" Heat flared in his chest. He clenched his fist against his thigh.

"Yeah, that girl—"

"Ms. Montgomery." *Not Julie.*

"Yeah. She had a few bruises on her wrist. She covered them up real good, but I know what it means when you have concealer rubbing off on your shirt sleeves."

"She ever mention who hurt her?" Petrosky asked.

Baker squinted at him though the screen. "Why? Is she dead too?"

I chewed my cheek and typed in another batch of dismissals. Engineer Ernie Smack was not nearly as intimidating on paper as his name suggested he'd be if I tried to fire him in person. Luckily, Noelle had let him go this morning and I was just helping her play catch up on her files. Not that I minded; I needed something to keep my brain busy so as not to end up in a padded room.

So far, my efforts were working. Over the last week, things had been so quiet at the shelter that my panic had finally subsided. And it was looking like the first victim was completely unrelated to the shelter or to me. When I saw her unfamiliar face on the news—bleached blond hair and polar bear white skin—I was so relieved that I didn't even mind when Jake snapped the channel back to his lame car race.

This ride on the paranoia train happened all the time, and I wished I could stop buying tickets. I once freaked out for three weeks after the news reported a tall man with dark hair had strangled a female store owner whose face kinda looked like mine. Which obviously meant that he was trying to find me and got confused. I tend to be a paranoid jerk and not the cute kind that can feign innocence about it. At least I'm aware of it, I guess.

The horned owl on my desk glared at me. *I should break his other ear off. Or get a plant for him to hide under.*

I looked up at the sound of heels clacking on the floor. Noelle stood at the entrance to my cubicle, smiling, her lips shiny from a fresh coat of gloss. "What's up?" she said.

*Just contemplating torturing an inanimate ceramic figurine. Also, someone might be after me and killing girls I work with at a place you don't even know I go to.*

92

"Not much. Crushing people's dreams and occupational aspirations with the touch of a few buttons."

"Eh, I'm sure Dominic has a reason."

I stared at her, trying not to think about lying beneath Jake's naked body the other night, eyes squeezed shut, swallowing Mr. Harwick's name while Jake moaned in my ear. "You're on a first name basis?"

"Well, no. But hopefully I will be soon." Noelle winked.

My face grew warm. Subject change time. I nodded at the other side of the room and lowered my voice. "How are things with Ralph? He seems bummed, and he's been watching you all day."

Noelle shrugged. "He wasn't what I was after, I guess. Boring, you know?"

There was something else in Noelle's eyes, but it passed before I could get a handle on it.

"Anyway," Noelle said, "how about we let off some steam after work? There's a club downtown that I've been dying to check out. They keep sending me ads. Maybe it will give me a little practice for the boss, or at least help me find someone more interesting than Mister Excitement over there." Noelle jerked her head in Ralph's direction.

I needed to stop chewing on my lip before I ate it clean off my face. One day, Noelle was going to get tired of asking me to go out with her. Maybe she'd even go find another friend altogether. *Shit.*

"I'm not sure... I mean, I don't know if Jake—" My wrist throbbed. I cleared my throat. "I can't."

"Girl, it's fine. Next time, okay?" She waved her hand in that universal shooing-a-fruit-fly gesture.

Ouch. I hoped I had better than fruit fly status—buzzing, fruit-stealing, poop-eating, assholes. Did fruit flies even eat poop? A biologist I was not.

"Yeah, next time," I said to the owls since Noelle was already gone.

My cell phone rang. I grabbed it out of the bottom drawer. "Hey, baby. What's up?"

Jake was chewing on something, and the wet crunch of chips or pretzels made me want to gag. In the background, the television chattered about leasing a car.

"Just working," I said. *Like you should be doing.*

"My mom wants us to come over for dinner tonight," Jake said.

"By 'we' do you mean 'you?'"

"Why do you always do that?" he demanded.

I took a deep breath. He was right. I was in a horrible mood and in no shape to be around his mother. Not that my heart ever swelled at the prospect of sitting in her living room, choking on cigarette smoke, watching her glower at me. *I should run off with Mario, my silent but poisonous plant—or Horny the rage-faced owl.*

"Sorry, I just… don't think she likes me very much."

"She likes you fine. I just think… I dunno, I think maybe she wishes we'd gotten married before we moved in together."

*I'm pretty sure she just thinks you can do better.* I rose and peeked at Noelle, on the phone in her cubicle. Maybe making plans with someone less fruit-fly-like. My heart squeezed. "Actually, I'm going to work late tonight. I'll get dinner before I come home. You go ahead."

"Fine," he spat.

*Don't be mad, don't be mad.* "There's some extra money in the drawer in the kitchen. Why don't you grab some drinks and dessert for you and your mom? I won't be too late."

The channel changed in the background. Game show. Judge show. News show.

*How do you get your boyfriend to do sit ups?*
*Put the remote between his toes!*

There was a pause, then a sound like Jake was rummaging in a drawer. The shuffling stopped. He must have found the money.

"Well, okay." His voice was softer. "Don't spend too much on dinner."

"Okay." *Like you should have any say where I put my*

*money.* "See you when I get home. Tell your mom I said hello."

"I will. Love you."

Not mad. Thank goodness. "Love you too."

The line clicked, taking the chatter of the television with it. I tossed my cell back in the drawer and headed to Noelle's cubicle. "Change of plans," I said, my heart twitching with nerves or maybe... excitement.

Her hand pressed against her chest in mock surprise. "You mean Little Miss Goodie Two Shoes is actually going to go out and absorb some nightlife?"

"I guess so. I just need to make sure I get back early. Like, maybe dinner, and then we can stop in at the club but head out after an hour or so."

"Aw, but no one's out at five, Hannah."

Jake's mother usually slugged back half a dozen beers and smoked a pack before she took Jake home. Last time I went to visit her, we got home at midnight—not because we were having a blast, but because his mother had fallen asleep on the couch and Jake said she'd be angry if he didn't say goodbye to her. "If we can get out of there by ten thirty, I should be fine."

"Okay, Cinderella, I will return you home punctually and as virtuous as when you left." Noelle's eyes said she would do anything to break that promise if I was willing. She smiled. "You won't regret it."

---

Robert ate a late dinner at Johnny's, an Italian pizza kitchen around the block from his house. The food was good but not great, eaten over a nondescript tablecloth and served by a nondescript waiter. Despite his obvious boredom, the waiter looked expectant when he handed over the check, like he thought he deserved a tip.

*He's going to be disappointed.*

The car ride was no better. Every accident within sixty

miles was clustered along his route to the club. Robert bit back his rage as best he could, though it didn't stop him from aiming expletives and obscene hand gestures at an elderly woman in a neighboring car. Her horrified eyes improved his mood considerably.

Thomas was waiting for him at the entrance to the parking structure a block from the club, eating something fluorescent from a small plastic bag in his palm.

As Robert approached, Thomas held the bag out in offering. "Gummy bear?" Thomas's tongue was green.

*Imbecile.* "You look like a fucking leprechaun," Robert said.

The drone of music and lively chatter swelled as they neared the club. Each drew IDs for the muscled door attendant who was hulking behind rope chains and currently squinting at the license of a skinny blonde wearing stilettos and a miniskirt that left half her ass hanging out. *Slut.* The bouncer waved her through and stared Robert down over the top of his fake license. Robert stiffened.

"Twenty apiece, pay at the door." The guard handed Robert's ID back and nodded at Thomas.

They walked to the entrance, handed the cover charge to a grim-faced skinhead with barbed wire tattooed around his left bicep, and entered the club.

Inside, the warehouse-like expanse stunk of stale smoke and the rank tang of sweat. The place was already teeming with bodies, a mix of men and women in sharp business attire as if they had come straight from work, and casually-dressed young people who gave off "regulars" vibes. A few slouched men in cargo shorts and women in spaghetti straps scrutinized other patrons as if deciding whether anyone there was worth fucking.

At the bar, a young woman in a tight halter dress approached a stodgy Tom, Dick, or Harry in an expensive suit. She rubbed her breasts on his arm and whispered in his ear. Robert narrowed his eyes in disgust. The succubus always found her prey early.

"There's a table near the back," Thomas said. "It must be our lucky night."

They threaded their way to a small table with a wraparound leather bench across from the bar. The polished wooden tabletop was littered with empty glasses and wrinkled napkins. A few tiny stirring straws were set up in a tic-tac-toe formation in the center.

"Wanna play?" Thomas gestured to the straws.

"Nah. I hear leprechauns suck at that game."

Thomas stuck out his tongue and it glowed eerily yellow under the black lights. He really was an idiot.

A redheaded waitress appeared wearing tight pants and a harried expression. Her lithe hands scurried like rabbits, clearing the table into a brown bin. She set the bin at her feet and whipped out a small pad of paper from her back pocket. "What can I get you?"

"Vodka and Red Bull," Robert said.

Thomas shrugged. "Whatever you've got on tap."

She scrawled the orders, shoved the pad into her pocket, and flashed them a tense smile. "Be right back, guys."

Robert watched her over Thomas's shoulder as she walked away, her hips sashaying more than seemed necessary. Maybe that was for his benefit. Maybe not. He frowned as she disappeared into the back with the bin and their table scraps.

Thomas was focused on the televisions behind the bar. Robert glanced at the screen where a common-looking woman in a blue suit yammered into the camera about something surely as tiresome as her flaring nostrils.

"CNN, huh?" Robert said.

Thomas met Robert's eyes and grinned. "Nothing says it's time to party like stock market updates."

Robert looked past Thomas again, but the redhead did not reappear. When he drew his gaze back, Thomas was staring at him with knowing eyes, and Robert resisted the urge to throttle him.

"You looking for our waitress?"

Panic chilled Robert's marrow. "Yeah, I'm thirsty."

"Aw, come on, man! You were staring at her when she walked away. Not that I blame you." He winked, tarnishing her.

No, he could not let Thomas take this away from him, not if she was The One. There was no time to dwell; Robert felt her return in every cell of his body. She emerged through the doors, eyes alight with passion and the promise of resurrection, of atonement, of a chance to prove himself worthy and noble. He had been noble once.

He could do it again.

*For love.*

And he had loved her, if only for a day during his senior year in high school. Mindy Haliburton. Each twist of her fingers, each bite of her lip had been a sure indication that she was trying to control herself. But she was Reverend Haliburton's daughter.

They were in the Reverend's basement when Robert had pushed her to the floor. "Don't worry, Mindy. I understand," he whispered

Of course he'd understood. He understood that by fighting him, by making the lust his alone, she might absolve herself of guilt and save herself from Hell. He understood that her thoughts were as deep as his, or she wouldn't have asked him there. And he surely understood that she wanted this, no matter what she had to say to protect her reputation and her soul. Each desperate sound she made mirrored his own desperation, their mutual desire mingling with fear of repercussions, their need for one another overriding their terror.

"No! Robby, stop!"

But he heard what she really meant: *Yes! Robby, harder!*

When it was over, she lay still, eyes bloodshot, face ashen and laced with tears. He stroked her cheek and ran his tongue over her bottom lip.

*You're welcome.*

He had admitted to the rape, despite their mutual need. He had saved her from her own sins by sacrificing himself to hordes of inmates who had offered no remorse, no leniency, no forgiveness. There was nothing more noble one person could do for another.

Pride welled in his heart.

"Here you go, guys."

Robert refocused his attention on the redheaded waitress as she set Thomas's glass in front of him. She had a tinkling voice that grew a little hoarse as she increased her volume to be heard, as if Pollyanna were trying her hand as a phone sex operator. Robert met her eyes. She did not look away. He touched her wrist as she put his drink down, and electricity zipped up his arm, through his chest, and down into his groin. She pulled her hand away, too quickly. Her eyes, once warm, now emanated surprise and fear—and revulsion.

She knew. She could feel it in his touch.

"Can I get you anything else?" she asked, her voice suddenly not so much sultry as irritating. Robert shook his head.

"No thanks," Thomas said with an idiotic smile, oblivious to the whole exchange.

But Robert was not. *I am a doomed man*, *and she knows it*.

The waitress picked up an empty cup, her eyes wide. Watching him. Marking him. The mark of Cain.

*No one will ever offer me forgiveness.* He kept his gaze on her, memorizing her features as she retreated.

*Especially her.*

"Earth to Jim! You hear what I said?"

Robert blinked at Thomas.

"Two just walked in, our age, both of them gorgeous. The blonde looked right at me."

Robert ground his teeth together. They'd surely sense his wickedness and mark him like all the others. But if there was any chance, any at all…

His jaw relaxed.

"They're in the booth next to us. We should say hello."

"Yes," Robert said, plastering on his best come-hither

smile. "It would be cruel to make them wait."

The Hangout was a posh establishment, but the bouncer shooed Noelle and me in without asking us to pay the cover, which made me feel attractive and also a little like a prostitute flaunting her wares to save twenty bucks. The music pounded through immense speakers and strobe lights pulsed flashes of red and yellow, green and blue, in time to the music. Noelle stood on her tiptoes to scour the seating situation, then dragged me to a back corner booth across from the bar. The vacating couple was still collecting their drinks when she clambered into the seat. I waited until they disappeared into the crowd, and sat as our waitress approached.

Noelle ordered a daiquiri. I got a cranberry juice with lime.

"I better take it easy on these," I said when the drinks were delivered. "I don't want you to have to carry me out of here."

Noelle laughed, but it was hard to hear her over the music. I watched her face, trying to decide if I was supposed to be making conversation as she scanned the room. I settled for working on my drink.

Within minutes, the booth began to feel like a prison. A gopher in my chest clawed at my ribcage. I pictured the rodent from *Caddyshack* and squinted at the subtitles on the muted television behind the bar, half expecting Jake's face to leap onto the screen, eyes radiating disapproval. *I really need to get out more.*

"Hey, need some company?" Two men stood next to our table, drinks in hand. The one who spoke was blond, with chiseled features and a wide mouth. His taller, darker companion looked like he had just stepped off the cover of *G.Q.* His eyes were sharp like a hawk's and ringed with aqua, the unique coloring visible even in the dim light of the club. As our eyes met, a pang of memory flittered across my mind and disappeared. My breath caught, but I could no longer remember why.

"Sure." Noelle scooted toward me in the booth and the blond slid in beside her. I moved to the end to avoid being squished.

"I'm Thomas," the blond said, offering his hand. Noelle took it and smiled at him.

"I'm Jim," said Mr. G.Q. He was watching me, presumably waiting for me to tell him my name, but my mouth was too dry to speak. When I said nothing, he parked next to Thomas.

Noelle raised her voice over the pounding music. "I'm Noelle, and this is my shy friend Hannah."

Thomas waved, and it was so exaggerated and goofy that I almost smiled. Jim bowed his head once. "Nice to meet you, Hannah."

I picked up my juice and put it to my lips instead of responding. Social awkwardness was a bitch. *Dammit, Hannah, act normal*!

Noelle glanced at me and turned back to the guys. "So, Thomas, what do you do?"

"Yoga." Thomas's voice was strained, speaking over the music, but it was still mellow somehow. Calm. "I also play on the jungle gym whenever possible. Buy catnip. Not for me, mind you, but that doesn't make it less true."

Noelle laughed. "No, for work."

"We're both in the automotive industry," Thomas said, pointing to Jim. "Being in the Motor City, it was between designing cars and starting a Motown boy band. But I can't dance."

Noelle's eyes were on Thomas's face as she shifted toward him and put her hand on his arm. "Original. Most guys just go for 'I'm a big-shot lawyer' or 'I'm an engineer.'"

Thomas's smile was infectious: straight, white, genuine. "I have to play to my strengths. I'm better at creative dialogue than dancing anyway."

Noelle laughed harder than I'd ever made her laugh and a pang of jealousy hooked my stomach.

"Did you go to school here?" Noelle asked him.

"Yep. University of Michigan," Thomas said.

My head throbbed in time to the music. I set my glass on the table next to Noelle's.

As if remembering there was someone else at the table, Noelle took her hand off Thomas's arm and sat back in the booth. "How about you, Jim? Where did you go to school?"

Jim sipped his drink and watched me like he hadn't heard her. It was probably my overactive imagination, but it didn't stop the niggling at the base of my skull. There was hunger in his fixed stare, like he wanted to eat me alive.

"Cal Tech," he said finally.

I turned my head and looked across the way, behind the bar, toward the television again—anywhere to avoid Jim's eyes. The view wasn't any better over there. On the flat screen, a spunky young newscaster feigned seriousness while, behind her, police officers walked by with a black body bag on a stretcher. It was the same shot that had been on replay for weeks as the media exploited the murders of two young women. Jane and what's-her-name. Meredith. I winced.

"Scary stuff," Jim said.

I turned toward him but kept my eyes on his forehead.

"Don't worry, they'll catch him," he said.

"What makes you think it's a him?" Noelle asked.

Jim's head cocked to the side. "It always is, isn't it?"

Noelle's face darkened so briefly that I thought I imagined it.

"Things aren't always as they seem," Thomas said, and his voice was solemn, all trace of humor gone.

The hair on my arms stood.

Jim painted an abstract in the condensed water on his glass. "I mean, it's always some dude who is so fucked up in the head that no one else wants anything to do with him. Look at Dahmer. Same story, different guy."

Noelle elbowed me lightly. "Hannah, you okay?"

I cleared my throat. "Yeah, I guess I... feel a little sorry for some of those guys. Not the murdering part, but the part where they're so desperate that they think their only option is to kill someone."

There was a pregnant pause. *Did I just say I feel sorry for murderers?* If only I were a magician so I could disappear. Behind us, the black lights flickered off and neon strobes swept over the room, like searchlights seeking to highlight my stupidity.

"Hey, how about another round of drinks?" Thomas asked, summoning the waitress with his trademarked goofy wave. Noelle giggled and nodded her agreement.

Thomas was my new personal hero. *I'll call him Captain Awkward and he can come to my rescue in ridiculous social situations.* It was an ingenious plan. So why was my skin still crawling?

I twisted toward Noelle but she was whispering in Thomas's ear. In my peripheral, I saw Jim, openly staring at me, his eyes alert and sharp and... famished. My heart backflipped. *No. Don't panic. Not now.*

Too late. I couldn't breathe. I grabbed my cranberry juice to loosen my vocal cords and the cup slipped, splattering juice down the front of my shirt.

"Shit."

*Well, at least you can still talk.* "I'll be right back," I croaked like someone who had just turned from a princess to a frog but without any of the royal pizzazz. I squeezed through happy women, angry women, and dancing couples to where a hand-painted wooden sign decreed *Ladies* above a little stick figure of a person in a dress. I was wearing jeans. I considered using the men's bathroom to make a point but jerked open the door to the ladies' room.

The bathroom was crowded but only for the stalls. In an alcove off to the side, I found a place at the sink and scrubbed at the stain with a wad of wet paper towels. The stain spread. I scrubbed harder, trying to avoid the buttons so I didn't tear them off. Other women walked by to the other sink, but none acknowledged me. I kept my eyes on the bleeding stain.

*Why couldn't you just have a vodka tonic like everyone else?*

*Because you can't handle being out of control even a little bit.*

A little more water, some soap, and a ream of paper towels later, the spot had faded from maroon to a sickly pink—still visible, but better. My heart had slowed as well. I looked into the mirror.

*Shit.* Under the florescent lights my cream-colored blouse was almost completely see through. *Shit, shit, shit.* At least the stain had covered my undergarment. Now, the outline of my bra was clearly visible to everyone.

I stepped to the hand dryer and jabbed the button, half squatting and stretching the blouse as best I could to get the fabric under the airflow. The dryer stopped humming. I pushed the button with my elbow and frantically tried to get the material back into the perfect place before the hot air stopped again. By the sixth round, I was smashing the button, less worried about the shirt and more consumed with the desire to kick the dryer into space. Why couldn't the thing just keep going? Like anyone's hands really got dry in one push!

"Hannah? What are you doing?" Noelle stood in the doorway, eyebrows raised. I desperately wished for a sudden power outage so I could make a groping, awkward run for it.

"I was… trying to get this blouse to work again." Out of the corner of my eye, I caught a glimpse of myself in the mirror: hair askew from the errant dryer wind, cheeks flushed with exertion, and that fucking shirt stretched and hanging off my front, a disarray of transparent ripples.

Noelle began to laugh. I joined her, and once I got going, I had no ability or desire to stop. Tears rolled down my face and mingled with the sweat of panicked shirt drying. Three other women walked into the bathroom and tossed each other knowing looks. *Wow, look who's already had one too many*, their pursed lips said.

I wiped my eyes with the back of my hand. "Can we take off, please? This is enough excitement for one night."

"Aw, come on! We've only been here for an hour! Plus,

with your invisible shirt, you're finally in something club appropriate. Maybe you'll even get laid when you get home! Nothing like a little ooh and aah to make the embarrassment worth it, right? Though I'm not sure Jake knows how to get you to make those noises anyway."

*Point taken.* "What's the difference between ooh and aah?" I said.

Noelle raised her eyebrows.

"About three inches."

We collapsed into laughter again. Noelle was the first to catch her breath. "Let's get our stuff. I already got their numbers, but I want to say goodbye. Here, take this."

She handed me her cardigan. I pulled it on and followed Noelle out of the bathroom toward the table. The guys stood when they saw us—impressive, actually—but it didn't change anything.

"I'm sorry, gentlemen, but we have to head out," Noelle said.

Thomas's face fell. "But it's so early! Is there anything we can do to change your minds?"

Noelle shook her head. "We had a little wardrobe malfunction."

Their banter faded in my ears. Jim's eyes roved over me, as engaged as if I had suggested we strip naked and hula hoop. The prickle of goosebumps I'd felt earlier returned with renewed ferocity. I touched Noelle's arm and jerked my head toward the door.

"Hopefully we can get together again soon," Jim said.

I tried to force a polite nod, a grin, some kind of acknowledgment, but my body was shouting *no way in hell.* Noelle and I weaved toward the exit through throngs of club-goers smelling of Axe Body Spray and desperation. It wasn't until we reached the street that I felt my body relax as if an invisible wire had been cut.

"Why the hell would it be okay for you to go to a club?"

My face was on fire. "I wasn't there for long and I didn't dance or anything like that."

"Did you talk to anyone?"

"Well, yeah, but—"

"What the fuck is wrong with you?"

*Why did you tell him, Hannah?* "The club was next to the restaurant. I just—"

"Who'd you go with? Are you fucking around?"

I put a hand on the table behind me to steady myself. "No! I... saw Noelle, this girl who works with me in HR. She always asks me to come out with her, and I always refuse because I know you wouldn't want me to. But I was right there. I thought she might get suspicious or something if I said no."

"Suspicious?" A flash of understanding. Not enough.

"I mean... I don't know." My back was dewy with sweat. *The table. Focus on the table.*

Jake stepped toward me, face inches from mine. "Are you fucking listening to me?" I could barely hear him over the thudding of my heart.

He grabbed my arms in both hands. "Look at me, goddammit!"

"I'm sorry, I'm so sorry, Jake, I just thought that—"

"Why do you make me do this to you?" He released me, violently. My tailbone hit the table and I yelped.

*Just get it over with. Be done.*

"I need to get the fuck out of here to calm down," he said. "You're fucking worthless, you know that?"

I watched him stalk into the hallway. The door slammed.

*You're worthless. I am the only one who appreciates you. Let me show you how much I care about you—*

I ran through the living room to the bathroom and dropped to my knees in front of the toilet. One of Jake's pubic hairs stuck to the seat. My stomach muscles lurched, but nothing came up. The world wavered. I gripped the sides of the toilet bowl.

*In, out... in, out...*

I shouldn't have told him where I had gone. No, I shouldn't have gone somewhere that I wasn't supposed to be. I was a damn liar and nowhere near clever enough to do the right thing or avoid pissing him off. Maybe I should stop working at the shelter too, before he found out and had another reason to get angry.

A scar on my ankle throbbed wetly. In the past, it had been worth bleeding the dejection from my veins with a straight razor. The pain had worked to clear my mind because it released calming endorphins, though I suspected the hurt also served as a distraction from my shitty life. But I wasn't that girl anymore.

*Maybe if I did just a little. It wouldn't take much to make my head stop spinning.*

*I won't go back.*

I stood on wobbly legs, leaned against the counter and stared into the mirror. Pale cheeks, like Casper, but not as adorable. See? As long as I could crack a joke, I would be okay. I smiled shakily at my reflection.

*You're okay, Hannah.*

I splashed my face with cool water, toweled dry, and walked out to the living room. All was silent except for the television that had been left on low. The whole place felt utterly abandoned. I touched a large brownish stain on the armrest of the empty couch. *Sticky.* I sighed instead of crying.

Beer bottles and old magazines littered the coffee table. I was bending to pick them up when a cold chill shivered down my spine. Someone was watching. I jerked around, envisioning a figure emerging from the shadows, but the room remained empty.

*Outside.* The curtains were open, window cracked— probably so Jake could smoke a bowl without me knowing— but now the darkness beyond taunted me with far more terrifying unknowns. I clasped the papers to my chest and moved closer to the window, peering down at the empty street below. What would happen to me if Jake left for good?

*Get it together, Hannah. There's no one there. No one's*

*going to come after you, you're not that important.*

*I was important enough to him. And I'm sure I made him furious.* I slammed the window shut.

The living room took half an hour, the bedroom another forty minutes. When all was tidy, I finally felt like I could breathe again. As I brought dirty rags back to the kitchen, I stumbled over my purse on the floor and grabbed the wallet off the top. But I already knew—my cash was gone.

---

Through the glass front door, the man saw Jake rush out of the stairwell and into the lobby. The man had no time to escape across the street without drawing attention to himself, so instead he grabbed the front door handle as Jake emerged.

"Pardon me," the man said.

Jake glared back, his stained T-shirt showing beneath his wrinkled, open jacket.

"A friend of mine is having a party here tonight, but I seem to have left the address at home. Can you tell me where Sandra Henson lives?"

Jake snorted. "How the hell would I know?" He scurried down the walk without waiting for a response.

The man held the door, watching Jake's back until it was swallowed up by the night. Then he let the door swing shut and crossed the street to a building that had once been a family home, but was now a tailoring service for children's clothes by day and vacant every evening after six o'clock. He ducked under the awning and considered the boyfriend.

An unexpected encounter, but not concerning. Jake would be less apt to think it strange when they met again.

And they would.

His breath hissed steadily in and out, merging with the brisk, dry air and the twigs that skittered across his path. A short distance from his shoes, the grass shimmered under the glow of the streetlight. He wore the shadows without concern for passersby; she lived on a street populated with people who went to bed early. Was it by chance, or by her conscious design? Probably the price. And the fact that there were fewer people to hear her boyfriend yelling at her like a Neanderthal.

And then there she was, a silhouette against warm lamplight, moving, almost dancing as she wiped the glass. She had stayed up late, as if she knew he'd be there.

He inhaled the crisp scent of leaves and musty earth. Interesting how quickly he had found her once he began looking in earnest. It was equally intriguing that he wasn't yet sure whether he would kill her, whether he would pull out her insides and watch her writhe like the others.

Usually, he knew a woman's date of death from their first meeting. This time he felt the question throbbing between his ears, wrapping his mind in a conundrum.

"Hannah." He let the name play on his tongue, tasting the syllables, savoring this single piece of her he now possessed. Hardness strained against his zipper. He watched closely as she spun from the window, clicked off the lamp, and disappeared into the blackness of her apartment. Satisfaction tingled around the edges of his brain.

The night birds squalled as the light in Hannah's bedroom turned on. She did not pass the windows, no more bustling around trying to forget her useless boyfriend, not even a shadow as she dressed for sleep. Perhaps she was already in bed. The wind pulled at his jacket, the cold sharpening his focus on her window until the song of the night birds faded in his ears. He could almost hear her breathing. And still the light remained.

Hannah must not be sleeping well. He suspected it was because of him.

## MONDAY, NOVEMBER 1ST

*What a difference a weekend makes.*

On my desk, a vase of tulips brightened my cubicle with silent but sincere apology. Three were already wilted, but they did their job all the same, even if they had been bought with money from my purse. At least I hadn't had to pay for the deliciously long back rub that had lulled me to sleep last night.

*I should pick up something special for him on the way home. Maybe condoms.*

I was the most romantic girlfriend ever.

Also on my desk, three stacks of new hire packets fluttered in the dry heat from the vent. I blinked hard to wet my corneas and an eyelash stabbed me in the eye. I tried to blow it off. It stuck. I brushed at it until the stubborn bastard came out, then finished entering the last of the new employee data from the second stack.

I took my completed work to the filing room and found Noelle already there, shoving personnel files into the cabinets with practiced precision. "Hey there, stranger! What's been going on?"

"Same old, same old," I said, trying to sound casual but feeling guilty as hell for not calling Noelle back this weekend.

She squinted at me. "You okay? What happened?"

"Jake was a little pissed about the whole clubbing thing, but we made up. No biggie."

She wiggled a file into place. "I just don't understand what you see in him. I keep thinking about what you told me when my dad died. All that stuff about it taking more than blood to build a relationship, so I wouldn't feel bad for hating his ass. But all Jake ever gives you is grief, and you don't even—"

"I really do love him." My pulse quickened and I swallowed hard. "He's had a tough time finding work so I think he's stressed." I just needed to talk to him more. Be more understanding. At the least, I could avoid intentionally doing things that I knew would make him upset.

Noelle touched my hand. "Hey, I'm sorry, okay? I didn't mean it. I'm just a little tired."

My heart slowed at her backpedaling. But... Noelle, tired? There were no bags under her eyes, and the whites were clear, probably more clear than mine after my renegade lash incident. She looked... peaceful. Happy, even. "You're tired? Why? Did you go over and mess around with Ralph? He looks like he could go all night long." I tried to smile.

"I went out with Thomas last night."

Jim's creepy, weirdo eyes flashed across my consciousness and disappeared. "How did it go?"

"Dinner was good." Her words caught almost imperceptibly, like a leaf hitching on an underdraft that doesn't ultimately possess enough power to change its course. Noelle closed the drawer and bent to open the one below it, but kept her face buried in the files. "He's an interesting guy. Really... different from any other guy I've met. He's funny but not like he's trying to be."

"Did you... you know?"

Noelle closed the file drawer and straightened. "Nope. He came back to my apartment but he didn't even try to get in my pants."

"Really? I mean, he likes women and everything, right?"

Noelle laughed at my joke, but not as hard as she had laughed at Thomas's. "Yeah, he likes women. He's just... nice. Cautious, you know? Respectful. Plus he's kind of a homebody. Would rather hang out in the woods or at home than be out partying."

I took her place in front of the cabinet and opened a drawer. Noelle was happy with a homebody? She wasn't determined to drag him out clubbing with her?

*Or is it just... me that she needs to take out? Am I not*

*interesting enough on my own?*

I stuck a couple folders into the drawer. "So what did you do at your apartment?"

"Talked for a few hours. And ate ice cream."

I closed the drawer. "Come on, Noelle. You have to do better than that. How else am I supposed to live vicariously through you? I need details!"

"If you feel like you need to live vicariously, then that just proves you're missing something in your real life. Jake seriously needs to step up his game. Or you need to make better friends with your vibrator."

———

Hannah laughed, but her eyes glazed over as if she were thinking something she didn't want to say. Noelle's stomach clenched.

*Note to self: Don't talk about Jake.* Just the mention of that jack-off made Hannah's mouth tighten up.

Noelle ground her teeth together to keep from screaming at her friend to kick his ass out. She knew Hannah wouldn't, and she no longer cared why.

"Good enough," Noelle said. *Good enough if you don't care about being happy.*

She avoided Hannah's eyes.

*There has to be a way to get him away from her.*

———

I took a bite of the roasted vegetables I had made for dinner. "I just can't believe I got everything done today. I'm glad I was able to sneak out of there on time."

"Well, I know you're good at your job. You're good at everything you do. I appreciate the way you always take care of me."

His words softened a touch of the frostiness I had felt when I walked in and found beer bottles all over the kitchen counter and the garbage overflowing. But being angry at him wouldn't push away this feeling I had that someone was after me, and it certainly wouldn't help if I pushed him away and ended up alone. I stared at the table and wielded my fork like a bayonet as I finished my veggies. Better the carrots than a person. Probably.

*I should buy myself some more flowers.*

After dinner, he slothed off to the living room, though sloths are cuter than the face Jake makes sucking on his after-meal cigarette. Maybe instead of Mario the philodendron I would get a tree, so Jake could hang out in the branches all day on his machete claws, looking dull. Doing nothing.

I washed the dishes with irritation burning in my chest like a nasty infection you couldn't scratch lest you make it spread. I tried to picture the flowers on my work desk. I should have brought them home so I could be more easily reminded of the good things. Things like the way he used to hold me when I was too afraid to sleep, though he thought I was just an insomniac. And the compliments, used sparingly, so I knew he really meant them. And what about that time he spent all day cleaning the apartment after he got angry and… well there were other good times too. Lots of them.

When the last dish was clean, I poked my head into the living room where Jake was glued to the TV, eating what looked like a fast food apple pie from a paper sleeve. "I'm going to get the mail." My voice dripped annoyance, but if he heard it, he didn't acknowledge it.

"Mm-hmm."

*He even talks like a sloth.* I rolled my eyes and yanked open the apartment door, but glanced back toward the living room once more as if really expecting to see a sloth lounging on Jake's recliner. The television droned on, flashing lights on his face as he chewed with his mouth open.

I squared my shoulders and hurried down the hall and downstairs to the wall of mailboxes. A slip of white paper poked from the corner of my box, probably an advertisement for housekeeping services. Or pizza delivery. Maybe a new takeout restaurant. My keys clattered against the metal doors as I unlocked the box and grabbed my bills and the rogue paper. A scent like lilies wafted into my nose, but it was sharper, more acidic. Citrus. Oranges, maybe. *Weird*. Perhaps I'd be a scent detector if this thing at Harwick didn't work out. But they already had German Shepherds for that. Doggie jackasses, stealing all the good jobs.

I opened the mystery sheet.

> *Jake*
> *Miss you, babe! Come down tomorrow after she leaves for work. I picked up that lingerie you like and some whipped cream. xoxo*
> *~Me*

*Jake*? Snakes in my stomach awakened and writhed. Acid climbed to my throat. Behind me, someone entered the building, and the blast of bitter air turned the dew on my skin to ice. I fled to the stairwell. My feet on the metal stairs thudded like an executioner's drumbeat.

*How could he do this to me*? I reached my floor and grabbed the door handle, but it was heavy, much too heavy.

*No one else will ever put up with me the way Jake does. Maybe I shouldn't say anything about it at all.*

I let go of the door and collapsed on the top stair, face against the dilapidated railing. My tears tasted metallic.

*Just leave. Run. Start again.*

*Stay. Don't say anything. It's not worth fighting.*

*I won't make it on my own.*

*So what? What have you got to live for anyway?*

My hiccuping gasps echoed around me, then, from the phone in my pocket, a text message plink: *Baby, where'd you go*?

The snakes lashed themselves against my esophagus. I wiped my tear-stained face on the sleeve of my shirt and stood, fist clenched around the letter. Lingerie. Whipped cream. I had never had a chance.

The apartment door clicked softly closed behind me. Sometimes the beginning of the end was a whisper. I resisted the urge to throw myself at his feet, begging him to stay.

"Where'd you go?"

I stared at my shoes, the wall.

"What's in your hand?"

"The… mail." No use delaying the inevitable.

He snatched it from me. "What the fuck is your problem?"

Paper rustled. I walked around him into the kitchen, and turned back to face him, my butt against the dining table.

"What the hell?"

Jake flicked the letter with two fingers. "I have no idea who this is! It must be for someone else." His face was flushed, neck corded.

*Don't talk.* Tears slid down my cheeks. I swallowed back bile.

"Baby, it isn't for me! Someone is fucking with you. I want to marry you! I've asked you a dozen times!" His hands clenched into fists when I didn't respond.

"How could you even… so what, it's over now? We're not going to get married? I have to start all over?"

I clamped my lips shut, stealing glances at him, gauging his distance.

*I'm sorry, forget I said anything, please don't hurt me!*

*I don't care who you screw, please don't leave me alone!*

His knuckles were white. "You're going to believe some stupid note over me?" His voice grew louder with each word, escalation steeped in rage. "We've been together for years and you're just going to throw it away on this shit? What the fuck is wrong with you?"

*Don't speak. You'll make it worse.*

Jake's fist unclenched and everything around us slowed until there was only the motion of his hand, reaching along the counter. A weapon? A knife? My heart slowed too, then seemed to stop, the throbbing of my chest replaced with white noise so deafening I couldn't even hear what he was shouting, though spittle flew from his moving lips. Then movement, sudden as lightning. He grabbed a plate from the stack of drying dishes and I flinched, preparing for the pain, for the shattering glass to embed in my skin. It flew past me and the breath from the hurtling dish whispered in my ear: *Run. Run away.* I flattened myself against the table. *Don't move. Watch the wall. Nothing but the wall.*

Footsteps pounded toward me, reigniting the furious beating of my heart, and then he was there, his breath hot with rage and reeking of tobacco. His fist slammed into my temple with a dull, wet thud. Stars exploded behind my left eye and I was falling, plunging over the edge of the table, crashing against the linoleum. Pain roared up my side.

He panted above me, breathing fast, much too fast. I curled into a fetal position and squeezed my eyes shut. I waited. No more blows landed.

"I'm done. I'm fucking done," he said. I heard footsteps stomping away from me, and then the door slammed.

As my tears puddled around my throbbing head, I wondered if I would survive without him.

***

It was dark, as it had been in his younger years, though he no longer waited in patient silence for the feathery kiss of tiny legs to climb over his dirty bare feet. Nor did he listen for the disembodied groans coming to him through the closet door, or the wet *thwack thwack thwack* of skin-on-skin, those strange songs that had once held a faint promise that maybe he would eat tonight.

He stretched his eyes wide, adjusting to the gloom. As a child, he had once wondered if he could develop superhuman sight if he strained hard enough against the dark; comic book super heroes certainly had no less outlandish ways of acquiring power. But he had dismissed the idea just as quickly, even then. Most children will believe anything. He'd believed nothing.

Moans filtered through the memories and snapped him back to the present. The drugs must be wearing off. The man on the table groaned again, louder this time. He could get as loud as he wanted; no one would find them here.

The cement building had long been abandoned, each stinking puddle of rat urine a tribute to all the wretched lives that had once spent time in these rooms. Crumbled walls, crumbed dreams. From the windows on the upper levels, a power plant lit by feeble floodlights was visible in the distance, belching eerie clouds of grayish smoke into the obsidian sky.

Cities like Ash Park were punctuated by isolated pods of despair where the silence was so complete that even vagrants seemed to avoid them. Here, a child could go undiscovered for weeks on end before anyone in the apartment building noticed the smell of their mother's rotting corpse. These streets felt like home and beckoned that quiet child back into focus.

But he was not a child anymore.

Around him, the basement room had retained its shape, unlike the rubble-strewn rooms on the above floors. A lantern in the corner cast the floor and ceiling in amber. His captive was on his back, supine and naked, stretched across a four-by-four-by-six concrete table constructed from cinderblocks and covered with a clear plastic tarp specifically for this occasion. The filthy gray cement made Jake's pale skin stand out in striking contrast, though he was still jaundiced by the yellow glow of the lantern. Above Jake's head dangled a single, unlit fluorescent light bulb in a battery-powered goose-necked lamp. A flick of the switch turned it on.

Jake opened his eyes in the sudden blinding light and worked his mouth behind the duct tape, squinting like a woman readying herself for a beating. As his mother had. As perhaps Hannah had. But there would be nothing so trite as punching happening here tonight.

With latex-covered fingers, he reached for the small

instruments he'd lined up on the floor. Scissors, chest clamps, nails, scalpel. *Scalpel. No, stopwatch.* How could he forget? He reached for it and pushed start, betting on fourteen minutes and twenty-two seconds with a forty-five second margin of error before Jake stopped screaming. Only once had he miscalculated, but that had been enough.

He grabbed the scalpel and held it up. Jake's eyes bulged. Behind the tape, his captive leaked a whining screech, the squall of a bird seized by feline jaws.

He moved the scalpel to Jake's clavicle and slowly, slowly, sliced ribcage to sternum. A bright red line appeared and swelled to a garish stream that gushed down Jake's sides and formed slick puddles on the plastic tarp. Grunting and huffing, now fully alert to the precariousness of his situation, Jake strained against the cuffs—arms, then legs, then both in a helpless dance.

He peered into Jake's eyes. The expression was familiar, and he stopped mid-cut, the scalpel buried in hair below Jake's belly button. They all made that same face at the end. Fear? Anger? Maybe the look of recognition when someone realizes they are about to die. Desperation, perhaps.

Desperation would not save him, though. Nothing would.

He returned to his task, cutting the thin skin of the abdomen and cleaving slowly through flesh and fat and down to the muscle. The struggling man shivered as the muscles split under the blade. He set the scalpel aside. Jake's muffled howling disintegrated into thin yelps and squeals.

*It won't be long now.*

He peeled the layers of skin back and secured them in place with hardware nails, then pressed his fingers into the cave of Jake's belly, prying the ruptured muscle back to expose the cache of organs beneath. He wrapped his fingers in a coil of intestine and pulled.

Jake panted through his nostrils. His eyes rolled back in his head, his breath erratic and fast.

*No more screaming.* Satisfied, he dropped the spiral of intestine and pushed the stop button on the watch, leaving a bloody fingerprint on its face. Thirteen minutes, fifty-eight seconds. *Still within the margin.* He smiled and picked up the scalpel.

Drawing his attention back to the tangle of organs that had once been a man, he picked up a length of intestine and sliced it open, watching the yellowed, pus-like contents drip into the open abdominal cavity. The scalpel slid smooth as silk—not the slightest hesitation in the tissue, as if it wanted nothing more than to give up its treasures.

But no insect.

This time he had waited several hours after forcing the roach down his victim's gullet, so perhaps it had already made it through the small intestine. He should at least be able to spot the legs and shell; roach exoskeletons were admirable in their ability to remain at least partially intact through the duration of the digestive process. He remembered that well enough from his childhood, along with the way they smelled: that oily, musky odor that set his mouth watering even now.

It was an amazing thing, how a human being could survive and function on so little nourishment. How a handful of cockroaches every day and the occasional loaf of bread could sustain a child for years at a time.

*Simply incredible.*

He ran a finger over the soft, slippery tube of intestine as if it were Hannah's cheek, envisioning her face when she heard the news: her eyes getting hazy, then overflowing, her arms reaching for him.

*She might cry out of genuine sadness.*

He dismissed that possibility, giving it twelve-to-one odds in favor of tears of relief—if she cried at all.

Jake was a waste of a human. It made no logical sense for anyone to miss him.

## TUESDAY, NOVEMBER 3RD

Dawn's light shone sickly and dim against the windowpane. I dressed and applied makeup over the deep purple bruise that stained my temple. Then I went through the house and filled a box with Jake's things—so he would have no reason to go through the rest of the place—and left the box in front of the door where he'd trip right over it. If he came back at all.

*I can't turn into one of those women.*

*News flash: you already have.*

Decisive actions, but everything was foggy, confusing. I blinked back tears all the way to work. At the office, my fingers sat leaden on the keyboard until I forced movement, and even then it was slow. Each file I entered brought me another minute closer to the end of the day and an empty apartment.

"Hey, girl!" Noelle was smiling when she poked her head into my cubicle, but her eyes widened when she saw me. "What the hell happened to you?"

I looked away, the explanation catching in my throat, blocked by shame. A tear escaped from under one lid. I swiped at it with my sleeve.

Then Noelle was there beside me, her hand on my shoulder.

"It's almost lunch time," she said. "Come with me."

I stood unsteadily and followed her from the room.

We sat at the picnic table near the lake. The sun had been swallowed by deep clouds. Frosty air blew off the ice that was creeping along the edges of the water. I shivered. "He's... cheating on me. I found a note."

"That's why he hit you?"

"Yes."

"But this wasn't the first time."

"No," I whispered.

"When did it start?"

"He never did it until after I moved in with him." He used to be so supportive, so kind. What had happened to that guy?

"Why didn't you just leave the first time it happened?"

"I don't know. I should have. I know I should have."

"Oh, no, it's not your fault, Hannah."

But it was. "I just kept pushing and I knew better. I tried not to say anything about the note, but he knew something was wrong and I just—"

"Jesus, Hannah, would you fucking listen to yourself?"

*What's wrong with you, Hannah?*

*You're an idiot, Hannah.*

Angry bees swarmed my stomach and stung my heart. I hung my head.

"Aw hell, Hannah, I'm not trying to get on you. You just shouldn't blame yourself. You need to leave him."

"I think he's gone for good. He said he's done with… me." My tears were hot in the icy breeze. He'd never said anything so terrible, even during our worst fights. But there hadn't been another woman before either.

*That I know of.*

*Oh god, that's probably where he stayed last night.*

"I put his stuff by the door so he could grab it and take it over to her place," I said. My ribcage felt constricted. I pulled frigid air through my nose. "I don't want to be there when he comes back."

Noelle walked around the table and wrapped me in a bear hug. It felt good, safe, even though bears were more known for their mauling than their hugging.

"Hannah, I am so sorry." Noelle had tears in her eyes. "You don't need that worthless asshole."

*If he's worthless, what does that make me if I can't even hang on to him?* Noelle's sympathy made it clear that she was oblivious to this point, which only made me feel worse.

She held my hand. "Come out with me tonight. I was going to meet Thomas and Jim downtown at The Mill at six. There's an art show down the road. Jim was going to bring someone, but she cancelled."

My mouth dropped open and I tasted lake air on my dry tongue, metal and mud. "I... I can't just go out—"

"What are you going to do? Sit at home alone and wait for him to come back all pissed off? Be out of the house. You can even sleep at my place if you want. If he's really leaving he should be back to get his things while you're gone. And if not, the extra day will give him more time to cool off."

We'd broken up less than twelve hours ago and all I wanted was to curl up in my bed and cry. But as Noelle watched me, the throbbing of the bruise on my cheek was slowly awakening something else: rage. I could feel it bubbling under the fear and the loneliness. And I didn't want to be alone in that apartment. I found myself nodding. What kind of a person does that? Maybe I was destined to be a tramp.

Noelle beamed. "I'll get you some makeup before we head out. We'll need to do better with that eye."

"Or I can just go with the raccoon look. Quick, punch me in the other eye." My voice cracked.

Noelle gave me another one-armed hug.

I visualized angry bears again, and somehow that comforted me.

Noelle looked like she wanted to maul Jake.


We met the guys at The Mill and ordered two pizzas topped with pepperoni, onions and extra cheese. I hadn't eaten all day, but I was still surprised when my stomach grumbled.

Jim raised his eyebrows at me. "So, are you totally single now?"

Noelle stiffened beside me.

I froze, a pizza crust halfway to my lips.

122

"It's just that I thought I remembered Noelle telling us you were involved with someone. It's none of my business, really—"

"We… broke up." The words felt foreign on my tongue and I realized I had never had to utter them before. I took a deep breath. The pizza in my stomach lurched around like it was alive and angry at being trapped.

"Sorry to hear that," Jim said, but the twinkle in his eyes said he was anything but.

*Placid. Think about the lake. Or Botox.* Maybe I should get that. I'd look chill all the time. "These things happen," I said over the thumping of my heart. I grabbed my root beer, glanced at my yellow blouse and wondered if this restaurant had better hand dryers than the club we'd gone to. I set my glass down again.

"If you ever need someone to help take your mind off it, I would be happy to oblige," Jim said.

I shot a panicked look at Noelle. She rolled her eyes.

I turned back to Jim and cleared my throat. "I might need a little time, you know?"

He inclined his head, but slowly. "Of course."

"So how many artists will be at the show tonight?" Noelle said.

The men took turns answering her questions while I sagged against the plastic booth. I wanted to kiss her for changing the subject. Still, she had been right; this was preferable to sitting at home on my kitchen floor, trying to forget my own worthlessness while listening for the creak of the floorboards in the hallway.

---

Robert liked the way her mouth moved as she spoke, the minute quiver of her lips that she probably hoped no one else noticed. The faraway look in her glorious green eyes. She was sad, perhaps conflicted, but not a single tear. That was admirable. He had underestimated her strength the first night they met.

Her sadness would surely escalate in the days to come as she worked through her loss. And he would be there to pick up the pieces, to analyze her desires and become them, making her ache for him, driving her to the brink of insanity and back again before she collapsed desperately into his arms.

But slowly, he cautioned himself. He couldn't push her. She wasn't like ordinary women, wonton and shameless. She was better. She was pure.

He smiled.

What could he do to repay her for the wonderful thing she was going to do for him? What gift was there for the salvation of his soul?

He turned to Noelle. Her hair fanned as she tossed it over her shoulder, her sweater struggling to restrain her creamy breasts as she moved. He smiled more broadly.

Noelle smiled back.

*What a whore.*

## WEDNESDAY, NOVEMBER 4TH

Petrosky threw the newspaper down hard enough to spill his coffee. This media bullshit wasn't going to help him any.

In the last week, he'd spun his wheels questioning everyone who knew either of the murdered women, but he'd gotten nothing more than a few vague details he could have figured out on his own. They had both suffered some pretty violent beatings at some point in the weeks before they had died, but that was commonplace with prostitution. There were no leads on common acquaintances, dealers, or johns.

He dropped his eyes to the paper. Front page. Two days old already:

*In an update on a recent story, the killer responsible for two murders in the Ash Park area may have used even more horrific methods than first speculated. According to an anonymous source, the victims were surgically opened while still alive, enduring the dissection of intestinal walls, and possibly the stomach, before perishing. Police have no strong leads. If you have any information, please contact the Ash Park police department.*

Now they needed someone to cover the false confessions from the crazies. Fuck it, he'd have Morrison get one of his buddies do it. Or he'd just give the crazies the number to the goddamn newspaper office.

Petrosky slammed his fist against his desk. "Hookers are killed every day, and they pick my case to publicize? Why do they care all of a sudden?"

But he already knew. *If it bleeds it leads.*

Morrison looked up from his desk across the aisle and shrugged as his phone rang.

Petrosky righted his upended coffee cup. "I swear to God,

125

if I find out who the hell—"

"Petrosky!"

He startled at the strain in Morrison's voice.

Morrison was already out of his chair and pulling on his coat. "We've got another body."


"This doesn't fit, boss."

The building was a skeleton of a factory. In some places, towering pillars of cement and steel reached toward the sky; in others there were only piles of rubble. Petrosky grimaced at the steel ribs as he passed underneath, wondering how much jostling it would take to make them fall.

The basement seemed sturdy enough, at least for now, with steel support poles like the kind found in an underground garage. The concrete roof was cracked in places, but intact, blocking the elements and protecting anyone inside from the falling debris of the upper stories. Off the main area, smaller rooms with cement walls offered even more privacy— probably why their killer had chosen it, along with the building's distance from the more populated areas of the city. It was dumb luck that some homeless man had snuck down here during last night's snowstorm and found the body.

Petrosky followed the murmur of voices to a back room. In the center, a man lay on a bloodied plastic tarp on top of more cinderblocks, his eyes closed, his mouth open in a silent scream. At each of the four corners of the makeshift table, bolted-in metal cuffs secured the man's wrists and ankles. A straight cut ran down the center of the body. The man's intestines were piled on his scrawny bird chest in filmy coils.

Crime techs bustled around the concrete blocks, dusting the restraints with fingerprint powder.

"Got an ID?" Petrosky said.

A dark-haired, darker-skinned tech stood from where he'd been crouching behind the concrete block. "Jacob Campbell. Wallet was in his pants pocket."

"He's not wearing pants, tech."

"They were in the corner, *detective*."

Petrosky glowered at the tech until he crouched behind the cement wall again. "Any sign of a poem? Lettering?"

Another tech, who was working on something on the floor, shook her head without looking his way.

Petrosky peered at the ceiling. "Too far away for anyone to hear much. But to know the basement was down here… he knows the area. Gotta be a local."

Morrison nodded stiffly.

All of this was shit they knew already. What they didn't know was why they had a new victim who didn't fit the original pattern. Looked like McCallum was wrong about their killer having a type. What else had he been wrong about?

The medical examiner arrived with a stretcher and acknowledged Petrosky with a twitch of his bristly jaw.

"Wait a second." Morrison said it so softly that it took Petrosky a minute to figure out who had spoken. Morrison rifled through his notebook, brows furrowed, until he tapped a sheet with his index finger. "Got it, boss. His address is the same one I pulled the other day from the domestic violence shelter file."

"Why was his address in the files for a women's shelter?"

"His wasn't. It was the girl we talked to there, a" —he ran a finger down the page— "Hannah Montgomery."

*Shit*. Since meeting Hannah at the shelter, Petrosky had been wrenched from sleep night after night, sheets soaked through with sweat. Each nightmare was the same: a trail of blood leading him to a field where he came upon Julie and Hannah, arms around each other, throats slit. Fuck it, he wasn't going this time—seeing Hannah was the last thing he needed. His brain was already hazy enough from the midnight shot of liquor he'd used to lull him back into a tortured sleep.

Petrosky slipped out of the room, Morrison scrambling after him.

"Who've we got that can go to Montgomery's place?" Petrosky said.

"Boss?"

"She's not a suspect, Morrison. We don't need to do recon on the bereaved." Their shoes echoed along the cement hall. A breeze blew down from the open ceiling.

Morrison stopped walking. "But—"

Petrosky's footfalls were heavy, angry. "We just need someone to let her know what's going on, keep an eye on her. I'm going to follow up this afternoon after we check out the apartment building and get a little background on Campbell."

On Campbell. And on Hannah Montgomery, the girl who knew two of the victims, one intimately. She had to know something, even if she wasn't aware of it. Petrosky pushed away an image of Hannah's wide, frightened eyes. She wasn't as ignorant as she pretended to be.

She was in danger. And she knew it.

The apartment manager was a wiry man who looked to be in his sixties, though time may have just been remarkably unkind. Dark brown khakis and a button-down shirt hung from his gaunt frame. His shiny skull was speckled with patches of brown age spots, some of which looked too dark not to be malignant.

"Detectives? I'm Samuel Plumber." His thin lips parted to reveal teeth the same yellow as the whites of his eyes. Liver failure, perhaps, and yet he was still wandering the halls of this shithole.

Petrosky and Morrison followed him into a tiny office. The room was messy, but in a neglected way, not a busy way. The particle board desk was piled high with folders and crumpled papers, the wastebasket overflowing. No photos, no coat hook, no boots in the corner. Petrosky wondered which unit Plumber lived in, or if he lived there at all.

On the wall above the desk were two small television screens above three VCRs. The recording equipment looked as old as the desk and the cracked vinyl chair, though a crocheted afghan slung over the back of the chair appeared relatively new.

Plumber sank into his seat and Petrosky and Morrison crowded in behind him to look at the television screens. "I tried to get them as close as I could to what you were looking for. You're lucky you called when you did; I reuse these tapes every three days."

"We'll be taking the tapes with us." Petrosky squinted at the grainy images. One screen showed a stairwell, and the other, the mailroom right outside Plumber's office.

"Is that him?" Petrosky asked as a dark-haired man sprinted down the stairs.

Plumber nodded. On the other screen, the man emerged from the stairwell into the mailroom and disappeared from view in the direction of the front entrance.

"He's in quite the rush," Morrison said.

Plumber stayed silent. He pushed a button and the clip froze on the empty mailroom.

"What about the outside of the building?" Petrosky asked.

Plumber shook his head. "I just keep an eye on things in here. I expect the cops to take care of things out there." He picked up another tape. "I did find some with his girlfriend, though." But he made no move to insert the tape into the VCR.

"Problem?"

Plumber looked up at Petrosky's question. "It's just that she seems like such a good girl, and—"

"Mr. Plumber, Ms. Montgomery is not a suspect at this time. We just need to put together a chain of events for the evening. This was the last place Mr. Campbell was seen alive."

Plumber pursed his lips. "I must admit, he was trouble. I got calls about him yelling and carrying on all the time. Even yelled at other tenants in the hallway."

"He yell at his girlfriend?"

"Yeah. One time, someone heard glass breaking or something and I went up there. She said she dropped a bowl. But ain't no reason to cry over a bowl." Plumber sniffed and turned back to the screens. "That boy didn't do anything good for anybody, from what I could see."

If Campbell was a shithead, that could be the beginning of a motive. But the girls? It didn't feel right. The set of Plumber's mouth was off as well, stubborn, almost defiant, not a trace of regret. Petrosky's back stiffened. "Mr. Plumber, are you implying that Mr. Campbell deserved to die?"

Plumber looked up at him, his eyes earnest. "No, sir. It's just that I don't know of anyone who would be worse off at having lost him."

The tapes showed Hannah rifling through the mail, then fleeing up the same stairwell that Campbell had run down several minutes later. She had cried on the metal stairs for what seemed like an eternity before going back inside her apartment.

Petrosky was not sure what to make of her actions, but seeing her broken up like that tugged at a tender place in his stomach where this morning's coffee was still trying to settle. He vowed to think about it later. Or never. For now, recon.

He and Morrison started at the top floor and worked their way down to the residents on the ground level. Many of the apartments were empty this time of day, and Morrison used his notepad to track who would need follow-up calls.

The few residents who were home were of little assistance. In one unit, a young woman in a white tank top and dirty jeans stared blankly at them until they thanked her for her time and left. In another apartment, an older woman with a set of reading glasses on her head and another set of glasses on a chain around her neck asked them four times who they were before shuffling off to her living room. Petrosky closed the front door for her.

"What do you think, boss?"

"All it takes is one neighbor to hear something. This last floor won't take too long to finish up and then we'll head out."

"You think Campbell was killed by the same guy who

killed our female victims?"

"Looks like it. But with the press leak on something like this you never know if you're dealing with a copycat. It's not likely—but it's possible. It happened once about twenty years back, some tweaker beating the shit out of dealers with a flathead shovel. Press got wind of some of the details, but not all, and a week later we had a crack dealer beaten to death with a spade. Small differences, but enough to find the second guy and clear him of the first few crimes."

"What about the first guy? The serial?"

"It's probably still in the cold case file."

Morrison pulled open the door to the ground level hallway. "It's disconcerting that no one knew either Campbell or his girlfriend."

"If he was roughing her up, that isn't a surprise."

"I got that. Sickening."

"Life's not all rainbows and surfboards, California."

Morrison's mouth tightened. Instead of responding, he rapped hard on a door.

The knob turned, the door opened. "What the hell do you want now?"

Petrosky balked and recovered.

Janice LaPorte wore a pink and yellow flowered housedress that undulated around her thin frame like a pair of parachute pants. Her thin mouth was done up in a horrible shade of maroon.

"Ms. LaPorte."

She frowned.

"We have a few more questions."

She stepped aside. "Fine." Her was voice as stiff as her shoulders.

Petrosky and Morrison followed her into a sparse, but clean, living room with flowered furniture in shades of green and orange, still covered with heavy duty plastic furniture covers. The wooden coffee table was old but polished to a mirrored sheen. She waved them to the couch and the plastic squealed in protest under their butts. Morrison pulled out his notepad.

She sat across from them in a wingback armchair with a lacy crocheted blanket draped over the headrest like a doily. LaPorte saw Petrosky looking at it and fingered a corner. "Made it myself."

"It's nice," Morrison said.

Petrosky glared at him until he turned his eyes to the notebook. LaPorte watched the exchange with narrowed eyes.

"So did you meet Ms. Montgomery here?" Petrosky asked her. "Pretty coincidental that you both live in the same building."

LaPorte's jaw stiffened. "No. We didn't meet here."

"What about—"

"Is this about that poor girl again? I haven't seen anything since we last spoke."

"Ma'am, this is about another resident of the building. A Jacob Campbell."

"Hannah's Jake." LaPorte's eyes hardened. Her voice was cold.

"He was found dead this morning," Petrosky said.

Her left eye twitched, and Petrosky's hackles rose.

"I... I had no idea."

"Anything you can tell us about the night before last? Anything out of the ordinary with either Mr. Campbell or Ms. Montgomery?"

LaPorte shook her head. "Not that I recall."

"How were they as a couple?"

She hesitated. Petrosky saw a flash of agitation in her eyes before she looked away. *She's a killer. Don't forget what you're dealing with.*

"She doesn't open up much." Her face was a blank slate.

"Did she ever mention Mr. Campbell?"

Morrison's pen scratched. LaPorte stared.

"Ma'am?"

LaPorte shook her head again. "When she did, it was in passing. I remember thinking she might have been afraid of him."

132

"Fights?" Petrosky asked.

LaPorte looked away from him, toward the window. The hairs on the back of his neck danced, though Jacob Campbell hitting his girlfriend was hardly a revelation. And why was Campbell dead? If their killer was picking off abusers, he'd have taken Meredith Lawrence's boyfriend down instead of Lawrence herself.

"She never fought with him," LaPorte said. "He yelled at her sometimes though. Just him. I never once heard her yell." She sighed. "Poor dear." Her voice was soft, but tight. Irritated.

Morrison's pen froze.

Poor dear? *What do you know, Ms. LaPorte?* Was LaPorte in danger here? Was Hannah? Were the other girls at the shelter? Petrosky shifted his weight and lowered his voice. "Poor dear, as in Mr. Campbell, the man who was brutally killed?"

"If you ask me, officers, anything that happened to him he brought on himself."

<hr />

I blinked sandpaper from my eyes and shut the desk drawer for the fourth time. I should have brought my cell phone to work. I probably would have if I'd thought I was strong enough to ignore Jake's calls. If he ever called. So far, he hadn't even come by to pick up his things.

*What's the difference between boyfriends and condoms? Condoms have changed. They're no longer thick and insensitive.*

The office phone rang. I jumped.

*It's him!*

*It's not him.*

It rang a second time. I grabbed the receiver.

"Ms. Montgomery?" The voice was deep and gravelly—familiar, but I couldn't place it.

My back tensed. "Yes, this is."

"Detective Petrosky. Ash Park PD. I would like to speak with you as soon as possible regarding Jacob Campbell."

"Jake—"

*Oh God.* Someone must have called the police about the other night after all the yelling… or maybe about my eye. I stared accusingly in the direction of Noelle's cubicle but only saw the empty cork board, which wavered as my vision blurred.

*Shit. He's going to be furious.*

"Ms. Montgomery?"

"Yes. I… can I just drop the charges over the phone?" I gripped the receiver harder.

There was a pause on the other end of the line. "Ma'am?"

My hand cramped. I tried to loosen my grip. "I mean, everything is fine, I just… I mean, I'm fine. I don't want to press charges."

This time the pause was longer. Dread thickened in the pit of my stomach. Maybe I was the one in trouble. Maybe it was all my fault. Maybe the cops already knew that.

"Is he there with you already?" I asked. "If it's about his stuff, he can come get it. I wasn't trying to, like… steal it. It's all by the front door."

"Ma'am, Mr. Campbell is dead. I'm sorry, I thought someone had already been by to tell you."

The room expanded around me, then vanished as if it had been an apparition. The suddenly thin air didn't want to fill my lungs. The phone clattered against the desk and dropped to the carpet, but the sound was muffled, as if I were underwater.

A hand on my back. "Hannah?" *Noelle.*

A small, tinny voice buzzed from the receiver. I reeled it in and put it back to my ear. Everything vibrated: my chest, my legs, my hands.

"Ms. Montgomery? Hello? Are you there?"

"Yes," I whispered. Noelle squeezed my shoulder.

"I know this is difficult, but we need to speak with you. Can you make it to the station, or would you like us to meet you at your home?"

"Um… I don't… the station." *Where all the cops are. Where it's safer.*

"Can you come now?"

I nodded.

"Ma'am?"

*Oh, right.* "Yes. Yes, I can come."

"Do you have someone who can look after you?" His voice was softer now—kind, even.

I met Noelle's eyes. "Yes."

"Good." The line clicked.

I dropped the receiver and fled the office.

"Hannah!" Noelle's voice faded halfway down the hall. I threw myself into the bathroom, locked a stall door and sat on the toilet seat. The stall pulsed around me in time with the knifing beats of my heart. My breath wheezed out of me, dissipating, disappearing into the air, and I was jealous, so jealous of this ability to… vanish.

*I'm safe right now.*

*You can't stay in the bathroom stall forever.*

I pushed my hair from my face with shaking hands.

*You have nowhere to go.*

The room went black at the edges.

*He's found me.*

<hr />

Petrosky considered Hannah—Ms. Montgomery—through the two-way mirror in the interrogation room. She seemed fragile, dwarfed as she was by the large metal table.

She looked just as innocuous on paper: Hannah Montgomery. Born in Vermont. Parents: divorced. One sister. Employment history began five years ago at an Ash Park convenience store, then at Harwick Technical. No arrests, no warrants. Not even a speeding ticket.

Beside him, Morrison toed the linoleum, face drawn up with just the right amount of sympathetic concern. Petrosky crushed his empty coffee cup, wishing he had something stronger to drink, and reread the notes off the file in his hand. It had taken two hours for her to arrive, which had given the medical examiner extra time to get his shit together.

There were significant differences between this crime and the others. This one had used metal cuffs instead of leather restraints, and nails instead of silver clasps to hold the skin back. There was no note. They had also found a pair of tread marks in the room, though those could have been left behind at another time.

The two hours had also given Morrison time to go poking into Montgomery's whereabouts over the last week. What he had told Petrosky was interesting to say the least.

"You think she's got something to do with it? That whole double dating thing is pretty coincidental," Morrison said.

Petrosky stared at the notes in his hand, written in the flowing script you'd expect from an English major. "We'll see. You did good, California."

"Thanks, boss."

In the interrogation room, Montgomery folded her hands in her lap.

*She's just a grief-stricken girlfriend.*

*She was on a date hours after he died. The facts won't go away just because you don't want them to be true.*

"I'm going in. Watch. Take notes. You're good at that."

"Right on, boss."

Petrosky tossed the cup into the garbage and entered the interrogation room. Montgomery straightened, her dark hair falling over her shoulders. He had tried to braid Julie's hair into pigtails once and she had ended up looking like Medusa. *Fucking hell, Petrosky.*

He cleared his throat. "Thank you for coming, Ms. Montgomery. Do you know why you're here?"

"Because Jake—" She shivered, closed her eyes, then opened them again. "You said you wanted to talk to me."

Petrosky nodded. "I'm sorry for your loss."

"Thank you." Her lower lip quivered and Petrosky

smothered the rush of warmth in his belly that tried to well up for her.

*Focus.* He stood on the other side of the table and put his hands palm down on the top. "I need to know about his movements in the days before his death. Tell me anything you can remember."

"I think he went to his mother's. Dinner the night before, maybe." Her brows furrowed. "Everything is so… fuzzy."

"Try."

"I think dinner with his mom. That's all I know about. He… I… I work during the day. I don't really know what he did when I was gone."

"Why didn't you report him missing?" Petrosky kept his voice even, trying not to scare her into silence. Three days was a long time not to notice he had disappeared.

She shrugged. "I didn't know he was missing, I guess, not really."

"Neighbors say you had a disagreement the night he disappeared."

She stared hard at her lap.

"Quite the bruise you have there." He waited for a response, and when none came, he switched tactics. Maybe he'd surprise a real answer out of her. "How did you not think he was missing when he didn't come back home for three days?"

Finally, she met his eyes. "He was moving out."

"That must have made you pretty upset."

"I… I don't know," she whispered. A tear dripped on the metal tabletop where it formed a shiny little bead.

Petrosky wished he had a tissue. He pushed the thought away. "You were angry enough to go out with someone else the day after he disappeared."

Her eyes widened with surprise. She choked back a sob and gripped the sides of her chair as if she were trying to hold herself upright. "It was just a friend thing. I didn't want to go home."

Guilt jabbed at his chest.

*Do your fucking job.* He balled his fists behind his back. "Where were you on the night of October tenth?"

"October tenth?"

Petrosky froze. Repeating phrases was a classic sign of lying.

"I don't know," she said "I mean probably at home with—"

"How about the first of October?"

He waited for a telltale twitch, a flash of guilt. She just shrugged.

"Anyone else who might have seen you on those dates in October?"

Montgomery shook her head. "Maybe at the apartment? I don't know."

"I'll look into it. What about your friends?"

Silence. Again. *Talk to me*, *dammit.*

"Anyone else who may have wanted to hurt him?"

Montgomery jerked her head up and her eyes were brighter, her mouth open in stunned realization. "Maybe. He had another girlfriend. She sent him a letter the night he left."

That was what she had found in the mailbox that night, the note that had sent her sobbing to the stairwell. "What's her name?"

"I'm not sure."

"But you knew he was messing around on you?"

Her face crumpled.

Petrosky wiped his own face with a beefy palm. *She's not Julie, for Christ's sake. Get it together, Petrosky.* "Do you have the letter?"

"Um… no, I don't think so. He took it."

"Did you look at the postmark?"

"It didn't have one. It was just slipped into the side of the box." She was gripping the chair hard enough to turn her knuckles white. Her eyelashes were wet.

Petrosky looked away. "I'm going to look into your alibi and check some security tapes. I'll also need to look through his things, check out your apartment."

She stared at him. "All his stuff is in a box by the door."

"He do that?"

"No. I did." Her voice shook.

It sounded like she couldn't get away from him soon enough. "Do I have your permission to search or do I need a warrant?"

"You can look."

Petrosky pulled a page from the folder and unclipped a pen off the cover. "I'll need your signature here. Until we sort this out, don't leave town."

She left without another word. He strode to his desk and rummaged in the top drawer for a pack of cigarettes and a lighter. They had been there for six years, since the day he'd promised Julie he'd quit.

*They're bad for your health.* His daughter's voice echoed in his head. He could almost see Julie, her face tilted toward the sun, her dark hair shining. He wondered what she would have looked like had she been allowed to grow up.

*Probably a lot like—*

He ground his teeth and tore open the pack on his way to the parking lot, trying to shut out the voice that told him he had just badgered an innocent girl. Julie had been innocent, too. She had died innocent.

He walked out into icy drizzle, feet squelching on half melted snow and parking lot sludge. He yanked a cigarette from the pack and lit it. Acrid smoke burned his throat.

*Sorry, honey.*

## SUNDAY, NOVEMBER 8TH

Some days I missed him so terribly I could almost taste the despair. Other days, I hated myself for feeling relieved that Jake's murder was connected to the others. "Serial killer," the news said. I still cried myself to sleep, wondering if my actions had caused him to leave, caused him to die, but the idea that he was killed by a stranger and not as a direct result of my past made me almost giddy. And my guilt at this almost giddiness weighed on me like a ton of rock. It was a vicious cycle.

*If I weren't so paranoid, so afraid, would I have wanted him to die?*

This morning, as I applied makeup over my still-bruised face, I was thankful to the person who had taken him even as I feared that the creaking footsteps in the hallway outside would stop at my door. It was all too much. I could almost hear the moment I shut down and separated from myself, like the clank of a bank vault.

The detachment accompanied me to the grave of my murdered almost-ex-boyfriend. I stood still and silent in my black funeral attire with dry eyes and a fluttering in my chest, like a sparrow trying to escape, though it was someone else's chest, someone else's bird. Beside me, Noelle clasped my numb fingers, and though I gripped her back, it still felt like she was holding someone else's hand.

Jake's mother stared daggers at me across the gaping hole in the frozen earth as they lowered the casket. The hem of my wool dress flipped in the breeze, and arctic air bit at my ankles. I smoothed the dress and pressed my feet together in a halfhearted attempt to warm them.

To the side and a dozen feet behind Jake's mother stood

Mr. Harwick, solemn in a black suit and wool overcoat. He raised his eyes from the casket, focused on me, and my mouth went dry. I looked away.

The casket found the bottom of the hole and the straps kicked up ice and sludge as they were removed. The *shh* of the straps on the ground sounded like the earth trying to breathe.

A wailing, like a wounded animal, split the air as Jake's mother threw herself on the ground at the graveside, tearing at the dusted snow with her fingernails. The priest tried to restrain her. I looked away, dropped Noelle's hand, and stepped back.

Noelle raised her eyebrows. *Want me to come?* the look said.

I shook my head and escaped across the cemetery. The wails faded, replaced by the crackling of frozen leaves. I was halfway to the car before I realized that I wasn't alone. Another set of footsteps ground ever closer, stalking through the snow behind me. I stopped. I was too far from the gravesite for anyone to see us, but maybe they'd still be able to hear me scream and send help. I whirled around, hands fisted at my sides.

"I didn't mean to startle you." Mr. Harwick's ice blue eyes met mine, kind and sincere.

I relaxed my hands, heart still in my throat. "No, it's okay. I just didn't know it was… you."

"I gathered. Shall we?" He gestured to the gates and I nodded. Our feet crunched across icicles of grass, leaving a trail of brown footprints.

"I was saddened to hear of your loss, Ms. Montgomery."

"Yes… I mean… thank you." What the hell was wrong with me? I tried to avoid looking at his mouth. I failed. A branch caught my foot and I was falling, the ground growing closer, my arms windmilling—

Strong hands under my arms righted me and sent currents of pleasant electricity through my chest. "Oh, uh… thanks," I said as he released me. So much for electricity—my face felt like it had been seared by a blowtorch.

He met my eyes. "If there is anything you need, you know where to find me. And you are welcome to take some time off past the bereavement period. Just apply and I will approve it."

"Thank you."

He nodded once and turned toward the front entrance once more. I watched the back of his head as he walked over the hill and through the wrought iron gate at the front of the cemetery.

Behind me, new footsteps drew closer, but their rhythm was familiar, as was the clank of Noelle's jewelry.

"What was that all about?" Noelle asked.

"Wanted me to know I could take some time off if I needed it."

"You going to?"

I considered my empty apartment, Jake's toothbrush moldering in the bathroom, the prickling of my spine every time I passed the living room window, the heart palpitations every time a floorboard creaked.

"No. I'll be back tomorrow."

Petrosky's desk chair groaned as he leaned back in it. He tapped Morrison's smartphone and rewound the video again. Morrison had taken Plumber's apartment surveillance tapes and installed them into some fancy ass thing on his phone. *An app,* he'd called it, which wasn't even a whole fucking word, and yet the damn thing was working pretty well.

Petrosky tapped play and squinted at the tiny screen as the wall of mailboxes appeared. Then came the girl—at least he thought it was a female. Small, lithe and fast. She wore a long jacket with a hood pulled over her face. Dark blue or black jeans. And she was watching. Back and forth, scanning, nervous. What was she scared of? Was she looking for Hannah, her lover's girlfriend, afraid of getting caught? Then the letter from a coat pocket. He zoomed in. She wiggled it into the slit in the door of the box and pulled her hood tighter over her face, shielding herself from the camera. She had known where the camera was; knew her actions would have consequences. It would be tricky without a face, without even a hair color, but they'd find her.

Morrison rushed into the bullpen and headed toward him.

Petrosky tossed him the phone. "Nice work, California. Now to find out who she is."

"I'm on it. But we've got a situation. Jacob Campbell's mother is here."

Petrosky followed Morrison down the stairs to the public section of the building where citizens came to whine about their neighbor's dog. Ms. Campbell stood in the middle of the waiting room wearing a pink muumuu over a black tank top, the straps cutting into her bared, pudgy shoulders. No coat, despite the snow. She had a cigarette tucked behind one ear.

143

Petrosky approached her. "Can I help you, ma'am?"

She turned glassy eyes in his direction. "Yeah, you can fuckin' help me. I need to know how to get around this shit." She thrust a sheaf of papers at him. "It's like all the government wants to do is fuck over good tax-paying citizens while they give everything to those bitches and their welfare babies."

Petrosky took the papers and gestured toward a door that led to their interrogation rooms. "Follow me, ma'am."

Morrison sat at the head of the table. Ms. Campbell sat across from Petrosky and glowered at him as he looked over the paperwork. It was notification of a monetary settlement to be paid to Mr. Jacob Campbell. The amount was nearly thirty-six thousand dollars.

"I'm not sure I understand what you're trying to do, Ms. Campbell."

"What I'm trying to do? That money should belong to me."

Petrosky turned the page, trying to figure out why she was there instead of at her lawyer's office. But he'd be damned if he suggested she get a lawyer before she told them something useful. "Why didn't Mr. Campbell have the money before now?"

She shook her head. "It's in there somewhere. There's a bunch of shit."

Petrosky passed half of the pile to Morrison and they spent the next few minutes looking over the information. Morrison spoke first. "It looks like there's a provision to turn the money over to Mr. Campbell when he gets married or turns thirty, whichever happens first."

Ms. Campbell shrugged. "Yeah, what the fuck ever."

"And in the case of death, all monies go to the closest living descendent or relative," Morrison said.

He and Morrison looked at her.

"Ma'am, you did realize this is a motive for murder?"

Petrosky asked.

"For who?"

"For his closest living relative."

She gnashed her teeth. "It isn't me. It's his fucking kid."

Petrosky set down the papers. His kid?

"He always said that bastard wasn't his, but she put his name on the certificate. Now the lawyers want to give the money to him once he's big enough."

Petrosky's mind raced.

She pulled the cigarette from behind her ear and stuck it in her mouth. "So, what do I have to do to get my boy's name off that fucking birth certificate?"

Shellie Dermont lived just outside Pontiac on a side street carpeted with last season's leaves and the oily residue of hopelessness. Even the house she lived in appeared to be frowning, its filthy awnings drawing furrowed brows over sagging window eyes, its front door a yawning howl of a mouth. Tax forms indicated she was broke, but stable, supporting herself working two waitressing gigs in the area. Still, people killed for a lot less than thirty grand.

Petrosky stood in the living room. Dermont sat on the couch, paperwork on her knee, finger moving in time with her lips. "I don't understand what this is." The black ring in her nose matched the heavy metal T-shirt she wore. In the next room, a boy rolled a toy truck back and forth under a rustic dining table right off the cover of one of those shabby chic magazines Petrosky's ex-wife used to read.

Morrison pulled out his notepad and sat at the table. Petrosky glared at Morrison until he stood, then turned back to Dermont. "You've never seen this before?" Petrosky asked.

"No." She held the papers out to him. He waved them back and she laid them next to her on the couch.

"It was sent certified mail to an address on Carper," Petrosky told her. "But it was never signed for."

145

"I only lived there for a few months. There were roaches in the cupboard and the landlord... I guess you don't need to know that, huh?"

"When was the last time you talked to Jacob Campbell?"

She laughed. It was a melancholy sound. "Not since Jayden was born, so around five years. He came to the hospital to see us. Took one look at him and bolted. Never even held him."

Petrosky waited for Morrison's pen to stop scratching on the notepad. "So you were separated before the baby was born?"

She nodded. "He was... mean sometimes. I didn't know I was pregnant when I left, and after I found out, I couldn't bear the thought of—" Her eyes moved to the boy who was now lying on his back, feet in the air. "Anyway, I told him about Jayden and he wanted a paternity test, so I had one done."

"Did you file for support?"

She shook her head. "He never had a job while I was with him and I didn't expect that he would suddenly get one after the baby came. I didn't want him around, anyway. He was always pushy, always asking me to marry him, especially when he found out I was pregnant. He got mad when I said no. It was kinda... scary." She shuddered.

"In what way?"

"Just the way his eyes got. Like he wanted to hit you."

"Did he?"

"A few times. After the last time, I left."

"Good for you."

A sad smile flashed and was gone.

"Hear anything else about him? Through mutual friends?"

"We didn't have mutual friends. When I was with him I didn't have friends at all. He kinda made sure of that."

Typical abusive bullshit. "I see."

"I know, it was stupid. At the time I just didn't... it's hard to see when you're in the middle of it, you know?" She looked at her hands. "To be honest, when I saw the story on the news, I wasn't all that... sad. I mean, it was a shock, but not all that sad."

There was a scuffling sound behind Petrosky as the boy ran to his mother and put his head in her lap. She stroked his hair. "Hey, Care Bear, you want to go get a book? We can read before I have to go to work."

"Stay home, Mama."

"I can't, baby. But Ms. Ross is coming and you always have fun with her, right?"

He shrugged. "I'll find the dog book."

"Okay." She watched him scamper off down a back hallway then turned back to them. "What else do you need to know? I have to get ready for work soon."

Petrosky and Morrison exchanged a glance. "We're almost done, Ms. Dermont," Petrosky said. "Were you aware that Mr. Campbell had an insurance policy that reverts to your family in the event of his death?"

Her eyes narrowed. "I don't understand."

"Mr. Campbell had an insurance policy from his father. He was to receive thirty-six thousand dollars after he got married."

"That's why he wanted to marry me?"

"I don't know."

"Well, I didn't marry him, so—"

Jayden skipped into the living room carrying a book and leapt into his mother's lap. "Found it, Mama!"

She smiled and kissed him on the cheek.

Petrosky waited until Dermont looked back up. "In the event of his death, that money reverts to his closest living relative."

"His mom, huh?" She smirked. "She always hated me, but she'll be happy now."

"Not the way it's written. In this case, children get precedence over parents."

Dermont stared at Petrosky, open-mouthed. "Wait, are you telling me that... that Jayden..."

"I am. Which is why I need to ask you a few questions about your whereabouts on the days around Mr. Campbell's death."

She sniffed. Her face had gone tomato red. "Ask away. I'm never anywhere but work or here, and I have a few neighbors who can verify. Ms. Ross lives across the street. She watches Jayden when I'm at work and keeps an eye on everything and everyone the rest of the time." Her voice was choked with emotion. A few tears slid down her cheeks and onto the top of Jayden's head.

"Hey, Mama! Stop! Stop! All wet!"

She held him close to her chest.

"You're going to college, baby."


Ms. Ross was old, wretchedly mean, and honest. She wouldn't let them in the house, but she had plenty to say: the kids in the neighborhood were too loud, Morrison's hair was too damn long, and there was no way that Shellie Dermont was anywhere but where she'd said on the nights in question.

Petrosky was quiet as he slid behind the wheel.

Morrison cleared his throat. "You think our killer believes he's helping people?"

"Helping?"

"Yeah, like offing people who are getting in the way of other people's happiness?"

The car's engine grumbled to life. "I doubt the families in question would have chosen that path," Petrosky said.

"Well, obviously they wouldn't have. Maybe that's why he intervenes; he thinks he knows what's best for everyone else. Like a nosy old lady." Morrison nodded at Ms. Ross, who stood on her porch in her bathrobe glaring at them.

"If we've got a killer out to rid the world of assholes, he'll have to kill a lot more."

"As it is, I don't see him stopping," Morrison said.

Petrosky put the car in reverse and nodded to Ms. Ross who squinted harder at him but touched her door handle like she was considering going inside. "No, he won't stop."

Their killer had planned this. Chosen a poem. And he'd

gotten off clean so far, which would only whet his appetite for more slaughter.

"The killings are coming fast," Petrosky said. "But this one with Campbell feels... different. We're missing something."

"Besides the poem?"

Petrosky's hands tightened on the wheel. Yes, the missing poem. Between the poem and the restraints and the type of victim, there were too many differences. That didn't sit right, and it intensified the disquiet already eating at him. "If we don't get a handle on this soon, we'll have another family to notify."

"At least the next family might not cry, if what we've seen so far is any indication," Morrison said.

Petrosky braked hard enough to lock the seat belts. "You a fan, California?"

"No, boss. Just saying."

*Just another month and you'll have enough cash to get out of here.*

*You don't really have to leave. This has nothing to do with you.*

From my desk, roses and lavender filled the air with a subtle sweetness. The elaborate vase had come after the funeral and graced my workspace every day since, a constant reminder that Jake had never given me anything so beautiful. That I was really better off without him. I had cried fat, guilty tears at those thoughts, but it hadn't been enough to make me remove the vase. It was enough to make me toss the note, though:

> *If there is anything I can do to be of assistance, please let me know.*
> *In sympathy, Dominic*

I had torn the note from the vase the day I got it, both in panic that I might have to take off work, and out of fear that I'd spend my life rereading it, extracting meaning that had never been there to begin with. Plus, I worried that if someone came to search my place again, they would misconstrue his words.

*Let me be of assistance. I want to help you.*

*Yes, sir.*

"Hannah…" Noelle's trembling voice floated over the top of the cubicles. I followed her gaze. Detective Petrosky was at the glass doors to the office, staring in at me.

*He thinks I'm a murderer.* I walked to the door on shaky legs, my stomach trying to dance a jig and succeeding only in

150

making me want to vomit.

"Ms. Montgomery." He nodded.

"Detective Petrosky."

"Can you spare a moment or two? Maybe take a fifteen-minute break?"

I glanced back into the office. Noelle was staring openly at us. Ralph wandered past, pretending not to look, but failing miserably.

"Maybe… um… a walk," I said.

We sat at the picnic table by the lake, my face toward the water, his face toward me. Half a dozen mourning doves crooned by the lake's edge, pecking at icy thistle and casting hopeful glances at us.

The detective's face did not look as hopeful. "I'm sorry to bother you at work, Ms. Montgomery. I just had a few follow-up questions."

*I swear I didn't do it! Ask someone else!* "Okay."

He pulled two pages from the folder and slid them across the table. Photos, black and white and glossy, of someone in a hooded jacket. "Do you recognize this person? Maybe the coat?"

"I can't see their face." I leaned toward the pictures and plastered them to the table with my fists when the wind tried to whip them away. *Was this taken in my mailroom?* "Is this… her? The girl who left him that note?" Hopefully, the detective would understand if I puked on his shoes.

"I think so, ma'am."

I touched the photo, her hood, her shoulder. *What did she have that I didn't? What made her so special?* I could feel my heartbeat in my frozen ears.

"Ms. Montgomery?"

"You think she was the one who… did it?"

"We're looking into it. You're sure you don't recognize her?"

"No, I don't. I doubt she would ever have wanted to meet

151

me."

He took the pictures back and put them in the folder. "Were you aware that Jake had a child?"

My mouth dropped open. Jake *was* a child. "I... No, there must be a mistake."

The detective's expression remained deadpan like he hadn't just blindsided me. "No mistake. He had a five-year-old son."

"But... he never said anything. I don't think he ever paid support—" My neck muscles went rigid. "You think this has something to do with his death?"

"Not the child support, but perhaps the inheritance from Jake's father."

I shook my head, hard. Now I knew they had it all it wrong. "He never knew his dad—"

"Maybe, maybe not. The money was to be paid when Mr. Campbell got married or when he turned thirty, whichever came first."

*Let's get married, baby. I want to take care of you.*

*Maybe we can just go see the judge. You know I love you...*

It had always been about money. My jaw clenched.

"Something wrong, Ms. Montgomery?"

"No. I'm just... I'm starting to feel like I didn't know a lot of things about him." Like the fact that he had an inheritance. That he had a fucking child. Maybe he'd always preferred store-bought spaghetti sauce to the homemade shit. All bets were off now.

Petrosky's eyes were soft. "Don't feel too bad," he said. "This is not information that many others had."

"Did his mother know?" Of course she did. No wonder she was pissed that we didn't get married before we moved in together.

"Yes, but she didn't think the child was his."

I blinked back the sting of tears. They had all known. Everyone except me. "But the baby is his? For sure?"

"He is. We have the tests to prove it."

I stared at the doves, who were obviously not worried

about anything but preening their feathers. Petrosky's voice came to me in snippets, something about keeping this quiet, not leaking to the press.

I met his gaze. "Why does this even matter? Wasn't Jake killed by the same person who killed those women? That's what they keep saying on the news."

His eyes darkened, like he was angry at me for asking. "We don't know."

The ice swept through my chest, hardening my lungs. "What do you mean, you don't know?" *No, no, no. This could still be my fault.*

"There were… inconsistencies with your boyfriend's murder. We can't rule anything out."

His face swam, blurring in my prickling tears.

I thought of the eyes on my back as I walked around my apartment, heard the crunching of footsteps in empty alleys behind the shelter. I blinked hard to hide the fear that must have been written across my face.

*I'll find you, baby. We will always be one.*

"So Jake's killer… might not have killed the others? He might have just killed Jake?" My voice cracked. "If you thought it was all connected you wouldn't be asking me about some woman in a picture, right?"

Petrosky searched my eyes. I resisted the urge to close them.

"Just covering our bases. Have you given any more thought to who might have wanted to hurt him?"

*Jake's dead because of me, and knowing it makes me an accessory.*

*I don't want to go to jail.*

"No, sir. I can't think of anyone."

Petrosky stood. "Thank you for your time, ma'am. If you think of anything else—"

*You already know more about the man I lived with than I ever did.* I nodded at the tabletop and waited, my heartbeat wild and hot inside my icy body. His footsteps crunched over the snow toward the parking lot.

I looked back out at the water, took a final deep breath and stood. *I hope I can save enough to run again before he kills me too.*

⸻

It had been hours since the police came to their office, but Noelle was still unsettled. She assaulted her fingernails with her teeth and winced when she drew blood.

Through her windshield, barren maple trees cast clawing shadows on snowy lawns that rolled up to neat, uniform houses. The homes were red or gray brick behind small cement porches and topped with aluminum-sided second floors.

Thomas's house was in a cul-de-sac at the end of a winding asphalt road. Bay windows protruded from brown brick on either side of the entrance. It was a nice home. A *family* home. But you couldn't just take a house and magically make a happy family any more than you could take just any self-centered jackass and make him a good father.

He opened the door before she knocked, his smile wide. "Hey! You found it!"

"I did."

He grabbed her hand and led her into the house. "You smell good. What is that, lemons?"

"Orange-mango."

"I like it." His lips were frozen in a permanent grin. "Come on in. I was just feeding the cat."

Noelle's boots squeaked over the light oak floors. The foyer walls were painted a deep green. A narrow table sat against one wall of the entry, topped by a small, sickly plant. Brown leaves littered the tabletop.

Thomas saw her staring at it. "Wolverine's kind of a jerk to plants."

They entered a large cheery kitchen with matching white appliances and light oak cupboards. He opened one and grabbed a bag of cat food.

154

She followed him through to the living room. "Holy shit."

"Oh, yeah. I forget that not everyone is a fan."

The entire room was painted a deep electric blue, making the light floors and suede couches seem larger. Small wooden tables topped with glass sat on either side of the sofa, and a leather chair faced the television on the wall to her left. The TV on the wall was at least sixty inches, flanked by large black speakers that looked as if they could blow the house apart if Thomas got carried away. Behind the couch, the far wall was entirely covered in a stretched canvas painting of huge, muscled-up green giant charging into the room, fist outstretched as if in attack, face twisted in a grimace. Droplets of cartoon saliva flew from his half-open mouth.

"It's… interesting." Violent and angry, but interesting. "I didn't even know you could get art like that."

He laughed. "I painted it. It was that, or tack up a poster."

"You painted it?" She studied it more closely. *He's kinda good.*

"Yeah, like I said the other night, I needed something to do with my time instead of football. Plus, the Hulk is more reliable companionship for a geeky kid than school buddies anyway." Thomas stooped and poured the cat food into a glass dish. "Hey, there he is!"

A fat orange tabby entered the room from a hallway in the back corner and slunk toward them, staring at Noelle with suspicious green eyes. Thomas scratched him behind the ears. Wolverine purred like a rumbling motor.

Thomas righted himself and offered his arm. "Shall we?"

She took it. "Lead the way."


*He is never picking the movie again.* Noelle glared at the screen. *Seriously, who cares about this superhero bullshit? I mean, except…*

Thomas's face was a mask of childlike excitement. Even the way he wiped fake popcorn butter on his khakis was endearing. What was wrong with her? Was she falling for him? Maybe it was the way he just seemed so damn happy all the time. He had probably had the perfect childhood outside of that whole being-small-and-bullied thing.

*Maybe that's why he likes this stuff.* She pictured him as a small, dejected boy in a Spiderman T-shirt, pouring over comic books, losing himself in another world where he was more... well... *super.*

Noelle's phone vibrated with a text message. She pretended not to hear it, though it seemed impossibly loud in the sudden quiet. On the screen, a guy in a neon blue leotard pressed himself against a brick wall. Very incognito.

She yawned and rested her head against Thomas's shoulder. He smelled like shampoo and something that could only be cat hair. She sneezed.

"Bless you," he said.

"Thanks." Her phone vibrated again.

"Do you need to get that?"

Noelle shrugged, fumbled in her purse for the phone, and checked the messages.

*You're such a bitch.*

She sighed. Ralph had been going back and forth from *I hate you* to *Please forgive me for whatever I did to upset you* for weeks. He had even left her a six-minute voicemail telling her that he knew she lied about having a brother, like she gave a shit.

"Everything okay?" Thomas whispered.

"Everything's fine." She turned the phone off and vowed to change her number tomorrow. He'd get tired of harassing her soon, if he was anything like the others. Their anger never lasted forever. She wondered if anything did.

Thomas put his hand on the armrest. She covered it with hers, leaned her head back against the chair and closed her eyes.

"You're missing the best part," he whispered.

She dragged her lids open. "Oh, I was just—"

"I know, resting your eyes." He chuckled. "Hey, there's no accounting for taste. Or for people staying home because they're afraid of a little snowstorm in the forecast." He nodded to the nearly empty theater. "I think the reviews were pretty bad, though. That's the first thing Jim said when I told him where I was taking you."

Noelle glanced at the screen, where two guys were engaged in a seemingly intense conversation about what it takes to bring down a superhuman. She rolled her eyes. Maybe next time Jim would get through to Thomas and save her from this nonsense.

"How's he been? Jim, I mean."

"Good. On a blind date. I get the impression he's just wasting time until Hannah is ready to go out with him. Every time I mention that I'm seeing you, he asks about her."

*Poor Hannah.* Noelle's stomach rolled. An explosion lit the room as the hero threw a car. Then he tripped over a fire hydrant and went sprawling, his blue leotard making him look like a flattened smurf. Noelle laughed and her stomach settled. *Okay, this isn't all bad.*

Thomas beamed at her, teeth shining in the light from the screen. "Maybe we can double with Hannah and Jim, once she's ready. I'll let you guys pick the movie."

Her stomach gurgled again, hot with equal parts guilt and fury. She had been glad when Jake and Hannah split, excited that her letter had the desired effect. She had not been sorry when he died.

*But—*

*He was not supposed to hit her.* She hoped his death was horrific. And slow.

Thomas was still waiting for an answer.

She squeezed his hand tighter and watched leotard guy leap from one skyscraper to another. He brushed his lips against her cheek. Her heart slowed.

"Noelle, you okay? I'm sorry if you hate double dates or something. We don't have to do it if you don't want to."

"No, I'd like to double. Hannah might be upset for a while, though. She's pretty torn up."

"Maybe." Thomas shrugged and turned back to the movie.

"Who knows? Things aren't always what they seem."

Noelle wasn't sure if he was whispering it to her or to himself.

I chewed on my cheek, trying to ground myself in the pain of it. The thought of leaving tonight and having to find another shelter in another city made me sick to my stomach. I just had to save a little more cash so I could legitimately start over, on my own two feet. Because whether or not Jake was killed by the same person as those other women, *someone* killed him. Someone who could be watching me right now. I felt like I was losing my mind. Maybe I was paranoid, but that didn't mean that someone wasn't out to get me.

The owls smirked at me from under my pointless blank cork board. No puppies, no babies, and I had never even picked my nose behind the partition. I should start, so that when I was old and gray in a rocking chair on a porch somewhere with an owl on a perch next to me, I would at least have this one small thing I could say I took advantage of when the rest of my life fell apart. I looked at my finger.

"Ms. Montgomery?"

The finger disappeared under my desk.

"May I sit down?"

"Yes. I mean, yes, sir." My heart quickened and slithered up my throat like an agitated python.

He took the seat across from me, his black suit and lavender tie too good for here. He stuck out like a penguin at a Bar-B-Que.

*An incredibly handsome penguin. Do people fuck penguins? That seems ill advised, and yet...*

Weeks of subpar sleep were creeping up on me and manifesting as slap happy absurdity.

"Something funny?" he asked.

I had not realized I was smiling. *I really am losing my*

*mind.* "No, sir."

"Please call me Dominic."

"Yes sir… I mean, Dominic." I put my fingers to my mouth to stop the goofy-ass grin.

"I hope you have been able to cope with the events of the last couple weeks satisfactorily."

"Uh… I've been okay."

"I notice you didn't take any time off. I was frankly surprised that you came back so quickly."

"I know, I just… feel better staying busy."

"If you need more time, a week, a month, the offer still stands."

"Thank you. Thank you for the flowers, too. They were gorgeous." *Oh my god*, Hannah, *stop babbling.*

"Is there anything I can do to help?" he said.

*Yeah, teleport me out of this state. Maybe out of the country. Or off the planet.* "No."

He studied my face. "Let me know if you think of anything," he said quietly.

"Yes, sir. Thank you."

"Dominic." He smiled. His teeth were the straightest I had ever seen.

"Dominic."

And as abruptly as he'd arrived, he was gone. My stomach dropped a little. I told myself it was hunger and not disappointment.

"Hannah! What did he say?" Noelle's head appeared over the cubicle. Would she miss me after I packed up and left? Maybe I would call her one day, years from now, from another state. From another life. More likely, I'd stare at her number and wonder what ever happened to her.

"Hannah?" She was watching me, eyebrows raised.

"He didn't say much. Just wanted to remind me that I could take time off if I needed to. You know with all the… stuff that's happened."

"He came down here personally for that?"

"I guess."

Noelle pursed her lips.

"He's just being nice. He cares. He's a good boss."

"Yeah, he is. But the way he looks at you is a little more than standard employee appreciation."

"It's not like that." But something flitted around in my belly as I said it. Excitement? Fear? Hope?

Noelle reached down for the owls and tapped Horny on the top of his fake head. "You still have these things?"

"Yes, I—" My sinuses tingled with something subtle and sweet and familiar. The back of my neck was suddenly very hot. "New lotion?"

Noelle put a hand to her nose, apparently unaware of the quaver in my voice. "Yeah, you like it?"

A hornet in my ear buzzed angry violent songs of love notes and cheating and perfume. Noelle had always put Jake down. Always tried to get me to go out, knowing it would make him angry, knowing it would pull me away from him. Because she was... what? Sleeping with him? But that didn't make sense.

"Hannah, you okay?"

"I—" *No*. "Not really. I feel sick."

"I know you've had a rough few weeks, but come out with Thomas and me tonight. Jim will be there too. Maybe it will get your mind off of everything."

"I can't." *Last time I went out, someone filleted my boyfriend.*

"You're going. Don't leave me with two strange men at a dark Greek restaurant."

Sweat leaked from under my bra and trickled down to my belly button. "I can't, okay?" But uncertainty nagged at me. Noelle was dating Thomas. She hadn't been after Jake. She hated Jake. And already Noelle had the same look that acquaintances got in elementary school when I told inappropriate jokes. I could see it like a rocket ship countdown: confusion, irritation, disconnection and *bam*! I was alone.

I couldn't lose her, not yet. Not before I had to. Surely it was possible that a skin care company might have made more than one tube of citrus-scented lotion in an insane attempt to turn a profit? I mean, *duh*, as the kids would say.

A few more weeks, that's all I needed. A few more weeks to suck everything I could out of our friendship so I could wrap the memories around me like a blanket when I was in some new, lonely place. If I made it that long.

Noelle pulled her hand back and the smell of oranges bombarded my nose like someone had thrown a bushel of them at me. My heart ached from pumping so furiously.

It was crazy anyway, to think Noelle would ever do something like that. I needed to stop looking for reasons to mess up the few good things I had left. God knows I had messed up enough already.

I inhaled through my mouth. *It isn't her. It wasn't her. And going out is safer than hanging out at home, right?* I pulled a pencil from the drawer, trying to hide my quaking hands by tapping it on the desktop. "You know what they say about the Greeks," I said.

Her eyes danced. "Big kabobs, small olives?"

"You got it." I swallowed hard.

"I'll pick you up at eight."

I watched her walk away, convinced I was finally, officially, going insane. I needed help. I glanced at the owls, and they glared back. I flicked Horny in the head and watched him topple over the edge of the desk. We were all just one good push away from breaking.


"You're sure I'm not crazy?" I asked, though I knew the answer and further knew that Tammy Bransen, shrink extraordinaire, didn't have enough information to make any kind of accurate assessment at all.

"Magical thinking, anxiety, depression." Tammy ticked them off on her fingers. "They are all part of the normal grieving process and you need to give yourself permission to move through those feelings. You need time to heal. Your wounds are still fresh." She pushed her horn-rimmed glasses up her nose and tucked a lock of straw-colored hair behind her ear.

We had met at the shelter, after one of the monthly group sessions Ms. LaPorte arranged for the women. Ms. LaPorte had thought it might help me after the abortion. Her relief when I agreed was a good enough reason to show up. Sometimes I even felt good coming here, like I was doing *something*, despite the fact that I hid the stuff that really mattered.

"I just feel so… paranoid. About everything."

Tammy shook her head. "Hannah, it is expected that you would have strange reactions to other people, what with the way your relationship with Jake ended. The fact that it was a sudden death makes it all the more difficult to bear, and the… type of demise, and the police questioning… well—"

"The whole thing just seems so unreal. Like tomorrow I'll wake up and find out it was all a nightmare."

"How has your sleep been?"

I sighed. "Not great." It was never great. And I still wrote about it, every morning, waiting with bated breath for that notebook to help me the way Tammy had promised me it would.

"Have you noticed any patterns in your sleep journal?"

"Nope, just the usual crappiness. It did get worse after Jake died, I guess. More trouble dozing off, more waking up scared."

Tammy nodded sympathetically. "That's quite common after experiencing such a loss. All very normal."

"Is it normal to believe your best friend tried to steal your boyfriend?"

Tammy raised her eyebrows.

*Oh*, *Jesus*. "Hypothetically. I have the craziest thoughts sometimes."

"Racing thoughts are normal. They're from the anxiety, and they're, by definition, irrational. So is the magical thinking thing."

I squinted at her and waited.

"Magical thinking is where bereaved loves ones convince themselves that they were responsible for the death. They feel like a final argument, or a missed phone call, somehow triggered the event. Again, irrational and completely untrue, but very common."

The room swam behind my tears. "I need it to stop. I just want to be normal." Not that I'd ever been normal.

"It takes time to heal, Hannah. Don't rush it."

"I just feel so nervous around other people lately. I feel like I always want to run."

*You have a good reason to run.*

*No one else knows that.*

*You don't have a reason. It's magical thinking.*

*That doesn't mean you shouldn't pack up and leave.*

Another nod. Maybe Tammy's head would wobble and detach, roll over to my shoes and spout off semi-supportive drivel from the floor.

Tears fell on my clasped hands. "I'm so tired of being so scared."

Tammy walked around the desk and offered me a box of tissues. "Don't push too hard, but allow yourself room to find a new normal, a new way of doing things that will benefit you. You may need to be around others to prove that people are not as frightening as you think they are. Go out if it helps, show yourself that there is nothing to be afraid of. Do whatever you think you need to do to heal. Don't just sit at home alone in the dark."

That struck a chord. *I hate the dark.*


By eight thirty I was fiddling with my fork and inwardly cursing Tammy's stupid face. *It's all part of the healing process. I just have to stick it out and prove how silly this all is. And when that doesn't work, I'll pack.*

We ate lentil soup that I could barely taste while Noelle and the guys chattered about their favorite restaurants, and recent movies, and which of their current supervisors were dickheads. I listened halfheartedly and avoided Jim's penetrating gaze.

They quieted as the waitress appeared with plates of garlic paste, hummus and warm pita bread. My mouth watered despite my initial ambivalence about dinner, and the food proved to be savory and spicy and just plain awesome. Had I really not eaten a full meal all week? *That's about to change.* I reached for a grape leaf and accidentally brushed Jim's fingers. Electric current zinged up my arm, and all my hair stood on end.

Next time I went to therapy, I was going to punch Tammy in the nose.

*It's all part of the process,* I told myself.

But I didn't believe it.

## FRIDAY, NOVEMBER 13TH

Petrosky ground his teeth together to avoid calling Chief Castleman a fucking asshole. Next to him, Morrison was stiff, the muscles in his jaw working in a decidedly un-surfer-like way.

"You can't be serious," Petrosky said.

"Detective Petrosky, Detective Morrison, this is not an attempt to freeze you out." Castleman squared his chubby shoulders. "But we have a serial killer on our hands and the Mayor doesn't want to take any chances. A screw up is the last thing this city needs right now."

"And I'll screw it up?"

"This has the potential to go national, Petrosky. The only reason it hasn't yet is that someone bombed a bus down south and killed a bunch of grade-schoolers. But that story won't stick around forever. We don't find this guy, they'll crucify us... and you."

"I understand, but—"

"No buts. The FBI has far more resources at their disposal. And it turns out that Meredith Lawrence was the royally fucked-up niece of a radio show host up in Dryesdale. He's making a big stink."

"A radio show host? How the fuck does a radio show host get to tell us—"

"I expect complete cooperation on this. Agent Bryant Graves is waiting for you in the conference room with his men. Get down there and give them what they need."

Dismissed, Petrosky left the chief's office and stalked down the hall, Morrison beside him. Framed photos of dead cops stared at them from the walls with solemn expressions, as if they knew that one day he and Morrison would be underground too, their snapshots also mounted like prized deer heads. Petrosky wanted to mount Chief Castleman on the wall too, along with Agent Bryant fucking Graves.

"Was Graves the one in charge of that case in Frankfurt last year?" Morrison asked.

"How the hell should I know? And how do you?"

"Heard about it from Zajac over in traffic. He used to live up there. The name sounds familiar, but I could be wrong."

Petrosky stopped. "You hang out with the traffic boys, too?"

Morrison stepped past him, leaning against the wall under a picture of an officer with brown eyes and an arrogant expression. He pulled out his phone and tapped a few buttons. "I met him at the gym… okay, same guy." He pocketed the phone. "Zajac said the case was a couple of kids making pipe bombs. Burned two teenagers and a father unlucky enough to open his daughter's mail. Turned out that the kid making the bombs was the mayor's son. The evidence was pretty substantial against him, but they ended up shifting the blame to the kid's friend. There was a lot of suspicion within the department that Graves might have taken a bribe to keep quiet about it."

"Sounds like a winner." Petrosky glanced at the conference room and drew himself up as tall as he could. "Let's go meet this asshole."

Bryant Graves stood at the conference room window, phone to his ear, eyes narrow with concentration—or rage. "What do you mean, no one asked before?" He stared at Petrosky and Morrison as they sat across from two other men, presumably, Graves's agents. The bald one exchanged a knowing look with the asshole with a buzz cut. Petrosky hid his clenched fists under the table.

"Call you back." Graves slipped the phone into his pocket, his eyes radiating accusation. "Detectives." He nodded to Petrosky's side of the room. "Shall we skip the niceties and get down to business?"

Graves gestured to the white board at the head of the table, where pictures of the three victims stared at them. Solemn mug shots for the girls, and a photo of Campbell in a red sweater from his mother, grinning at them with a much more optimistic expression than any photo in the hallway. "Meredith Lawrence, Jane Trazowski and Jacob Campbell. Since this type of killer does not usually have such wildly different victims, there must be something that connects our working girls to Mr. Campbell. The first two had similar lifestyles and drug habits. Jane Trazowski and Jacob Campbell were both connected to Hannah Montgomery in the last six months."

Petrosky's temple throbbed. "Trazowski showed up at the women's shelter after an altercation with a john. Apparently he roughed her up pretty good; she was scared enough to leave her apartment."

Graves glared at him. "Have you found the john?"

"No."

"How about any connection between Hannah Montgomery and Meredith Lawrence? They may have met at some point due to Ms. Montgomery's position with the shelter, particularly in light of Lawrence's extensive domestic violence history."

"We weren't able to find any connections."

"Then we're missing something."

The throbbing wrapped around his forehead and expanded until Petrosky could feel his heartbeat in his eyeballs. "We questioned Montgomery about it, but the night of Trazowski's murder she was working at the shelter. We verified it with the woman she works for and with another woman who was staying at the shelter that day."

Graves's lips tightened, nostrils flaring like he smelled something foul.

"We also have video of her apartment building. She was inside the night Campbell was killed," Petrosky said. *Reading a note from her boyfriend's lover and sobbing.* But he'd let these haughty fuckers find that out for themselves. "She's not a suspect here."

"No one thinks Montgomery is a suspect, detective." Graves leaned forward and put his hands on the tabletop as heat rose in Petrosky's face. "But just because she didn't do it doesn't mean there's no connection to her. We need to go over everything again."

Of course she wasn't a suspect. He was letting his emotions fuck with him. *Goddammit, Petrosky, get your shit together.*

Graves stood. "Hernandez!"

Baldy straightened, light reflecting off his scalp. "Sir."

"Find out what you can about Trazowski's background and see if there are any more questionable activities we should be aware of."

Petrosky stiffened. "That information is in the—"

"Paulson!"

Gray buzz cut turned toward Graves expectantly.

"I want more on Campbell. Friends, exes, family members. And double check the movements of Meredith Lawrence in the weeks before her death."

Paulson nodded.

They were wasting time. All of this was in the file. Petrosky met Morrison's eyes and Morrison raised one shoulder, maybe acquiescing, maybe feeling helpless, or maybe wanting to punch the condescending look off Graves's face.

Graves turned to the other two men at the table. "I want you to research the poem and double back on Shellie Dermont. And see what you can find out about Montgomery. Since two of the victims knew her, we may do well to keep a tight watch on who she sees and talks with. There may be a link between her activities and the way the victims are being chosen."

Graves turned to Petrosky. "Coordinate with these guys and fill in the gaps. We'll need your knowledge of the area and any insight you may already have. Let's get it closed before this ends up splashed all over the national news."

"Or before he kills someone else," Morrison said.

Silence. Graves turned away, toward the window. "Yes," he said finally, voice softer and lower and thick, like a perp making a confession. "That too."

Radio silence. Static. Then the pillow was ripped from my hands.

His face was red, split by a flash of white teeth.

Panic tightened around my throat like a scarf. *Run.* But I was pinned beneath him.

"No, please—"

He put his mouth to my ear. "Shut the fuck up, you little slut. You've been coming on to me for years, and now you tell me that it's wrong? That I don't have a right to give you what you've been begging for?" Droplets of saliva clung to my cheek, hot and wet.

*I am a slut. This is all my fault.* "Please, I'm sorry, I—"

His hand smashed into the side of my face. My ears rang. "Shut. The fuck. Up." It was the quiet, husky tone he'd once used with my mother and it had made her sit motionless on the couch until he'd left.

I tried to stay still like she had, tried to focus through the wavering orange that had settled across my eyes. I felt my pants sliding over my thighs, but distantly, as if in someone else's nightmare. He forced my legs apart with his knees. *No.* I kicked in a futile attempt at freedom.

"You wanted this. Don't you ever fucking forget that." He leaned close to me, his breath warm and putrid.

The world twisted and faded. He forced himself into me and the hurt pounded through every part of my body, hot and sharp and raw, until I was nothing but the pain. He laughed and heat in my chest exploded into furious panic.

"Stop! No! I'm going to tell!" *No! Shut up, Hannah! You'll make it worse!* I bit my tongue until I tasted blood.

"If you want them to die too, go ahead," he whispered in my ear. "Just ask that bitch of a mother how her new husband

171

is doing."

"You killed mom's—"

He sneered down at me. "You'd do well to keep that to yourself. Just knowing about it makes you an accessory. Between jail and death, I'd pick door number three." He moved his hips. I felt like I was being ripped in two. "We will always be one, Hannah. I won't ever let you go. And if you leave, I will find you. And I will fucking kill you."

Numbness seeped in where I once held only adoration. I floated outside my body near the ceiling, looking down at my prone figure draped in the angry profile of my father as he raped me, tearing the tapestry of trust and love and kindness that had taken my entire childhood to build. Blood-tinged semen dripped onto the bed. I prayed to a God I didn't believe in, but understood that help would not come, not now, not ever.

Nothing would ever be the same again. And it was all my fault.

I jerked upright, the air cutting like shards of ice into my sweat-covered skin. My shirt was soaked through. My teeth chattered.

The nightmares. I had thought they were over. I was wrong.

On the end table, the clock glowed three-fourteen.

I should go see my shrink again, maybe on Monday. But I had no words to describe my pain. And when I didn't know what to say, Tammy would say something like, "Let it out. Openness leads to less difficulty over time." Complete bullshit. There was no faster way to screw things up than to open your mouth.

Maybe I could tell Tammy about my mother leaving us for her boss, the dentist, the summer before I entered fourth grade. And about her husband's death the following year from ingesting something he was allergic to, and how my mother never came back to visit, even when she didn't have some mouth-poking, tooth-filling, wrinkly man to climb on top of. Maybe I could tell her how I had retreated to my father's room, wanting to ease his heartache. How some days he seemed happy and I rejoiced, as if finally there was something I could do correctly. But what would she say to what came after?

The night he put his hand on my thigh, I had not resisted. When his mouth found mine, I had brushed aside the nervous tingling at the base of my skull and reminded myself that he was the only one who believed I was worth anything. When his fingers parted me gently, I wasn't sure it was wrong. It felt weird, yet somehow nice. And as I lay naked and felt the searing, intense pain of him deep inside me, he had held me and whispered in my ear: "It's okay, baby. Daddy's here. Everything is okay."

I had believed him, from elementary school and all through middle school, though to say that out loud now seemed insane. Even more so when I considered that the more often I found myself in his arms, the more I knew I was completely and totally in love, a notion that was not contradictory to what I'd been taught in rudimentary sex education classes. Sex was for people who loved one another. Check. Sex happened between people in committed relationships. Check. Sex needed to be based on trust. Check. It all made sense.

In the teacher's defense, it was unlikely she suspected anyone in the class would be fucking her own father.

It was great until it wasn't. Sometime in high school, awareness crept up on me like cold centipedes on my arms, a million tiny legs groping me. It was in the way he avoided hugging me in public like other fathers did. The way he hid the cordless phone in his pocket and never let me answer it. The way he sometimes called out my mother's name when he came.

I knew there were legal penalties for adults who engaged in sexual activities with minors, but I also knew I was already in too deep. It was too late to go back.

I was not normal, and never would be. I loved him too much. And I had to remain silent or he would end up in jail and I would never see him again. At some point, panic gave way to dread that settled in my chest like a stone, growing heavier with each passing day until I knew it would crush my lungs.

And then I talked. It was such a simple question he'd asked: "Hey, Hannah banana, what's wrong?"

I could have said I was tired. That I was worried about a test. That I was on my fucking period. Anything. Instead, I sobbed into a pillow.

"You... we're not supposed to—" I had choked on the words, as if saying it out loud would somehow make it true. *You're not supposed to have sex with your daughter.* It was applicable to everyone else in the world, but not to us.

Then radio silence. Static. And the pillow had been ripped from my hands.

Honesty gets you nowhere. Openness is fucking crazy.

*Focus, Hannah. He's not here. Not now.*

I peeled myself out of bed, the wet top sheet still clinging to my skin. Every night home alone seemed worse than the one before it. Maybe tonight it was because of that electricity I'd felt when Jim's fingers brushed against mine. Or maybe it was the knowledge that I was now completely and utterly alone. Vulnerable. Small. With no one to help me if he finally came sneaking in from the hallway with that awful hungry look on his face, lips peeled back in a sneer, eyes dark and glittering with excitement. Maybe he even knew about the baby.

Maybe he was pissed. More pissed than he'd been at mom's husband, and he'd poisoned him, right?

My breath caught in my throat and I tried to think of something that would make it better, make it funny, make it bearable, but there was nothing besides the fear and the urge to retch as if I could purge all this vile stuff from deep inside.

I left the bedroom, made my way to the living room window on jelly legs and drew back the curtain. Below, the streetlight cast ghostly shadows onto sidewalks covered with wisps of powdered sugar snow. Empty as it always was, but hell, I was a paranoid freak, right? It had been five years, surely he wasn't coming tonight.

I dropped the curtain.

*Stop, Hannah. Just stop.* I kept my hand on the couch to steady myself, then the counter. In the kitchen, I pulled a lonely Pabst Blue Ribbon from the fridge and drank it in front of the sink in case it made me throw up. I gagged once, but swallowed again and again, and tossed the empty can in the sink. That would buy me four or five more hours of sleep and tomorrow I'd jot down notes about my shitty night, just enough to make Tammy shake her head and say: "Mm-hmm. And why do you think that is?"

I staggered back to my bed, the room wavering at the edges, and pulled the blanket up to my chin. Beside me, the deserted spot where Jake used to lie felt like a living thing, breathing into my ear.

Alone. So alone. But did I miss him or just the body that provided some respite from being so vulnerable? Had I ever wanted him or was I a terrible person who just needed someone to be there because I was so fucking afraid?

Probably the second. In a perfect world, I would have chosen someone more supportive. But that didn't mean Jake deserved to die. My eyes filled and I wiped them on the blanket. If I'd just held my tongue, Jake wouldn't have left that night. Though he'd still be here if he had been more… calm. Patient. Understanding. Or if he hadn't fucked someone else.

*Let me know if there's anything I can do…*

Dominic's flowers were still on my desk, probably wilting and filling my cubicle with their sickly sweet perfume. I'd have to get rid of them soon, though I didn't want to. How dead would they have to be before Noelle began to tease me for holding onto them?

I closed my eyes, pictured Dominic's face, and slipped my hand into my panties.

*There must be something I can do for you, Hannah.* His voice in my head was deep and smooth and reassuring.

175

*Maybe if you just stayed here, just for a night, I could get some sleep.*

*Shall I sleep on the couch?*

*No, why don't you stay with me in the bed. I'm sure we'll both be more comfortable...*

I ground my hips against my fingers. Nice, but not earth-shattering like what you read about in those Cosmo-type magazines. I focused on the mellow warmth of the alcohol coursing through my system. Not orgasmic, but sort of nice.

Panting and nauseous, I rolled over and glanced at the clock. Four thirty. I needed to sleep so I could head to the shelter later. One of the only places outside of work where I wasn't as alone, wasn't as afraid, wasn't as fucked up.


I stifled a yawn and knelt before a little boy who was bouncing on the balls of his feet. Ash blond hair glinted above huge brown eyes and cherub cheeks that I would have pinched if it wouldn't have made me look like a huge weirdo. He was the kind of kid you see and think, *aw, I could eat you alive!* but you try to keep that to yourself because it's super creepy to talk about eating children.

"What's your name?" I asked him.

He smiled broadly. "Timmy."

"Nice to meet you, Timmy." I held out my hand and he took it. "Would you like a hot dog? Your mother said it was okay."

"Yessssss!" he said, drawing out the word as only a five-year-old can.

"Follow me, sir."

He skipped behind me to the cafeteria tables, clambered onto a bench and grinned up at me as I retrieved a plate of food from the kitchen. "You're pretty," he said.

I froze, though I wasn't sure why. What the hell was wrong with me? I swallowed hard. "Here you go." I put his plate and fork in front of him and went back to the kitchen to take care of the women who were waiting patiently for their plates.

*Hot dogs, baked potatoes, canned green beans. Hot dogs, baked potatoes, green beans. Dogs, potatoes, beans.*

Timmy's mother, Antoinette, stood next to me, efficiently wielding a pair of tongs. The bruise on her cheek and the gouge across her lip had almost healed from the altercation that had brought her to the shelter last week. Her blond hair was up in a clean ponytail, and freckles were visible along her nose and at her neckline. A pair of perfectly matched bluebirds on either shoulder aimed inwards toward her collarbone. Antoinette twisted to grab another stack of plates and there was something in the set of her shoulders—high and straight—that suggested she hadn't been born into a life of abuse. What had changed for her?

A little voice piped up from behind the counter. "Momma, can I have another one?"

Antoinette stood on her tiptoes and peeked over the partition. "Did you eat the beans?"

"Um—" Timmy scampered back to his plate.

"Kids," Antoinette said with a grin.

"He seems sweet." I set the last plate on the counter.

"He really is. He's an angel."

"Momma, all done!" He was back with his empty plate.

Antoinette put another hot dog on it. "Here you go, hon."

He frowned. "Ketchup, please?"

She smiled, squirted some on the hot dog, and he ran off, eyes on his food.

"So what do you have planned for next week?" I asked. Unless no one else needed the rooms, women could only stay one week. Right now, we were full.

Antoinette shrugged and took off her apron. "I think I can go back to my old apartment."

I nodded uncertainly. "I hope it works out. But if it doesn't—"

"I know where you are." She wiped her hands on her jeans and went to the front room to sit with Timmy.

Out the front window, the last of the dying sunlight had

faded to dusky black, making everyone in the dining room stand out in stark contrast. I watched Antoinette ruffle Timmy's hair and kiss his cheek, and my stomach turned like I had eaten something bad. I turned away and headed for the dishes in the sink.

The back door clanged open. I lifted a frying pan like a club and held it at the ready until I heard the pecking beeps of someone entering the alarm code. Then Ms. LaPorte entered, hugging three paper grocery bags to her chest. I rushed to her side and grabbed them from her, still gripping the pan.

"Thank you, dear." She shrugged out of her down jacket, hung it on a hook and opened the fridge by the stove. "I got everything for tomorrow's breakfast. Even found some bacon on sale."

I set the bags down and handed Ms. LaPorte a gallon of milk. Her hands were warm and comforting, but my stomach was still tight. I took a deep breath.

"Everything going okay here?"

"Dinner's winding down. Nothing else to report. Pretty quiet, actually." *Quiet and gloriously boring.*

"Ah, we can all do with some quiet nights." Ms. LaPorte bustled back and forth between the fridge and the cupboards. I started on the pots and pans with a stainless steel scrubber. By the time I set the third pan on the sideboard to dry, my stomach felt almost normal.

"Hannah, why don't you go home for the night?"

And the nausea was back. My hand shook. I dropped a clean pan onto the sideboard and it clattered like it was going to break the counter. Ms. LaPorte shoved something else into the cupboard and either didn't notice or didn't mind the racket I was making.

"I'm okay for now." I fought to control the tremor in my voice. "I figured I would help clean the after-dinner dishes."

"You've been here all day, dear. Time for you to get home and get some rest. Everything will be fine. I won't take no for an answer."

*Everything will be fine.* Of course it would. It wasn't like

I could live at the shelter. I set the last pan on the sideboard. "I'll be back early tomorrow evening. Right after work."

"No hurry, dear. You take your time."

I exchanged my apron for my coat. "Like I said, I'll be back early."

I cast one more glance at Antoinette, who was wiping Timmy's mouth. She saw me looking at her and waved. I waved back, zipped my coat and exited the building, letting the door swing shut behind me with a clang that echoed through the deserted lot. No... not deserted—

I dropped my keys but I was frozen, unable to retrieve them.

A figure crouched next to my car with a long slim object. *A knife!*

My lungs stopped working. *No a... coat hanger.*

*He's trying to get into my car!*

He jerked upright and made a break through the trees at the back of the lot.

His gait. The way he walked. I had not seen his face, but I didn't have to. I knew.

*He was going to get in and wait for me... and then—* My insides turned to water. I thought of Jake, of those women. I did not want to know what my father had planned for me. And if he was here... maybe he had killed those other women too, just to scare me.

*Or to practice.*

I could never come back here. Ever.

*I am not crazy.*

Detective Petrosky's sad bulldog eyes flashed in my brain. *He thinks I'm a murderer.*

*He's right. Knowing who killed Jake makes me an accessory.*

*It's all my fault.*

I retrieved my keys and leapt to the car, my heart shuddering in my ribcage, my mouth dry as I gasped for nonexistent air. I was out of time.

*What the hell am I going to do?*

## MONDAY, NOVEMBER 16TH

Scorched air huffed from a vent under the psychiatrist's desk. Petrosky had been there five minutes and dampness was already creeping around his armpits.

"The change in victim is concerning," McCallum said. "It doesn't fit the mold. Not only do you have a completely different victim, but you have a completely different type of restraint system. Then, there's the fact that there was no writing at the scene." He grabbed a pen out of his desk drawer and clutched it in his meaty fist.

"We purposefully withheld the poems from the public in the first two murders. It suggests copycat, but with the similar dissection styles it's hard to say. We're still pushing the same killer to the public either way, though. One is less scary than two."

McCallum nodded.

But Campbell was killed by his guy, Petrosky could feel it. So why would he vary his pattern? And why Campbell, some loser nobody, with no connection to the other victims?

"Let's hash this out. I need to think." Petrosky leaned forward in his chair. "If we're dealing with the same killer, he had a very specific reason for choosing Campbell. I just can't figure out why. Did Campbell piss him off? Did he see something he shouldn't have? I could get behind our guy just being in the mood to slit someone's throat, but he had all his dissection shit with him. It was premeditated."

Petrosky's gut was a hot mess of too many chili dogs and too little Jack Daniels; the nip he'd had before coming here wasn't nearly enough.

McCallum tapped the pen on the desk. "If we're looking at the same killer, there's clearly some connection between the third death and the first two. If Campbell knew something, he'd have to have been there to see something, or know someone who was. Did he go out much?"

"Nope. DUI a few years back, no license, no car. He does have one common acquaintance from the shelter, but she only knew one of the female victims, not both."

"This girl… is she a suspect?"

"No. I mean, I don't think so."

McCallum's eyes bored into him. "You're worried about her."

Petrosky sighed. "Yes." It sounded dirty to say it out loud—dirty but honest.

McCallum set the pen down. "Do you have reason to believe she's involved?"

"Not really. I can't see a motive for the women, and we have the tapes of the lobby, so she has an alibi for Campbell's murder. Unless she went out the window."

"What's your concern?"

"I'm… not sure." His stomach roiled.

"She's not Julie." McCallum's voice was low but he might as well have shouted it.

"I know she—"

"I understand, Ed. Julie's on your mind. Always will be. It's grief. It's trauma. It's complicated. But it's a mistake to assume that any suspect who looks like Julie must be innocent. You're generalizing, maybe even seeing resemblances that aren't there because you *want* them to be there. You want to save Julie and you can't do that, so you're trying to save someone else. But not all these women deserve your sympathy."

"She just lost her boyfriend. She deserves something." Petrosky wiped a hand over his forehead. It came away wet.

"Katherine Delacrois deserved your sympathy too, right? I'm sure you remember her."

Petrosky clenched his jaw. Katherine had been just as lovely, with the same huge eyes and dark hair. She had been soft-spoken and tearful when he questioned her, and he'd felt so guilty about making her upset that he defended her to the other officers. A week later she had quietly, and just as tearfully, admitted to brutally stabbing her boyfriend thirteen times in the chest.

"This isn't—"

"No, it's not. But it wouldn't hurt you to remember that *this* girl is not *your* girl either."

"I don't have all day to bullshit about old news." Petrosky clenched his fists under the desk, something sharp as a fish hook tugging at his heart. "I need to figure this out before he kills someone else."

McCallum sat back in his chair, eyes tight but not surprised. "If you insist. Back to your case."

He tried to ignore the twitch at the corner of McCallum's mouth, but his back tensed anyway. "I need to look at the victims more." Maybe there were similarities he had missed, not that he'd ever give Graves's the satisfaction of admitting that.

"Their attraction for your killer may not be as obvious as it seems."

"The attraction to the working girls seemed pretty obvious until Campbell."

McCallum put his hands flat on the desk. "Look deeper."

Petrosky stood and started for the door.

"Ed?"

He turned back.

"You know what you need to do. Find the links between the victims and you'll figure out how he's choosing. You can't focus on things you know aren't leads; you can't focus on this girl. As you said, you don't have the time. He's out there. And he's hunting."

<hr>

All night I sat at the dining table, staring at the door with a kitchen knife in my hand, imagining I'd be ready the moment I heard him picking the lock. While I waited, I considered my options. One: leap into the car and run with the couple hundred bucks I had in my wallet. But I wouldn't get far. Two: take the bus with that same money and probably get farther. But since he obviously knew that I had stayed in a shelter the first time, he'd surely look at shelters this time and find me right off. So that was out, and I had no idea how I'd find an apartment without someone like Ms. LaPorte looking out for me. I had never even used my name to open a credit card. Three: there was no three. For the life of me, I could think of nothing else to do.

The next day started on autopilot. My hands trembled as I lathered my hair, but I still washed it. My stomach lurched at the thought of food, but I still made toast. And when the hallway creaked ominously outside my door, I threw on my shoes, peered into the hallway and raced for my car like I was running from a burning building.

At least at work my heart could relax to a dull roar in my ears, white noise instead of the heavy metal drummer that had blasted away in my skull all the way to the office. I'd never been so grateful for the guarded doors, the security locks, and Jerome, somewhere in the building looking out for shady characters.

But I couldn't stay here for the rest of my life, in this building, with the incessant clacking of fingers on keyboards to help me keep my composure. I peeked over the partitions at Noelle but the back of her head wasn't very comforting. Nor was the way Ralph was leering at her from across the room. I collapsed back in my chair and tried to lose myself in my work, punching in information as fast as I could until my shaking fingers refused to type any longer.

*Let me know if there is anything I can do.* His words rang in my head until there was nothing left but his voice, and the hope trying to seed itself within me.

I shoved my chair back. File folders crashed to the floor.

*Maybe he can help.*

*No, certainly not.*
*Tell him a joke! He likes those!*
*Not like you have anything to lose.*

I threw open the office door too hard, caught it, and closed it gently, glancing over my shoulder through the glass wall at Ralph and Toni and Noelle. No one looked up. I ran to the staircase and ascended, my shoes on the metal steps almost as fast as my heartbeat.

The top floor was another world—leather armchairs and cherry wood furniture, and abstract art. Doubt seeped into my chest like a river of burning oil. Desperation burned hotter.

*What's the worst that can happen?*
*He'll think you're crazy.*
*So what?*
*He'll fire you.*
*Joke's on him—I quit!*

The secretary had steel gray hair and black-rimmed glasses like an old-fashioned schoolmarm. Her bony fingers kept typing away on her keyboard even as she stared me down.

I smoothed my hair. "I need to speak to Mr. Harwick, please."

"Name and appointment time?"

"Hannah Montgomery. I don't actually have an—"

She smiled, but her gaze was one you'd give a naughty child. "Then I am afraid he cannot see you."

My body felt suddenly heavy, like I was wrapped in a wet blanket of hopelessness. *Of course he can't see me.* I was an idiot. "Can I make an appointment to see him today?"

The woman punched a few buttons on the keyboard and squinted at her screen, eyes flat and disinterested. "How about three weeks from tomorrow?"

I put my hands on the desk to steady myself. I couldn't breathe.

*I'll be gone by then.*
*Or gutted like a fish.*

"Please, I just… please—" My voice rang shrill, foreign,

hysterical. Back spots floated around the edges of my vision. My lungs were on fire.

"Ma'am, you're going to have to—" The secretary's voice grew distant. My fingers, splayed on the cherry wood, slid toward me in slow motion as I gasped nonexistent air and fought the haze at the edges of my vision. Everything went black.

*He held me, cradling me like a child as he walked me to my bedroom.*

*Shhh, it's ok, baby...*

I opened my eyes with a start. I was half lying, half sitting in a leather armchair, knees over the arm. Near my feet, a sculpture made of colored glass reached toward the ceiling with intertwined bands of red and yellow.

"You're awake." Mr. Harwick rose behind an enormous desk of glass and stone.

I tried to pull myself up, but my sweaty hands slipped on the leather.

"Just relax for a moment."

I stopped struggling and wilted in the chair.

"Are you hurt?"

I shifted in the seat. My legs were asleep, but I only felt pins and needles, not pain. My elbow stung with what was probably rug burn. My lungs were working again. Nothing felt too sore or wrong, though I did seem to have a mass of creepy crawly things teeming in my stomach.

Then everything came back to me.

*I need help. My father killed my boyfriend and it's all my fault.*

*Shit! Don't say that!*

He perched on the arm of the other chair, concern etched across his features.

I swung my feet to the floor.

*Tell him.*

*I don't know what to say.*

185

"I… need help." It came out a whisper.

"What can I do for you?"

His cologne was biting, earthy, masculine. "Uh…" In all the hoping I'd done I had not thought to plan out what to ask of him. I wanted to punch myself in the head.

*You can't tell him.*

*You have to tell him. You can always deny it later if he tells anyone.*

"I… my um… father…" I looked down. "He wasn't very nice when I was growing up. I ran away." *Why are you still protecting him*?

I took a deep breath. "I… I'm afraid he may be trying to find me. I am… I don't know what to do, but I can't… I think he's been following me."

"Did you call the police?"

My heart caught in my throat. *They'll arrest me for not telling them who killed Jake.*

"No. I mean, I think I might be in trouble too. I… uh… took some things from the house when I left." *Yeah, like your clothes. Look at you, super thief! First your clothes, then an old cafeteria table, and tomorrow a bank so you can actually manage to avoid homelessness wherever you end up.*

His forehead wrinkled. "I see."

"Maybe… maybe I can take out a loan against my next paycheck? Or I can just borrow a little bit so I can get started in another state? I'll pay you back, every cent. I'll work two, three jobs if I have to. I just need enough to get away and set up somewhere else."

*Here it is. Now he'll tell me to get out and I can go pack my apartment.*

"I can help you."

*You can… what*? I blinked at him.

"You don't have to leave, Hannah. If he found you here, he'll find you there. Then in another year you'll be back in the same position. Let's give it a week or so to assess the situation."

"But—"

"Did he come to your home?"

*Not yet.* "He will."

"I can help you get an apartment in another name."

"He's been following me. He knows my car." *Oh, God.* He probably knew where I ate dinner, where I shopped for groceries.

"I'll drive you, or I will have a car sent."

I did a double take, heart twitching. "What?"

"Or you can stay with me for a few days. I've got an alarm and a big dog."

*You can't help me, no one can help me. You'll die just like Jake did.* "Mr. Harwick, I—"

"Dominic."

"Dominic. We don't even… I mean, we don't know each other all that well."

"I know you're scared, but I can help you. And if in a week you still want to run, I will give you some cash and a new license plate."

Something was obviously wrong with my ears. *He doesn't understand the gravity of the situation. If he did—*

"Are you sure you don't want to call the police? We can do it from here." He reached for the phone.

"No! I mean… I don't know."

*They'll lock me up too, just for knowing about Jake. They'll blame me.*

*Would Dominic?*

I had nothing to lose anymore. My eyes filled with tears. "I just feel so… broken. Like I don't even know what to do to be normal anymore."

His eyes were far away. "My dad always used to say, 'Pretending to be normal is the best way to make people think you are.'"

I wrung my hands, every nerve in my body twitching. Pretending, I could do. It was what came after the pretending that worried me.

"You're strong. You'll get past this." He touched my arm softly. "Everything will be okay."

*Everything will be okay.* Was that true? *Everything* encompassed so very much and it felt like it was all flowing through me in that moment—the unrelenting stress of the past few months, the pain of my childhood, the guilt and the grief and the panic—until I feared I would burst or lose my mind completely. *Everything.* I needed everything to be okay, if only for a moment.

His eyes bored into mine. "Hannah, you're shaking. It's all right. I'll help you." He was so… confident, his eyes calm, patient, understanding.

I threw myself into his arms and sobbed into his shirt as he stroked my hair.

"I… thank you."

*I'm safe here.*

Then, there was more than gratitude. It began like a fire in the pit of my stomach and crept lower, heating the space between my thighs. *Something's wrong.* I pressed my legs together, but the smoldering ache swelled and spread.

I tilted my face upwards and he captured my mouth with his, silencing the remnants of fear. But then the fear reemerged, burning panic mingling with something feral, clawing at me to get out.

*I can't do this.*

I put a hand on his chest, prepared to pull away, but he wrapped an arm around my back and liquid warmth spread through me.

*He'll hurt me too.*

But his hand in my hair was soft, gentle, kind. He did care for me. Maybe he always had. I could hear my heartbeat in my ears, feel the throbbing of it between my legs, sweet and unrelenting.

He had come to the funeral. Not for Jake, not for just another employee, but for *me.* He'd sent me flowers. Came to see me in the office. He cared, and not because I was an employee, not even because I was pretty—I surely hadn't been ten minutes ago with snot streaming down my face. No, he cared about… me.

I clutched his shoulders as if letting go might cause him to disappear and I would be left desperate and lonely again. I was so focused on his mouth, his scent, the hardness of him against my pelvis that I didn't feel him moving me toward the desk, but there I was, the glass top cold under me as he laid me down and guided my arms above my head. Then my mouth was free, my lips still swollen with the taste of him, as his tongue trailed along my jaw, down the side of my neck, over to the top button of my blouse. He unbuttoned my shirt slowly and brushed his lips against each patch of newly-exposed skin. I closed my eyes.

*Everything will be okay.*

He put his hands on my knees and moved upward under my skirt, each stroke leaving tender, tingling flesh in its wake. A low moan escaped me, primal and hungry, a sound I didn't even know I was capable of making. The past months—all my worries, all my mistakes—vanished. There had been nothing before this moment. Here, with him, it was safe to be born again.

*Everything will be okay.*

Then he was inside me, filling me, and I raised my hips to meet him. His tongue flicked against my nipple, and I could feel every gentle suckle in my loins. I wrapped my legs around him as if I could erase everything else by pulling him deeper into me. He thrust, again and again, his fingers stroking me at the apex of my thighs.

*Everything will be okay.*

An unfamiliar sensation took over my body, and there was no more control, no time to be shocked, only pulsing, shuddering waves crashing over me as I clung to the desk and screamed Dominic's name. He covered my mouth with his, joining the two of us in blissful silence that spoke volumes. He cared about me. He wanted me. And I wanted him back, desperately, furiously, in that moment, and for as long as he would have me.

*He will protect me.*

*Yeah, as long as he never knows how fucked up you really*

*are.*

Swallowing the thought, I wrapped my legs around his hips and fastened myself to him as if he were an anchor, one steady thing in a sea of hurt.

## WEDNESDAY, NOVEMBER 18TH

Robert seethed. *This is not possible.*

He sat with Thomas at the deli down the road from their office. A ham and swiss sandwich too big to fit in his mouth sat untouched on his plate. The completely oblivious bastard across from him was making short work of his own turkey and cheddar.

*She betrayed me.*

It was a simple thought, one that shouldn't have surprised him, and yet it did.

*Women are whores. Liars. Vile.*

But not this one. This one was supposed to save him. With every part of his being he rejected the idea that she had left him before granting him absolution.

"When did this happen?"

Thomas shrugged. "This week, I think? Apparently, Hannah just packed up and moved out of the blue. Noelle was totally shocked when she found out."

Robert cursed himself for biding his time instead of actively pursuing her. But a sudden move did not seem like typical behavior for the demure woman he thought he knew. The girl he needed would not have given herself so easily to anyone. And it was not possible that one could change so suddenly.

He sat up straighter. What if she had been tricked? Perhaps she was merely the unwitting victim of a cunning adversary. He could save her from him, give her a gift, and in return, she would cleanse him, grateful for his selflessness.

A pastoral voice sounded in his head. *Therefore, confess your sins to each other and pray for each other so that you may be healed.*

Without her there was no one who could absolve him. He felt himself sliding into the grips of desperation, each breath more difficult than the last.

Thomas bit into his sandwich and chewed, the sound wet and thick and infuriating.

"Who the fuck is he?" Robert asked as soon as he could speak.

Thomas's eyes were boring a hole into him and Robert wanted to rip them out of Thomas's skull.

"That's the craziest part. The boss man."

Robert squinted. "The boss? Like, the head of Chrysler?"

Thomas laughed. "Nah, I don't think she aimed quite that old. The owner of the contract house we work for. Harwick."

Robert leaned back in his chair and gaped. He had worked there for years and had never even met Harwick. "I didn't know they knew each other."

"Yeah, I think they work in the office with him," Thomas said, nonchalantly, clearly missing the blinding rage and despair emanating from the man across from him.

*Dominic Harwick.* Robert clenched his teeth together, jaw aching with the pressure of it.

*She is my only hope of salvation.*

*I cannot fail.*

## WEDNESDAY, NOVEMBER 18TH

He crouched underneath the table, not because he was scared, but because she had screamed at him to do it. The john didn't want him in the closet while they were in the bedroom. There was apparently no worse buzz-kill than the sneeze of a small child.

He waited while the moans from the bedroom accelerated and finally stopped. A shirtless man walked out to the table, kicked under it until his foot connected, and left the apartment.

He watched the door close behind the john and rubbed his throbbing shin.

Then her face appeared, nearly purple with rage. She reached under the table to grab him, as he had expected, and jerked him into the open. The splintered linoleum tiles slashed at his legs as she dragged him across the floor. She slapped him in the face and his cheek lit up with pain. Her foot connected with his stomach. He tried to breathe but the blows came too quickly.

Still, he remained impassive, yielding. It was better this way, faster too. Maybe he'd even pass out. When he came to, it would be over.

"You prolly just cost me fifty bucks, you little piece of shit."

Her words were slurred. She kicked him hard in the thigh. The air returned to his lungs. Much better. Much more—

He was weightless for half a second. Stars shot into his vision as he struck the cabinet with his head and crashed to the floor on his stomach. There was a loud snap as a bone in his ribs gave way. Pain flared in his chest. He gritted his teeth and lay still.

The front door slammed.

He struggled to his feet, panting through his nose as the ache in his side intensified. In the bathroom, he climbed gingerly onto the sink and peered into the mirror. Blue and green marks stained his skin. He touched his side, swallowed the pain, and watched his face. His eyes stayed as empty as the kitchen cupboards.

He brought the edges of his mouth up like the hero did in the comic magazine he had found. He frowned.

That wasn't it.

He tried again, willing the corners of his eyes to move as well.

The door slammed. A man's voice muttered something. Then a clink of glass—they'd stopped in the kitchen. He scrambled from the bathroom sink, gasping against the stabbing pain in his side, and ran to the bedroom, into the closet.

Maybe if she came for him again, that smiley face he'd been practicing would help him. It certainly seemed to help the man with the cape.

He shook his head at the long-ago memories. Superheroes never lasted, nor had that vulnerable boy who had once dreamed of becoming one.

She wouldn't last either.

The woman paced the alley on legs run through with purple veins. Her stomach was too thin to have seen anything but blow in the last week. He wondered if the boy housed in the apartment upstairs was as malnourished as she was. He could almost smell the child, dirty and sweating, hiding in a closet, cowering in a corner. But no matter. Soon the boy would be free of his bitch mother.

Her artificially yellowed hair shone under the single streetlight like a beacon as she tossed it over one shoulder. Business was good tonight; he could tell it by the bounce in her step. So much the better. Her good mood would make her that much more trusting.

*Fucking idiots. Like oysters led to their slaughter.*

He emerged from the shadows and let her see him. She grinned, revealing yellowed teeth with wide gaps.

"Hey, honey, you looking for something?"

He nodded, feeling the cool wetness in the hand he held behind his back. Chloroform always made the taking easier. Plus, it let them awaken for the best part.

He squinted, beckoning another face into focus, a reminder from the past.

*There you are, bitch.*

She walked toward him on precariously high heels.

He readied himself, pulling his lips into his best superhero smile. Though she was not the one he wanted, for today, she would do.

No one would miss her. No one at all.

## THURSDAY, NOVEMBER 19TH

When I opened the door to my apartment, the first thing I saw was the box. Jake's box, brown and sad and lonely. *Forgotten.* That seemed the worst kind of slight. The air itself seemed itchy, like someone was picking at my skin.

"Hannah?" Dominic set a stack of pre-folded boxes against the dining table and straightened. His khakis matched the boxes. His sweater brought out the subtle flecks of green in his eyes. I wondered if he'd done that on purpose.

"Oh, sorry. I was just thinking, I should bring that box to Jake's mother."

"I'll have it sent." His eyes scanned the kitchen and the living room beyond. "You've had company."

I followed his gaze to the kitchen, where white powder dusted the cabinets. Two of the upper doors still hung open. By the fridge, a piece of blue tape clung to the countertop.

"They were already in here right after Jake died," I said uncertainly. They must have come back for... something. What had they been looking for that they didn't find the first time?

I scratched at my arm, too hard, but stopped short of drawing blood. Maybe they knew my father was after me. Maybe they knew he'd killed Jake. Maybe they'd be back to arrest me any day. I stared at Jake's box and tried to avoid retching.

"I'm sure it's just routine. I heard the FBI is taking over the case, so I bet they're double-checking everything."

Of course. It wasn't all about me, was it? I was as narcissistic as the world's most irritatingly self-centered rappers. Maybe I'd even name my child after a direction in honor of the kid's importance, so whenever anyone said, "Go left" I could hear, "Go, Left!" and rejoice in the universe's unrelenting support of my child.

"I'll take this box to the car and let you get started up here."

"You're leaving?" *But you're supposed to protect me!*

"I'm walking to the car, Hannah. I'll be right back."

"But—"

He closed the distance between us and hugged me tightly to him. "Everything is fine. You haven't even been here in three days. No one is crouching in a closet waiting for you to show up."

Something in my chest writhed and tightened around my lungs.

"Have I steered you wrong yet?" He let me go and peered down at me. "Have I done anything inappropriate or even remotely dangerous?"

*Inappropriate.* I took a deep breath and could almost feel it crackle over my dry tongue, like winds across a desert. Was sleeping with me inappropriate? If so, I wished he'd been *more* inappropriate. The past three nights I had slept snuggled against his back and he hadn't even tried to touch me. *Why doesn't he want me anymore?* Maybe something was wrong with me. Maybe he realized that he had been a total dolt bringing some strange girl home with him. Or maybe the sex just hadn't been as good for him as it had been for me and he was loathe to repeat it.

And yet, sleeping next to him, I had felt safer than I had in years. Tammy would be thrilled at the change reflected in my sleep journal. I'd even occasionally wondered if all my fears had just been me being crazy about nothing. Maybe the man in the parking lot had just been someone trying to steal my car stereo, as Dominic had suggested. This possibility did seem more likely than my father showing up at the shelter. Too much coincidence. And if they thought the killings were related to dear old dad, wouldn't the police have called me to get some information on him? As Dominic said all the time, logic ruled. I wondered if Dominic would kick me out if I decided to stay in town after all. Maybe he'd kick me out just for being nuts.

"Hannah? Do you trust me?"

I swallowed. Nodded.

"Good." He hoisted the box to his shoulder. "I'll be right back to help you finish and we'll go out to lunch after. I know a great Italian place."

I watched him go, licked my parched lips, and tossed an empty box onto the kitchen floor. Plates and bowls. Silverware. Cups. Some got wrapped in paper towels. I picked up Jake's favorite mug, the one he had always chugged beer out of while I cleaned the kitchen. I left it on the counter. Noelle would have thrown it in the trash. *Noelle.* I should call her.

The door clanked and packing tape squeaked.

*He came back!*

*Of course he came back.*

"I'll set these next ones up and secure the bottoms," Dominic said, unfolding a box. "I'll tape that one when you're done."

"It's done." I pushed the box toward the door and Dominic taped it shut. "Thanks."

One box of choice items was enough for the living room, too. In the bedroom, I stared at the dresser drawers, sighed, and upended one after another into a cardboard box before turning my attention to the bedside tables.

The bed hulked in the middle of the room, a reminder of things I didn't want to think about—and much closer to the dresser than I remembered. It was like the room had gotten smaller, collapsing in on itself now that the world was missing Jake's energy. But I wasn't sure I missed him. I took his pillow from the bed, put it to my nose and inhaled the faintest trace of cigarettes. I threw it against the wall.

Footsteps approached, but there was no menacing squeal of rubber, like that which accompanied the shoes my father wore, only the soft clack of moneyed leather.

The tension drained from my neck. I flipped the

cardboard box closed. "Last one."

He scooped it up in one arm. "I can send someone for the furniture."

"Don't bother."

"Are you sure?"

*It won't fit in my car anyway.* "Too many memories."

I followed him to the front door and down the stairs, calling quiet goodbyes to my life here; the hallway, the stairwell, the smell of socks and putrid onions.

"Did you want to invite some of your friends to lunch? You haven't seen anyone in the last few days."

My toe caught on a stair. I righted myself on the railing.

"Are you okay?" Dominic stopped and turned back, the barest of smirks on his beautiful mouth.

"I'm fine. And no, I don't want to call anyone. They won't even miss me yet."

He started back down, shoes lightly smacking the stairs. "I just want to make sure you're staying in because you want to and not because you're frightened. I'm sure Noelle misses you."

"Maybe." My face heated. "Lately, I haven't wanted to hang out with her."

"Why?"

*Because I suspected her of screwing my dead boyfriend and now I feel guilty.* "I—I'm not sure."

"I see."

He shifted the box to his shoulder and held the lobby door for me. The room was barely brighter than the stairwell, dust particles playing in a beam of sunlight that shone through the tiny window.

"I find being around people is helpful during trying times," he said. Tammy said things like that too, but the words felt different coming from Dominic. Almost… believable.

I glanced at the mailboxes, ominous and dark, and remembered the letter. *That girl.* Jake had probably been thrilled every time I left. *Maybe Dominic wants me to go out, too.* "Do you want me to make plans to get me out of the

199

house?"

"Of course not. I just don't want you to feel like you have to stay home all the time." He smiled and I forgot the mailboxes.

"Okay. But just so you know, I don't usually make big plans. The only thing I did on a regular basis was volunteer, and I can't go back there."

"The place where he tried to get into your car?"

"Yes."

"You think he'd be brazen enough to do it again?"

"I... maybe."

"I can hire someone."

"Hire someone?"

"To check the lot. Or to drive you. Either way, you can't let fear hold you back. And it's not too late to call the police."

I shook my head. "No. Thanks, but no."

He opened the door to the parking lot. "Hannah, I just want you to live your life normally. You need to do the things that make you happy, not spend your life afraid. I'll help you."

A beam of sunlight fell on my arm. "Why are you doing this for me?"

"I made you a promise. I'm keeping it." He shoved the front door and it opened, screeching in protest.

Air blew against my face, cold, crisp but somehow sweeter than it had ever been.

*I made you a promise.*

I followed him out into the sunshine.

## Friday, November 20th

Petrosky dumped coffee grounds into the filter, his gut heavy with old hurt and yesterday's donuts. Julie's nightlight glowed over the sink.

*Fix this. Save someone else's girl. It's the least you can fucking do.*

He ran over the cases in his head. The women had been young, urban prostitutes who used their hard-won funds to feed drug addictions. Jacob Campbell had been a white boy living in the suburbs with a pretty girlfriend and an absentee kid who was taken care of elsewhere. It didn't fit. But that wasn't the problem.

The killer was methodical, intelligent. Maybe angry.

*He has a plan.* So why wouldn't he leave a message at Campbell's scene?

Petrosky punched the countertop, relishing the ache in his knuckles.

The clamps. The nails. The dissections. There was a reason for everything. Had to be.

The scene had been scoured by crime scene techs and FBI agents alike, and each board and piece of trash had been examined. They had printed and moved and touched and tagged. Yet they'd found nothing.

*Did he run out before he could finish the note?*

Petrosky shook his head at the thought. They would have found another body if someone had interrupted him.

*Look deeper.*

*Fuck.* He yanked the nightlight off the wall and hurled it in the sink next to six empty beer bottles. The coffee pot percolated like a lazy asshole. Petrosky walked back to the bedroom and jerked on a pair of jeans and a sweatshirt.

Halfway to the car, he stopped in the driveway and stared at the ground, then returned to the kitchen and retrieved the nightlight. He wiped it on his shirt and plugged it back in.

*Sorry, honey.*

He shot the half full coffee pot one final glare and kicked the front door shut behind him.


"What are we looking for, exactly?" Morrison stared at the cinderblock mass in the center of the underground room where they had found Campbell's body. Small chunks of cement had been chipped away, probably by their forensics team.

Petrosky knelt at the back corner of the room and ran his fingers along the line where wall met floor. "Not sure. Anything different." He hated the strain in his own voice.

"Different like what, boss?"

"Different like…" Petrosky stood and wiped his fingers on his jeans. "Shit, I don't even know anymore."

Morrison prodded the side of a cement block with his thumb. "It's crazy that there was a body on here. It doesn't have blood on it or anything."

*Anything different…*

"There was a tarp here, right?" Petrosky pictured the blood-stained table in the westside basement and the cemetery concrete that would forever smell like copper. This guy had never used plastic before. There had to be a reason now.

He knelt and laid his head against the floor, exploring the bottom of the structure with his fingers, then heaved himself upright and sat back on his heels. "There's no way. A cement mass this size has to weigh, what? A thousand pounds?"

"I doubt it," Morrison's voice echoed against the concrete. "I worked construction in college. Cinderblocks are usually hollow."

Petrosky stared at the table. "Hollow, but still pretty heavy."

Morrison bent down beside him. "Yeah. He'd have to be strong to shove it even a short distance. Or he has a partner."

"No, no partner for our guy." Petrosky stood, rubbing his forehead with his fingers. *How did he do it?*

Wait. The treads. *Of course.* "He had a dolly. And he didn't shove it. He needed a way to lay it down without marring the words." If there were words. There had to be words.

"There's no way he lifted this whole thing with a dolly alone."

Petrosky squinted at the rows of cinderblock that made up the top. "Could you hold those top pieces up with something besides other blocks?"

"Metal supports, secured internally and run from one side to the other could do it." Morrison stared at the concrete. "Do you think the killer put it together himself?"

"In this whole place, there isn't a single other intact structure. I can't believe we missed that."

Morrison frowned. "But if he painted words in Campbell's blood under there, he couldn't have done it before he killed Campbell. And he couldn't have built the structure underneath the body afterwards—the blood splatter on the tarp and the surrounding ground was consistent with Campbell being killed where we found him."

Petrosky walked around the cement table, probing the mortar between blocks. "All this was dry when we were here, right?"

"It was. I talked to the techs and they pulled samples from the blocks, side and top. Someone would have noticed wet cement in the crevices."

Petrosky's chest was tight. He kicked at the base of the block in front of him. Solid. He took a step to the right and kicked again. No give.

Morrison lowered his eyes and followed suit. *Kick*, *pause*. *Kick*, *step*. *Kick*. "Boss?" Morrison disappeared below the side of the structure.

Petrosky stepped around the blocks. Morrison was

pressing on one of the lower bricks with the beefy part of his palm. "There's a little give. Not much, but the bottom should be the most solid and there's definitely some wiggle here."

Petrosky knelt on Morrison's right, pulled his Swiss Army knife from his back pocket and scraped at the mortar, where a hairline crack was already widening. A chunk of mortar fell, revealing dead space between the bricks. Were they all like that? Mortared thinly on one side to save dry time? No. That tricky fucker had left himself a way to get in, then patched the outside to make it look solid. You don't do that for no reason.

Petrosky shimmied the knife into the mortar over the brick to the left, but the mortar there was thicker. Morrison pushed at the first brick. A crack appeared down the left side. Petrosky followed suit on his side until the block was free of the rest of the structure, but there was still no room to get his fingers around it.

"How would he get in there to write?" Morrison said. "The space is too small to even see what you're doing."

Petrosky shoved his knife into the space between the bricks and pried, heart hammering in his ears. It shifted, but nowhere near enough to free it. *Shit*. They were so fucking close. If only he had a sledgehammer.

Morrison stood and positioned one bull shoulder against the table and gripped the top with the other hand.

"What are you—" Petrosky began, but Morrison's face was already reddening, his fingers white against the structure as he heaved his weight against the top row of bricks. Petrosky followed suit, shoving the side with his shoulder until the mass lifted, just enough for Petrosky to get his fingers around the brick and slide it out with a grating sound like an angry rattlesnake.

Morrison grunted and lowered the table.

"Looks like all those gym visits were good for something, surfer boy. We didn't even need the dolly."

Morrison sat beside Petrosky and pulled his phone from his pocket, wiping his brow on his sleeve.

"Who you calling now?"

"Flashlight, boss." He tapped a few buttons and handed Petrosky the phone, which now glowed from the top with a single beam of LED light.

Petrosky set it next to the opening to illuminate the inside and lay on the floor, his belly fat crushing his organs. The concrete dug into his cheek and cooled his fiery forehead. He scooted closer and pressed his face into the opening, the sound of his labored breath raspy in the tiny, hollow space. Above him, the metal rods Morrison described held up the tabletop bricks. Their guy had built himself a structure after all. And he'd left his card behind: a single sheet of paper, reflecting the brilliant white light.

Petrosky jerked a glove from his back pocket, lifted himself onto his elbow and pulled the paper out, disgusted by how much his hand was shaking. The poem was printed in the same block script as the others, the words the deep carmine color of dried blood.

> *Long has paled the sunny sky:*
> *Echoes fade and memories die:*
> *Autumn frosts have slain July.*

Sweat dampened his neck. He handed the note to Morrison and pushed himself to his feet. "Call Graves and get some techs over here. There's a reason this one was special. We need to figure out why."

*I love you Daddy, please...*

*You'll like it. It won't hurt if you just lie still.*

I struggled against him, but he held my wrists tight, his face contorted in a grimace. He pushed closer. I cried out, yanking at my hands, throwing my knees up, gnashing my teeth when he lowered his head.

*No, not again, no, no, no...*

"Hannah, stop."

The voice was not his. *Daddy? No...*

My eyes flew open. Someone was on top of me, pinning my wrists to the mattress. My breath came in ragged gasps.

"Stop." His face swam into focus, nose inches from mine. Dominic.

*He'll help me get away.* I was still trying to hit him. I stilled.

Dominic released my arms and climbed off the bed. His skin glistened under the waning moon that shone through the skylights as he headed for the bathroom.

*Daddy.*

*Dominic.*

I touched my face. It was wet, but my heart was slowing.

*Stop.* It didn't work when Tammy said it, or when I tried to tell myself to knock it off. But somehow, it was different coming from Dominic.

He returned, stretching an arm out to me. "Come on."

"What?" I took his offered hand and let him lead me across the room, around the stairs and into the weight room. A chill brushed my damp shoulders and I shivered. "What time is it?"

"Doesn't matter. Put your shoes on."

"I think they're downstairs."

"I put them here, where they go." He gestured under the bench.

*What the hell?* I tied them quickly.

"Treadmill."

I gaped at him.

"Trust me."

I got on, sleepy muscles protesting.

He stood at the head of the machine and pushed the button. It hummed to life. "Start slow and tell me when you feel warmed up."

I walked, faster, faster, shrugging and rolling the tension from my shoulders as the stiffness in my leg muscles eased.

"Ready?"

I swallowed hard. "Yes."

He punched the button. I ran, breasts flopping all over the place under my tank top. Thank goodness I didn't have torpedo tits or I'd give myself a black eye. Maybe he liked torpedo tits. Maybe that's why he didn't want to touch me. But I couldn't think about it because the track was flying beneath me.

Sweat poured down my back. I gasped for breath.

"Dom… I… maybe—"

"You can do it. Keep going."

*I can't.*

He stared hard at me. I stared back and ran until there was nothing else, nothing but the treadmill and his eyes.

The machine beeped twice and skidded to a halt. My heart thudded in my temples.

"Weights."

"I've… never done… weights before," I panted.

"Good time to learn."

"In the… middle… of the night?"

He shrugged and held out a barbell. "You're stronger than you think."

*Am I?* He kept saying it, so maybe it was true. I took the weight and let him lead me through a set of curls. And another. My muscles shrieked and burned.

"Last ten."

I pushed harder.

"Now squats."

"Dominic, I can't."

"Stop saying that and do it."

I did. One. Another. Ten. Twenty. My jelly legs threatened to buckle.

"Stop," he said, and my muscles seemed to skid to a halt in response to his voice.

"How do you feel?"

"Like a bowl of pudding. And now I want pudding." I rested my face on the glass and saw his eye twitch in the mirror. Saw the smear on the glass from my sweaty face. I peeled my forehead from the mirror and stood. "Sorry, I'll get that later."

He nodded and held out his hand.

*What now?* Much more and I'd pass out.

"Shower. Then bed. I doubt you'll have more dreams."

My dream. I had forgotten all about it.

Under the shower's hot spray, my muscles melted. He stood behind me and soaped my hair. I leaned back against him.

"Turn around." His hand slid over my breasts, down my ribcage, between my legs. Another hand teased my nipple, flicking until it was hard. A fire rose in me, an intense liquid heat that spread through my belly and settled between my legs, pulsing and wanting. So this was passion. Real passion, something I had never experienced, something I had been so worried was just a onetime fluke in Dominic's office. Somewhere inside me, a dam was breaking. His fingers slid into me.

I moaned and turned to him. He lifted me by my thighs and pressed me against the shower wall. The spray from the dual showerheads caressed my hair and sent rivulets of water down my body, awakening the nerves beneath my skin. And then he was inside me, hard but so gentle, so warm, massaging me from the inside. He captured my mouth with his.

I felt. I felt him. I felt everything, every wave crashing over me, every beat of our hearts throbbing in time to my lower body. My insides convulsed, shuddered, released. I screamed his name, over and over again, unable to close my mouth, unable to think.

I didn't feel the shower turn off. I only vaguely felt his hands wrapping a towel around my back, carrying me to the bedroom, laying me on the bed. The cotton felt like silk against my back as he climbed in next to me and stroked the tender nub between my legs. Even in the dark, the colors of the world seemed brighter, each muted shade of gray more vibrant than I remembered. Through the skylight, stars glimmered, dazzling but nearly unrecognizable as if every star I had seen before tonight was a different, duller breed. My eyes prickled in spite of myself.

Dominic stopped touching me and shifted his weight to the side, moving his hand near my shoulder. "Are you crying?"

I wiped my eyes. "I worried that it was just luck or something. At the office."

"Luck?"

"No one has ever made me... well, you know."

He touched my cheek, trailed his fingers down over my neck to my chest and circled my nipple with his thumb. "They've been doing it wrong." He climbed between my legs and slid into me. My hips rose automatically, seeking him.

He put his mouth to my ear and rotated his hips, slowly, sensuously. "Had I known you had this concern, I would have proven it to you before now. I assumed you wanted to get acclimated to your surroundings." His breath was feathery against my earlobe.

He had been waiting for me to be ready. He cared. My feelings mattered. "And today? Now?"

He rose above me and smiled. "I thought it might help."

"Oh, it did." I really did feel okay with him. I wasn't sure exactly what that meant, but it had to mean something.

"I'm glad the shower helped you feel better," he said. "It didn't do anything bad for me, either."

"Well thank goodness for that."

He thrust slowly, deeply, every inch of him exquisite, then faster, more urgently. I flung my legs wide and let him take me, clinging to him, pleasure surging through me until I was sure I would burst. When I could take no more, we fell asleep side by side, my leg hooked over his hip.

---

When Dominic awoke, he was alone in the bed. He sat, listening. Not a sound save for the gentle tapping of rain or sleet against the skylight, a wake-up call far preferable to the muffled crying and swift kick to the groin that had woken him last night. The skirt and blouse he had laid over the chair last night were gone. He climbed from the bed and padded into the weight room. Her face print had been wiped clean.

*Curious.*

A clatter arose downstairs. He followed the noise to the kitchen.

She was standing at the stove with her back to him wearing a pair of flannel pajamas and fluffy yellow socks. The dishwasher stood open, but empty.

Hannah turned as he approached, her cheeks flushed with the heat from the pan, a spiral notebook clutched against her chest. She slid the book onto the counter behind her back, eyes locked on his. "I was making a spinach and mushroom omelet for you. Looks like you're up too early for breakfast in bed."

"Looks like I'm awake too early to pick up the clothing from last night as well."

Alarm flashed across her features. "Sorry I—I like things clean." She looked down as if that were something to be ashamed of—as if the world wouldn't be a better place if everyone picked up their shit.

*More curious.*

"I do too," he said simply.

She grabbed a spatula, cut the omelet in the pan and slid two almost symmetrical halves onto a pair of plates, then put the pan in the sink.

In the dining room the table was already set with orange juice, coffee and sliced melon.

Yes, he could get used to this. Perhaps he'd let her stay forever.

## MONDAY, NOVEMBER 23RD

*It's quiet here.*

An hour from Petrosky's usual domain, far from the brick and mortar of the city, the howling wind lashed against fields of dead grass and grain. While nearby areas were covered with higher-end condos and lakefront housing developments, this town just outside Lapeer had peaked and declined well before his killer had made the trek out here.

The run-down barn was tucked in the back corner of an abandoned wheat field, at the end of a gravel drive. To his right he could make out a trailer park in the distance, though it was too far for anyone to have heard much.

*I'll question them anyway.*

In the middle of a pasture on his other side, an enormous metal chicken loomed, the only thing around that appeared to be in good repair, despite deposits of graying snow on its beak. *Fucking country folk.* Maybe his killer had a sense of humor.

The barn itself was missing boards, like many of the other barns in the area. Through holes in the ceiling, frosty sunlight speckled the straw-covered floor. The air was redolent with damp hay and the iron scent of freshly spilled blood.

The girl was laid out on a wooden table at the back of the barn. Like the other girls, her wrists and ankles were secured by leather restraints which had been fastened to the table legs. Her stomach had been sliced neatly in half, like two sections of a broken heart. The pieces lay on top of her chest, the remnants of her last meal teeming with ants. Jumbled corkscrews of intestine dangled from her belly down onto the sawdust and what might have been the top of an ant's nest below the table—they'd probably been hibernating when they were disturbed by the dripping of warm bodily fluids. The techs bustled around the perimeter of the room, either done with the table or simply avoiding the mess.

"The location is different," Petrosky said finally. "This rural thing isn't his style."

Morrison's face was green. *Rookies.* You never knew when they were going to lose their cool, or their lunch. Here it was probably the bugs, the way Morrison was staring at them.

"Well… yeah, boss, the location is different, but the building is just as dilapidated. And the place itself probably has the same number of people within a two mile radius as those old housing projects. The modus operandi is consistent with the first two as well."

"Modus what?"

"It's Latin. It means—"

"I don't give a fuck what it means, surfer boy. And breathe through your mouth before you throw up."

A winter bird, blue and orange, squalled and fluttered out through a gap in the ceiling above. Petrosky watched the bird disappear into the frigid sky.

"Maybe our killer ran out of places in the city," Morrison said.

*Or he's escalating, broadening his territory.* "They know who the girl is?"

Morrison looked at his notes. "Working girl, same deal. Bianca Everette. Her driver's license was under the table. Not bothering to hide their identities, is he?"

It was a dare, a tease. "This guy's fucking with us," Petrosky said.

"We've got something over here." A tiny wisp of a woman with a tattoo behind her ear and short-cropped platinum blond hair waved a flashlight from the front corner of the barn.

Petrosky headed her way, leaving Morrison by the body.

"What've you got?"

She pointed near the corner where a splintered piece of plywood leaned against the wall. "Behind it. I was dusting above the board and touched it to secure my tape, and—"

Petrosky squinted in the dim light. "Show me."

She pinched a corner of the board and lifted it away from the wall. He peered into the space, past threads of cobweb strung with sawdust. There were marks there, uniform, deliberate.

"Need a bigger light over here!"

The crime tech slid the plywood out of the way.

Morrison shone a thick flashlight beam onto the words, dark brown now, hard to read against the grime. With a blood tracking LED, they'd light up like Christmas.

> *Children yet, the tale to hear,*
> *Eager eye and willing ear,*
> *Lovingly shall nestle near.*

A tech behind him snapped a picture.

"What do you have?" Graves ducked into the barn, boards squeaking under his shoes.

"Poem, in blood, like the others. He's trying to tell us something, but I just can't—"

"ID?"

"Bianca Everette."

"Where's she from?"

"Close to here according to her license."

Graves whipped out his phone, tapped the screen and put it to his ear. "Hernandez? I need you to do a background on a Bianca Everette. Look at newspaper ads in the Lapeer area and anywhere nearby. And I need someone to pull all escort services in a fifty mile radius. Have something for me when I get back." He slid his phone back into his pocket.

Petrosky's muscles vibrated with tension. "What the hell was that about?"

"They're already in front of a computer, Petrosky. Tricky guys. Can crack into anything to get what we need in ten minutes."

"So can my guy, Graves." He gestured to Morrison. Morrison straightened, jaw set.

"It's under control, Petrosky."

214

Rage burned in Petrosky's chest. "This is bullshit."

Graves glowered at him. "If you're so anxious to make yourself useful, go to her house. Find her next of kin. Go talk to her mother. Get us something we can use this time."

Petrosky sucked down three cigarettes in the six miles to the Everette house. He tossed the last butt into a swath of pine trees in the front yard. The house was tiny, maybe eight hundred square feet, with two windows—the one on the left probably for the living room, and the one on the right belonging to a single bedroom, as evidenced by a pillow and a stuffed bear smashed against the inner screen. From the front porch, Petrosky could have reached out and touched either one.

Morrison stood behind him, as irritatingly calm as he'd been on the drive over. Apparently, year-round sunshine made you care less about FBI shitheads. Petrosky breathed through his nose like a bull and fantasized about goring Graves, or at least breaking his jaw. It almost made him forget that he was there to give a mother news that would fuck up her life irreparably. Fast and direct. That was the best way to do it. Coddling wouldn't make a kid any less dead. Still, he felt like a truck was sitting on his chest. *Dammit.*

He knocked.

The front door opened to reveal a woman with papery thin eyelids and a strawberry bun streaked with white. A boy of about four sat on her hip, his thumb in his mouth, his shirt dirty with the remains of breakfast. The wind huffed freezing air at them through the open doorway and the kid buried his face in her neck.

"Donna Everette?" Petrosky said.

"Yes?" Her voice was low, soft, cautious.

He flashed his badge. "Detective Petrosky. We need to speak with you, ma'am."

She blinked rapidly. "Is it… Bianca?"

"It is, ma'am."

She put the boy on the floor. "Go play in the room."

He clung to her leg.

"Gavin, now!"

Gavin let go and scurried away.

They squeezed into the living room with the one window. She sat on a futon behind a large electrical wire spool topped with a plastic bowl of milky Cheerios. No other chairs. Petrosky stood across from her, Morrison in front of the door.

"What happened?" she asked finally.

"We found your daughter this morning in an abandoned barn off of Chickesaw."

"By the hen?"

"Yes."

"Is she—"

*Fast and direct.* "She's dead, ma'am. The local coroner will have you make a positive identification, but her wallet was found with her. I'm sorry."

Everette's face didn't change. "Will I have to go to the courthouse to identify her, or do ya have a picture? I don't have time to be driving all the way to town right now."

No surprise. No sadness. Petrosky clenched his jaw to keep it from dropping.

Morrison pulled out his phone and turned the screen to Petrosky. He'd gotten a shot of just the face—pale and dead, but none of the grisly mess. Petrosky nodded and Morrison handed the phone to Everette.

Her face was impassive. "That's her." She handed the phone back.

"Gramma?" Gavin stood in the doorway, eyes wide. "When's Mama coming home?"

"Get in the room, now! Ain't you got no sense?"

Morrison startled and dropped his phone on the carpet. He bent and wiped it on his shirt before sticking it back in his pocket.

Petrosky watched the boy walk backward into the bedroom and close the door. "I take it you two weren't close?"

"How could anyone be close to that?" Her eyes narrowed. "You shoulda seen the things she did."

Disgusted by her own daughter. His killer would be smart enough to at least act upset, but Petrosky wanted to haul her ass down to the precinct anyway. "But she did live here?"

"Sometimes, when she couldn't find somewhere else. I didn't see her much."

Morrison's pen scratched on his notepad.

"Anything unusual in the last few weeks?" Petrosky asked.

Everette cocked her head as if she had no idea what that sentence meant.

"Any bruises? Mentions of anyone violent? A boyfriend?"

"Oh, she had boyfriends all right, but never for more than an evening. Some of 'em beat her, some didn't, but I don't think she cared as long as she got her money. Not that she ever brought it back here."

"Where did she go when she wasn't here?"

"Hell if I know. She just left."

"What about friends?"

"None that I know of."

Something hit the bedroom door and thunked against the wall.

"Is Gavin her child?"

Everette snorted. "*Her* child. She pushed him out all right, but ain't never bothered with him since."

"She didn't support him, then."

"Nope, she sure didn't. She didn't even know who his father was. Didn't do much of anything except sell her crotch to the highest bidder. I used to hope she'd get smarter, better, but she was just always bad."

"Maybe she was just always desperate."

She glared at him, lips tight.

Petrosky gave her a card. "If you think of anything, ma'am, please give me a call. We need to do everything we can to find the person who did this to her."

Everette crumpled the card in her palm. Petrosky nodded

to Morrison and they let themselves out.

"What was that all about?" Morrison asked as their shoes beat against the frozen earth. "You think she hates her own kid?"

"Don't know, but McCallum suspects that whoever is doing this had a disaster of a childhood. Mommy issues." Not that they could really check. Most abuse went unreported, and even foster homes were a crapshoot when it came to safety.

"Do you think Graves knows—"

"Don't worry about that asshole," Petrosky snapped.

"Boss?"

"Fuck him, Morrison."

"Yeah, boss. Okay. But this is important."

Petrosky yanked the car door open. "What?"

"The poem. It's out of order." Morrison pulled out his phone, tapped it a few times and handed it to Petrosky. "We're missing one verse."

> *Still she haunts me phantom wise,*
> *Alice moving under skies*
> *Never seen by waking eyes.*

Petrosky passed the phone back and slid behind the wheel. "We're not missing a poem. We're missing a body."

## MONDAY, NOVEMBER 23RD

The itch was back. Robert had felt it as a child when he rolled around in the grass under the hanging tree, picturing the bodies dangling precariously above him as verdant blades irritated his skin. But he had not been back there since high school. And this itch was not one he could scratch.

He would have been what she needed. Whatever she needed. And now he couldn't get to her.

Thomas sat on an adjacent bar stool, staring at him like an idiot with dopey eyes in a dopier head. Robert wanted to punch him. Probably would punch him before the night was over.

"What's going on, man? Sounds like the boss has been getting on your case. You need help?" Thomas sucked back his beer, too righteous to wait for an answer before he tended to his own needs. He'd be doing the same thing if Robert hadn't been there at all.

But Thomas's question made him uneasy. Robert needed to slow down, get his head straight. Two in the last week, poor substitutes, but he'd had no choice. It was the only way to release the pressure.

He spent every waking moment obsessing over Hannah. He lost himself in her eyes even as his boss berated him for mistakes on his projects, mistakes he never should have made. He couldn't even recall designing the projects in question, let alone fucking them up.

"I just need to concentrate. Been having some trouble sleeping. Too much coffee."

Lies. He was turning into an animal—growing claws and teeth, almost rabid with desire. He shook with the constant, desperate need to find the next, to take her, to slake his lust, lest he implode before he could beg Hannah to love him, to forgive him.

He had waited too long. Someone else had taken his Hannah.

Thomas raised a finger to order another round. "Maybe the beers will help, eh?"

Robert plastered a smile on his face, the face he needed to have to survive, to fit in. To keep them from knowing. "Perhaps."

"I'm meeting up with Noelle in a little while. You want to join us?"

"On a date?"

"Kinda. We're just going bowling. But you seem a little down, like you could use some company."

So, Thomas wanted to share his woman. Use her, throw her to the lions, watch her squirm. "I'm sure she'd love that."

Thomas grinned.

*Imbecile.*

"Maybe if you show her how charming you are she can hook you up with Hannah. You keep going out with all these other women, but you never see them again. What's not to love about blond hair and tight pants? What'd they do to piss you off?"

The itch. His back crawled with the prickling of a thousand needles. "How do you know that?"

Thomas sipped, swallowed. "Know what?"

"What they look like?"

"I know you. You've got that photo on your desk of some woman."

"Are you crazy? That's my mother."

"Yeah, your mother. They say we all look for someone like our moms."

"Who's 'they'?"

"I dunno. Scientists."

Behind the bar, the television flickered, taunting Robert with laughing newscasters. He looked away, heart hammering, half expecting Thomas to turn on him after some prim news anchor flashed his photo with a list of his sins laid bare for the world to see. And if Thomas saw his picture and was warned, Hannah would also see his face staring at her, telling her to stay far, far away from him.

He needed her more than ever. He could not lose her.

The thorny sensation on his back subsided. Perhaps if he found his way to someone close to her, someone she loved more than her abominable ex-boyfriend, he had a chance. He would be careful. Very careful. His efforts had not been tenacious enough, methodical enough. She had not been hurt enough to fall into his arms. She'd need to hurt in order to see. It was the only way she would find her way to him.

"Bowling sounds fun," he said.

She'd hurt. He could make it hurt.

And then she would be his.

## TUESDAY, NOVEMBER 24TH

Icicles seeped from the metal table through the thin gown I wore. I shivered, wrapping my arms around my exposed abdomen. The child would be cold too, if I didn't leave.

A woman walked in rolling an expensive-looking ultrasound machine, her eyes bright with animosity. An elaborate array of blue, green and yellow cables sprang from the front of the machine, and next to it sat a television monitor and a white cord attached to a small paddle.

The woman grabbed a tube of bluish jelly and squeezed a frigid glob onto my abdomen. "Watch the screen." She shoved the wand against my belly. I bit my lip and tried not to shrink from her piercing stare.

"There's the heartbeat," she said, not even trying to hide the disdain in her voice. "Still beating right now."

*Please… please stop.*

"Here's her head… her feet."

The world was closing in. "Her?"

The woman kept her eyes on the screen. "Sure you want to go through with this? You can still change your mind. There are other options."

*Want to*? I *had* to. And I had to do it now before it was too late.

Through a veil of tears, I nodded. "I'm sure." I was prone, captive, and totally vulnerable. And I was nothing to her.

The woman thrust the wand back into its holder on the machine and started for the door. "The doctor will be in shortly. God bless that poor child." She made the sign of the cross and softly closed the door behind her.

I didn't notice the doctor entering, but suddenly, there she was, only a jet black ponytail visible between my knees. I stared at the ceiling, removing myself from the pain as I had so many times in the past. When I couldn't pretend any longer, I let the tears fall, soaking my hair with salt.

One final surge of suction, and I heard a familiar voice: "All done."

I watched in horror as the doctor stood, but it wasn't the doctor anymore. It was *him*, holding the tiny child, my child, by the leg, its face grotesque and bloodied, its scrawny arms and legs flailing against my father's wrist. He wrenched the child's head, snapping her neck bones in one fluid motion. He laughed, and it echoed through the room, inside my head, even when his mouth stopped moving.

I scrambled backwards on the table.

"You thought you'd get away from me that easily, did you? You will always be a part of me." My father lunged toward me, extending the mangled infant slick with my blood. "We're a family now, Hannah. Take her, love her the way I loved you." The child's skin brushed my face. Cold, so cold.

I screamed and bolted upright, shivering from fear and the cold sweat that soaked my T-shirt. My hand settled on my flat abdomen. *A dream. Just a dream.* Just another shitty night to write about in my notebook.

I felt his gaze on me before I saw him, seated in a leather chair in the corner, obscured by shadow. The nightmares were surely too frequent for him to ignore. How often had I woken him up in the last week?

I crossed the room and settled awkwardly on the arm of the chair. "Sorry."

He shrugged, his face impassive.

"Did I wake you?"

"Yes," he said, like he had just agreed to a bologna sandwich. Did he not care about being awake or did he not care about… me?

*I'm going to lose him.* Spoors of panic took root in my chest and multiplied, crushing my lungs and ribs. It had been acceptable for Jake to think I was a little nuts—he had been a jerk either way. But, Dominic was genuinely kind. And he

223

actually cared. I didn't want to push him away by keeping things from him.

*So tell him.*

*Is damaged better than crazy?*

I stared at the floor, the words rushing out before I could stop them. "About five years ago, I ran away from home. My father… he… I was pregnant with his child. I aborted. I had no idea what else to do."

"And you wish you had done it differently?" His voice was neutral, serene even. He was probably relieved that he had a good reason to kick me out.

"No." My voice cracked.

"Deciding not to carry an infant you know you can't feed seems perfectly rational. What were the other options? Force the child and yourself into a life of poverty? And for what? If anything, you did everyone a favor, including that incest-derived embryo whose mere presence would have served as a constant reminder to you of all that is wrong with the world." He stood and took my face in his hands. "Would you like something to drink?"

I stared at him. "Uh… sure."

"I'll be right back."

I barely noticed him leave the room. Had he really just said that the things I'd spent a lifetime hiding were… acceptable? I must have misunderstood.

"Here you go." He was back already, handing me a glass. "Orange juice. I thought you could use the vitamin C. With all that worrying, you're going to end up sick."

Was I dreaming now? *He doesn't hate me?* I sipped, despite my lurching stomach. Sweet, with a slight bitter tang of peel—probably fresh squeezed. The good stuff.

He looked at me, almost expectantly, but I wasn't sure what he wanted me to say.

I lowered the cup. "I'm sorry."

"For what? Everyone has a past. Children have only so much control."

My stomach churned, hot with shame. "I mean… it's a lot

to take in. I've never told anyone. And I wasn't a child when I had the abortion." I waited for him to say something, anything, but he just squeezed my hand and watched me. "Don't you feel anything about all this?"

He shrugged. "Not really."

And when I searched his eyes, I saw no disgust, no anger. He understood. Calm, pure and blue, ran through my abdomen where stabbing anxiety had held me prisoner for so long.

*He doesn't hate me. He doesn't think I'm a terrible person.*

He led me to the bed. I lay there, wrapped in his arms and let the tears fall as years of pain melted into acceptance.

As I fell into sleep, I wondered how I had gotten so lucky.

*It's time.*

Robert stood at the bottom of the bed. The whip unfurled at his side, dangling over his shoulders like the cross he bore, the leather warming with his body heat. His knee squeaked against the plastic mattress cover. He jerked his wrist and a noise like a firecracker reverberated through the room.

She screamed, but all that came out was a muffled whine. *Pathetic.* Handcuffs clanked against the metal headboard. He cracked the whip again and shook his head in disapproval. She stopped moving, her face a mask of fear behind the duct tape that held her lips together.

*She knows. And she hates me for it.* The knowledge of his exposure swarmed his brain like a cloud of locusts, gnawing away at his self-control.

They all knew. Except one. Except *her.*

*And she's with* him.

He brought the whip down against the whore's ribcage. She flexed and moaned. *Crack*! *Crack*! Slices appeared in the shaved skin at the apex of her thighs.

The fear in her eyes drew out his own.

*I'm a marked soul, every mistake inscribed on my face. But love can erase it all. Love can save me.*

He needed Hannah. And soon.

His heart rate accelerated. He cracked the whip harder and watched a long line of blood weep from beneath pale ivory as skin gave way. She wheezed a ragged sigh through her nose.

He brought the implement down, again and again, crosshatching the skin of her thighs, her breasts, with oozing red.

She would bear the marks too.

Satisfied, he tossed the whip aside and climbed between her legs, positioning his face above hers. Pancake makeup dripped down her face on beads of sweat.

*Look at me, bitch.*

She did, as if she could hear his thoughts.

He ripped the tape from her mouth and thrust into her roughly, feeling the resistance that she couldn't will away, even for the money he was giving her.

Pinpricks of crimson on her lips grew until the blood trickled down her chin.

"Please, stop—"

"Close your fucking mouth."

"But—"

Robert only wanted the words of one woman. *I forgive you, Robert. It's okay, Robert. I love you.*

"Please—" Her voice was nasal and petulant and vile. And she was not Hannah.

He backhanded her, the sting on his hand and the clack of her teeth offering some comfort, some consolation, though not enough.

"Anything else?" he said.

She stared at the wall.

Robert squinted, blurring his vision so her thin face dripped away like a Dali painting, oozing, shifting, reforming, solidifying. *Hannah.* Dark hair swirled around her lovely face, the green of her eyes pulling him into her.

She smiled at him. *I forgive you.*

He moved his hips faster, with renewed passion.

*I can take the pain away. I can help you.*

Over and over he thrust, feeling *her*, smelling *her*. When she moaned louder, the screams were Hannah's as he brought her to the peaks of passion with him, rewarding her for saving him, for loving him, for releasing him from a lifetime of dread.

Shaking, he wiped tears from his eyes with the back of his hand. His knuckles burned. The whore's sweat and blood clung to his skin.

He climbed from the bed and left the room, careful not to look at her. He did not want the reminder that *she* was not there with him.

"Soon," he whispered.

She'd be with him soon enough.

"They froze me out." Petrosky resisted the urge to kick McCallum's desk.

"I heard. How did that make you feel?"

"You know how the fuck I feel about it. They didn't even call me. Just went out there themselves and ran the scene." From what he'd heard, Alice Putrus had been found under a manhole cover, her stomach torn open, a dog gnawing on her bloody shirt. She'd been there for a few days, definitely killed before Everette. And his guy had done his homework—there was no way her name was a coincidence.

"Where's Morrison?"

"Getting what he can from the brass. Or from his workout buddies."

"He's better with people, isn't he?"

"Doesn't take much to beat me at people pleasing."

"There's some truth to that."

"How insightful. Some shrink you are." He paused. "I'm going to solve this fucker."

"That's why you're here?"

"Yes."

The doctor raised an eyebrow. "No other reason?"

"Goddammit, McCallum, knock it off. This isn't about me. This guy is good. Meticulous. He might not be the best at dissection, but he's certainly the best at getting in and out of there clean. Even used a rake to obliterate his footprints in that Lapeer field."

"So we're left with what?"

"The type of victim. The poems." The poems bothered him more than he cared to admit. Especially Campbell's. Had their killer hidden the poem on purpose to throw doubt on his identity? If that was the case, why write it at all? Maybe he was messing with their minds. Or maybe it was as simple as them missing the fact that they could move that brick.

"The other poems were hidden too, but not nearly as well," Petrosky said. "I mean, he actually risked bringing a large piece of equipment in to lift the cement and hide the paper. He used different restraints, too. There has to be something special about that killing."

McCallum nodded. "I agree, though the reason it matters might not be as deep as you think. Have you found anything to indicate that Campbell knew any of the other victims?"

"No."

*Just her.*

"McCallum tapped his pen against his desk. "If he hadn't gone right back to the old pattern, I would say it was a sign of escalation; a game. But he just picked up where he left off, though he's clearly accelerating his pace."

Petrosky resisted the urge to grab the pen and hurl it across the room. The dull throbbing in his temples was turning into a full-blown ache.

"Anyway," McCallum continued, "the similarity in the victims before and after continues to scream past slight. I would bet that Campbell's death was for another reason. Either he knew something he wasn't supposed to, or he was getting in the way somehow."

Petrosky gritted his teeth. "How would he get in the way? He never did anything! He didn't work and hardly left the apartment except to walk down the street to get cigarettes. He didn't even have a car to get close to any of the places the killings occurred."

McCallum shrugged. "Maybe he had something the killer wanted."

"We've considered the money route, but the only people who would have benefitted are his ex-girlfriend and her son. They have alibis."

"Plus, one of them is five." *Tap. Tap.*

*Joke it up, asshole.* Petrosky clenched his fist to avoid

229

shoving the pen through the doctor's twinkling eye.

"Money isn't everything. Your killer had something to gain by Campbell dying." *Tap, tap, tap.* "Figure out what it is and you'll be one step closer to solving this case."

"I'm doing my best." Petrosky stood.

"Where are you off to?"

"Staff meeting." He pulled his coat off the back of the chair and hauled it on, one of his shoulders creaking in protest. "Might as well make an appearance before Graves tries to throw me off the case altogether."

"You and I both know that wouldn't stop you, Ed."

"Yeah, probably not. But it'd sure make getting into the donuts more difficult."


Morrison was already in the conference room. Petrosky sat next to him and swallowed bitter precinct coffee, casting envious glances at Morrison's stainless steel mug. He always brought the best joe from home. In the front of the room, someone had transferred the victims' photos to an oversized cork board, neon green sticky notes tacked beneath each picture, connections between victims outlined in thread. Next to the cork board, the original white board listed their victims:

*Meredith Lawrence: October 1st*
*A boat beneath a sunny sky*
*Lingering onward dreamily*
*In an evening in July-*

*Jane Trazowski, October 11*
*Children three that nestle near,*
*Eager eye and willing ear*
*Pleased a simple tale to hear—*

*Jacob Campbell: November 3*
*Long has paled the sunny sky:*
*Echoes fade and memories die:*
*Autumn frosts have slain July.*

*Alice Putrus: November 18*
*Still she haunts me phantom wise,*
*Alice moving under skies*
*Never seen by waking eyes.*

*Bianca Everette: November 22*
*Children yet, the tale to hear,*
*Eager eye and willing ear,*
*Lovingly shall nestle near.*

Graves stood at the front of the conference room, his eyes much too cool for the occasion. *Prick*.

"As most of you know, Alice Putrus was discovered this morning on the eastside, hidden under a manhole," Graves said. "Preliminary data indicates that she died around November eighteenth. Our killer is moving faster. That means more chances he'll make a mistake."

Graves looked out the window as if he expected to see the killer grinning up at him from the parking lot, holding a dead hooker and waving a bloody Q-tip. But their killer wasn't going to trip himself up. Not this guy. Petrosky pushed his coffee away as his stomach soured.

Graves turned back to the boards and pointed at Campbell's picture. "At the Campbell crime scene, a note was recently found underneath the table. It appears to have been placed there using a dolly to lift the blocks after the killing. Like the others, it was written in the victim's blood."

Petrosky bristled. *Was recently found*. No recognition for his discovery, not even a nod in his direction. Looked like Graves didn't want everyone to know his guys were goddamn useless.

"Why it was hidden is still uncertain. He may have been trying to lure authorities into thinking we had a copycat, at least until the writing was discovered. The different restraints may have been a part of this. Officers are looking into the November second press leak, in the off chance the information was leaked by our suspect to encourage the confusion."

*The off chance.* It wasn't an off chance. The killer was fucking with them. Bloody words smeared themselves across Petrosky's brain. There was a reason for everything. There was a reason for Campbell. And if there was a reason for Campbell—

*She's in danger.* It was a gut feeling he couldn't shake.

*Maybe she knows more than she thinks.*

*Don't focus on her or you'll blow the whole thing.*

Graves was still talking but Petrosky was no longer listening.

*One last visit can't hurt.*


Hannah sat waiting for him at the picnic table, her face as placid as the glass pond. He crunched toward her over frost-streaked grass and the occasional frozen leaf.

"Ms. Montgomery."

"Detective Petrosky."

He stopped walking, his back stiffening, but not with cold. Her squared shoulders and erect posture were a far cry from the skittish demeanor she'd had at the shelter. Something was different. *She* was different.

He sat across from her, tense and wary.

"What did you need to see me about? Did something else happen?"

He shook his head and watched her, gauging her reaction. Her features stayed even. Detachment, maybe? Had everything become too much to bear? "I understand you've been cooperative with the FBI, answering their questions about the other victims. I thank you for that."

She nodded. Not speechless, not nervous, just matter-of-fact.

Muscles along the back of his neck tightened and cramped. "We have recently come across new information. I was wondering if you might have some insight."

"I'll help any way I can." She looked him straight in the

eye, not past him or at the lake like she had before.

"What I am showing you has to remain confidential."

"Of course."

He pulled out the list of poems, watching her face for a hint of recognition or understanding. "Do these words mean anything to you?"

She took the page, scanned it, and met his eyes again. "No."

Not a single anxious twitch.

"Are you sure?"

"Positive."

He appraised the calm of her face, the evenness of her mouth. "If you happen to think of anything else—"

"I'll call you."

Maybe she didn't need help after all.

He felt her eyes on his back as he walked away. Her boyfriend was gone, but as both LaPorte and Plumber the apartment manager had said, she certainly didn't seem worse off having lost him.

---

The very air I breathed was different, lighter somehow, as if a suffocating fog that had always been wrapped around my face had suddenly lifted. Even the snow on the pond seemed to sparkle through the detective's questions about a poem. A poem he insisted was connected to the killings. My father didn't know anything about poetry, but that wasn't what made my heart soar.

It was all because of Dominic. He knew my secrets now, and he still accepted each and every part of me, even the parts I had once thought appalling. I felt like a whole new person.

*A better person.*

I practically floated to the filing room to finish up a few things before our monthly staff meeting. If I could find a way to float to the meeting, Dominic and I could giggle all night about the shocked looks from his other employees. *Oh no*!

*It's a ghost!* In my current state, I'd make the least terrifying apparition ever. Which was kind of okay.

Noelle crouched by the bottom file drawer and squeezed a folder into place. "Morning!"

A twinge of guilt pricked my stomach. I'd been awful to suspect her, to avoid her the way I had. But that was in the past. It was all in the past.

"You getting a jump on the filing, too?" I asked.

"Yeah, I want to make sure I get out of here on time tonight. Got a hot date." She closed the drawer.

"With Thomas?"

"Yep." Her cheeks flushed. "Though I must admit, I don't usually let myself get carried away like this."

I knew what she meant. It was both exhilarating and terrifying when a guy could make you feel drunk and giddy at the mere thought of him. I opened my mouth to tell her how I felt about Dominic, how fast I'd gone from a crush to adoration, but there was no way Noelle would trust my judgment about relationships—after all, I had chosen Jake and professed my love for him even when he was causing me pain. "Looks like you're falling for Thomas," I said instead.

"Yeah, I know." Noelle squinted at me. "Hey you've got something on your—" She gestured to my chest.

I looked down and brushed off a few dark hairs. "Duke, Dominic's dog. He's almost always just wandering around the backyard, but we were wrestling this morning before work." I closed the drawer and it latched with a soft *click*.

"Quite the happy family over there, aren't you?"

"It could be worse." *She had no idea.*

Noelle stared past me at the wall. "Yeah, it could definitely be worse," she muttered.

We both turned as Ralph entered through the open door. Noelle coughed and slid past him out into the hallway. He watched her go, shoulders slumped.

Ralph always looked so… hurt. Sad. Maybe I could talk to her about making amends with Ralph. Maybe she'd trust me about him. No one could say I didn't understand what it

234

was like to be hurt.

I followed Noelle, trying to ignore the tightness in Ralph's eyes as I passed him. Looked like he wasn't taking nearly enough Xanax.

By the time our staff meeting was over, I had almost forgotten about Ralph and his agitated gaze. Perhaps it was the conference table loaded with coffee and pastries. Maybe it was the banner behind the podium that demanded *Imagine!* in rainbow colors. Or maybe there was simply nothing as relaxing as listening to your supervisors drone on about teamwork for an hour.

*Well... almost nothing.*

The phone on my desk was ringing when we got back to the office. I raced over and snatched up the receiver, glad my hands had finally steadied.

"Harwick Technologies, Human Resources, this is Hannah," I said in the higher pitch that I hoped screamed customer service.

"Good afternoon." Even on the phone his mellow baritone gave me chills.

"What are you doing calling me at work? My boss will be terribly irritated." I couldn't keep the amusement out of my voice. I hoped he could hear it.

Dominic laughed on the other end of the line. "I won't keep you. I just wanted to know if you were free Saturday evening. I have tickets to the symphony downtown. I thought we could go to La Roseo right down the street first."

"I would love to. But... I'm not sure about the symphony."

He was silent for a moment. "Do you have other plans? Maybe another kitchen reorganization?"

"I thought you liked my mad organizing skills!" I wondered if anyone else in the office could feel my happiness radiating out at them, tickling their backs.

"I do. Just don't organize my man cave."

I rolled my eyes. Only Dominic would refer to a workout

room that way. "I wouldn't dream of it. I just don't have anything to wear to the symphony."

"That is not a problem. We'll go shopping first. Maybe hit the salon. On me."

Shopping? The salon? I usually trimmed my dead ends in the sink. "That's... I mean, I don't want you to have to pay to dress me." Even as I said it, my uncertainty dissolved.

"Trust me, dressing you would be my pleasure."

*I'm sure you'd enjoy undressing me more.*

"Do we have a date?" he asked.

I had a choice. I had control. And he cared about me. Maybe. Probably. My heart was as full as those jelly donuts. "It's a date," I said.

"Good. And I'll meet you out front at five-thirty. I'm making dinner tonight, so don't be late. You've done enough cooking this week."

I smiled into the phone. "I don't mind."

"Neither do I. And I'm pretty good at it, if I do say so myself."


He wasn't lying about being able to cook. The smell of warm butter and garlic permeated the air as I entered the kitchen later that evening. Dominic was putting the finishing touches on two plates.

"What's all this?"

"Pan seared duck with rosemary, roasted potatoes and caramelized beets with green salad."

I watched, high on endorphins from an hour on the treadmill, my hair still wet from my shower. A spark of apprehension twittered in my chest. I was falling too fast. We had not known each other long enough. But I couldn't help it; I was completely and totally smitten, and all he was doing at that moment was spooning potatoes onto a plate. He hadn't even minded when I set up Romeo, my new philodendron, in the kitchen and accidentally smashed his crystal vase. "These things happen," he had said.

"It looks amazing," I told him.

He put a sprig of parsley on top of the potatoes. "I hope it tastes amazing. I spent an hour on it."

"Sounds like someone needs a hobby."

He abandoned the plates and wrapped his arms around me. "I have one now."

We ate by candlelight in the dining room, each bite more delicious than the last. When I could eat no more, I sat back and stretched, yawning.

"You sure you're okay?" He laid his fork beside his plate.

"Just a little tired."

"I'll make sure you sleep well tonight."

"I bet you say that to all the ladies."

"I am an expert in putting women to sleep. It's my electric wit." He smiled around his glass of sparkling water.

"Or… this." I raised my foot under the table and rubbed my bare toes against his crotch.

"Just what every man wants to hear. 'Darling, your penis puts me right to sleep.'"

"The sleep is just a happy byproduct. And what woman doesn't love a nap?"

"I think we can do better than napping. And I don't need to use my penis to relax you." He stood. "I want to show you something."

"I'll bet you do."

"No, not that, though I'm sure I could be persuaded later." He led me through the living room, past the right archway and opened a large wooden door that I had assumed was a closet.

I followed him inside the room and gasped. It was humongous, like every other room in the house, but it felt like another planet: cozy in spite of its size, and rich and majestic like an old library. Wait… it *was* a library, the entire back wall covered by floor-to-ceiling bookshelves. The other walls were paneled with deep wooden planks each about a foot across, their rough surfaces dull despite the stain. I ran my hand over the surface and feathery splinters pricked my palm.

"The wood came from a turn of the century barn that was

on my father's property," he said. "The people who wanted to buy the house after he died were going to demolish it."

"It's… beautiful. All of it." I glanced to our right at two perpendicular leather couches. Between them sat a coffee table fashioned from an enormous piece of driftwood topped with a carved chess set, the pieces arranged haphazardly on the top.

"You play chess?" I asked.

"No."

"But—"

"It was my mother's."

"Sorry. It looked like you were in the middle of a game."

"We were. That was the last move she made." He touched a pawn. "I was six. Cancer. My father died of cancer also, just a few years ago. He went quickly, in line with his wishes. He believed that pain was not an acceptable end to a life well-lived."

"Dominic, I'm so—"

He continued as if he hadn't heard me. "My mother loved chess because it was full of possibilities. The plays themselves may not fall the way you think they will, but they always work out the way they should, especially if you're paying attention." He straightened. "I've always thought that this still board is like a version of the end in and of itself. No one else will ever play on it, but all the pieces are where they should be if you just accept them."

Acceptance. Healing. His parents had taught him well. And now he was teaching me.

He walked to the bookcases that covered the back wall and pulled a book off a shelf. "How do you feel about Rabindranath Tagore?"

I raised my eyebrows. "Who the what now?"

He smiled and sat with me on the couch. I relaxed into his chest, feeling his heart as if it were mine, matching his breath, inhaling the earthy scent of good leather and wood.

His voice vibrated through me as he read:

"I seem to have loved you in numberless forms, numberless times...
In life after life, in age after age, forever.
My spellbound heart has made and remade the necklace of songs,
That you take as a gift, wear round your neck in your many forms,
In life after life, in age after age, forever..."
*He loves me. He'll protect me.*My breathing deepened.
"You and I have floated here on the stream that brings from the fount.
At the heart of time, love of one for another.
We have played alongside millions of lovers, shared in the same
Shy sweetness of meeting, the same distressful tears of farewell-
Old love but in shapes that renew and renew forever."
I closed my eyes, hoping against all hope that I could stay here forever, relishing the heavy peace that had finally, finally settled in my chest.
*I love you.* I allowed sleep to envelop me before I could dare to say it out loud.

## THURSDAY, NOVEMBER 26TH

Timmy sat on the ground behind a huge tree stump, the only one on the dark, abandoned playground. He ran his finger over initials someone had cut into the wood and peered into the night. The tree shouldn't have been there, surrounded by concrete.

He shouldn't be there either.

He leaned against the trunk while his mother finished her business behind the wall to the side of the old school playground. If only the school behind him was still full of students, with other kids just like him. He would go every day if he could. He pictured walking to school, hair spiked and gelled, backpack slung over one shoulder the way the cool kids did it on television.

*Hey, Timmy!* they would call, smiling at him as he walked by.

*Want to come over tomorrow?* they would ask.

He covered his ears in case she made any noises—he always felt dirty for even hearing them. And he wouldn't need to listen for her calling him. She had given him the same old speech: "I'll be right back, honey, okay? Don't talk to anyone and don't move. I'll come back for you when we have enough for groceries."

He crossed his legs on the frozen ground like the good boy he was.

*Hey, Tim! Will you play with me at recess?*

*Hey, Tim, let's swing together!*

He took his hands off his head. It was suddenly quiet—too quiet. A chill ran through the puffy coat he wore. He grabbed the blanket his mother had left with him, climbed to his feet and cocked his head, listening.

Nothing but the wind.

"Mom?" he called softly. Maybe she was finished working and was waiting for him. His stomach grumbled. He was ready to go too.

He squinted into the blackness.

"Mom?" he called, a little louder. His heart beat faster as he took a few sneaky steps, knowing he wasn't supposed to bother her while she was working. The wind whistled around him, bit at his numb hands and froze the tip of his nose. The building loomed above him.

She wasn't done, or she would have come to get him. They probably went in to get out of the cold, he thought, congratulating himself on solving the puzzle. He braced himself against the bitter wind and crept toward the old school to warm up while he waited. If he was quiet, they would never even know he was there.

## THURSDAY, NOVEMBER 26TH

He had strapped her down on an old cafeteria table. Though convenient this time, it wasn't his favorite type of work surface; the metal grooves in the table collected the gore and made everything slippery. Not that she'd minded. Or even noticed.

He watched the cockroach wriggle inside the sheath of her stomach, its legs twitching as it fought to survive in her meager juices. Even after thirty minutes and twelve seconds, the bug still lived.

*These fuckers will outlast us all.* He touched it with the point of the scalpel and the bug writhed away from him, perhaps alarmed.

*Creak.*

He turned around. A blanket dropped to the floor as the boy hiding behind it stared, open-mouthed, brown eyes wide.

"Momma?"

In two strides he was upon the child, slicing through fascia and muscle along the front of the boy's throat. The hole in the child's neck gurgled, a last attempt to suck air though a severed windpipe. A waterfall of life spurted down the child's jacket. Then the eyes closed and the boy collapsed backwards. A tear drop peeked from under one dead lid like a single cell trying to escape demise.

He removed the boy's jacket, tossed it aside and carried him to the table. The cockroach stuck in the woman's body was still struggling, but slower, sluggish. Perhaps the boy's stomach acid would be more robust, paralyzing the bug in moments if he were to place it directly into the child's gut.

He glanced at his watch. *No time.* But there was always another boy, another day.

He arranged the child on top of the woman, snuggling his lower half among her disordered intestines as if she were trying to pull him into the gaping hole.

*Back from whence you came.*

He positioned the boy's head on her chest, between the two abominable bluebird tattoos near the front of her shoulders. The birds appeared to be flying headlong into the child's hair.

He dropped the bloody scalpel into a plastic bag, an inconvenience but a necessary one. The police would be getting closer now.

The wind howled through the silent building. He dipped a latexed finger into the gore that had settled in the metal grooves on the table top and scrawled bloody calligraphy along the bench.

> *In a Wonderland they lie,*
> *Dreaming as the days go by,*
> *Dreaming as the summers die:*

His work complete, he walked out listening to the wind singing an eerie lullaby to the boy nestled peacefully in his mother's final embrace.

I cut another slice of turkey for the women in the shelter dining room and grinned at the plates like a sappy idiot. Apparently, nothing made me giddy like a good night's rest and a morning eating Dominic's leftover turkey, mashed potatoes, and pie.

Pie made everything more awesome. And the way Dominic had woken me up wasn't half bad either.

I flushed and glanced at Ms. LaPorte, who was faring less well. She slumped and shuffled, head hung low as she slopped potatoes on the plates, like someone had sucked all the energy from her bones. Holidays did that to you. I didn't usually make coffee this late in the afternoon, but there might not be a choice if I wanted her to make it through dinner.

"Are you okay?" I set the last plate down and laid my hand on her arm.

She turned to me, her eyes watery and bloodshot.

*Oh shit.*

"I knew she had some trouble, but that boy… that poor boy." She wiped a tear with the back of her hand.

My chest, my throat, everything constricted. Another murder? "Ms. LaPorte? What happened?" Please let it be something else. *Anything else.*

Her eyes widened. "Hannah, have you not been watching the news?"

My mouth was too dry to speak. I'd been avoiding the news, avoiding all the sadness and the hurt out there.

"Do you remember Antoinette? Her little boy Tim?"

Ms. LaPorte grabbed my hands as realization sank into my stomach like a knife. I shook my head in disbelief.

"Hannah, I know you've been through a lot lately. If you

don't want to know—"

"Please… what happened?" My voice had gone shrill and my heart was hammering so loudly I worried I might not be able to hear her. I gripped her hands to steady myself but it didn't stop the trembling in my legs.

She leaned close to me. "Someone came here this morning, looking for Tim after he missed a visit with his social worker. They were only here for a few minutes. And then we heard the sirens at the school across the street, and I looked out the window—" she choked back a sob. "It was just horrible. Those black bags…"

I shivered. Cold. I was so cold.

*He's a good kid.*

*Momma can I have another hot dog?*

I sucked air through my nose, my mouth, but there wasn't enough oxygen in the room.

*That poor kid.*

I let go of Ms. LaPorte, grabbed the serving dishes from the counter, and retreated to the sink.

Ms. LaPorte followed me. "You look a little pale, dear. Maybe you should take off." She blew her nose on a paper towel.

I shook my head. "No, I want to be here. To help you. I… just can't believe it."

"Me either, dear. And to think all these killings have something to do with girls from our shelter."

"Did the police say that?" My voice was hoarse. My nerves vibrated.

*Dominic will protect me.*

"No, but they implied it. Told me to watch out here. Be careful leaving."

*This has nothing to do with me. Nothing at all. It's just a terrible coincidence. But—*

I couldn't be here. But I had to be here. Maybe I'd take Dominic up on that private bodyguard thing.

"I think we need to shut our doors for a few weeks," Ms. LaPorte said.

"You're sure?" *Thank goodness.*

She held up a hand. "I know; they need us. But if someone is taking these women from here, like the police seem to think, I don't want to put them in harm's way. I already told Brandy she could stay with me for the time being."

Relief. Guilt at the relief. I nodded, mute.

"Will you be okay, Hannah?"

"Yeah, I just need... I don't know what I need." A baseball bat. A place to hide. Something to whack a killer in the balls. *I need to call Dominic.*

⁘⸺⸺⸺

Petrosky grabbed an antacid from the roll on his desk and chewed it slowly. His hands shook. It was probably from too much coffee. He worried it was from not enough booze.

Another one from the shelter. The scene had been horrific, but the aftermath was making him even more anxious than standing in that empty school cafeteria, the tinny scent of blood and human waste hanging in the air like thick perfume.

*And that kid—*

He ground his teeth. She had been another hooker, one that fit the victim profile to a T. But this time, there had been two victims. At least this time he had found out about the scene before the bodies were put in bags.

Ms. Montgomery would be frightened; she had been scared the first time. And maybe she should be.

Petrosky slammed his desk drawer closed and walked down the hall to the conference room. Graves stood looking out the window, still apparently waiting for their killer to come to them. Outside, snowflakes melted to slush in the salted parking lot.

"Sir?"

Graves turned.

"I have a bad feeling about this one."

"A bad feeling about a dead woman and her kid, huh? Go figure."

Petrosky could feel the irritation building in the pit of his stomach. "Is there any way to increase the presence around Ms. Montgomery?"

"We've already surveilled her, and she's alibied on the nights in question. We don't have the manpower to keep following a suspect who we know isn't one."

Petrosky frowned. "I'm more concerned that she's a target."

"I doubt that. And anyways"—Graves shook his head—"we've already freaked her out enough."

*What the fuck?* Petrosky raised his eyebrows.

"One of your officers decided to go rogue and search her car while she was at work. She saw him, but—" Graves sighed. "We don't need the illegal actions of one force member compromising the integrity of the entire case." His eye twitched.

*Liar.* It had probably been one of Graves's agents who'd broken into her car. Maybe Graves had even put the guy up to it.

"Dammit, we have to do *something!* What about the poems? There's only one more verse."

"We have nothing to indicate that Ms. Montgomery is in danger at all. If anything, she's an unlikely target: employed, no children, no history of drug use or prostitution. Yes, half of the victims happened to spend time at the shelter she volunteers at, but there aren't that many domestic violence shelters around. And the other victims frequented shelters that are completely unconnected to her."

"What about her boyfriend?"

"Maybe Campbell's secret fuck buddy was one of the other victims and he knew something about her killer. We've got men on it now." Graves's jaw was set. "We just can't afford any more bad publicity on this."

"Wouldn't it be worse publicity if she dies?"

Footsteps approached. Graves broke eye contact and nodded to someone behind Petrosky.

Petrosky's phone buzzed in his pocket.

"Paulson, expand the library record searches on that book to cover fifty more miles. It's a stretch, but this guy likes to play. I want every copy back here and checked for markings, notes, anything. Then take a partner and see if you can find any links to other women's shelters."

Graves was grasping at straws. Wasting time. Petrosky's phone buzzed again.

"Yes, sir," Paulson said.

No one acknowledged Petrosky as he walked out and mashed his phone to his ear. "Petrosky," he snapped.

"It's Shannon."

"What are you doing working the day after Thanksgiving?"

"Why, is it a holiday or something?"

"Not around here." Petrosky glanced back toward the conference room door but no one emerged. Graves and Paulson were probably both staring at the parking lot like a couple of fuck sticks. "So what'd I do this time, Taylor?"

"Nothing."

"How'd you get this number?"

"Morrison."

"You calling my rookie in your off hours?"

"That's not your business, Petrosky. What *is* your business is the tip I'm about to give you on your serial."

Petrosky accelerated his pace down the hall. "I'm sure you heard the Feds are on it now, Taylor," he said. "Why'd you call me instead of Graves?"

The phone crackled. "Everyone over here has been pretty pissed about how it was handled. And Graves is a piece of work in his own right. I heard two of his last three cases were solved at the expense of some uncooperative witnesses who turned at the last minute, testifying with information that put them in danger one way or another. Pretty convenient, if you ask me."

Pretty convenient, indeed. Maybe those witnesses had even had someone break into their car.

"Either way, I trust you. I might have to call him

248

eventually but I can plead busy for a few more hours. Actually, fuck it, you tell him if you want him to know."

Petrosky entered the bullpen and yanked a pad of paper from his desk. "Hang on." He ignored Morrison's raised brow across the aisle and dropped into the chair. "Okay, I'm listening."

"Got a colleague prosecuting a Xavier Kroll, K-R-O-L-L, heroin addict, small-time crook. Kroll apparently knew Antoinette and Timothy Michaels. Says he lived with a woman who was friends with Antoinette's mother."

Petrosky scrawled the name. "Interesting."

"Kroll says Antoinette lived at his girlfriend's house with the kid. Off and on, never for longer than a few months, but she was there recently. I doubt you'll see that address on any forms."

"Where's it at?"

"Chapman. 4587." She paused. "The guy might be full of shit, trying to swing a plea, but the prosecutor was going to follow up anyway. I convinced him to wait until after you checked it out."

"Why'd he agree?"

"He's friends with Morrison too."

"California, huh? The boy gets around," Petrosky said as Morrison approached his desk.

"Don't we all?"

"Thanks, Taylor. Give me a few hours."

"No problem. Tell Detective Morrison I said hello. And tell him I saved him some of yesterday's pumpkin pie if he can get free for dinner."

Petrosky glanced at Morrison. Morrison grinned.

"Tell him yourself, Taylor. I'll keep you posted." He pocketed the phone and stood. "Got a lead, ten minutes out. I'll call you with whatever she gives me and get you to run it from here. In the meantime, get me a background on Xavier Kroll."

"On it, boss." Morrison looked at his watch. "You want a granola bar for the road?"

"I wouldn't want a granola bar if I was fucking starving. By the way, Taylor has some pie for you."

"Really?"

"Yup. And how the hell do you know everyone in the prosecutor's office?"

"They like granola too." Morrison winked.

"Save it for your girlfriend, surfer boy."

## SATURDAY, NOVEMBER 28TH

Saturday dawned frigid, but clear. I spent the morning alternating between staring through the skylights, working out with Dominic, and scratching behind Duke's ears while Dominic finished some paperwork.

Everything was… peaceful. Or had been since last night, when Dominic talked me down from my freak out over the shelter. "I'm sure those girls got into all kinds of things they shouldn't have," he had said. "And Jake too. But you're not in danger any more than I'd be in danger of a contact high for knowing other CEOs who snort cocaine. And you don't have to go back until the police sort this out. No use worrying before there's something to worry about."

I had balked. "You know people who snort cocaine?" He'd just laughed, and my anxiety had evaporated.

After lunch, we left to get my dress for the symphony. Dominic drove us around the lake where ice gleamed off the edges of the water and dusted the sparse cattails that had not yet called it quits. They were apparently stubborn bastards, like the cats for which they were named.

We fought traffic for a few miles, then turned off the main drag. The shops were tucked back from the street, off a long, curvy road that wound through fir trees heavy with snow. I hadn't even known this place existed.

*His world. I'm in his world.* I wanted to press my forehead against the window, relishing the sight of every jewelry store, every suit shop. We parked in front of a large window filled with oil paintings and expensive-looking pottery.

Dominic led me down the walk and through a wooden door carved with a fairy tale scene: a woman in a ball gown singing to a bird. Hokey, but somehow perfect. Inside the

251

dress shop, row upon row of luscious fabrics lined the walls. I fingered an ornate blue gown wrapped in a layer of creamy lace.

From the back room, a woman with thin lines around her eyes approached us, her smile painted in candy-apple red. "Can I help you?" she asked me. I looked at Dominic.

"Tell her what you want. I will take a walk while you decide."

*Wait... what? This isn't my world!* My heart pounded in my throat as he handed the woman his credit card, stooped to kiss my cheek and headed out the door.

*Everything's fine. He'll be right back.*

The woman looked at me expectantly.

What did I want? "Um... I don't... it's for the symphony."

She put a finger against her lips, appraising me.

I fought the urge to run.

"Come with me," she said finally. "I have a lovely organza that I think will suit you nicely."


An hour later, I left the shop with a garment bag over my arm and found Dominic on the sidewalk outside.

He took the dress. "How did it go?"

"Pretty good, I think." Salt crunched under our shoes. "Why did you leave me alone in there?"

He kept his eyes on the walk in front of us. "I'm not sure what you mean. They didn't have anything in my size."

"What?" *Just laugh, let it go.* No, I could tell him anything. I cleared my throat, my face hot. "I... sometimes don't do that well with new people."

"You are stronger than you think." He squeezed my hand.

I snorted.

"You got the dress, didn't you?"

I squeezed his hand back, the warmth draining from my cheeks.

Dominic stopped in front of a set of double glass doors,

pulled the handle, and led me inside a room with high ceilings and four separate hallways leading toward the back of the building. Cinnamon and orange peel tickled my nose. I was still taking in the photographs of serene waterfalls when Dominic addressed the woman at the front desk.

"We have a four o'clock appointment with Genevieve."

"Right away, sir." The brunette behind the counter glanced at me, then back at Dominic. "Will you be accompanying our guest today?" A smocked attendant wandered by, grinning cordially with huge white teeth. I tried to smile back but it might have looked like a grimace.

Dominic met my eyes. "Yes," he said.

*Thank goodness.*

We took the blue-gray corridor on the far right and emerged into a large salon, complete with leather seats and sea green towels that looked plush enough to sleep on.

A tall blonde wearing high heels and a skin-tight black sweater approached and held out her hand. "I'm Genevieve," she said. "Welcome." The corners of her lips turned up and it made her look younger, friendlier. Her hand was warm.

I relaxed into the cushioned back of the chair as she pushed the foot pedal to raise it.

"So, what would you like to do today?" she said.

Dominic smiled down at me. "You need me for this, or shall I leave you to it?"

His eyes showed no irritation, only confident support. I sat taller, suddenly more self-assured. "Go ahead."

My heart raced as it had in the dress shop, but this time I was ready for it. I watched Dominic's broad back in the mirror as he retreated down the hallway.

*You're stronger than you think.* I glanced up at Genevieve, sure that I would see some sign of contempt at being kept waiting. She smiled kindly.

*I can do this. I am in control.* I took in the green of my eyes, the milky hue of my skin, the mahogany of my hair. Somehow it all felt wrong. In the lighted vanity, the colors lent themselves to a face that looked far too much like... *him.*

I set my jaw. "You know, I think I may be up for a change."

Genevieve reached for a comb.

I smiled at the mirror. *I'm not his little girl. Not anymore.*

---

Petrosky stood in the middle of the room and tried not to touch anything. All goddamn day yesterday she had been gone, and now that she was finally here, he hoped he hadn't wasted his time. Not that he had more pressing engagements since Graves had hijacked his fucking case.

Margaret Garner sat on the couch, a maze of tiny blue veins creeping across her nearly translucent chest like spiderwebs. "I just can't believe she's gone," she said over the dry whir of the space heater.

Petrosky studied Garner's face. He saw sorrow there, expected from someone who had been closer to his victim than her own estranged mother. But her eyes were purely sad, no twinge of surprise, no disbelief. Had Garner expected something to happen to Antoinette Michaels? What had she seen in the last three years that Michaels had been her off-and-on roommate?

"And Tim... oh God." She collapsed into sobs.

*There's her surprise.* No one ever expected kids to die.

Petrosky watched Garner pick at a plume of stuffing peeking through the threadbare arm of the couch, her tears leaking onto her pants.

"Tell me about the last few weeks," he said.

Garner sniffed and swiped at her eyes with a tissue. "The usual. She was trying to get back on her feet. She always got clean for a few weeks, then every time, back into the life. She worried constantly about Tim, about how she was going to get him into a good school district or whether she'd have enough money for food."

"Nothing out of the ordinary recently?"

Garner shrugged.

"Then why did she go to the shelter?"

"Oh, *that*." Garner ran a hand through hair slick with grease. "Someone beat her up, and pretty good too. But it's all… I mean, it happens with what she was doin'."

"Do you know who the guy was?"

She paused for too long.

Suspicion corded Petrosky's neck.

"I—I don't think he was a regular, but I don't know. I haven't done anything like that since I found my boyfriend." Her lips twitched into a half smile, but the corners of her mouth trembled.

She was lying. But was she hiding something relevant to this case? "I'm not here to arrest you. If I were, I'd be packing up that needle on the kitchen counter and hauling you in."

Her mouth dropped open, eyes flicking to the kitchen.

Petrosky stepped closer. "I have no interest in your drug use, your occupation, or anything else besides finding out who killed Antoinette and Tim."

Garner's shoulders slumped, eyes on her lap. "I did… I mean, I can't get in trouble for taking a message, right?"

Petrosky stared hard at her until she met his gaze.

She licked her lips. "I took a message for her." Her sour breath hung in the air between them.

"When?"

"The night she got beat. Like I said, he wasn't a regular, he just left an address because I told her she could use my car for the evening."

"He left you an address?" That didn't make sense. His killer wouldn't just throw his address to anyone who asked for it. The guy was smarter than that, he could feel it in his bones.

"Well, he left *her* an address." Garner swallowed hard. "When I answered I was hoping it was… a friend of mine and—"

"You tried to take the job."

She stared at him. "He got the number from one of us. I didn't know if it was her or me. So I just pretended to be who

255

he was looking for."

"But he asked for her?"

Silence.

"Ma'am?"

She sighed. "Yes, he asked for her. But these guys won't leave their information with anyone besides the girl who's coming, and most of the time they don't call back. I was tryin' to help her out. I didn't mean for her to get... for Tim to get—" Her chest heaved and her eyes slid back to her lap.

"This wasn't your fault. But if you have information, any information, you need to tell me now. Help me catch him, Margaret."

She raised her eyes and her breath was slower, more controlled. "Like I said, I just took a message. Told him I'd be... I mean, *she'd* be over in a little while."

"Do you still have the address? A name?"

"Course. It's good business to keep 'em if things get slow later." She grinned, then shook her head, her proud smile faltering. "I've got an address for you. They don't leave names, though, not that we need 'em. We ladies never forget a... face."

Petrosky called Morrison on his way to the precinct. When he stopped behind the building, Morrison ran out and jumped in the car, his beach-boy face flushed from the winter chill.

"The address belongs to a James Clark," Morrison said, talking so fast his words were almost unintelligible.

Petrosky sucked on a cigarette and furrowed his brows. *James...* He exhaled in a burst and jerked his head backwards. "The guy Montgomery was out with the night after Campbell was snatched?"

Morrison looked like a cat that just ate a fucking canary. "It gets better. Apparently that's not even his real name. James Clark, AKA Robert Fredricks, has a pretty significant record. Did a prison stint for two counts of first degree rape at age eighteen. Got out about five years ago."

Petrosky's muscles shivered with excitement. At least he hoped the shakes were from excitement and not because the bottle of Jack Daniels under the passenger seat was still full. He should have emptied the liquor into his coffee before he got to the precinct.

Morrison opened his window and waved the smoke away from his face. "Should we go in and tell Graves?"

Petrosky took another drag, blew it out violently and crushed the cigarette into the ashtray. "Let's take a drive first."

An hour later they pulled into a small neighborhood near the Everette crime scene and squeezed their car down deeply rutted dirt roads that were barely wide enough for one vehicle. Petrosky could see the shore of a small, tranquil lake within walking distance of the street, but the cottages surrounding it were anything but quaint. Peeling paint was commonplace, some of the homes had shutters swinging from single rusty hinges, and behind one rickety fence, a Doberman snarled at them as they rolled by.

The car bounced over a particularly deep rut in the frozen dirt road. Petrosky hit his head on the roof, swore, and gripped the wheel harder.

"Gotta watch that, boss. Maybe you should be wearing your seat belt."

Petrosky rubbed his smarting head. "This is it." The difference between this house and the ones around it was remarkable. It was small, but freshly painted, with doors and windows in good repair. The roof looked new. The flower beds, now frozen, contained neatly-trimmed evergreen bushes, and not a single leaf peeked through the snow that covered the lawn.

Well-maintained.

Meticulous.

*Careful.*

The front porch had been swept clean of snow and salt

granules crunched under their feet. Morrison picked up the door knocker and dropped it. Somewhere, water on ice ticked steadily.

The hairs on the back of Petrosky's neck prickled. He knocked with his fist. Nothing. He tried the knob. Locked.

Petrosky pulled his Swiss Army knife from his back pocket and wiggled it into the door jamb. The lock gave way with a click.

"Boss—" Morrison began, but Petrosky was already turning the handle. "We've got one shot, surfer boy. They'll be all over the place giving us the run around as soon as we call it in." He nodded to the mat. "Wipe your feet."

Petrosky stepped inside. Morrison followed and closed the door.

The front entryway opened into the kitchen, strong with the scent of lemons. The stainless steel appliances and porcelain floors gleamed in the light streaming through the spotless windows. Framed black and white photographs hung on the walls—copies, but good quality ones. *Expensive.*

Morrison was still standing by the door, shifting his weight from foot to foot like a nervous first grader. Petrosky left him and wandered farther into the house. To the left of the kitchen, an archway opened to a small but nicely furnished living room with a big screen television. He stole past leather sofas into a hallway. The first door opened to a small, tidy bathroom—spotless, like the rest of the house.

From there, he entered a huge bedroom with a king-sized bed. Four poster spindles nearly touched the ceiling, each one painted to appear old or tarnished. Shabby chic bullshit.

*No*, he thought as he moved closer. *They're actually marked.*

He touched the headboard. The black iron was gouged with slivers of silver. Metal scored by metal? *Did you handcuff them and torture them here first, you sick bastard?*

He opened the nightstand drawer. Toenail clippers, remote control, phone charger. He closed the drawer and turned on the closet light.

Boots creaked on the carpet behind him. Morrison whistled at the wide array of suits and ties.

"Nice of you to show up." Petrosky squinted at the ceiling—smooth. No shelves on the upper walls. "Any wisdom to offer?"

"Well, this dude obviously has money. Why would he be living out in the middle of nowhere in a neighborhood full of thugs and crime?"

*Dude? Fucking surfers.* Petrosky fingered a silk tie. "In these neighborhoods, people mind their own business." *Which hopefully means they won't notice we're here.* He ran a hand behind the wall of shirts. Nothing. He scanned the floor. A corner of brown peeked from under the shoe rack. Petrosky crouched, grabbed the corner—a shoebox—and pulled it into the light.

Morrison edged around him.

The box was full of photos. The one on top showed a blond woman lying nude on the bed in the same master bedroom. She was handcuffed to the iron posts, her eyes wide with terror, irises colored in with red marker.

Petrosky's heart faltered, then hammered painfully against his ribs.

He pulled out a stack and rifled through them. Here, another blonde was bent over the bed, her right wrist handcuffed to the bedpost, her face turned toward the camera. A piece of duct tape covered her mouth. In another, a woman was cuffed face down on the bed, her back and buttocks slashed with weeping, bloody wounds. From a knife? A whip?

Petrosky's stomach rolled, but he kept flipping, faster and faster. There were other young girls with their legs spread wide on the bed and their arms attached to the posts. In some, the camera had snapped shots from above: girls with male genitalia in their mouths, duct tape still hanging from the sides of their lips. Some were blindfolded but unrestrained. Others had their ankles tied to either side of the bed. In every photo, their eyes had been colored in with red, making them look demonic.

Petrosky flipped another photo.

Morrison gasped.

Antoinette Michaels stared back at them, arms handcuffed above her head, mouth covered in duct tape. The beginnings of fresh bruises on her cheek were obvious in the picture as was the horror etched on her face.

He had no doubt they would find photos of the other victims there.

Petrosky's skin crawled with electricity. He put the pictures back in the box and covered them with the lid. The box shushed as he slid it back under the shoes.

"Boss, what are you—"

Petrosky put his hands on his knees and pushed himself up. "We broke in, California. Without a warrant we can't use them anyway. Right now, we need to get out of here, get a warrant, and stake this place out before he hurts someone else."

They hurried back through the house and out the front door. Petrosky locked it behind them, his heart throbbing in his ears. Outside, the only sounds were the steady drip of melting ice and the wail of the wind.

"Find a good parking place down the road," Petrosky said, sliding into the passenger seat. "Make sure we can see the house."

"Aye aye, boss." Morrison put the car in gear. Tires crunched over ice and salt and rocks.

Petrosky stared at the phone. He had no choice.

"Graves here."

"Sir, we have some new information." Petrosky explained as Morrison pulled behind an abandoned house a block from Clark's place.

Graves was silent on the other end of the line.

"Sir?"

"You're there now." It was not a question.

"Yes."

"He home?"

"No."

"Take off. Now. We'll get a warrant and retain him for questioning."

Petrosky's heart sank. "But, sir—"

"If we fuck this up, we lose the evidence we need to nail him. We'll put out an APB on his car and watch him if we see him sneaking around another abandoned building tonight. Now, get out of there before you scare him off."

Petrosky hung up the phone and shook a cigarette from his pack, his muscles twitching with the desire to leap from the car and hide in the bushes to wait. "Head back to the station."

Morrison maneuvered out of the neighborhood. Petrosky dragged smoke deep into his lungs and watched the house recede in the rearview mirror.

They had their killer.

Now where the hell was he?

## SATURDAY, NOVEMBER 28TH

Thomas lay on the couch, his face drawn and pale.

"You all right?" Robert said. "You haven't moved since we got here." He sat in a chair across from Thomas, head cocked, eyes on Thomas's face.

Thomas shook his head weakly. "I'm not sure. Ever since lunch it's just been… shit." He leaned over and vomited into the bucket next to the couch.

Robert averted his eyes until Thomas had finished puking.

"I can't go tonight," Thomas said, collapsing back onto the couch. "I feel like death."

"I'm sorry." Robert swallowed a smirk. "I wish I could do something."

Thomas cast his eyes down, defeated. "It took me two weeks and three hundred bucks to get that reservation." He sighed. "Noelle seemed so excited about it too—Hey!" Robert could almost see the light bulb turn on over Thomas's head as he looked back up. "Jim? Is there any way you might do me a favor?"

Robert tried not to smirk. "Anything. Just name it."

Noelle had sounded disappointed on the phone, but she'd insisted on coming over to Thomas's place. Now she knelt next to the couch.

Robert watched from the kitchen.

"Let me take care of you." She put her hand on Thomas's head.

*They all think they're fucking nurses.* Robert pictured her in a nurse's uniform as she bent to pull up the blanket, and his groin throbbed impatiently.

"No, really, there isn't anything you can do. I just need to get some rest and—" Thomas's eyes bulged. He retched again.

Noelle winced and stood.

"Seriously, honey, I just want to sleep. Let me know if the place is good enough to take you to in another month, okay? I had to bribe the maître-d to get in before February and I'll be pissed if we waste the reservation. I'd rather my two favorite people use it." He smiled thinly. "Just don't go falling for Jim." His eyes closed.

Noelle turned toward the kitchen where Robert stood waiting, keys in hand.

"I'll drive," he said.

She followed him down the stairs. "I hope Thomas feels better soon."

"He will." Robert smiled. *Eye drops only make someone ill for so long.*

---

I was a whole different person. A better person. A person I barely recognized with my long, white-blond hair and a chartreuse gown that brushed my legs with silky fingers. A person who held hands with the love of her life and sniffed through a melancholy symphony, relieved that her current life felt so normal, so damn happy, in comparison to whatever the composer had been going through when he wrote the music. And I couldn't keep my hands off the emerald pendant Dominic had picked out for me as Genevieve worked on my hair. By the time the last note rang out, my eyes were dewy with joy, just from the opportunity to be there, with him.

Holy crap, I was turning into a ball of mush.

We drove back to his house in silence, but not uncomfortable, awkward silence—just the shared I'm-cool-with-you-not-talking silence. I stole fleeting glances at him as he steered the car through the quiet streets. Once, he caught me watching him and smiled and a slow heat rose from my abdomen into my chest. Those eyes. So full of comfort and understanding. Eyes that never seemed to show uncertainty, or anger, or fear. I wondered if he could make me more like that, like him.

*Actually,* I thought, *he already has.*

When we arrived at the house, he took off his jacket and shoes in the mudroom and walked into the kitchen. "Would you like some water?" he called over his shoulder.

"Yes, thanks." I kicked off my shoes and ducked into the half bath. I unzipped my dress, shimmied out of my nylons, and unhooked my bra, laying everything on the sink.

When only the emerald necklace remained, I padded into the kitchen. Dominic's back was to me. I ran my hands up his back to his shoulders and kissed his arm through his shirt.

He turned, two glasses of sparkling water in his hands.

The edges of his mouth curved into a smile. He abandoned the water and wrapped his left arm around me as I arched into him. He reached between my legs. I was already wet.

*I love you*, I thought. Maybe tonight I would tell him.

---

Noelle had only agreed to go with Jim because Thomas was so bummed out about wasting the reservation. But without Thomas there, the whole restaurant felt a little awkward and business-like. Jim was reserved and kinda boring, a gentlemanly cliché, holding doors and pulling back chairs and talking about appropriately mundane work topics. But it wasn't as bad as she had anticipated, especially after a couple of daiquiris, and the tinkling notes of the in-house pianist filled any gaps in their conversation. With Thomas she wouldn't have needed the piano; he'd surely have been ready with some weird story about his elementary school or a parallel between politicians and Wolverine. The only thing that made Jim's eyes light up was talking about Hannah.

"So how long have you and Hannah known each other?" Jim said over after-dinner coffee.

Noelle washed down molten chocolate cake with a sip of her Kahlua and cream. The booze warmed her insides. "A year or so. She was my first friend when I moved here." Her only friend, really.

"Are you two close?"

She nodded.

"Thomas and I are pretty close friends, too." He lowered his voice. "Plus, I hoped you'd put in a good word… you know, if she ever drops that other guy."

*Poor guy. He really does care for her. But he doesn't stand a chance now that Dominic's in the picture.* Noelle smiled and hoped it looked more like kindness than pity. "Will do."


Jim drove them out of the restaurant lot, Noelle's after-dinner drinks still sloshing hotly in her stomach.

"Should we go back to Thomas's and check on him?" she asked.

Jim nodded at the clock on his dashboard. "It's a little early yet. Maybe we should find something to do for an hour or two so he can get a little more rest."

She looked at the clock. He was right. They had only been gone for two hours and Thomas had just been dozing off when they left. Not that she couldn't go snuggle up beside him and spend a few hours smelling the sour stench from the bucket on the floor. Eh, later. She shook her head against the fuzziness that was settling in her vision.

Jim kept his eyes on the road. "Want to take a drive? I found a cool overlook not too far from here. One of those scenic view type places. I wanted to bring Hannah up here back when I still had a chance, but…"

Sympathy tugged at Noelle's chest as she imagined how hard it might be for her to lose Thomas. She looked at the clock again and shrugged. "Sure, why not?"

"Great!" Jim squinted at an upcoming red light and turned down a side street. "Faster this way," he said.

The neighborhood homes glowed under bluish-white light

from the street lamps. They emerged onto another, dimmer, main street and turned left. "Maybe you can take Thomas up here when he feels better." He grinned, cutting the wheel right onto a sparsely lighted road where the homes were set far back from the street. Above them, the moon shone through a film of murky clouds. "Thomas is always looking for weird, out-of-the-way places. I think they remind him of the lab where they hid the Hulk... or maybe planet Krypton."

Along the road, the evergreen trees had thickened into a solid wall of iced needles, the ground beneath them heavy and black. She smiled but it felt forced. "You're probably right about that. But you'll have to draw me a map so I can find it again."

Uncertainty pricked at the edge of her subconscious but she brushed it away. *Thomas really would love it out here. Hopefully he'll be feeling better when we get back.*

Noelle took her cell from the purse at her feet. The battery flashed red. One percent. She let it thunk back into the bag.

They emerged from the woods and into a small clearing that ended in a chain link fence at the edge of a cliff. A small lake surrounded by tiny cottages twinkled below the edge of the precipice. The moon tucked itself behind a cloud and winked back again, turning the scene into a sleepy, sparkling town straight out of a children's book.

She leaned forward. "It—I mean, wow." *If only Thomas were here.*

She didn't register that Jim had moved until she felt his hand on her shoulder. Crystals of fear began at his fingertips and radiated through her, chilling her blood, encasing her lungs in ice. His face, suddenly so close to hers, thrummed with an anxious energy that bounced around her like a thousand bits of hail. His eyes, that just hours ago had been so friendly, glittered darkly with madness or... evil.

"Jim?"

His hand slithered down her back. His fingers wound tight around her arm, digging into her flesh.

Noelle screamed, the trees and moon her only audience.

## SATURDAY, NOVEMBER 28TH

Petrosky knocked before he could change his mind. Biting, midnight wind whistled from the lake and around the monstrous concrete building. There were no sounds coming from inside the house.

*Either these walls are really thick, or no one's home.*

"Wait for me, boss!" Morrison ran up the steps.

"I thought you were waiting in the car before you got fired."

"I figured you could use the moral support. Plus, there's always Cali."

"You mean California?"

The door opened. A tall, dark-haired man, presumably Dominic Harwick, looked the detectives up and down. He wore only a pair of silk pajama pants, his bare, washboard abs glinting in the porch light. Another gym rat, like Morrison. Petrosky sighed.

"Can I help you?" Harwick stifled a yawn.

Petrosky showed his badge. "I'm sorry to disturb you at this hour, but we're looking for a man who works for your company."

"Officers, I have thousands of employees. Surely you don't think I can keep track of—"

"We believe Hannah Montgomery knows him personally and this was the forwarding address given at her apartment. Is she available?"

"She's resting." Harwick paused, then opened the door wider. "Come in and I will get her." He glanced down at their shoes, thick with snow.

Petrosky knocked the snow off on the stoop, Morrison followed suit, and they squeaked into the biggest living room

267

Petrosky had ever seen.

"Can I offer you gentlemen something? Coffee perhaps?"

"No thank you, sir."

Harwick gestured to a set of enormous leather couches. "Make yourselves comfortable. I will be right back." He walked to the back of the room and disappeared through an archway at the far corner.

Morrison goggled. "Holy shit, this place is crazy!"

"Looks like Hannah is moving up. A few months ago she was dating our suspect and now—"

Petrosky stopped talking as a striking blond in a blue silk robe emerged from the back hallway. She strode to the couch and sat across from them, posture erect.

"Evening, ma'am," Morrison said.

"Evening."

Petrosky did a double take. "Ms. Montgomery?" Some detective he was. His head swam. Maybe it was the shot of Jack he'd had when Morrison got out of the car to piss, but he didn't think so. This wasn't normal. She wasn't normal. People don't just change, not like that. If there was a magic formula to boost someone's self-esteem and quell anxiety overnight, McCallum would be out of a fucking job.

"Oh, yeah." She touched a blond curl. Her face shone. "I changed my hair." She looked at Petrosky. "What can I do for you?"

"James Clark is wanted for questioning. Do you have any idea where he might be?"

Now her face paled. "Is this about the murders? Jake?"

"Yes, ma'am."

She twisted the hem of her robe in her fist. "I... oh my god, no, I mean, I haven't seen him. Jesus."

"Is everything okay here?" Harwick marched toward them and Petrosky's hackles rose.

"Yes, sir," Morrison said.

"When was the last time you spoke to him?" Petrosky asked her. "If you have any idea where he might be, any information at all... it's important that we locate him."

She twisted her robe harder, the fabric tightening against her thigh like a coiled snake. Harwick sat beside her and put his hand on her knee, gently stroking her with his thumb until she dropped the hem of her robe. Her shoulders relaxed. "I have no idea where he is." Her voice was soft, but crisp, without a trace of the anxiety they had just witnessed.

*Harwick must be one hell of a goddamn guy.* Not that it took much to be more stable than her ex. Montgomery looked at Harwick, expectant, as if waiting for him to make everything all better. Petrosky's eyes narrowed. Then again, being too dependent was how abusive relationships got started. And she was vulnerable to that abusive bullshit, if her relationship with Campbell was any indication.

Petrosky eyed Harwick. Harwick watched Montgomery, hand still on her leg.

Protective, or possessive?

Montgomery shot to her feet and Petrosky reared back on the couch. "Wait! Noelle might know. She was going out with Thomas tonight."

She padded into the kitchen and returned with her cell phone at her ear. "—it's really important. Okay, bye." She sat and leaned against Harwick, phone in hand. I had to leave a message."

Petrosky held out his business card as he and Morrison stood. "If you think of anything else—"

Harwick took the card. "Detectives, if he shows up for work on Monday, I will have security bring him down and detain him. Do you have any reason to think he would show up here?"

Petrosky hesitated.

"No, sir," Morrison said.

Montgomery put her head against Harwick's shoulder.

*It's more than happiness,* Petrosky thought. *She knows she's safe.*

*If only I could have given Julie that kind of security.*

*But* feeling *safe doesn't actually mean you* are *safe.*

Petrosky's stomach churned, acid rising until it felt like it was burning a hole straight through to his heart.

Harwick led them to the front door. "Thank you for your diligence. I hope you find him soon."

*Suave mother fucker.* "I hope so too, sir."

The door clicked shut. Petrosky paused on the porch, listening for anything amiss—a scream from inside or a subtle thud. But there was only the wind, howling around his ears. Maybe Harwick really was a decent guy. Maybe she really was secure and content and happy.

Morrison snickered as they climbed into the car. "It really is amazing what a rich guy can do for a woman."

Petrosky jerked his cigarette pack from the console. "No wonder my ex-wife left."

"I thought she married a construction worker."

"Thanks a lot, *dude.*"

## SUNDAY, NOVEMBER 29TH

My back was still tingling the next day, as if Dominic's fingers had etched their imprint on my skin. I barely noticed the stiff chair in Tammy's office, or the way her lips were pursed with displeasure. Thus far, we'd covered the usual rigmarole about how I was feeling about Jake's death, how work was going, and what else was new. What was new was that things were generally... okay. It felt good to say that out loud and actually mean it. I'd been a little worried when I'd gotten Noelle's voicemail again this morning, but Dominic had assured me she was fine. She'd probably just slept over at Thomas's. It was silly to worry before you had something to worry about, he'd told me. Tammy might have said that to me in the past, but when Dominic said it, I believed him.

"Are you sure you've been okay? You missed your last appointment." There was a hint of disapproval in Tammy's voice.

I prepared myself for the guilt. I felt none.

"I feel like things are going a lot better," I said, instead of apologizing. "I've definitely been feeling better overall. More optimistic, I guess."

Tammy made a note in the file in front of her. "How about your sleep?"

"Better, at least sometimes."

"What about the rest of the time?"

I shrugged. "It's hard to say. Some nights I sleep better than I ever have. Some nights I have bad dreams and wake Dominic. He seems to have a calming effect on me, though." *And he actually knows about my past and understands me, unlike you.*

Tammy nodded thoughtfully. If something ever happened

271

to my shrink, someone could make her life-sized bobble head twin and it would be just as effective as she was now.

"It is possible that his presence makes you feel safer. It is also possible that the days you sleep better are the result of less outside stress, maybe fewer work issues. Is this increase in quality sleep usually on the weekends?"

I furrowed my brows. *Was it?* No, some days I showed up to work in the middle of the week, ready to take on the world. And sometimes, I had to sleep in on Sunday because I'd tossed and turned all night long. I shook my head.

Tammy put a finger to her lips. "Before attributing these improvements in sleeping patterns to another person, perhaps you should look in your journal, at your sleep recording exercise. I don't want you giving all the credit to someone else."

*Like, someone besides you?* "I'll look, but so far, I haven't noticed any patterns. Seems random."

Tammy stood. "Take another look and see what you can find. We will talk about it next week."

*Why do shrinks use shock treatment?*
*To prepare patients for their bills!*

"Next Saturday, nine o'clock? I can't do Sunday again."

I nodded, but I was already tuning her out.

*I don't need her anymore. I only need him.*


I drove back to Dominic's house and let myself in. *No*, I corrected myself. *Our house.* My heart felt as if it had sprouted wings.

I glanced at the clock on the oven and caught a reflection of my face, grinning like an idiot. It was only ten. Dominic wouldn't be home until eleven-thirty.

What to do?

I could watch TV, but I wasn't really in the mood. I could try Noelle again, but I didn't want to be all stalker-y, especially since she was probably busy with her boyfriend. Even Duke was out at the groomer's.

I frowned and peered across the living room, toward the far archway. After Dominic's twilight poetry reading, the library was fast becoming my favorite room. I could still hear his voice in there if I concentrated: *I seem to have loved you in numberless forms, numberless times... In life after life, in age after age, forever.*

Maybe I could find something beautiful to read to him.

The library welcomed me with the subtly sweet scent of old books and furniture polish. *I wonder where he stuck that poetry book.* I headed to the back wall of shelves and ran my finger along the spines, each uniform ridge a smooth transition to the next book. *A History of the World. Economics: Past, Present, Future. Global Transactions.*

A little much for light Saturday morning reading, I thought, though picturing him reading the educational stuff made my heart swell. That was the side he showed to the world: the businessman, the intellectual. His softer side he showed only to me.

*Thump.* My hand stopped at a thick text sticking out further than the rest on the top shelf. I pulled it down. *Poems for the lovestruck, here I come!*

I looked at the cover and frowned.

*Through the Looking Glass? That does not sound like poetry.* The pages rippled when I leafed through them. Nope, not poetry.

Or maybe it was?

> *Tweedledum and Tweedledee*
> *Agreed to have a battle;*
> *For Tweedledum said Tweedledee*
> *Had spoiled his nice new rattle.*

Hmm. So some regular story, some poetry, and the occasional photo of chessboards or rabbits or obese children. Weird, but whatever. It had to be better than *Economics* and I could always find a romantic poem later.

I walked to the couch, stretched out with my back against the arm rest, and dove in.

"Any signs of physical harm?" Petrosky asked.

The baby-faced rookie shook his head. "Nah, she just freaked out when he tried to get fresh. Went running into the woods. A group from a nearby house was out there roasting marshmallows and saw her before he even caught up. He did have handcuffs in his trunk though, so who knows what he had planned."

"Thanks for calling Morrison before you called Graves."

"Hey, you guys are dicks less often. Not a *lot* less, but still."

"I'll get you a donut tomorrow."

"Make it a cruller."

"Deal." Petrosky dismissed him with a wave and tapped the file with his thumb. James Clark, born Robert Fredricks, had completed his engineering degree during his five-year prison stint, and had somehow managed to score a respectable position at Harwick Technical Solutions. He had been up here in Michigan for less than two years: plenty of time to get comfortable and to explore out-of-the-way places to dump half a dozen bodies. And it took a cool head to go to work and smile every day with some woman's blood still under your fingernails. *Manipulative. Calculating.* Then there were the photo souvenirs.

Everything fit. Almost too nicely.

Petrosky squinted at his suspect through the one-way mirror.

Fredricks's face was impassive, his fingers laced on the tabletop in front of him. His blue eyes raked the room as if looking for something. Probably someone else's daughter.

*Fucking bastard.*

Petrosky's fist clenched around the file. He squared his shoulders and marched into the interrogation room, letting the door slam behind him.

"So, Jimmy, I just got back from your place. You live a long way from the office."

Fredricks stared at him. "It's quiet there." His voice was bland, but with an edge, as if he were struggling to keep it even.

"Try again."

A manic rapping sounded under the table. Fredricks's foot. He was nervous, panicked even. How nervous had he been when he was slicing through his victims' bellies, torturing them, until they probably begged for death?

"I couldn't live anywhere else. I was supposed to report my residence and my status as a sex offender. Three neighborhoods petitioned before I gave up and went somewhere where no one would care."

That felt like the truth. He let it go for now. "How'd you manage to score such a ripe gig at Harwick Tech?"

Fredricks looked down at his hands. "I put in an application, I think. They called me and I went."

"Once you got here, you met some nice girls, huh?"

Fredricks's jaw worked furiously. His hands balled into fists on the table.

*Here we go.*

"How about Hannah Montgomery?" Petrosky's heart quickened at her name, but he snuffed the feeling and kept his eyes on the shithead at the table. "She's pretty, isn't she? Is that how you chose the other women? Did you follow her to the shelter?"

Fredricks's face twisted with rage. "She has *nothing* to do with this." Spittle flew from his mouth and landed on the table.

"We're going to make this easy on each other," Petrosky said. "You are going to tell me what I want to know. I am going to pretend that I didn't see the pictures of all the little girls you have at your house. They don't take kindly to pedophiles in prison, though I suspect you already know that."

The blood drained from Fredricks's face. His body listed unsteadily and he caught himself on the table, knuckles white. "I... I... They all told me they were eighteen!"

*Fucking liar.* "And the dead girls?"

Fredricks stared at him. "What?"

"You're not fooling anyone. You have photos of each of the murder victims in your closet."

Understanding crept across Fredricks's face. His mouth dropped open. "Wait, hang on! I... those were just—" He collapsed into sobs. "I just liked the pictures, the excitement. I paid them all. They... they all went home. Oh, God—" He wheezed.

Maybe Fredricks would pass out and crack his head open on the floor. The thought was comforting.

"You have young women in your past who almost didn't go home. Remember Charlotte Ostick?"

Fredricks paled still more. His lips opened and closed in manic little movements as if his brain was working far too quickly for his mouth.

"She almost died too," Petrosky said savagely. "You didn't bring her inside a building, though. You anally raped her, beat her, and left her in a fucking field to die from internal bleeding. Would she have been your first, Jimmy? Did the fact that a twelve-year-old girl survived make you rethink your locations so a well-meaning farmer wouldn't find your victims before they were beyond saving? Maybe this shit isn't as satisfying if you think they may survive."

Fredricks's tears fell on his clenched, white knuckles. "I tried to stop." It was a whisper. "I... I couldn't. I hired people. I paid every one of them. They all agreed—"

"Did they agree to die?"

A muffled choking sound.

*Choke, fucker.*

"I didn't kill anyone!"

"It's all over, Jimmy. Let's work together and I'll make sure your sexual escapades don't get broadcast all over the prison mess hall. Deal?"

"No! I didn't do anything! I mean—I didn't kill them! You have to believe me!"

"Too late for that, Jimmy. Enjoy prison."

He'd let Fredricks sweat and come back later for his confession.

The bell rang again. The white shag rug was too soft under Noelle's bare feet, as if toying with her, teasing her with nice comforting things while she waded through the knowledge that she had almost been the next dead girl on the news.

"Noelle, open up!" Hannah's voice. Noelle had called her after Thomas had left this morning because she hadn't wanted to be alone. Now the pine door to her apartment seemed bigger than usual, alien.

The door squealed as Noelle pulled on the knob.

"I'm so glad you're okay!" Hannah threw her arms around her. "I can't believe this."

"Me either. It's just…" She really didn't want to talk about it. Not now. Noelle stepped back, her jaw dropping when she saw Hannah's face. "What happened to your hair?"

Hannah ran a hand through her blond waves. "Do you like it?" She sounded like she wasn't sure about it, or maybe she was just unsure of Noelle's reaction.

"I love it. Now we can be twins."

Hannah's face lit up. "I don't have the boobs."

"Now that you landed a rich dude, you can inflate those puppies."

Hannah shrugged. "Eh, Dominic likes them the way they are."

They sat on the loveseat bought with her late father's money, the very least he could contribute to her life. Noelle suddenly wondered if things would have been different if he were still alive. Would she have called him to tell him she was okay? What would he have done besides vow litigation and his firm's involvement in a high profile case? At least she had Thomas. He had stayed with her all night, holding her and apologizing for suggesting she go out with Jim. He'd probably never forgive himself. She understood that feeling.

Noelle's stomach knotted. "I still feel like an idiot," she whispered.

"Me too. To think that Jim might have killed Jake, that I might have played a part in that is just—" Hannah leaned back against the couch. "But there's no way we could have known. That guy fooled everybody. I used to get nervous around him and I still didn't suspect that he was... you know... that kind of crazy. And if Dominic hired him he must have been a damn good faker, because Dominic's no fool."

"It's one thing to see someone in a job interview and another to be in the same room over and over again and just not... see it. I'm so... stupid."

Hannah searched Noelle's eyes. "You're smarter than you think. Give yourself some credit, everyone else does. Hell, Dominic was shocked when he found out. Said you had a good head on your shoulders and that Jim must have been a really good faker."

"Yeah, maybe."

*Had Dominic really said that?*

"Plus, there's the way you strong-armed your way out of there. Like a freaking kick boxer."

Noelle almost smiled. "It was kinda bad ass." Thomas had compared her to Wonder Woman. "Hopefully I never have to do it again, though I think Thomas might be sticking around. So no more serial killer dates for me."

"He's not a no-good murdering psycho, is he?"

Noelle laughed. "I sure as hell hope not. He'd have a hard time explaining his comic book fascination to other inmates. Same with that cat."

"Thomas might have weird hobbies, but at least he was honest about them. He put his weirdness right up front. It's scary how Jim seemed so normal. But he must have just pretended so he could fit in."

Noelle shrugged. "Even psychos need to have a life, I guess."

Hannah squeezed her hand. "Everybody does."

## THURSDAY, DECEMBER 3RD

No out, no help, no hope. Robert's will to fight had disappeared the first day he'd begged his attorney to believe him.

"I'm not sure what to tell you," the troll of a man had said. "The evidence is pretty compelling. You don't have one single alibi. Pleading guilty should at least make the process easier on you."

"I didn't do anything!" He'd had to clasp his hands together to avoid grabbing his attorney and shaking the shit out of him.

"You did enough to kill any sympathy a jury might have had." The lawyer had tapped his foot, obviously eager to be dismissed and on to a case he had a chance of winning.

"But I didn't kill anyone! How can that not matter?" It was more critical than a lifelong prison sentence. It was a matter of eternity, of salvation versus writhing on a blistering bed of coals.

*If I can't get out soon, I will never see her again.*

*If I stay in here, I am doomed to Hell.*

The lawyer had merely shrugged his meaty shoulders. "Consider pleading guilty. It's your best bet." *Because you're bad, Robert.* His innocence was irrelevant. Any attorney he hired would see his depravity and seek to punish him.

That had been the beginning of the end. Each day his panic was replaced by a hopelessness that wound itself around his chest, growing tighter and tighter as days turned to nights and back to days again. His face itched from the dark hair that crawled across his lower jaw. There was no mirror in his cell, but he knew his eyes looked like hollow orbs, blank and eerily unexpressive as if the life had been sucked right out of him.

And it had.

He left his food tray on the floor of his cell, untouched. He spent his days sitting silently on the cot, searching the cinderblock wall for some answer to his plight, refusing to speak to another soul.

But he listened. He had always listened. And the more he ignored the world that had forsaken him, the louder the voices became.

*And into the gates of Hell, the sinners of the world shall pass.* A woman from his father's church whispered the words into his ear, her beautiful blond locks shimmering against his cheek, awakening the lust in his belly.

*Those whose hearts are pure are temples of the Holy Spirit.* He saw Mindy Jacobs writhing underneath him, her eyes vacant, St. Lucy's words crackling from her lips with the hiss of Hellfire.

He stood in the dark and pulled the sheet from his bed.

*Only the chaste man and the chaste woman are capable of true love.* And it was the girl in the field, her scrawny hip bones sharp under his hands as he threw her over a hay bale and forced himself into her, her insides rupturing, his thighs covered in her blood.

He looped the sheet around the pipe in the ceiling and tied a smaller loop close enough that his feet would not touch the ground when it was time.

*And your sins will follow you, casting you down away from those who sought the love of Jesus Christ, your immortal soul to be punished, writhing in agony for all eternity, for the sins of the flesh you cannot escape.* Hannah came to him now, his Hannah, smiling as he climbed the bars to the top of the cell. He gripped the pipe with one hand and slid his head through the knotted cotton.

*Do not be afraid; our fate cannot be taken from us.* All of them chorused in unison, each lustful apparition pleased with his penance as they'd never been pleased before. He deserved this. Always had. He closed his eyes and released himself into the abyss. Tightness seared his throat and he lurched, his

280

feverish fingers clawing at the noose as his feet kicked air. A rush of blood blistered his face as his airway constricted— demons preparing him for the heat of eternity.

He opened his eyes. Below him, his father smiled knowingly as Robert swung from the hanging tree in front of his childhood home, a final sunset blazing red in the distance like the blood that had been spilled there long before his time. The crimson orb sank silently into darkness. Above him, pinpricks of light twinkled into existence and swelled until he was blinded by their brilliance.

Robert raised his sightless eyes to the heavens and smiled.

## Friday, December 4th

She lay on the couch, arm extended, palm open to the sky as if she were begging for something. A needle hung from one swollen vein. He wondered if it would eventually rip free. If he stayed there long enough, he might get to watch it happen.

He knelt in front of her. She stared at him, unfocused, unseeing, not really there at all. In a way, she never had been.

A white crust clung to her blue lips, and a slippery trail of vomit ended in a milky puddle on the floor. Her chest rose and fell, again and again. Much too fast, much too shallow.

He touched her hand. Cold.

A single tear trailed a path down her face. He traced it with his finger.

He did not cry. He did not understand the gesture. As if watery eyes made bad things any less terrible. Not that this was bad.

He looked at the Mickey Mouse watch he had found, dropped by some john, the only thing that was just his. Twelve minutes, he guessed; it would take twelve minutes before she stopped breathing altogether. That was seven hundred and twenty seconds. Most five-year-olds did not know their multiplication tables, but he did, from counting out baggies of drugs and figuring out how long it took for her to sleep off a hit. It was safer to be hidden before she woke up.

He pulled a banana from a bag on the table, the latest delivery from the church outreach. They smelled even better now that he would not have to share them. Her breath quickened, then slowed abruptly. He peeled the fruit and counted out the seconds in earnest.

Five hundred and forty-two, five hundred and forty-three—

The life drained from her in a matter of seconds. He watched her eyes, trying to catch a glimpse of… something. But there was nothing. She was no less dull in death than she had been in life.

He sighed. Off by one hundred and seventy-seven seconds. He hated to be wrong, even if it was not by much. Perhaps eventually, if he practiced enough, he would get better at guessing things like that.

He took a bite of the banana and walked to the bathroom. It would be a few days before anyone noticed her missing. Probably around four days, six hours and forty-six minutes. He calculated the day and time he expected the first knock at the door, and wrote his guess in eyeliner on the bathroom mirror so he would be reminded of his success… or failure. He dropped the pencil in the sink—

And awoke.

He turned to the clock. *Five oh five*. Thirty-five minutes before the alarm. Too late to go back to sleep. He might as well get up and make coffee.

In the kitchen he scooped grounds into the espresso machine, blinking sleep from his eyes. A pillow of steam escaped with a raspy whisper.

What a strange dream. Or memory. Not that it mattered.

They had shielded his eyes when they removed him from the apartment, though any idiot would know he had already seen it. By then his mother's body had been a nest of ants on the damp, putrid sofa; even the bodily fluids had stopped leaking onto the untreated floor, though he had been surprised by how long that part had taken. *Three days, four hours, six minutes.*

The car ride to the hospital had taken twenty-four minutes. When they arrived, men in white coats tore the watch from his hand and forced him onto a bed. He had fought violently until a sharp prick in his buttocks made him slip away into nothingness.

Three days, twelve hours and thirty-two minutes later, he

escaped from his room and fled down the maze of hallways. When the trailing footsteps got too near, he ducked into a room in a dark back corner. The woman in the bed had reached for him, zombie-like. He'd watched, fascinated.

From the chair, a man's voice, not like his, but like his all the same. "That was a hug."

He did not respond, just watched the man with the buzz cut.

"My wife loves to hug. She likes to do a lot of things that never made sense to me. Her face was an open book that I couldn't read. I understand now, though."

He and the man stared at each other, playing a silent game of wits.

"You don't get it either," the man said simply. "We're not like other people."

He looked at the man's shoes. They were the shiniest things he had ever seen.

"You'll learn," the man told him.

The orderlies discovered him asleep in the chair next to the woman and took him back to his room. Twenty-six hours and five minutes later the man appeared at his bedside.

"My wife's dying," the man said.

They listened to the beeping of the heart monitor.

"Your mom's already dead." The man pulled a chair to the side of his bed. "You're on your way to foster care. I hear it's a pretty awful place."

*Beep... Beep... Beep...*

"So what did they do to you when you got here? Strip your clothes? Take your things?"

*Beep... Beep... Beep...*

The man nodded. "You don't feel a thing, do you?"

*Beep... Beep... Beep...*

"I understand. It works wonderfully in the military, being numb enough to shoot the enemy in the face or leave your comrade behind. But you need to use it differently out here."

"How?" His own voice sounded foreign after so many days spent in silence, avoiding the questions of the hospital staff.

"You'll learn," the man said again. "People like us always can."

The man sat in the chair for one minute and twenty-two seconds before he spoke again. "Would you like to hear a story to pass the time? It was my wife's favorite." The man opened the small brown book in his lap without waiting for a reply.

"The Walrus and the Carpenter
Were walking close at hand:
They wept like anything to see
Such quantities of sand:"

He closed his eyes and tried to pretend he was free and walking along the beach, or even just along the sidewalk. Anywhere but this place where he had no choice but to bend to the will of those larger and stronger.

"'Oh oysters come and walk with us!'
The Walrus did beseech.
'A pleasant walk, a pleasant talk,
Along a briny beach:'"

Maybe one day he would see sand, ocean, waves.

"'It seems a shame,' the Walrus said
To play them such a trick.'"

*The oysters were idiots to follow the walrus in the first place, he had thought. They deserved what they got.*

Three days, twelve hours and thirty-two minutes after his hospital admission he had run into Linda Harwick's hospital room. Six days, four hours and eight minutes later, he went home in the custody of Rupert Harwick. That period was the most vital nine days, sixteen hours and forty minutes of his life.

A final belch of steam poured from the espresso maker. Dominic grabbed a cup from the cupboard, poured a steaming mug and finished it with a squeeze of lemon.

His footsteps were nearly soundless on the stairs. The

upstairs rugs swallowed the tap of his slippers. In the bedroom, Hannah lay sprawled out on her stomach, the sheets pulled up to the middle of her back, her arms in disarray.

*Like a common drunk*, he thought. He noted the way her hair lay on her back in disordered waves, rising and falling as she drew breath.

He thought of Linda Harwick, her stiff form, the casket, the guilt-ridden mourners. Unlike his own mother, whose death had been of no consequence to anyone, Linda had apparently been useful to many, including her husband.

Marrying Hannah could work. That might be more useful in the future.

*But not nearly as much fun as watching her bleed.*

He sipped his espresso and peered through the skylight where the gray was just beginning to show through the freezing winter clouds. It would be so easy, so—

She rolled onto her back and wrinkled her nose. Her arm rested across her breasts now, the outline of her ribcage visible beneath the thin silk sheet. Her cheeks flushed pink, the warm color a beacon of vitality.

*She is lovely*, he thought. Like an antique vase, or a really nice leather briefcase. He wondered if she would keep that warm, elegant quality, or if it would fade immediately as she expired, her diminishing color turning her just as bland as anyone else. He guessed the latter. Time would tell. Maybe.

He glanced at her pale throat, incandescent in the dimness.

*Too easy*, he thought. When the time came, if the time came, he would draw it out. He would watch her recoil and thrash and writhe. And he would relish every moment. It wasn't as if he'd miss her.

## SATURDAY, DECEMBER 5TH

Snowflakes pelted the skylights and blocked out the sun, like the room was wrapped in a protective blanket.

Dominic was already awake and typing on his laptop, his eyes jumping in concentration. From across the room I took in the curves of his toned body in flannel pants and a white T-shirt. That tiny curl of dark hair that sometimes snuck to his forehead. *Delicious.*

He looked up.

I smiled. "Morning."

"Good morning," he said. "I didn't wake you, did I?"

"No." I rolled onto my side toward him. "Though I wouldn't mind if you had."

He set the computer aside, a touch of a smile at the corner of his mouth. "I have meetings all day, and then this evening there's that new-hire welcome I told you about last week."

"But it's Saturday."

He chuckled, climbed into the bed next to me and leaned close to my ear. "Let's say I wake you up appropriately, then come back home and put you to bed even more nicely?"

I snuggled against him. "Anything you say, sir."

His fingers sank into me and I forgot everything else.


I was still in bed when he emerged from the closet dressed in gray pin-stripes and a tailored blue shirt that set off his eyes.

"Hurry back."

He pinched my nipple. "You know I will." Then he was gone.

I stretched my still-throbbing muscles and headed to the weight room, nude.

My workout clothes hung from the hook on the wall, where they belonged. I tugged them on, climbed on the treadmill and appraised my face in the mirror. I looked different, and it wasn't just the hair.

I smiled. My reflection smiled back. Then I turned up the speed, pushing myself harder than usual, testing my limits.

*I can do it.* I had dealt with trauma and grief, with a crazy father and a crazy boyfriend and a psycho killer colleague. I could deal with running just a little faster.

An hour and a half later I was showered, exhausted and satisfied. I toasted a couple of English muffins and made a beeline for the library. I had a feeling eating in there would be frowned upon, but what he didn't know wouldn't hurt him.

*Such a rebel.*

I laughed aloud.

I set the plate on the end table and walked to the shelf to grab my book, still tucked into the same place it always had been so Dominic wouldn't know I was reading it. Every time I opened my mouth to tell him, my face got hot and I changed the subject. Maybe I was embarrassed for reading a little kid's book when he was reading about economics. Or maybe it was because every time I touched the leather cover, I had a fit of nostalgia, as if I was rediscovering some missed thing from my childhood.

*Maybe it* is *something I missed. While everyone else was reading stuff like this, I was—*

I pushed the thought away. I wasn't that girl anymore. I was here now.

The couch beckoned, soft and warm. Even the frozen chess game seemed comforting, a piece of memory steeped in love that I could almost share by being nearby.

The worn book cover was satiny under my fingertips. I took a bite of my muffin and flipped to the page where I'd left off, wondering what Alice would do next.

The department was still riding the wave of praise for catching Robert Fredricks. Graves spent his time strutting around and grinning like a fool for the cameras, but the continuous press conferences were starting to give Petrosky a headache. He assumed that things would die down once the trial began.

Or maybe not. There was plenty of sensational evidence, more than enough to create a media circus. The search warrant had unearthed the photos plus two sets of leather restraints and a bloody scalpel found underneath the kitchen sink behind some cleaning supplies. DNA tests had confirmed the blood belonged to Antoinette and Timothy Michaels, Fredericks's final victims. The case would be open and shut. Everyone was expecting a conviction, even the court-appointed attorney who'd reluctantly agreed to represent him.

Petrosky closed his notepad and headed for the front of the building where yet another question-and-answer press conference would be held. Graves had given him the opportunity to address the public this time. Maybe because Morrison had told the chief that they, not Graves, had found the lead on Fredricks. Or maybe Graves didn't want to risk stonewalling them and causing a scene when Petrosky hit him in the mouth. Either way, it was about time he got a little respect, even if he'd have preferred a mention in the paper instead of having to give a speech. Maybe that's why that fucker had offered him the speech.

Petrosky pushed the glass doors leading to the outdoor pavilion and the steady buzz of the journalists swelled in his ears. But there was another noise… flashbulbs? No. Footsteps.

Petrosky turned and raised an eyebrow as he watched Morrison dash toward him up the hallway, red-faced and panting.

"Petrosky! Wait!"

"Come on, dude! Looks like someone needs to hit the gym."

289

Morrison grabbed the door handle. "We need to talk."

Petrosky glanced at the throng of reporters. "You earned it, Petrosky," Graves had said. It might have been bullshit, but it felt damn good.

"Right now?" Petrosky asked.

"Yeah, now." Morrison released the door handle. "There's not going to be any trial."

The place reeked with the noxious mix of urine and feces that hadn't yet been cleaned from the floor. Directly above the small puddle hung remnants of white cloth, presumably the bed sheet that had been looped around ol' Jimmy's neck before they'd cut him down.

Petrosky took a breath through his mouth. *Not good.* "So where is it?"

Morrison grabbed a single sheet of paper from the now bare mattress and handed it to Petrosky.

> *Pity, like a naked newborn babe,*
> *Striding the blast, or heaven's cherubim, horsed*
> *Upon the sightless couriers of the air,*
> *Shall blow the horrid deed in every eye,*
> *That tears shall drown the wind.*

Petrosky rubbed his temple. "What the fuck is it with this guy and the rhymes? Who does he think he is?"

"Shakespeare," Morrison said.

Shakespeare. Not the final bloody verse from the poem he'd left at the crime scenes. An uneasy ache settled in Petrosky's stomach. *What the hell was this guy doing?*

He passed the page back to Morrison. "So, Mr. Big Shot literature major, what the hell does it mean?"

Morrison furrowed his brows. "It's about the death of an innocent."

"Lots of innocent women died at his hands." The tattered bed sheet mocked Petrosky from the ceiling, twisting in the draft from the heating vent. The murky light from the hallway stippled the cotton with glaring yellow eyeballs.

290

Morrison stared at the poem. "Yeah, they did. It could be a confession, I guess. A way to say, 'Hey I killed a bunch of innocent people.' But I don't think he thought those women were innocent."

If not the girls, then who? The kid? His killer had found the women repugnant; had to in order to tear them apart like that. And from what Petrosky had seen, the killer wasn't sorry, either. There had been no tears to drown the wind. A tourniquet ringed his abdomen, squeezing bile into his throat.

*It's not a confession.*
*It's a warning.*

## SATURDAY, DECEMBER 5TH

The hotel ballroom teemed with three hundred or so local engineers already under the umbrella of Harwick Technical Solutions. They milled around like sheep, jostling one another to get to the hors d'oeuvres. And the drinks. Dominic eyed them disapprovingly, but never long enough for them to notice.

A few came up to shake the hands of the other managers. The more daring employees approached him as well, and were rewarded for their temerity with a handshake and a broad smile that was convincing enough. They'd not recognize his disdain, not while they were half drunk and clambering for his approval. They were all broken, troubled, sick, each with something to prove. And the right level of disturbance paired with the right job ensured he would spend his days watching his bottom line climb ever higher, even as his workers cried themselves to sleep or fucked little kids or beat their wives or sliced through their own skin with razor blades. Some of them were even like… him.

And numbers never lied.

He listened to snippets of conversation as he walked to the bar.

"Did you hear about Jim? I met him at a quality control meeting last year—"

"Yeah, that was crazy. He looked totally normal in his picture—"

Dominic ordered a sparkling water and scanned the room.

Jim had seemed totally normal, but guys like that never changed. Dominic had counted on that when he sought the man out. If Jim had suddenly done a one-eighty, it would have been a statistical anomaly. Dominic had put his money on the math. And on the tracking chip he'd installed on Jim's—Robert's—car.

He took his drink.

"Did you hear that wasn't even his real name?"

"I heard he changed it before he sent in his resume—"

The game had been fun while it had lasted. But there would always be time for another round as long as he examined the opportunities around him. Stayed one step ahead of the rest. His father had shown him that much—that, and how a dismally boring existence could be transformed the first time you held someone's still pulsing organs in your hand.

As Dominic walked back to his table, the sea of people parted for him. A man wearing a dark blue suit jacket and a hopeful expression sidled up to him. Dominic forced himself to look pleased.

*Idiots.* He shook the man's hand. *Fucking Oysters.*

⊶⊷⊷⊷⊷⊷

Something molten scorched my insides, the flick of a lighter before the flame. On the table next to me, the English muffin had long since grown cold. I reached for it blindly, registering the clatter of the plate on wood, but it seemed far away. The book sat open on my lap, the page invisible despite how hard I stared at it.

*It isn't possible.*

The book closed in slow motion, as if my hand were disconnected from my body. Then the bookcase was before me, the book sliding into its place, though I didn't remember getting up.

*Books. So many books.*

*Anyone could have that book. It's just a coincidence.*

I took the plate to the sink, scrubbed it with shaking hands and turned to the dishwasher. The plate slipped and shattered against the marble floor.

*The broom. The sweeping. Don't think.* I took slow,

293

deliberate breaths into quivering lungs. My chest hurt.

*This is ridiculous. Talk about an overreaction.*

*It's okay. Just go read something else.*

*Yeah, something not connected to a series of violent killings.*

*Stop it, Hannah.*

I dumped the glass shards in the trash. The kitchen was alive, pulsing in time to my heart. My legs wobbled and I grabbed the counter. I really was crazy.

I staggered into the living room over white marble that suddenly seemed cold and rude and indignant. *It's just a floor, Hannah.* The nearly invisible seam up on the ceiling watched me, waiting to distract me with the hidden television.

*I need to rest. Just rest.*


I awoke to a high-pitched voice talking about a flood in Indonesia. The last thing I remembered, I had been watching some game show.

I pushed myself upright and brushed matted hair from my face.

*Note to self: No sleeping on leather.*

*Why do I feel so strange?*

On the screen, a swirling torrent of water crashed into the side of a building, obliterating the foundation and washing it out to sea. The scene shifted to a woman in a newsroom saying something about requests for aid.

*There are plenty of people far worse off than you.*

*Yeah, because nothing is wrong with your life.*

I squeezed my eyes shut.

*One little coincidence and I almost lost my shit.*

"In breaking news," the woman said, "New information has been released on the man responsible for seven deaths in or near the Metro Detroit area. His violent killing spree began on October first with the murder of a prostitute in Ash Park and culminated on November twenty-sixth when another woman and her young child were found brutally murdered in an abandoned school."

*November twenty-sixth...*

"Channel Eight is here on the scene where sources say that Robert Fredricks died earlier this afternoon—"

I put my hands over my ears, but the thoughts kept coming. I grabbed my phone off the coffee table and pulled up my web browser.

*Don't do this again.*

*October first, November twenty-sixth...*

I punched in keywords until I found what I was looking for. Dread bloomed in my abdomen. I ran to my purse and yanked out my journal, flipping through scribbled sleeping notes. Here, I slept. There, I didn't.

*A coincidence, just a coincidence.*

My sleep hadn't changed until I had moved in here. I ran a shaking finger down the pages.

I slept better when other people were dying, and in the days leading up to those times.

*Gotta have time to case a victim.*

*Stop it, Hannah. You're just a little tired today.*

*Does that mean someone else is dead?*

It didn't even make sense. How do you get someone to sleep on demand?

*You hold their hand and bring them orange juice. Or make them dinner.*

But that would mean he... what? Drugged me?

*No. No way.* I dropped the journal and put away my phone.

*You're crazy, Hannah.*

But I couldn't stop thinking, couldn't stop moving. What if I was wrong? I had been wrong about Jake. Maybe I was wrong about... everything.

My feet flew through the living room and up the stairs, independent of coherent thought. In the bathroom, I tore through the medicine cabinet like a possessed raccoon, tossing bottles and scattering toothpicks, cotton balls, gauze.

*Nothing.*

I snatched at the drawers underneath the sink and

rummaged through the linen closet. In the bedroom, I searched under the mattress, behind the bed posts, around the night tables.

My heart slowed.

*This is crazy. You're crazy. It has to be a coincidence.*

But it wasn't. I knew it in my core, somewhere unmentionable and primitive, just as I had known my love for my father was wrong. A nest of weasels in my chest scampered into my brain, into my lungs, until their clawing feet were all I could hear, feel, sense.

Then his voice. *Just don't clean my man cave.*

I ran. The bright light of the workout room assaulted my eyes. I wrenched open the closet door. Bleach, towels, rags, buckets. The buckets were empty. Towels flew over my shoulder, cleaning rags ripped from their resting place. Dull thuds, empty swishes of cloth, and then, the telltale clatter of plastic on rubber. I fell to my knees next to a small, unlabeled, orange bottle and poured a few of the pills into my shaking palm. Small and blue. No telltale markings that made any sense to me.

*It's probably just a painkiller for if he overdoes his workout.*

*Unlabeled in the back of the closet?*

I pulled out my phone, fumbled it against my thigh, and called up photos for medicine identification. There were thousands, but you could narrow it by shape and color and type. Blue. Oval. What helped you calm down? Tammy had recommended them once and I'd refused. *Shit.* Narcotics? No. *Benzodiazepines.* I stopped scrolling.

*Xanax. Five milligrams.*

It was identical.

*Maybe he was suffering from anxiety and I had accidentally ingested the pills.*

*Then why were they in the closet, the one place I had been told not to go?*

The bottle went into my pocket. I watched my numb fingers fold the towels and put them back on the shelf.

*Run, Hannah! Run!*

I folded the rags and put away the buckets.

*What the fuck are you doing? Get out now!*

When everything was in place, I walked downstairs to the living room, my legs not quite connected to me, but moving, still moving. I opened the flue and started the gas fireplace. Then I retrieved my journal and flung it into the hole.

Oily flames licked the cover and the cardboard crinkled and disintegrated. The urge to reach in and salvage the burning pages tugged at my arm, as if by keeping the journal I could save what was left of my dreams. When the inner pages curled in the heat, I let the tears fall. Fear thrummed through my veins, thick, liquid, and scorching.

*No one can ever know.*

My lungs cracked and shriveled, wrenched in an iron fist of hopelessness. As much as I tried to wish it away, his secret was mine now, locked forever in the ashes on the fireplace floor. I wiped my tears with the back of my hand. If he was a monster, then I was just as much a monster for loving him so much.

*I have failed every man I ever loved.*

*I cannot fail again.*

I sat on the couch to wait for him.

⁘⸻⸻⸻⸻⁘

Petrosky sucked smoke deep into his lungs and blew it at the no-smoking sign on the wall next to his desk. He needed a stiff drink—several, actually. But he couldn't bring himself to leave.

Since discovering Fredricks's body, he'd gone over the case again and again. Fredricks had to have been their killer. It was the simplest explanation, the obvious explanation. They had a mountain of evidence.

Just not a confession.

Fredricks's eyes blazed in his memory—and the way he'd turned hostile when Petrosky had mentioned Hannah

Montgomery. Hostile but almost… protective. Their guy was supposed to be a sadistic psychopath, removed from all human emotion. But Fredricks had *cared*.

Maybe he was a good faker. Petrosky had seen that before. *Or maybe you're wrong.*

He flicked ashes onto the floor. If he was wrong, then the real killer must have followed Fredricks, preying on the women he abused after he was done with them. That left Jacob Campbell—the biggest question mark in this whole ordeal. Fredricks had a motive to kill Campbell, if only to free Montgomery for himself. If he was lonely enough, desperate enough, crazy enough to think no one else would do… Petrosky could see it. And who else had that motive? Certainly not her new guy. That high-horse-riding mother fucker only had to look at her and she would have followed him home, just like most of the women in America.

Petrosky sighed. Something wasn't making sense.

*You're losing your shit, Petrosky.*

*Hannah isn't Julie. Hannah's fine.*

Trying to ignore the gnawing in his gut, he shoved the folders into the drawer, slammed it closed, and marched out of the precinct. He would not waste any more time driving himself fucking crazy. He was already close enough.

## Saturday, December 5th

I stood by the wall of windows, veiled in moonlight.

Dominic stepped into the middle of the room, ten feet away, though it felt like a chasm separated us. Even in the dark, the moonlight reflecting off the white marble illuminated him like a figure in a shadow box and I could see nothing else. The howl of the night wind faded. I could sense his very breath sucking the air from the room.

"Hannah?"

His voice was almost enough to undo everything I had been thinking.

*He has been so good to me.*

He stepped forward, and terror buzzed frantic through my body.

"Hannah, are you—"

"Why?" It came out a choked whisper, like my brain was trying to tell me to just shut the fuck up before I gave away what I knew. But my heart needed to hear his confession, needed to know for sure, so I didn't spend my whole life wondering whether this was nothing but the wild imagination of another fucked-up girl with a fucked-up daddy.

"Why what?"

I tossed him the bottle. He snatched it out of the air.

"You drugged me."

He pocketed the bottle. "I thought you needed more sleep."

*He's lying. They all lie.*

"Did you ever love me?"

*If he loves me, maybe everything is going to be okay.*

*Hannah, that's crazy.*

*He's never hurt me.*

299

*Just drugged you senseless.*

"I needed you," he said.

*He needs me. Maybe I can help him. If he knows it was wrong, we can make this better together. No one else has to know. I can fix this.*

"I need you too," I whispered, taking a step forward. We had each other. It wasn't too late.

"You may be misunderstanding the situation," he said.

The air in the room changed suddenly, like a draft from an open window freezing my marrow as it crept up my arms and into my chest. But there was no window, no opening to the elements that would have caused such a chill. "I know you did some things that were—" It stuck in my throat. I didn't even know what the words were for something like this. "You're not a bad person. Let me help."

"You did help," he said softly. "You made me normal."

I couldn't breathe. Jesus fucking Christ, I couldn't breathe.

*Emotional thinking never leads to anything good.*

*But... don't you feel anything about all this?*

*Not really.*

*Pretending to be normal is the best way to make people think you are.*

"That's why you gave me the pills. So you could... leave?"

He watched me, silent.

"And I would be your alibi because I didn't know any different."

I waited for him to tell me it wasn't true, but he didn't deny it, just fixed his gaze on me as my heart thrashed in my frozen chest.

"Did Jim help? Did he talk you into it?" Hope sputtered, tried to catch.

"Jim can't keep his dick in his pants. He never could."

"But that doesn't—"

"Jim was predictable in his compulsions and statistically likely to fuck up. Sometimes people don't do what you expect them to, but when they do, there is nothing more rewarding." A corner of his mouth turned up. I couldn't tell if it was a smile or a snarl.

Outside, the frozen moon ducked behind a cloud, casting us into dusky shadow. A shoe clacked on the floor, and another. The moon reemerged and he was nearer now, six feet and closing. His face was clear, as beautiful as a marble sculpture. I fought hysteria. "He could have killed Noelle!"

Dominic crept forward. I slid backwards on my fluffy socks.

"I doubt that."

"What are you—"

"His wasn't that kind of damage."

Hot coals in my chest fanned into flame and singed my lungs. "Did you choose me because I was damaged?"

"Yes."

"But you… you helped me, helped to fix me—"

But then I knew: helping me had been a side effect, not the goal. What was the goal? He clearly hadn't fixed those other women. Or Timmy. Or… Jake.

*He killed for me. He loves me.*

*No he doesn't. He's going to kill me.*

It wasn't a question. His face mutated into a mask of predatory excitement. Adrenaline zinged from me to him and back again, a ricochet like a wayward bullet.

My muscles coiled in anticipation.

He lunged, impossibly slow, as if the world had stopped spinning. I leaped sideways and pain shot through my skull as he dragged me by the hair, the room sliding past my socks on the marble as if I were walking on ice. I skidded, flailed, kicked, and pain blazed up my leg through my ankle under the distant sound of shattering glass.

The world wobbled. A dream, just a dream.

I clawed at his fist and he tightened his grip on my hair. Bright orange pain pulsed through the top of my head into my vision, dimming the shadowy white plaster of the moonlit ceiling. Then the white ceiling disappeared. A light flickered on, illuminating deep wood, and I could smell leather and books and my own rank sweat. Rugs. Wood.

He stopped at the bookshelf and reached for something. A sound like a slithering snake hissed in my ear, then a thunk as he threw something on the table. I clung to his arms, tears blurring my vision as the room pulsed black and focused again.

On the table, a box full of silver tools glittered sharply on velvet. A scalpel.

Panic screened my senses and tunneled my vision, and there was only him, the box and the scalpel he grasped. Then I was being dragged again, attached to his fist like a doll, flailing, clawing, kicking until my knee connected with something hard and a clatter reverberated through the room. Chess pieces rained off the table from the toppled board.

He stopped and stared, then jerked me toward him, my feet skidding against the hardwood as he raised the scalpel and plunged it into my upper arm.

Pain—hot, white, exquisite—shot through me. My arm weakened and my hand faltered against his.

He tore the scalpel free and the scent of copper thickened the air.

*The pain.* Endorphins poured into my bloodstream, smooth and warm. My vision opened. Air filled my lungs.

I wondered how long it would take me to die.

He pulled me out of the library and into the living room, and the ceiling swam, painted in bloody moonlight. Glass jangled around our feet as he dragged me through the kitchen toward the mudroom door.

*No, no, no, I cannot leave this house with him.* My fingernails dug into his skin, slipping in my blood.

"Dominic, please! I won't, I'll never—"

His chuckle told me there was no point. He'd just make it hurt more. Like my father had.

My pulse thundered in my temples. I could see, feel, smell the cold, dark room where sheets of poetry would be scattered over pieces of my body. Here a foot, there my ear, here my entrails shoved into my dead, gaping mouth.

*The pain. Focus.*

I drove my palms against his hand, every drop of energy pooling in my wrists, pushing away from his grasp on my hair. An audible grinding screamed inside my head as the roots of my hair cleaved a chunk from my scalp. Wetness dripped over my ear. I crashed to the marble, free.

*Run!* I scrambled toward the living room, glass from the broken sculpture tearing into my feet, my lungs burning, threatening to implode. His shoes crunched closer, closer. I cut around the couch, slipped and fell to my knees. My fingertips closed around a chunk of broken sculpture—sharp, jagged, deadly.

He bared his teeth and lunged, arms extended.

*You're stronger than you think.*

I lurched upwards with the piece of broken glass and thrust it into his belly. Blood bloomed across his abdomen in a vibrant red stain. *A dream, just a dream.* I plunged the glass into his flesh again, pushing until the hilt disappeared into the wall of his stomach.

He reached for me again but I leapt backwards, sliding on the glass and on blood that was probably mine, but maybe his too. I tumbled onto my left side and my head struck the floor. The world turned in dizzy circles—some nightmarish alternate universe where I had just stabbed the man I loved. He raised his arm above him in a final gesture of hope.

But the blackness didn't care about hope. It was trying to swallow me. Maybe I wanted it to.

*Why couldn't he just love me?*

I closed my eyes and let the darkness take me.

## SATURDAY, DECEMBER 5TH

Noelle pulled the blanket up to her neck, wondering if she should try to sleep some more or just give up and watch television. The nightmares had been decreasing, so she probably wouldn't have another tonight. But that didn't mean she felt like risking it.

The curtain whispered in the dark, rippling in the current of the heat vent. She took a deep breath and blew it out slowly. The attack itself was not what was bothering her. No matter what Jim had planned, she was alive. And he wasn't. The news story about him swinging in his jail cell had been oddly comforting.

All men were assholes.

*Well, almost all men.*

She exhaled, forcing her frustration into the air.

*What am I missing?*

She had slapped him when he tried to kiss her, then managed to get her knee in between them enough to pop the car door and roll out. Even in heels, she had torn through the woods until she found someone else, someone to help her. "Like a freaking kickboxer," Hannah had said.

That was the problem. Hannah.

Jim had cried when the police slapped the cuffs on his wrists.

"I need her, Noelle. Please, I need your help! I thought if I could make her jealous… I just love her so much."

As they'd ducked his head into the car he had stared straight at her, straining against the officers.

"I can save her from him! She will save me, too. Please! I can save her!"

Then he was gone.

Noelle rolled over. Her friend didn't need saving from anyone. Now that Jake was gone, Hannah could finally be happy like she deserved to be. With Dominic.

*Maybe I should call her.*

Noelle looked at the bedside clock. *12:10 a.m.*

She sighed. Hannah was fine. Waking her up wouldn't do anyone any good. Besides, what was she going to say? *That killer dude wanted to save you from... uh... not sure who?*

Thomas's scent clung to her pillow. Her stomach flipped. *Thomas had been Jim's best friend. What if—*

She shook her head. Jim was a serious whack job who'd fooled everyone, even his boss. And Thomas was the nicest guy she had ever met. The fact that he was charming, and friendly, and super smart didn't hurt either. Besides, he idolized Superman. How twisted could he be?

She fought the urge to get her phone.

None of this shit mattered anyway. That asshole was dead.

Noelle pushed aside the tingling that ran along the back of her neck and wrapped her arm around the pillow. She'd call Hannah first thing in the morning.

---

I felt like I was on a bed of hot coals, skin sizzling under me. The wet throb of my heart pulsed sharp, bright pain through my skull, into my arm and down over my ankle.

Asleep. I was just sleeping. Just dreaming. It'd be over soon.

I opened my eyes. Glittering pieces of broken sculpture peppered the living room. I'd have to clean that up later. And someone had spilled something on the marble, dark and shiny in the moonlight. That would stain if I didn't take care of it.

And... his legs. Unmoving. Still. Understanding crashed through me. I pushed myself to my knees, my injured arm twitching and throbbing—letting myself hope, for one exquisite moment, that he was not dead.

*No.*

Dizziness tried to pull me to the floor. He was just sleeping. Tired. Everything would be better in the morning, if only he could take this much needed rest.

*I should get him a blanket*, I thought suddenly.

But the deep, black pool on the pristine marble was a river I could never go back across. A river that separated who I was now from the semblance of sanity I had so briefly enjoyed. The glass in my knees no longer hurt and I longed for the pain. For now, anything felt like pleasure compared to this aching, pulsing dread that had settled into my stomach like a tumor.

Luminescent moonlight bathed the room, a room where I had been happy and in love just hours before.

Happy, because of him.

My scream echoed off the walls as if searching for someone else to hear, to understand that this was a loss so deep I could never truly recover. He had saved me in every possible way. He had proven to me that I was strong, and I had used that strength to cut him down with brutal finality.

I felt it then, a visceral snapping, a break in the rope that had held me to myself, that had bound me to a world where pain meant you were alive, if only you could put up with it. Dizziness pulled. I pushed back.

I inched forward on knees and forearms. Still-warm blood seeped into my pants, glazed my arms, my hands, my legs, until I felt like I was wrapped in a blanket of gore, coating myself in the essence of what he used to be.

I pulled myself onto him and laid my head on his bloody chest. His body felt warm against my cheek, but not warm enough. And he was still. So still. My heart seized. I gripped his shirt with quivering fingers, listening for any murmur within the recesses of his ribcage.

There was only silence.

Voices began as a tingle in the back of my mind and grew to such a violent swell that I feared they might erupt from my fractured brain and alert passersby to this horrible thing that I had done.

*Run, Hannah. Run. Save yourself.*

*There is nothing to live for.*

And suddenly he was there, too, a voice from the past resounding through the blackness in my soul.

*You're worthless to anyone but me.*

*Let me show you how good it feels to make me happy.*

I was five years old again, his arm around my shoulder.

*Do you love me, Hannah?*

*Yes, Daddy.*

Moonlight glinted off something in the coagulating pool near my knee.

The scalpel. I picked it up. In a way, it had ended him, but just as surely, it had ended me, or what I once had been.

I couldn't let everyone know he had done these things. They wouldn't... couldn't understand.

He had saved me. I had to find some way to save him, even a small part of him, in death.

There was resistance, a rip like paper tearing, as I brought the scalpel across his belly. His insides were warm, so warm, blood and gore and pieces of him oozing around my fingers as if they were still alive. I got hold of something and pulled. A worm, a tube. I was holding his—

*Jesus.*

I skittered backwards, feet slipping, stomach convulsing. I was halfway to the couch before I realized I was still gripping his intestines.

"I love you," I whispered, half expecting him to answer.

I tried to stand, but my limbs were heavy, like I was dragging myself through cement. I'd never make it upstairs.

*Help me, Dominic.* I inched through the living room. In the mudroom, I wrenched the doorknob and fell onto the back porch, the frigid air biting at my face and arms. I dragged myself across the porch, panting and choking on tears. The bathroom door came into focus. *Almost there.*

But someone was watching. Someone who knew what I'd done.

I swallowed bile and peered into the blackness. "Hello?"

No response. But I felt the unseen eyes burning into me

like hot pokers. Whoever was there was waiting, biding their time to attack.

*Move. Now.*

I lurched into the bathroom, slammed the door, and clawed the knob, blindly fumbling for the lock. My fingers were weak, but it clicked. I stumbled into the shower and collapsed against the wall, listening, waiting for the watcher to break down the door and take me.

There was nothing except my ragged breath wheezing in my ears. My oozing skin crackled and stung and throbbed. I braced myself against the wall and stripped off my clothes. Blood seeped from my mangled arm, but slower now. I turned on the water and whimpered, biting my lip as my skin shrieked from a thousand fissures. The basin went red.

I choked back a sob and turned under the spray as the cascade of water took some of the smaller shards, pushed others deeper. The basin turned pink. The wall of the shower wavered.

I turned off the water and peered out from the stall. All was quiet. The towel I wrapped around my breasts would be useless against groping fingers or a blade, but it might at least help stop the worst of the bleeding.

I unlocked the door and scanned the porch.

Nothing. But something. My heart surged.

Whether I ran, tripped or floated I wasn't sure, but suddenly my feet were on marble again. I heaved the deadbolt into place.

*Don't look.* Out the back windows, tree limbs twisted in the wind and I focused on them, let them guide me forward, past the glass, past the blood, to the stairs and up. I left the stained towel on the floor and dressed my deeper wounds with the bathroom first aid kit and a roll of gauze. Some other cuts were still bleeding but they were small, hopefully small enough to stop on their own.

*Don't think. Just move.*

Jeans and a sweater. Underwear. Shoes. Q-tips. The hazy room twisted as I sucked in a breath.

I watched the trees through the windows on the way back downstairs and retrieved the book from the library. It vibrated against my skin as I picked my way into the living room—or maybe I was shaking. I dropped the book on the couch and flipped to the last page. *If only it were all a dream, Alice.*

I picked up the Q-tip.

*Don't look. It's paint. It's just paint.*

When I was done, I laid the book and the makeshift pen on the ashes, stoking the embers with a nearby poker until a flame licked the leather cover, the orange and red caressing the pages, as sensual as his hands had been on my body. Greasy black smoke rose and disappeared into the dark void of the chimney.

*I will not fail you.*

I stood straighter, pulled by the strings of an invisible puppeteer.

*You're stronger than you think.*

*Everything will be okay.*

As the last of the leather curled and crumbled into ash, I retrieved my purse from the kitchen, pulled the duffel over my good arm, and unlocked the back door.

## SUNDAY, DECEMBER 6TH

*Focus, or she's dead.*

Petrosky ground his teeth together, but it didn't stop the panic from swelling hot and frantic within him. After the arrest last week, this crime should have been fucking impossible.

He wished it were a copycat. He knew it wasn't.

Anger knotted his chest as he examined the corpse that lay in the middle of the cavernous living room. Dominic Harwick's intestines spilled onto the white marble floor as though someone had tried to run off with them. His eyes were wide, milky at the edges already, so it had been awhile since someone gutted his sorry ass and turned him into a rag doll in a three-thousand-dollar suit.

*That rich prick should have been able to protect her.*

Petrosky looked at the couch: luxurious, empty, cold. Last week Hannah had sat on that couch, staring at him with wide green eyes that made her seem older than her twenty-three years. She had been happy, like Julie had been before she was stolen from him. He pictured Hannah as she might have been at eight years old, skirt twirling, dark hair flying, face flushed with sun, like one of the photos of Julie he kept tucked in his wallet.

They all started so innocent, so pure, so... *vulnerable.*

The idea that Hannah was the catalyst in the deaths of eight others, the cornerstone of some serial killer's plan, had not occurred to him when they first met. But it had later. It did now.

Petrosky resisted the urge to kick the body and refocused on the couch. Crimson congealed along the white leather as if marking Hannah's departure.

He wondered if the blood was hers.

The click of a doorknob caught Petrosky's attention. He turned to see Bryant Graves entering the room from the garage door, followed by four other agents. Petrosky tried not to think about what might be in the garage. Instead, he watched the four men survey the living room from different angles, their movements practically choreographed.

"Damn, does everyone that girl knows get whacked?" one of the agents asked.

"Pretty much," said another.

A plain-clothed agent stooped to inspect a chunk of scalp on the floor. Whitish-blond hair waved, tentacle-like, from the dead skin, beckoning Petrosky to touch it.

"You know this guy?" one of Graves's cronies asked from the doorway.

"Dominic Harwick." Petrosky nearly spat out the bastard's name.

"No signs of forced entry, so one of them knew the killer," Graves said.

"*She* knew the killer," Petrosky said. "Obsession builds over time. This level of obsession indicates it was probably someone she knew well."

*But who?*

Petrosky turned back to the floor in front of him, where words scrawled in blood had dried sickly brown in the morning light.

> *Ever drifting down the stream—*
> *Lingering in the golden gleam—*
> *Life, what is it but a dream?*

Petrosky's gut clenched. He forced himself to look at Graves. "And, Han—" *Hannah*. Her name caught in his throat, sharp like a razor blade. "The girl?"

"There are bloody drag marks heading out to the back shower and a pile of bloody clothes," Graves said. "He must have cleaned her up before taking her. We've got the techs on it now, but they're working the perimeter first." Graves bent and used a pencil to lift the edge of the scalp, but it was suctioned to the floor with dried blood.

"Hair? That's new," said another voice. Petrosky didn't bother to find out who had spoken. He stared at the coppery stains on the floor, his muscles twitching with anticipation. Someone could be tearing her apart as the agents roped off the room. How long did she have? He wanted to run, to find her, but he had no idea where to look.

"Bag it," Graves said to the agent examining the scalp, then turned to Petrosky. "It's all been connected from the beginning. Either Hannah Montgomery was his target all along or she's just another random victim. I think the fact that she isn't filleted on the floor like the others points to her being the goal, not an extra."

"He's got something special planned for her," Petrosky whispered. He hung his head, hoping it wasn't already too late.

If it was, it was all his fault.

# EPILOGUE

The pre-dawn humidity covered the freeway in frozen mist. I glanced at the clock. *Seven forty-five.* I should be there before nightfall. I set my jaw and fingered the emerald pendant that lay against my clavicle, warmed by the heat of my body.

A whimper rose from the backseat. In the rearview mirror, a massive black head eclipsed the back window.

"It's okay, buddy. Just relax. We'll be there in no time."

Duke slumped onto his belly on the seat and rested his head on his paws. On the dash, the panda bobbled, silly and childish and stupidly innocent. I backhanded it. It toppled to the floor.

I gripped the wheel tighter.

Before me, the brilliant red and yellow glow of sunrise streaked across the road and illuminated the tops of distant evergreen trees, lighting the sky with hope, with promise.

*It's not promise. It's power.*

I slid my hand underneath the bag on the passenger seat and let my fingers brush the cool metal of the scalpel. I squeezed. The sharp point bit into my finger. I pulled my hand back and watched a tiny crimson drop swell and drip onto the steering wheel. I smeared it with my thumb.

Duke whined, low and hollow.

"It's okay, boy," I said softly. "It won't be long now." The pavement whispered under my tires. I kept my eyes on the bloody dawn.

*Baby's coming home.*

Don't miss CONVICTION, the next book in the Ash Park series, available September 2016.

*Conviction means nothing when you're dead wrong.*

Shannon Taylor takes no prisoners—save the ones she tosses into lockup. Between convicting criminals as an Ash Park district attorney, dealing with her jerk ex-husband (who also happens to be her boss), and caring for her dying brother, Shannon is already stretched thin. So she's less than thrilled when new evidence from a closed case emerges—evidence suggesting she threw a young mother in jail for a murder she didn't commit.

Shannon knows the girl is hiding something. But whatever the secret, it is even more compelling than the hope of freedom—the girl won't talk.

When Shannon becomes the target of a series of cryptic and bloody warnings, she must find a way to protect everyone she holds dear. Will her persistence free an innocent woman? Or will her pursuit of the truth turn her family into helpless targets in a madman's game?

Conviction runs deep. Courage runs deeper. And nothing in Ash Park is as it seems.

# ABOUT THE AUTHOR

Meghan O'Flynn is a clinical therapist, writer, artist, wife, and mommy. She adores her amazing little boys, dark chocolate, tea, dirty jokes, and back rubs with no strings attached, in that order. She writes a psychology blog and creepy psychological suspense novels and is amazed that her wonderful husband still agrees to live with her after reading them.

If you want more on the regular (and you know you do) come check Meghan out on her Facebook page at
https://www.facebook.com/MeghanOFlynnAuthor/
Then sign up for her newsletter at http://meghanoflynn.com
to be first in line for new releases and other special offers. Meghan won't spam you. She's got better things to do.

If you want to make Meghan leap ecstatically about her kitchen, leave her a book review on Amazon or Goodreads. You can even follow her on Amazon so you won't miss a book release. There's probably dark chocolate or a back rub in it for you. Because, karma.

Printed in Great Britain
by Amazon